I0645801

SHIFTER GHOST

A WYRDOS UNIVERSE NOVEL

GWENDOLYN DRUYOR

SHIFTER SCHOOL BOOK TWO

Get your Bonus Wyrdos Book!

Want to know more about the Wyrdos world? Visit my website below and subscribe to get your complimentary copy of *Doug vs. The Boogeyman*!

Wyrdos.net

Enjoy!
Gwendolyn

1

"*B*oomtown, Jeffers!" The captain of the opposing team bounced off a bench to high five the seven-foot-something white guy who'd just jammed the basketball in the hoop on his second try.

Laylea yawned, her long, pink puppy-dog tongue curling at the end. She should feel guilty that she'd been napping under that bench when she was supposed to be on guard. But, so far, nothing exciting had happened other than Jeffers making a basket.

Jeffers giggled, "Boomtown." He liked the word.

"Means you did good, Jeffers." The captain, a small, gangly kid, executed a complicated handshake with the big guy.

"I did good. Nicky, I did good." Jeffers kept his head down, watching in awe as his hands danced with his friend's.

"Yeah, you did good. Here, the taco truck is giving out free taquitos." Nicky led the way over to the Latino man in a spotless apron handing the fried treats around to the players and everyone else hanging out in the South Side Chicago neighborhood.

Laylea watched Nicky help Jeffers adjust his retro sports goggles on their way there. There was something odd about that.

Laylea blinked. The captain's footsteps hadn't woken her so much as the sound of both teams on the neighborhood court cheering for the big man with mirrored, single-lens goggles that hid everything but his grin.

She stretched all four legs out and curled her paws back in. Laylea was a twelve-pound, fawn-colored terrier. Under the bench was the perfect place for her to watch the pharmacy. Or it would have been, if she hadn't fallen asleep.

The smell of grass, el pastor, and sweaty humans seeped into Laylea's sleepy dog brain, reminding her that she was on a job and really shouldn't have taken the nap. She peeked out from under the park bench to see if anyone else on the stakeout had noticed. Feet pounded across the recycled rubber basketball court. Lucio waggled his fingers at her as he raced by in his three-hundred-dollar sneakers.

She peered out beyond the taco truck to see Orin grinning at her from where he was tuning up his bicycle. Damn. Still, Morioka and Dee, the final two members of their crew, probably hadn't seen her nap because they were ensconced in the fake service van with cameras focused on the pharmacy. Lucio had learned, through some of his more questionable contacts, that the pharmacy was a major delivery hub for the rapidly dwindling supply of N in town. According to Laylea's contact at the records office, the building was owned by a corporation owned by a guy named Gorshkov. They added the corporation to the list of different organizations that owned the many buildings they suspected were being used to create N.

N was a deadly drug. It made normal humans feel as powerful as shifters and they would do stupid things, like try to fly off buildings or race train cars. Wyrdos who took it either experienced a surge in their powers or lost them completely until the drug wore off. Many shifter addicts lost the ability to shift at all.

Laylea and her friends had teamed up to help keep the city safe from supernatural threats like the Mesozoic-era demon that had brought them all together. They'd trapped that demon in a magical box. Meanwhile the "good" Pre-Cambrian-era demon, the one who'd helped them trap her mate, was currently sitting in the OnSite Car Repair service van with Dee. Regardless of how they'd come together, or the many tragedies they'd prevented since, the scourge of N had become the team's primary focus. It was tearing the city apart and the police couldn't really fight the epidemic if they could never find the kingpin. And since the kingpin behind N was clearly a paranormal being, that made N a Team Wyrdos problem.

Thus, five of them watching the South Side pharmacy. Or, rather: three watching, one playing basketball, and one napping.

In Laylea's defense, it was a boring stakeout. This was a nice neighborhood. Dozens of people were out, enjoying one of the first temperate evenings of spring. Winter in Chicago was brutal, and these people seemed determined to break out of hibernation. They greeted each other, grabbed food from the taco truck, and watched the game as little kids up way past their bedtimes wrestled with the tiny jungle gym. Sure, the basketball players trash talked each other, but it was all in fun. And if anyone's language got too strong, the old lady leaning out her window would let them know.

Lucio, Laylea, Orin, Dee, and Captain Yaksha Morioka had arrived separately and were supposed to hang on the periphery, blend in, and keep an invisible eye on the enemy stronghold. Orin had flipped his bicycle over on the handlebars and was giving it a tuneup. Laylea, easily the queen of blending in—as she was a dog most of the time— wandered around at will, getting scratches from the neighbors and cleaning up abandoned food. She'd skipped the droppings around the taco truck. There was something off in the scent of the roasting meats.

Dee and Morioka ended up together in the OnSite Car Repair service van Dee had fixed up with surveillance equipment. Neither of them was very good at blending in. Not because they were wyrdos. Neither Dee nor Morioka was very good at looking like anything other than a cop.

Lucio, however, had done either the worst or best job at blending in when he'd joined the basketball game. The man's brown eyes sparkled with mischief at all times. They were on a stakeout, but he grinned at Laylea as the game tore past her hiding spot again.

Half the players carried taquitos in one hand as they ran. A girl in duct-taped boots stole the ball and the game turned around. Everyone's heads spun back in the other direction. Laylea stretched, waking up more. A guy's high-topped sneaker shot out. He tripped the girl in the duct-taped boots. High-tops stole the ball. Duct-taped boots went rolling into Jeffers. He fell into the grass right in front of Laylea's bench.

"Oof." For a moment, the big man's face scrunched like he was going to cry. Then Jeffers spotted Laylea and he beamed. He walked his fingers through the grass to her muzzle and giggled when she nudged his hand to get him to pet her. He wasn't hurt.

Beyond him, the cheater wasn't so lucky. His high-top's laces popped out of their neat bows and tangled up. In his spectacular fall, the guy missed the soft rubber of the court and the grass surrounding it, stumbling instead all the way to the torn-up street where he shaved flesh off of several limbs and almost got hit by a car. Other neighbors goggled at the impossibility of his fall. Laylea wasn't fazed. That was just the sort of thing that happened when you behaved badly around brownies. She guessed it was Orin who had handled the karma, since Lucio's eyes were focused on Jeffers and Laylea.

Few players saw the cheater go down. Like Lucio, most of them watched the man laying full out in front of Laylea. Nobody was trash talking anymore. All the tough guy voices turned gentle as they called out.

"You okay, Jeffers?"

"He okay?"

"Jeffers, my man, you got to get up. We can't win without you."

"Hey, Jeffers!" Nicky, walking like he'd grown six inches in the last day and a half, trotted over to the big guy. "What you got there?"

Jeffers ran his hand over Laylea's head as gently as if she were a glass figurine. He took a moment to glance back at his friend, still beaming brighter than when everyone had feted him for making a basket. "Nicky. Kitty."

Despite the unintended insult, Laylea crawled closer so the guy could pet more than just her head. As she got near him, she saw that his grin was that of a kid, even though Jeffers appeared to be in his twenties. He smelled muskier than your average American man, too. Another odd primate scent wafted down from Nicky, along with the off-putting scent of the taquito in his mouth. Neither one of them was completely human.

As Jeffers turned away from Nicky, the late evening sun hit the single lens of his retro sports goggles at exactly the right angle. Laylea saw beyond the reflective surface. Her jaw dropped in a canine grin. She'd thought the glass was too shaded for an evening game, but now she understood. The goggles were his disguise. Jeffers was a cyclops. She was extra impressed that he had gotten the ball in the hoop at all with no depth perception.

He kept petting her gently, whispering that weird "pspspsps" thing that cats melted over until Nicky crouched beside him and explained, "That's a puppy, man. You say 'who's a good boy? Who's a good boy?'"

Lucio laughed over their shoulders. "Yeah. Who's a good boy?" Unseen by the others, he gestured at himself.

Jeffers changed his murmur to, "Puppy puppy puppy puppy," and kept petting her like he was accustomed to breaking things. Laylea licked his hand. Jeffers sucked in a breath and didn't exhale. His face glowed with joy.

"Come on, Jeffers. Let's get back to the game, man." Nicky checked the man's goggles to be sure they were in place as he pulled him away from Laylea. She sniffed, but didn't recognize Nicky's scent. She'd never run into his kind of wyrdo before.

Jeffers cradled his hand against his body while Lucio and Nicky led him back to the game. Nicky took the opportunity to shovel the last of his taquito into his mouth. Lucio turned him down when he offered him another taquito, from his pocket.

Jeffers took it. Before he shoved the whole thing in his mouth, he whispered, "Who's a good boy?"

Nicky and Lucio both chuckled.

"You are, Jeffers. You're a good boy," Lucio assured him. He added, "Lee's a girl."

Laylea's friends knew her as Lee Woodford because Laylea Hillen was in hiding. Unlike Jeffers, she didn't have to hide *what* she was, only who she was, because all her close friends were wyrdos. Just like Jeffers and Nicky, they were supernatural creatures making their way in the modern world of Chicago.

The boys returned to the game, everyone hurrying to swallow the last of the free fried food. Laylea returned to watching the pharmacy, the surveillance van, and Orin. The sun inevitably dipped behind the roofs of the close-packed apartment buildings, and darkness fell over the pools of streetlight not quite illuminating the whole court.

The pleasant evening was turned on its head as the world grew darker. The pharmacy door opened with a quiet tinkling of bells, followed by the rattle of many guns being cocked at once. The game ground to a halt as several players started fighting each other. Jeffers tore the net from the backboard as the girl with duct-taped boots slammed the basketball into the ground so hard it exploded.

Dee burst from the service van and raced for the court.

Testosterone flooded Laylea's senses, sending her hackles up. A particularly strong and familiar musk dragged her attention to Jeffers' not-so-small-anymore friend. He'd shifted into an ape. Something clicked in her brain as the gunmen from the pharmacy beelined for the taco truck. She finally identified the off-putting smell in the roasting el pastor smoke that had been bugging her all evening. It was N.

The complimentary taquitos the truck's owner had passed around to the basketball players had been laced with N.

By wild chance, or, as the brownies would insist, well-deserved karma, the wyrdos had come out to get proof against the pharmacy on the very night that a rival dealer had chosen to steal their customers away. And Laylea had fallen asleep in the middle of it instead of using her preternatural senses and saving all those neigh-borhood kids from being dosed.

Or shot.

Guns appeared in the taco truck's service window, and she felt more than heard as the truck's electric engine purred to life. All the drug dealers had to do was drive away to escape the cops. Laylea couldn't let that happen. It was her fault they'd succeeded in drugging everybody there. She scrambled to her paws and tore across the grass. In seconds, she was under the truck. A cable brushed along her raised hackles. She spun, bared her teeth, and latched onto it. Green salsa spurted from the punctures. Laylea blinked and tried to push the spiciness out of her mouth with her long tongue. She leapt for another cable. This time, the fluid that spurted out made her eyes roll up into the back of her head. She worried at the holes, throwing her head back and forth to widen the punctures until the greasy, black stuff poured out onto her face. She stumbled back and gagged, blowing air out of her nose to clear it.

A low whine rose in volume and pitch. The truck shifted above her. At the same moment, she felt the burning in her gut that often preceded a shift to her human form. The wheels around her started rolling. She would be seen. She couldn't be seen shifting. She couldn't let the truck get away.

In a panic, Laylea flailed out with her claws at the cables and hoses she saw all around her through the burning pain of brake fluid in her eyes. She stumbled along, staying with the truck as it rolled into the street. Liquids spurted out, drenching her fur in salsa, power steering fluid, pico de gallo, coolant, and a coppery substance she feared was liquified N. Finally, her claws reached a wire that sparked and incited a small explosion when she sliced it. The hum of the engine died, and the truck coasted to a halt.

She couldn't hear the gunfight, but muzzle flashes lit up her limited view from under the truck. Her ears buzzed with static and some kind of high-pitched wailing. She smelled burning fur. A snazzy pair of hand-painted Chuck Taylor high-tops approached, limned in gunfire. When Orin's bright green eyes appeared, his face crinkled with fear, she realized that the wailing was her. The burn in her eyes, on her fur, and in her mouth shifted to a fire in her belly. The fire spread like a flash throughout her body. In that instant, just as Orin got a grip on her neck, Laylea changed form.

And she healed. As her muzzle flattened into a human face and her legs lengthened into a small teenager's appendages, her paws changed to hands. Hands that gripped an electrical wire just as foolishly as her claws had. Orin's scream joined hers as both shook in the grip of the great god Electricity. Laylea shifted to dog, to human, and back again. She didn't know how many times she shifted, but she was never able to shake either Orin or the live wire.

The flashing lights of gunfire and the blue wash of city lighting suddenly blacked out. Laylea cried out for her parents. She cried out for Bailey and for the friends she'd made at Lincoln Park Shifter School and would never see again. An instant before she would have fulfilled her long-standing fear that she would die before age fifteen, the wire was pulled from her human hand. The taco truck flipped on its side, revealing her to the open sky.

"Puppy hurt!" Jeffers' voice rang over all other sounds.

Laylea's body instantly shifted her to dog to heal the internal burns. Her nose wrinkled at the sharp, terrifying testosterone wafting off of the cyclops. His eyeshade askew, the big man stood swinging an electrical pole at the shooters who had tumbled out of the toppled truck.

"Puppy's safe, Jeffers," Orin reassured the cyclops, scooping Laylea out of the lake of auto and taco fluids. "I've got the puppy. You go home now. Go home, Jeffers."

Orin didn't wait for Jeffers to comply. Laylea watched over his shoulder as Orin raced away from the chaos. Jeffers tossed his pole onto a pile of park benches, car parts, the basketball hoop, backboard, and pole all nested together in a small, but solid, wall rising between the armed pharmacists on one side and the taco truck terrorists on the other. Morioka had joined Dee in covering the gunmen with her service pistol. The bigger guys laughed at the little Asian woman, and all raised their guns.

The last thing Laylea saw as Orin tossed her in his bicycle basket was Lucio running in between the two cops and the many criminals. She howled at the uncountable gun barrels pointed at him.

"It's okay, Laylea. You know he's a brownie. It will be okay." Orin chanted the words in rhythm with the pedals going up and down as they raced north, away from the approaching sirens.

2

The next day started like a perfectly normal day. By nightfall, everything had changed.

When Orin dropped Laylea off at home after the disaster at the basketball game, she slipped in through the cracked window, since even though she remembered her apartment key she couldn't really use it without thumbs. Bailey wasn't home. She assumed he was at the library. He was always at the library. He took his premed studies pretty seriously.

When she woke, his backpack was on his desk chair, but Bailey wasn't in the apartment. She wanted to race to The Office to find out how many drug dealers Dee and Morioka had arrested, but it was unlikely anybody would be there this early. So, instead, she hopped onto the cushioned barstool beside the bed, bounced from the stool to the makeshift headboard, and up to the window where she could wriggle out into the crawlspace under the front porch. From there, she trotted out to the lawn to find the perfect place to take care of business.

Laylea didn't know it was her fifteenth birthday. If she had, she would not have been wasting her time searching for the right place to relieve herself.

By all accounts, a twelve-pound terrier could be expected to live twelve to fifteen years. Dee, the banshee who could see if a person was going to die soon, had told her she was safe. Still, the day would have gone differently if Laylea had known she'd reached her expected expiration date.

Instead, she was mincing through the snow-covered patches of grass in front of the three-flat, searching for a place to pee that wouldn't offend Nemo or Luna, but would remind Tippy that the house was Laylea's territory. Laylea didn't know where Tippy lived, but she knew the large fawn terrier didn't live in the three-flat. Their landlady, Madame Hu, and her teenaged granddaughter took up the top floor, Stan kept to himself on the main floor, and she and Bailey rented the tiny garden apartment. Still, Tippy's scent was everywhere around the converted three-flat, more than could be justified by the times she and Laylea hung out on the front porch.

Laylea's tail flipped up as the terrier in question came bounding around the Prairie Style Greystone on the corner. Tippy's face markings were as white as the snow falling from the bushes she brushed against. Laylea herself had a white diamond brightening the fawn-colored fur over her eyes. It faded to a pale birthmark on her human face. Tippy's diamond covered most of one side of her face.

Laylea's tail went into overdrive as her brother Bailey, in his ancient sneakers, tore around the corner, hard on Tippy's heels. Laylea scratched aside a little snow and peed over some uppity male dog's mark near the elm tree in the front yard. Then she bounded over to sing at her favorite human. She approved his new morning runs. Bailey tended to be a little overly focused on his studies and in a bit of denial of his particular abilities, magical and physical, but Laylea knew that he was just trying to find the answers that would keep him from ever hurting anybody again. She understood. There was a price that came with knowing that you were different—in his case, with knowing that you were possibly all-powerful.

The running was good. It gave him endorphins and made him get out of his brain for a little while every day. He'd made it a habit while she was gone last summer, condemned to attend the coolest high school in the universe, the Lincoln Park Shifter School.

Bailey paused to stretch out his calves against the first step leading up to the porch. He kissed the top of Laylea's head as he did. "I ran into Nemo and Brandy three blocks over. The chemo must finally be working if she's able to go on long walks again."

Laylea trilled at him in response. Brandy was Nemo's human.

"I thought that would make you happy. You're a good girl, Tippy. Go home. Go home, Tippy."

Tippy ignored him. She rolled in the grass before tearing down the alley beside their three-flat.

Bailey backed away from the porch and hopped down the steps to the door leading into their garden apartment. "Brandy said that Madame Hu has been helping her with the vet bills. Did you know that?"

Laylea barked in the negative. She hadn't known.

"Hey." Bailey held her up to eye level and looked at her sternly. "You have your key?"

She nipped his nose and dropped her jaw in a doggy grin. She used to forget it all the time. But he'd laid a spell on her key so she would always know where it was. She kept it in her collar, the one item of clothing specially designed so that she wouldn't lose it when she shifted between forms. Unlike typical dog collars, Laylea's was wide, with two zippered pockets spaced between cleverly hidden elastic bands that could expand when she was human and contract when she was a terrier.

Bailey laughed—again—and chewed on one of her ears like her fur brothers used to do before their birth mother had hidden them all. Out in the street, a garbage truck dropped a dumpster with a chaotic clanging. A spark of hot pain flashed in her gut, and Laylea suddenly felt the icy cold of the winter air on her bare, human skin. Bailey shoved the door open with her body and dropped her inside the apartment, listening with his preternatural senses for anyone who might have seen her shift. The laughter was gone.

"Lee. That's not safe." He scolded her in a tone colder than the wind as he slammed the door shut.

He stepped over her and stormed over to the galley kitchen as she sorted out her long, awkward legs and brushed short, dirty-blonde hair out of her eyes, struggling to get some control over her facile human tongue as she always did when she shifted. "Sorry, Bails. I am getting better."

He grunted in return and drained a glass of water. Then, without changing out of his sweaty running gear, Bailey plopped himself into his desk chair and woke the three screens covered in data and medical displays that looked like broken down sections of DNA. So, that moment of filial love was over.

Laylea's eyes caught on the envelope sitting in a homemade clay ashtray at the back edge of the desk. The ashtray had been a gift from their friend Kyle's daughter before Kyle had died. Anything in the ashtray belonged to Laylea. The envelope held their rent for April. Bailey had praised her when she put the envelope in there right after paying March rent. He didn't know that she'd saved up enough to pay the next six months. Which reminded her…

She rolled over to face the bottom shelf of their bookcase. A worn copy of Jack London's *Call of the Wild* was tucked in with other classic titles that Bailey would never read again. She flipped it open and pulled rolls of hundred-dollar bills from the hollowed-out compartment inside. She stuffed the cash in her collar, one roll in each pocket, and forced the zippers shut. The collar pushed uncomfortably against her throat. Hopefully, she wouldn't have to wear it that way for long.

She grabbed a pair of sweats and a sweatshirt reading "Go Cobs" from under the bed and wriggled into them. What with not having mastered shifting, Laylea didn't waste much time with fancy clothes she was guaranteed to lose out on the streets of Chicago. Misprinted tourist fare was her winter uniform, a sundress in summer. She had stashes of clothes hidden all over the city. There weren't a lot of size-one homeless, so she hadn't lost many of them.

Laylea pulled herself to her feet and dashed out the door, yelling over her shoulder at Bailey, "Be right back."

She paused just a second, expecting him to respond, "Don't forget your key." He didn't say a thing. Her brother was already brain-deep in his research. He'd never notice she was gone.

Which was one reason she was in charge of the rent. They couldn't set up a direct debit like most people because Bailey didn't want to risk opening a bank account, even with his fake identity. He had the papers. He'd used them to get into college. He said that was different. He trusted the school to keep their information private. So, Laylea paid their rent monthly, in cash. Their parents used to send money, but they hadn't written in a while.

She sighed as she swung around the railing from the cement stairs to the wooden stairs leading up to the porch. Their mother was a witch and their father was a super soldier. Bailey said they were fine, just being cautious. Laylea mostly tried to stay busy to keep from worrying.

She fished the enchanted key from her collar to open the front door. It wouldn't work on Stan or Madame Hu's doors. They had keys that worked on the front door and their own apartment doors. Laylea would love to know how that worked. She stared at the key as she bounced toward the stairs, trying to imagine how three different keys could open the same lock.

She was so caught up in her thoughts that she almost jumped into their landlady's lap. There on the fourth step up, Madame Hu sat quietly, a giggle on her theatrically-painted face.

Laylea screamed.

"Good morning, Wai-Sun." The giggle dribbled from Madame Hu's Kohl-lined eyes into her voice. "Coming to see me?"

"Yes, ma'am." Laylea stumbled on the words as she focused on tamping down the fire in her belly. A surprise like that would once have made her shift with no chance to stop it. She took it as a huge improvement that she hadn't just dropped into a pile of fur and poorly printed sportswear. "Are you okay? Why are you sitting here?"

Laylea wasn't accustomed to seeing older people sitting on the floor. She wondered if stairs counted as the floor and decided they did.

Madame Hu slid over and patted the step with her wrinkled hand. "I haven't seen Mr. Stan in several weeks, and he has been suspiciously reasonable in his recent email complaints. I was hoping to catch him on his way to work."

"He hasn't been running his trains as much since I got home." Laylea thought about it and realized that she hadn't seen the grumpy old guy in the flesh since then, either. It had been nearly six months with no slurred insults or weak kicks at her for merely standing near his path.

She sat beside Madame Hu and pulled her knees up to her chest. "As long as you're in concerned-for-your-tenants mode, I was wondering if you could let me pay you the rent in advance?"

"For April? I suppose that would be okay. Are you going away again?"

"No, I don't think so. I just…" She futzed with the zipper on her collar. "Ghost hunting has been booming this winter, and we've got a lot of cash in our apartment." It wasn't just ghost hunting, but she couldn't exactly tell Madame Hu about all the supernatural mysteries that she solved. Humans didn't know about the creatures that surrounded them. But most of them either believed in ghosts or understood that others did. It was a safe subject.

"I'm worried about getting robbed with Bailey so busy and focused all the time. He never remembers to pay the rent, right? So, I was hoping that you could take the next, say, six months of rent, since you have a bank account where it would be safe." She blurted the request while picking at the pink and blue bear cub printed on her sweatpants.

Madame Hu was silent for too long. Laylea glanced up to see the landlady examining her. She grinned reflexively. Her smile fell as she took in the worry in the old woman's eyes.

Slowly, Madame Hu shook her head. "I can't do that, Ms. Lee. Money is a delicate thing."

"My friend, Amal, says it's evil."

"He's not wrong. It can do evil things to people. But think of it this way, Wai-Sun." She took a deep breath and let it all out in a rush before continuing. "If you give me all this money and then Mr. Bailey becomes injured, you will feel horrible, coming to me to beg for your money back. A good girl doesn't beg, does she?"

Laylea shook her head silently. She had been raised as a dog for the first eleven years of her life. There was no higher calling than to be a Good Girl. "No, but Bailey doesn't pay attention to what's going on around him. If someone broke in, it could be very bad." Bad, in that Bailey would react out of instinct, and his magic could bring the house down on top of all their heads. Money, or a lack thereof, would be the least of their worries, in that case.

"Mr. Bailey's focus is admirable. He will learn what he has set his mind to. However, one of life's sneakier lessons is that what we need to learn is often quite different from what we think we need to learn. Your rent is low because you and Mr. Bailey help me with mainte-nance issues, yes?"

Laylea drew her brows together and tilted her head. "Yes, Madame Hu. Have we missed your calls?"

"No." Madame Hu smiled. "The fault is mine. Knowing how busy you both are, I have not called for you. I make you this promise: Fan will knock on your door more often, looking for Mr. Bailey's assistance. It will increase traffic to your door, as well as break into his unhealthy focus. And force him to interact with other humans," she added, guessing at Laylea's true concern.

"Thanks, Madame Hu." Laylea stood. "I understand."

"There are ways for a minor to open a bank account, you know."

Sure there were. It required a parent's signature and a social secu-rity card, birth certificate, or other proof that you existed. A dog license was hardly going to impress the banks. "Thanks, Madame Hu. I'll look into that." She started toward the front door and then glanced over at Stan's apartment. With a quick grimace at the landlady, she dashed over and pounded on his door. "Hey Stan! That pesky dog is peeing on your car!"

There was no response from the other side of the door.

She shrugged at Madame Hu. "I'd say he's at work already."

"Ah, well." Madame Hu accepted Laylea's help to get to standing.

"Thank you, Wai-Sun." She took hold of the the railing and started up the stairs as Laylea slouched to the front door. "I guess Fan will have to start knocking on Stan's door, as well."

"Yes, ma'am." Laylea was already deep into her own thoughts again. She had to do something about the money.

"Ha!"

Laylea stopped with the front door open, frozen by Madame Hu's sharp laugh.

The old woman smiled at her. "You have my permission to tell Mr. Bailey that I just compared him to Stan. If that doesn't shame him into being more social, I don't know what will." The old lady didn't wait for her response before heading up the carpeted stairwell to her own door.

3

---

*B*ailey didn't blow the house up when she slammed the door on her way back into the apartment. He didn't even jump. He did notice. "Slam it a little harder, why don't you?"

She thought of responding with Madame Hu's jab, but she wanted a favor from him. So, instead she said, "I couldn't possibly. I'm not as strong as you, my handsome big brother."

A grin ghosted his dimples. "What do you want?"

She rubbed her fingers along the tiny stuffed figure of a lizard's foot sewn to her collar. Sher had made it for her adoptionversary last May. "You know how you said you'd think about how the Mom charmed this to protect me from magic?"

"The Mom" and "the Dad" were how Laylea had thought of Sher and Clark back when she was just their pet. She'd never called them "Mom" and "Dad" because she hadn't shifted human until that very last hour she had with them.

"Yes. You want me to make lizards for your friends Oscar and KC?"

He'd guessed. She had never told him that. She'd told him about her best friends at the Lincoln Park Shifter School, but she didn't think he'd really been listening. "Yeah. Think you can?"

GWENDOLYN DRUYOR

"Lizards made by you might not work as well as yours. Yours is made out of Dad's bandanna and carries Mom and Dad's love, as well as all the memories you made with Mom's original patchwork lizard when you were a puppy. You carried that thing everywhere."

She'd left it behind when they ran away from home to hide from Walter and the Consortium. A wave of sorrow washed over her, and she found herself suddenly tucking her physical tail up into her furry belly. She'd shifted without even noticing that she'd done it. If she didn't take care, Bailey really was going to lock her in the apartment like he always threatened.

Her shame must have shown on her long, fuzzy face, because Bailey spun a 180 in his chair and reached for her. "No, sorry, that was my fault. I've been thinking about Mom and Dad a lot, and I'm sad, too. It is overwhelming."

Laylea wriggled out of her sweatsuit and hopped up into his lap. She stood her front paws on his shoulders to bury her nose in his neck.

"I don't know why they won't let you go home if Walter and Trask really are out of commission." He held her away so that he could look in her eyes. "It's not that they don't love you. You know that."

She licked his nose in a reply that didn't say she knew either way.

"This is why your lizard foot works so effectively," he said. "Love. All the love in the bandana, the memories, and Mom even thinking to make it for you when she's in the middle of a war. If you could get items with that kind of true magic built into them by the people who love your friends, I could maybe make them as strong as your lizard foot."

Laylea barked. She leapt from his lap and crawled between his feet to pick two red items from her basket of projects under the desk. She hopped back up into Bailey's lap to drop the origami crane and bracelet onto the desk. Oscar's mother, Sanna, had made the paper and folded the crane. Laylea had fashioned the bracelet out of a letter Sanna had sent to her son.

"Not here. I can't woogie anything with all this science staring me

18

in the face." Bailey scooped Laylea up in one hand and the bracelet and crane in the other. He took a step toward the bed and then froze. His face wrinkled up as if he were in pain and super angry about it.

But, Laylea had lived with Bailey since he was six. She knew that was just his deep thought face. Some pretty amazing adventures had come out of the deep thought face. She held still and tried to keep her tail from wagging at how silly he looked. It didn't work. Shifting and tails, neither were under her control.

"Sorry." He resumed animation and finished the short cross to the bed. "Science and magic aren't mutually exclusive for Mom. There's no way she could have made all those defensive devices without using both. So, where did I get the idea that I should keep them separate?"

He looked at her like either he couldn't see her at all or like she was supposed to have the answer for him. She'd only had four months of schooling in her life, and nobody at the Lincoln Park Shifter School even believed in magic. She dropped her head to the side in a doggy shrug. She did not drop her chin in a doggy grin at him using the word *magic*. He was afraid of his powers, and he avoided any mention of magic, using the Dad-invented word *woogie* if he couldn't avoid it.

"Right." He shook himself, like Laylea would do. "I'll go with the assumption that these aren't made with love."

Laylea barked and blew air through her teeth at him when he looked at her. Pffing was as good as an eye roll for contempt in her family.

"Not made with fourteen years of a mother's and father's love?"

She bobbed her head at him, conceding that point. If Sanna weren't addicted to N, Laylea would say the letter Sanna had sent Oscar held as much love as her lizard foot. Oscar and Sanna sent each other letters constantly. Only, Sanna's weren't really letters. She just mailed him blank sheets of homemade red stationary. Her mind was screwed up by her drug addiction, but her love came through loud and clear.

Oscar's father was a different story. He was on the Shifter Council. With his connections, he could have rescued Oscar from the school anytime. But he didn't. Not even after the school doctor sent the Council proof that the kids were being abused, having their blood taken and used for secret experiments.

But then, Oscar and Laylea both had it better than KC, whose parents didn't care about her happiness at all. They wanted to send her away to the wolf-centric shifter school out in Montana against her wishes. She'd saved up to pay her way into the Lincoln Park Shifter School, and that still didn't convince them how much it meant to her. Or rather, it didn't matter to them. KC had to run away, change her name, and lie about her species to escape them.

Oscar wrote about KC and Laylea in his letters. He'd told his mother everything. When she met her last October, Sanna had known who Laylea was without asking her name. She had known how much Laylea's lizard foot meant to her and had said, "A lizard foot for KC," when she gave Laylea the crane. It was soaked with a mother's love, if not KC's own mother's love.

It might not be as love-filled as Laylea's lizard, but any protection from the latent magic affecting life at the Lincoln Park Shifter School would be better than none.

She slipped back to watch as Bailey held the red paper items in his hands. He murmured at them and then blew on them, a warm breath that floated with golden sparkles over to where she sat with one leg thrown out to the side. She nosed at the sparkles like they were bubbles.

A memory flashed in her mind. She, Oscar, and KC had discovered a secret sub-basement of LPSS. The whole place glowed with magic. Bailey and Sher's magic was barely perceptible when they were performing an enchantment. There was never any residual hint of magic.

"Hey, I've got a question," she said, and then dropped her head. Again, she'd shifted without meaning to.

"Great job! You are getting better." Bailey cheered and added, "But, hold on a sec."

Laylea didn't correct him.

The golden glow brightened around the bracelet and the crane. Bailey turned each of them around to examine all sides. He held them up to his face to peer at them, sniff them, and even listen to them.

Laylea tilted her head. *Does magic have a sound?*

"Hm," Bailey grunted unhelpfully. "Where did you get this paper?"

"Sanna, Oscar's mom. What's wrong with it?"

"Nothing's wrong. It just sucked up the enchantment like you devouring a new book."

"And that's not normal?"

"This paper feels like it was made to be enchanted. Most things aren't made to be enchanted." He slid off the bed to grab Laylea's sweats from the floor.

She put them on as he relocated to his rolling desk chair.

His face lit up as he did, and he added, "It's easy to sit on a chair because it's made for sitting. It's much harder to sit on. . . a lamppost.

"When I put on this face," Bailey gestured to his delicate, pale features, "it's easy. I am magical. So doing magic to myself is easy. When I turn your hair blue..." He rolled over and brushed the tips of her short locks with his fingers. She felt a tingle as he changed her. "... it's harder. It takes more effort. This paper took the magic so easily, I had to make it visible just to be sure that my enchantment had worked."

Laylea ran her fingers through her hair. The blue didn't feel any different. "But I'm a werehuman. Aren't I magical, too?"

"I always thought so," he said. "But if being a shifter made you magical, wouldn't Mom's lizard foot keep you from shifting?" He didn't quite finish the last word before his eyes glazed over in deep thought face again. "Now, there's an idea."

He interrupted his own reverie to drop the glow on the bracelet and crane and hand them back to Laylea. "Those should work well enough for your friends to see that invisible raven, at least."

He meant Dizzy, the raven most of the students couldn't see. There was another mystery Laylea wanted to explore. First, she asked Bailey about the magical glow. "Every surface of the subbasement of the school glows like you just made these glow. Is that like a grunt witch thing? Like, a practitioner who isn't good enough to hide their magic?"

"No." Bailey frowned at her. "Just the opposite. It would take a witch of great skill to leave a permanent glow on her work. Could everyone see it?"

"It was just me and KC and Oscar down there, and we could only see it when we were connected to Mom's lizard foot."

"Then that's a message to other practitioners. The witch wanted other witches to see the enchantments."

"Could you tell, from the glow, what was done down there?"

Bailey thought about it for a moment. He glanced back at his screens. "I don't know. Mom could." He sighed. "I'll write them a letter and ask."

"I have to meet with the Wyrdos about last night, but if you write the letter, I can code it later."

All of their correspondence with their parents had to be coded. It kept them safe. Although, if Walter and Trask were out of commission, who exactly were they still hiding from?

"That's okay. I don't need you to encode my letters. I can take care of myself, Lee. I don't need you." To prove it, he turned away to his computer screens.

He didn't need her. Except to pay the rent and make sure he ate food. If Madame Hu was going to have Fan check in on him, maybe he wouldn't be so lost if Laylea went away for a while. She couldn't solve the mystery of the unknown witch's glowing message or the mostly-invisible Dizzy from here. She'd have to get back into the Lincoln Park Shifter School for those answers.

She didn't allow herself to think about the fact that she also had to go back if she wanted to see her friends, the only friends her own age that she'd ever had. Friends who understood the challenges of life as a shifter.

No, her only thoughts as she kissed her brother's head and slipped out the door, were how he'd never miss her, and it was only fair that she got to go to school, too, now that she knew of a school where she wouldn't endanger him by revealing what she truly was. She deserved it. And her friends needed her to help figure out all the mysteries going on in those underground halls. She had to find a way to go back to LPSS.

But first, she needed to know if Lucio, Dee, and Morioka had shut down the N trade on the South Side.

4

One thing that dogs and humans have in common is that both are easily bribed with food. Laylea had some pocket change, or rather, large rolls of collar cash, and she knew right where to get pastries good enough to get her out of hot water for last night's improvisation at the stakeout. The Flores Panaderia was right down the street from The Office, the bar where the Wyrdos met up.

Since she couldn't take public transportation for fear of shifting with nowhere to hide from the normal, unknowing humans, Laylea walked the four miles from their little three-flat to the Mexican bakery. Her knock-off uggs were definitely not made for walking, but she didn't even try to shift so she could run. It was easier to think logically with a human brain, and she had a lot of plans to make if she was really going to find a way back underground to the shifter school.

She felt confident in the two-week plan she'd arranged in her head by the time she got to the panaderia. She'd make sure the N trade was shut down, arrange for one of her friends to pay the rent and keep an eye on Bailey, and she would go to Oscar Luke's home and talk to his dad. She'd get him to explain why the Shifter Council hadn't stepped in to stop the abuse at LPSS or responded to Dr. Fenn's letters about the secret medical testing and how he could just leave his son there.

The whole plan flew out of her mind when she saw Sanna Luke sitting in the passenger seat of an illegally parked car.

"Mrs. Luke!" She ran over to knock on the window.

Laylea had met Oscar's mom just once. The woman had been skinny then. Now, she looked painfully undernourished with long, thin limbs drowning in swaths of fabric stained in the bright colors of Western Africa. Her high cheekbones accentuated the deep circles under her eyes. She'd cut her hair close to the scalp, which went a long way to reducing the crazy vibe she'd let off when Laylea had gone to her home last October. She and Dee had watched Sanna a few other times, hoping to catch the trail of the newest N dealer forcing the leopard shifter to stay addicted against her will.

Sanna looked at her blankly through the glass until Laylea reached into her collar and pulled out the red crane that Bailey had charmed that morning. Sanna had given it to her to deliver to KC. At the sight of the red paper, Sanna's dark eyes lit up with panic. She flashed a glance at the panaderia as she rolled the window down.

"Oscar's friend. You must go to school. Protect my son. He is not safe there." She shoved a stack of delicate red paper into her hands. "Take him these letters. You must help him save her."

The bright jangling of bells drew their eyes to the door of the panaderia. When Laylea looked back to ask Sanna what she was talking about, Oscar's mother had closed the window and gone back to staring vacantly into the distance.

The man coming out of the Flores Panaderia held their traditional pale pink box carefully away from his crisp clothing. He crossed to the car with his eyes scanning something on his armpadd. The instant he spotted Laylea at the side of the car, his gaze shifted to his wife. Where Sanna shared Oscar's fine bone structure and never-ending forehead, his father had gifted his son wide eyes and a determined expression that could easily be mistaken for haughtiness.

Laylea's psychic tail wagged with such joy at seeing her friend's familiar expression that it almost forced a shift. She gripped the red papers firmly and focused her human thoughts on the plan she'd just made. Instead of taking a few days to prepare her questions and corner the man at home, Laylea seized the opportunity and improvised.

"Councilmember Luke," she cried with a great big smile so that he would know she meant him no harm. "I'm a friend of Oscar's."

"How nice. You've graduated?"

"I'm on a bit of a break, you could say." She barreled on before he could ask any questions. "I could use your help. I'm new to the community and not doing great in Sociology. I've never heard of the Midwest Shifter Council before. Can you tell me what it's about? What do you do?"

The poor man looked around, as if there should be somebody nearby to rescue him from this impertinent pup.

Laylea let her thoughts pour out. "And if you know he's not safe there, why don't you use your influence on the Council to get him out?"

"Whoever is telling you Oscar isn't safe at LPSS is confused. LPSS exists to keep our children safe. It is our number one edict. Has been since the Phoenix Event. We must protect our children at all costs. The best place for you to learn more about our society and the Council is in school. And if you keep asking questions in public, I think you'll very quickly be sent back."

"You're funny, Mr. Luke. But seriously, why did the Council ignore Dr. Fenn's letters about the special medical testing going on in the school? Do you think secretly selling students' blood and medical data is the best way to keep us safe?"

Mr. Luke opened the driver's side door. "These are not matters for a little girl to be worrying about."

"Somebody thinks your son is in danger. Doesn't that concern you at all? Don't you care about him?"

The man paused in setting the pastry box on his unresponsive wife's lap. Laylea felt like maybe she'd gotten to him. The tension in the air sure felt like she'd gotten his hackles up. But the face he turned to her was smooth and emotionless.

"No. Oscar is exactly where he belongs." He pasted the politician's smile back on his face. "And I'm guessing you'll see him soon."

"Shall I tell him you miss him?"

"He broke the law. I don't care what you tell him." Mr. Luke shut the car door in her face.

Laylea stumbled back as the car pulled away. Her heart melted for Oscar. It must have been horrible growing up with that for a father.

"Lee!"

She spun around at the sound of a voice she wasn't accustomed to hearing in public and grinned at the man striding toward her from the entrance of the panaderia. He popped the collar of the purple flannel shirt he wore under an unzipped black sweatshirt as if showing off his new duds. Head down and hood up, his face was fully hidden, but if Laylea needed confirmation of who he was, she could simply look down at Kyle's Fox sandals, which he wore with socks. The only things remotely creature-of-the-night about him were the black leather gloves that protected his hands more from the sun than from the cold.

Laylea growled quietly. If he was hiding his skin from the sun, it meant that Kyle had been starving himself.

"Can you eat pastries?" She jogged over to meet the former Detective Kyle Nellwin at a spot of shade under the awning of the not-yet-opened-for-the-day Italian restaurant next door to the Flores Panaderia.

Kyle laughed. "Nah. I'm just befriending the counter kid. He needs a good influence in his life."

Laylea fanned herself with Sanna's red pages. "Woof. How bad are his other influences if his good one is a vampire?"

"Ha ha, Ms. There-But-for-the-Grace-of-Me-Go-You."

Kyle's maker had wanted to turn Laylea, the dog, into a vampire as well. Fortunately for Laylea, though unfortunately for his maker, the sexy vampire hadn't counted on Kyle resisting her charms and dusting her as his first meal.

Kyle pushed the hood back from his face and quickly flipped it back up again, squinting from the reflection of sun off the snow. He did not look healthy.

"You run out of bloodcicles, Kyle?" Laylea grimaced. "I've been working a contact at a blood bank up in Evanston. Do you need me to get on that for you?"

"I'm good, puppy." The vampire bumped her fist. "I just need to clear my head for a bit."

Laylea had helped Kyle through his transition, when he'd discovered that he absorbed people's memories when he drank their blood. He'd seen the truth about Bailey, about him being a witch, when he'd tasted Laylea's blood. He hadn't bitten her or anything. She'd been wounded by a possessed cat while he was still developing self-control. She couldn't blame him. Besides, he'd kept the secret to himself.

He looked up and down the deserted street. "Tell your friends the cyclops got home safe."

"How do you know?"

"I got him there. After the four four dragged his Bonobo friend away, I—"

"The four four?" Laylea had heard Dee asking around about a secret police code, 10-44. Was this the same thing?

"The shifter cops. The ones who get called in for things like a buzzard and bear trying to kill a puppy dog at the Lincoln Park Zoo," he said pointedly.

"Or a basketball player turning into an ape and tearing apart a food truck," she guessed.

"Right. A food truck with canine teeth marks on the brake fluid hoses and the electrical wires." He reached out to touch her face, as if to assure himself she was alright. "You could've killed yourself, kid."

"It seemed like a good idea at the time. Everyone else was focused on the pharmacy and the truck was going to get away."

"Are you going somewhere?"

"What?" The shift in conversation threw her.

"Why are you carrying so much cash around?" He slid his hand down to her bulging collar. "You're gonna get rolled."

"I'm trying to find a way to pay the rent if I'm not around."

"You're making plans for what happens when you die on one of these missions?" His hood fell back, and he didn't fix it. "That is not acceptable. Laylea. You need to take care of yourself. What happens when your bio-brothers finally find you, and you're dead? How about your mother? Sher and Clark? Do you think Bailey is going to stay sane if you die on his watch? What is wrong with you?"

"Dude!" Laylea grabbed his hood and pulled it back into place. "I want to go back to school. I don't want to die. I didn't mean to electrocute myself last night. It was an accident. I just didn't see any other way to stop the drug dealers before they got away."

Kyle stared at her as if he could suss the truth of her words by the force of his gaze.

She waved the red papers she still gripped in one hand. "I can give myself a paper cut if you want proof."

He stumbled a step away from her at the suggestion and then wiggled his fingers at her in a gimme gesture. "I'm taking the cash."

A door opened down the street. Nobody normal would have heard the quiet squeak of the hinges. Laylea and Kyle both glanced over to see Amal coming out of the Brownies' resale shop. Laylea hurried to pull the rolled bills out of her collar. Amal knew Kyle — had known Kyle. He didn't know that Kyle had survived the shooting. None of Team Wyrdos knew except Laylea, and she'd promised she wouldn't tell.

Kyle took the first roll of cash and tucked it away in an inside pocket of his hoodie. "No one's gonna roll me for your money. I'll keep it safe and get it to Madame Hu on time if you can't because you're in school." He took the second roll and tucked that away as well. "But, if you die, little girl, I will be there, and I will turn you. You will be the companion my maker wanted. Keep that in mind the next time you take a stupid risk."

Laylea felt tears welling in her eyes. She nodded. "I promise. Go. Amal will see you."

Kyle lifted her chin. "Because of your blood," he took a deep breath before he admitted, "I will always hear you. Whisper my name, and I will come." He dropped her chin and zipped up his hoodie. "Yell it, and people are gonna think you're crazy. Keep your tail up, puppy dog."

Kyle sauntered past the panaderia, waving at somebody through the door. He disappeared around the corner. A minute later, a tiny bat flew over the row of buildings, heading north with a light wisp of smoke rising from his tiny form.

"You've got to eat something, old man." Laylea whispered the advice she'd never tell him in person.

"Excuse me? I just had lunch."

Laylea whipped around at the sound of a voice so close she felt the man's breath on her neck. She hadn't heard anybody approach. It wasn't Amal.

She stumbled back at the vicious smile on the stranger's pale face. Something in her gut growled. Her body wanted to shift and run away. It was probably a mistake, but she held her shape and her ground.

5

*L*aylea tamped down on her desire to tuck her psychic tail under her belly. Her canine instincts had scanned the man with all of her senses and jumped straight to high alert. The human side of her took a bit longer to catch up. She didn't want to judge the man unfairly, despite the creepy way he'd snuck up on her. Her head tilted as she spotted the man's cane. She should have heard it. And he didn't look quite old enough to need it. While he was over-weight, he wasn't quite so heavy as to need the assistance. Beady eyes peered out of a round face. When he caught her gaze, the gleam in his eyes dimmed quickly from gleefully vicious to the muted gaze of a helpless dolt. But Laylea knew what she had seen. He smelled off somehow, and she had to stop herself from shifting to get a better whiff.

"I wouldn't call you an old man, sir." She showed her teeth, and if he mistook it for a smile, that was all to the good.

In response, a smile glommed onto the man's face that raised Laylea's hackles. She almost took another step back.

"As charming as I was told," he observed.

The man wore tweed top to bottom. His old fashioned houndstooth cap shaded a face crinkled in thought, his brown eyes examining Laylea from much too close.

Thanks to the many odd people she worked for as an investigator, she'd become good at dealing with socially awkward situations. She'd forgotten that she'd been good at them right from the start, being a terrier. She didn't back away.

She asked, "Do you know me?"

"You are Lee Woodford, the ghost hunter, yes?"

"I am Lee. Who are you?"

"I am Dr. Maurice Brock." He paused, watching her as if she might recognize his name. "I was told I could find you here, and you would exorcize my ghost."

"Well, I'm not a priest, Dr. Brock." She giggled.

He didn't.

She continued, "But, I do help people with a variety of paranormal issues. Are you in need of a communicator?" She slipped into the language that made it easier for her skeptical clients to express their self-labeled ridiculous suspicions.

"I need a ghost hunted."

A bitter scent emanated from the spittle sent flying by the man's over-enunciated Ts. Laylea stepped to one side.

Brock explained, "My house is haunted, and I was told you're the one to call. But, you don't have an armpadd."

"That is true. I generally just meet people at my friend's bar over there. Would you like to come in and chat about your problem?"

"There is a ghost in my house. That is my problem."

Laylea started walking toward The Office's blue door. Nobody could see out of the painted-over window, but she'd feel better if she were closer. The not-so-old man limped along beside her. He walked with a hunch that made him seem nearly as short as she was.

"Let's go inside, and you can tell me why you think you have a ghost, and I can outline the steps we can take to deal with your unwanted ex-person manifestation." She reached for the handle and pulled.

"No." He pushed the door of The Office closed and then yanked his hand back as if he'd been burned. "I can't go inside. I have an appointment to get to. I know you meet clients at Common Electronics. I live just down the street from there. Could you meet me in a couple of hours? We can talk then. Here's a retainer to reassure you that I'm on the level." He handed her an envelope that bulged with cash. "I'm not sure I can go home again unless you help me. I'm—" he swallowed and cleared his throat, "I'm scared."

He didn't smell scared. Still, a handful of cash meant she could stay at LPSS longer. And she wasn't making any promises to solve his ghost problem. All she ever agreed to do was try to help.

"Okay, Dr. Brock. No one should be afraid to go home. I'll meet you at Common Electronics at three." She reached for the handle again, the envelope making it a bit awkward.

Dr. Brock backed away with a grimace on his face. "Thank you. Thank you." He turned and practically ran for a sporty, two-seater car parked down the block.

Laylea thought she saw a figure waiting in the passenger seat, but she couldn't be sure with the shadows. She watched Dr. Brock until the door to The Office swung open in her face.

"Are you coming in or not?" A too-skinny man with scruffy off-blond hair and a smile that could light up a dungeon pulled her into the bar and into a hug that left her feet dangling.

"Guess I am," she mumbled into the thick weave of his St. Patrick's Day sweater.

Junior had discovered that ugly Christmas sweaters made people unreasonably happy. Since, as the boogeyman, he literally disappeared from people's vision when they got scared, he'd decided to collect ugly sweaters for every special day he could think of. Another Office regular with a knitting addiction was more than happy to oblige.

"Junior." Laylea used the hand she had wrapped around the boogeyman to tap him on the shoulder. "Junior, I can't breathe."

"Lee Woodford." He set her down and kept hold of her shoulders. "You can't work with us anymore if you're going to get yourself killed."

"How do you know about that?" Laylea's voice squeaked in protest.

He held up his right arm and pulled back the sleeve of his sweater, showing her his armpadd. Of course. Dee would have texted the team.

She turned away from Junior to scan the bar. It was pretty much deserted at noon on a Wednesday. Three people sat in the dark room. One huddled at the end of the oaken bar by the digital jukebox. One slept in a booth, her head leaning against the wooden wall. Ned, the knitting addict, watched Junior and Laylea as he worked at his usual two-top table, his huge fingers maneuvering the knitting needles like they were a pair of magic wands. He gave her a barely perceptible nod when she caught his eye.

"Hey, Ned." She looked from him to Seb, the owner, who stood on his riser behind the bar, polishing the already sparkling brass rails. "Hey, Seb."

"Scarecrow, you and the bairn should head to the back," he said in his charming Scottish burr. "You understand we've had some strangers in the place this week, Lee. I don't take risks like you do."

"I thought I was helping!" Laylea could usually count on a warm welcome from the barman. He was even shorter than she was and almost always knew the right thing to say when you were hurting.

She had been hoping for a cup of tea. Instead, she gripped Sanna's red papers in one hand, Dr. Brock's envelope in the other, and stomped past the long bar to the hallway that led to the bathrooms, storage room, and back courtyard. Laylea swung a left before the bathrooms and went into the storage room. In a corner by the closet that had once been stuffed to bursting with cleaning supplies, lay a red corduroy dog bed. The lowest level of the metal shelves behind it held a stack of sweatsuits and cheap boots. Beside them sat a canvas satchel much like the one draped over Junior's chest. Laylea had been collecting supplies in anticipation of returning to LPSS. She added the envelope and stack of red papers to the front pocket, which already contained an etch-a-sketch and a new dibs drive bracelet. She was about to look in Dr. Brock's envelope when a pair of long black arms, bare despite the cold weather, wrapped around her and squeezed.

"Don't you worry, little puppy." Amal's breath tickled her ear. "You just scared everybody. I can teach you about cars and which cables are dangerous and which will drench you in oily fluid."

Laylea shoved the envelope in with her school supplies and spun around to face the brownie. You'd expect brownies to be little guys who could easily hide in the forest. But this was modern Chicago, and wyrdos had to adapt. Amal had adapted far from the tiny species of brownie. When he wasn't kneeling to hug her, he stood six foot ten, topping Laylea by a solid two feet. He looked like he was in his early thirties, but he'd told stories about the Chicago World's Fair, so, like many of her wyrdo friends, she couldn't judge his age by appearances. His power, like Orin's and Lucio's, was instant karma. They could judge a person's karma and pay them back in all the traditional ways: cleaning your house, souring your milk, clearing your skin, or making you stink. He could also take money from one jerk's wallet and place it in a Good Samaritan's or any other payment or reward he could think of. Which had gotten Laylea thinking last night, before she fell asleep beside the basketball game when she was supposed to be on surveillance duty.

The Wyrdos, specifically Junior, had been keeping an eye on the "sleep lab" they'd discovered while searching for the N manufacturing center. It was run by the shifter enforcer, Adrien Denier. While looking for Laylea when he'd thought she was in kiddie jail last summer, Junior had found five more "sleep labs" all across the city. They'd been taking pictures and gathering as much information as they could on the sleepers, people hooked up to all kinds of machines. They'd discovered that some of the sleepers had been reported to the police as missing persons. Some had just dropped out of society, all activity on their credit apps and social media accounts stopping suddenly, without anyone making an official report. But they still didn't know why.

"I had an idea," Laylea blurted out.

"I had a thought," Amal echoed her.

Junior chuckled from where he leaned in the doorway. "I had breakfast for dinner."

They looked up at him.

"Just trying to contribute."

Laylea threw an off-brand ugg at him and poked Amal's chest. "Could you read the sleepers' karma?"

Amal's eyebrows shot up. "Yes. I can't believe we haven't tried that already. *I* was thinking you could apply your day job skills and see if there are any ghosts in the sleep lab. We know someone died in the Starwood lab."

"Oh." Laylea stepped off the bed. "Yeah. We had to run, so Dee couldn't help them cross over. There's a very good chance, if they were in the lab against their will, that their spirit is sticking around." She crossed to the broom closet. "Let's go."

Junior put up his hands. "Uh, I don't think you can go, Lee."

"Sure I can. I don't have anywhere to be until three o'clock."

"No, that's not what I mean. Um, you see, Dee kinda suggested…" He stopped, looking to Amal for help.

"Right." Amal laid a hand on Laylea's shoulder. "Dee ordered us to keep you off missions for a while."

Laylea gaped at her friends. She finally managed to choke out, "What? Why? Nobody got hurt because of me last night."

"You did," Junior pointed out.

"Only a little. I shifted right away. All better." Laylea healed when she shifted forms. It was a neat trick and came in handy.

Amal sighed. "Yeah, that was Morioka's complaint."

"Nobody saw me shift. You only know I did because they didn't find a fried dog under the taco truck." She headed for the door. "Where are they? I can convince them."

"They're still working the scene." Junior's words stopped her, even though he didn't block her way. If Morioka and Dee were still there, they were working the scene in their official capacity as cops. It must have been a bigger mess than she thought.

"Which means they're not here." Amal drawled the words, watching Junior out of the side of his eyes as he strolled over to the closet door.

"We have no backup if something goes wrong, if we get caught," Junior said.

"I don't even have to leave the closet to read the room," Amal said. "How about you, Lee?"

"Nah, I just need to be able to see into the sleep lab. I'll need both hands, but you can keep a hold of me, Junior, and if you sense any danger, you can transport us right back." Laylea shrugged, trying to act like it was no big deal. Her psychic tail was whipping back and forth, and she focused on her thumbs to prevent an untimely shift. It was hard to say no when her emotions wanted to wag.

"I don't want to get in trouble with Morioka. I've seen her mad." Junior picked an imaginary piece of lint from his sweater.

"She'll never have to know." Amal turned the knob.

Junior found a real piece of lint, but walked toward the closet as he flicked it from his arm. "Okay. But this mission is just between us. Agreed?" He held his pinky out to Laylea.

She hooked it with her own little finger. "Agreed."

He held it out to Amal, who rolled his eyes, but pinky swore just the same. "You know I'm telling Morioka nothing. Dee would flay us both alive."

The three of them stepped into the closet and held hands.

As a boogeyman, Junior could travel from any bedroom closet to any other. He didn't always choose a destination, but he'd gotten much better at reaching the right location when he did. The storage room closet counted because Laylea slept in the storage room from time to time. The lab closets were easy to find because each lab held around thirty sleepers. It put out a powerful signal.

Junior sucked in a deep breath and asked, "Ready?"

Amal replied, "Ready."

Laylea reached out and shut the closet door.

6

---

*L*aylea always expected flashing lights and quavering violin music when she traveled with Junior. But the shift from here to there was never so dramatic. One moment, they were in the neat—though small—closet in the back of Seb's bar. The next moment, she felt buckets against her legs and the handle of a cleaning cart pushing into her upper back.

Amal reached to open the door and bumped a mop from where it had been leaned against the wall. The mop knocked into a broom, and the pair fell right on top of Laylea.

Heat flashed in her gut and she shifted, rolling into the door, which burst open and spilled her out of the closet before they could determine if the sleepers were attended by anybody. She froze, listening and sniffing the air. She couldn't smell anybody awake besides Junior and Amal, who stank of adrenaline. That smell dissipated as Junior replaced the cleaning tools without causing any more racket.

"So much for staying in the closet," Amal whispered over Laylea's head. He stood in a low crouch, ready to protect her if there had been any doctors or techs in the room.

She bumped her head against his shin to show her thanks.

He laughed. "No worries."

"Can you contact ghosts as a dog, Lee?" Junior followed them out of the crowded closet and strode over to the nearest bed. He started taking pictures of the sleeper and all the equipment attached to her. "We can't stay long. Guards come through every fifteen minutes."

It was, in fact, easier to see clinging spirits when she was her dog self. But communication became all but impossible. That wasn't a problem if her only goal was to make them aware that they weren't alive or to give the ghost comfort. But Team Wyrdos needed a talkative ghost who would give Laylea all the details she could tease out of them.

Still, she wriggled out of her clothes and stepped to the aisle between the two rows of beds to circle slowly, shutting out the everyday worries of rent and Bailey and being banned from the Wyrdos. She turned east, south, west, north, acknowledging each direction. She turned west, south, east, and north, acknowledging all the directions in between. Finally, she turned widdershins again, opening her awareness. A veil lifted. She could feel a difference through her fur. The air, already quite cool in the medical lab, gained an icy quality, like freezing rain that hadn't started falling.

She inhaled and turned to the nearest spike of bitter that made the cilia in her nostrils ping. Her eyes were open, but the veil hung more heavily on that sense than her others. She listened harder and caught an echo that complimented the beeping of the heart monitors, which were all slightly out of rhythm around the room. Another echo thumped deep in her senses, contrasting the living machines. The soundtracks were the same. The ghostly sounds, while hollow and distant and not real to her, mimicked the very real wash of machine whine and motor drone around her as well as the ever-present *beep beep beep* of the monitors. The veil lifted further as her brain understood what it was she was hearing, smelling, and feeling.

Fighting fear with every breath, she forced herself to see the ghostly bodies sharing beds around the room. Her tail sank and tucked under her belly, but it wasn't enough. She needed tears. She found them dripping onto her human hands, the burn of the shift trembling against the bitter sting of adrenaline begging her muscles to run.

"What is it, Lee?" Junior's tender voice broke Laylea's paralysis. She sucked in deep breaths as she pushed herself to her feet to take her clothes from him. She left the boots by the closet door.

"They—" She swallowed against the choking sensation and allowed the tears to flow down her human cheeks. "Ghosts make their own reality. Some think they're still alive. Most think they're trapped in the place where they died. These poor spirits—" She broke off in a sob.

"You're safe, Lee." Junior rubbed the nape of her neck where her mother would have carried her. "You're okay."

"I am. They're not." She pulled herself together and walked from bed to bed, focusing to separate the comatose ghosts from the living, sleeping forms. One bed held four bodies. "There are more than a dozen ghosts here. They think they're still asleep. They're stuck here, and there is no way for me to help them move on."

She stopped at a bed that held only one form, the living body of a young Black woman. She couldn't have been out of her teens, or just barely. She was thin, malnourished, like Sanna. No ghost bodies lay on her bed. Just below the tubes taped to her arm, someone had tattooed two triangles tip to tip in deep black ink on her deep black skin.

"They're victims. Nearly all of these people have good karma." Amal's voice startled her. He stood at her elbow. "This girl is glowing with good karma — she-put-herself-in-danger-to-help-others kind of karma."

"Can you get a picture of her?" Laylea asked. "She's so young. But, she's the only one who's used this bed."

"Junior," Amal called down the row while he raised his armpadd to get a picture of the girl with the black tattoo. "Have we identified anyone in this lab?"

"Some." Junior stood at the foot of a bed holding another young girl. She was the only one of the sleepers who looked like she was getting fed enough. Despite looking younger than Laylea, her roughly shorn hair shone white under the fluorescent bulbs. "This is Deanna Amelia Gorshkov."

"Gorshkov? Really? The same name we've been seeing everywhere?" Amal asked.

"Yeah." Junior gripped the frame of the girl's bed with a white fist.

"Are they related?"

"No idea," he said. "There are no records, since Gorshkov went underground after being busted for Ecstasy and Methoin production."

"That was twenty years ago. This girl can't be as old as Lee." Amal's voice sounded tight.

Laylea hadn't heard about any of this. "Who's Gorshkov?"

Junior didn't respond.

Amal turned to the bed beside Deanna's, as if he hadn't heard her. "Who's this guy?"

A white man, not quite middle aged, lay in the shadow of a female ghost. His face and arms showed some badly healed scars. A couple pink slashes cut across a tattoo on his inner forearm. Two triangles joined at the tips, tattooed in white ink.

Junior barely glanced away from Deanna. "That's, uh, Brian Samborsky."

Amal laid his hand on the bare skin of the man's upper chest. The gentle wrinkles around Brian Samborsky's eyes melted away. "He's got the same fought-the-bad-guys-at-personal-cost karma as the teenager over there."

"They also have the same tattoo." Laylea pointed it out to the boys. "Do you recognize it?"

Amal ran a finger along the ink. "It looks familiar, but I can't place it. Junior?"

They both looked over when the boogeyman didn't respond. He'd returned his gaze to Deanna Amelia Gorshkov's sleeping face.

Amal put a little force into his tone. "Junior. Come here."

Junior blinked. He peeled his hand from the bedside and stumbled over to them.

Where he had been, a female figure now stood, as if he'd left a shadow behind him. Her nearly opaque hand gripped the bed frame just as Junior's had. Just as Junior had, she stared at Deanna Amelia Gorshkov. Bare feet and a hospital gown suggested she had been a patient when she died. But the fabric was decorated with storks. None of the figures in the beds had any decoration on their gowns. Her short, wet hair didn't move when she jerked her head to watch Junior backing away.

Laylea stepped between the spirit and the boys. The woman's eyes blazed, and Laylea felt the veil shifting again. The hairs on her arms stood up, much as her hackles would have if she'd had them handy. Though a frisson ran down her spine, she pasted on her client smile and forced some true warmth into her heart. This was a sad place. It was perfectly reasonable that this ghost would be sad, would share her sadness, would suck all the joy from the universe until life ceased to be. Perfectly reasonable.

"Hi." She took a single, small step closer to Deanna's bed. She had to think of it that way because there was no way she could have willed herself to take a step closer to the ghost. "I can see you. Would you like to talk?"

The ghost did not respond.

Laylea forced herself to feel the joy of lying on her dad, Clark's, lap while they flew in his little prop plane. She visualized that feeling as a green sweater and pulled it on over her head until it hung to her knees, protecting her from the ghost's overwhelming sorrow. She took another step away from the boys. She considered what to ask. They didn't have long, and her job here was not to help the ghosts cross over. She was here to get information about the lab. Laylea couldn't question the comatose ghosts.

Despite her overwhelming grief, this ghost was their best option, and she had wanted Junior to focus on the girl in that bed.

Laylea asked, "Did you know Deanna?"

The ghost turned her eyes to the bed, and the paralyzing sorrow lifted from Laylea. She kept her hold on her imaginary sweater anyway and took two quick steps closer, so she could still see the ghost's face. The woman was moving her lips, but Laylea couldn't hear any words. She took another step toward her. "What's your name?"

The ghost turned faster than a light switching off, enfolding Laylea in her pain. Trapped in the freezing dark and deafened by the poor woman's sobs, Laylea tried to suck in a breath and found herself inhaling bitter nails of ice. Reason drained from her and she cried out, mourning not her own death, but the torture of her daughter, Deanna.

7

*T*ime is a human construct. It has no place in the spirit world. Though subsumed by the dead mother's reality, Laylea was still human, still alive. She knew that such a thing as time existed. But, for all she could tell, she'd been standing at the foot of Deanna's bed for a lifetime. The cold freezing her limbs tasted bitter. The ice burrowed into the roof of her mouth and from there into her brain like a spike. It tasted like adrenaline. The ghost was panicking. Probably had been panicking for her entire death.

Laylea couldn't hear Amal, but she could see the general shape and color of him running to the room's main door, putting his ear against it, and yelling something at her. Junior joined Amal. He was just a splash of green passing through the blinding torment of watching her daughter trapped halfway between life and death.

Green. That was Junior's happy ugly St. Patrick's Day sweater. Laylea tore her attention from Deanna and fought to lift her hands up from her sides. She imagined the rough feel of wool against her skin and clenched her fists around the too-long sleeves of the imaginary joy sweater she had constructed out of the memories of her dad.

The very thought of a father figure blasted like a gas fire through the spirit's icy torment. She turned on Laylea, squeezing her lungs and sending spikes of ice into her skin. At the same time, a tiny, bright spike of reason burst through Laylea's paralyzing terror. If she was attacking her, the spirit saw her as a separate entity. Laylea could use that.

The ghost only knew panic. It couldn't differentiate her panic from anything else and that would be death if she dragged Laylea into her truth. Laylea's only chance lay in pushing the ghost to alter her own reality. It would be dangerous to convince the grieving mother that she was dead. But, if she could prove to the ghost that she was an individual, Laylea just might have a chance to survive.

Laylea reached out with her senses to keep Amal and Junior's distant voices alive in her reality. Then she mustered all her psychic strength and screamed into the muffling void, "Deanna loves you."

The change was instant. Laylea could suck fresh air into her lungs. She heard Amal and Junior calling her name, arguing over whether they could touch her. The ice pouring through Laylea's veins evaporated, and the ghost's grip on her became isolated to two electrified hands holding her upper arms.

Amal hissed, "Lee, the guard is coming."

Junior cried, "Tell us how to help you."

Laylea pushed her advantage. She pinned the ghost's wandering gaze, begging, "Who are you? What is your name?"

The ghost sucked in air, her throat rasping as her form took on more solidity. Her exhale slowly took on the form of a word, a name, "Aaaahhhhmelia."

"Amelia." Laylea repeated the name three times to make it stick. "Amelia. It's very nice to meet you, Amelia. I'm Lee." It was best to be completely honest with ghosts, but she couldn't very well give away her real name with Amal and Junior standing right behind her. And the fact that they didn't know her real name sparked a bit of guilt in her heart, down below her imaginary green sweater of dad joy. Amelia started fading as Laylea felt that guilt of dishonesty. She shoved it down.

"Amelia. Is this your daughter?" She knew it was.

Amelia released her death-grip on Laylea and took one step that transported her to the head of Deanna's bed. She brushed a hand along the girl's stark white hair.

"Do you know how Deanna came here?"

Fire burned in Amelia's eyes. She hissed, "Him."

"Him? A man did this?" She heard movement behind her but kept her focus on the ghost. "Who did this, Amelia?"

"Lee, hurry up." Amal touched her back gently. "The guard is at the door."

She nodded, not even aware that she had turned her head to acknowledge him. In that instant, Amelia moved.

Amelia's breath burned on Laylea's face. It froze her blood and blew her hair back. She could barely hear the buzz of the electronic lock disengaging on the door to the lab. Droplets of ghost spittle sizzled on her skin.

"He's at the school." Amelia's words grew louder until they were nearly incomprehensible. "He's at the Lincoln Park Shifter School."

She roared the meaning straight into Laylea's brain and then exploded into a million glittering fragments that floated into Laylea's being as Amal lifted her bodily and hauled her back into the closet.

The door slammed shut. Junior, Amal, and Laylea tumbled into a heap, scattering bottles of cleaning supplies all over the small closet in the back of Seb's bar. Amal hugged Laylea's skinny body to his chest. He rubbed her arms and blew hot breath onto her frozen fingers. "Talk to me. Are you okay?"

"Shift, Lee." Junior reached over the pair to pop the door open. He grabbed the fur-covered blanket from Laylea's bed, scattering her little treasures over the storeroom floor. "Shift and heal yourself." His voice trembled. Mist formed in the air as he spoke. Panic colored his actions.

Laylea pulled herself together. She had to help Junior. He'd never encountered a trapped spirit before. She was okay. She didn't even need to do a mental check. If she'd been truly injured, she would have already shifted. There was nothing wrong with her that a kind word and a couple hours of belly rubs wouldn't fix.

Junior didn't have it so easy.

She let him wrap her in the blanket and cuddle her between himself and Amal. It was easy to catch his eyes as he was desperately trying to catch hers. Getting his attention was a little more difficult. He kept asking questions and begging her to shift.

"Junior." She repeated his name a bunch of times until she caught sight of the illicit rawhide he'd given her for her adoptionversary last year, right before she'd gotten him shot.

She wriggled out of the men's grasp and scooped up the rawhide. Without thinking too much about it, she stuck it sideways into Junior's mouth. Amal sent spittle flying as he choked out a laugh. Junior finally stopped talking.

"Shush. You're alive. I'm—" She started to reassure him, but the sight of him with the rawhide in his mouth shot her back to the last time she'd seen him like this—when Diejuste, their goddess friend, had been digging a bullet out of his chest. Instead of trying any more reassurance for him, she flung her arms around him and babbled, "You're alive. You're alive. All the joy I need is that you're alive."

Junior lifted her from Amal's lap. He sat back and held her until her unexpected tears subsided. By the time she'd calmed, he'd calmed.

"Yeah," he said when she leaned back. "We're both alive."

"I'm alive, too," Amal put in from where he leaned against the closet doorframe. "I'm guessing you met someone who isn't, though?"

Laylea sighed. She rubbed a hand along Junior's sweater to keep the sadness at bay. "Deanna's mother is watching over her."

Amal's eyebrows shot up. "Was she a sleeper, too, before she died?"

Laylea shook her head. "No. And she wasn't much help. Junior felt it. She was trapped in a world of pain and sorrow. She could barely remember that she was a person once."

Junior shivered. "All I felt was shame. She was a mother, and she was ashamed. She needed to find a way to save her daughter, and she couldn't."

"That was panic. That's why your saliva is so bitter."

Junior's breathing slowed as Laylea said the words. His pupils contracted to a normal size. "Yeah. Yeah. She was caught up in panic."

"It took a lot for her to even remember her own name." Laylea glanced up at the clock over the door. She'd have to get going if she wanted to scout the neighborhood before meeting her client's ghost. A shiver ran through her scalp. Hopefully, the guy was a kook, and his *ghost* had a rational explanation. She really wasn't in the mood to meet another broken spirit.

"Do happy things today, Junior. That's an order. Go fill that lonely kid's closet with balloons."

Junior sighed. "Which one?"

Laylea crawled over to one of the items that had been flung away when Junior grabbed her blanket. She shoved the packet of balloons into his chest. "All of them." She looked down for a second and added, "Don't go back to the labs for a little while. Amelia might be restless."

Amal started gathering the rest of the scattered items, sliding them over. "Amelia is Deanna's mother?"

"Yes."

Junior scooped up Laylea's things and tossed them back into her dog bed, "And restless means dangerous?"

"Yes."

Amal pulled the blanket from around the two of them and fluffed it neatly within the bolster of the bed. "Did you learn anything useful from Amelia?"

"Yeah." Laylea reached past him to grab a pair of boots off her shelf. She put them on, wiggling her toes in the tiny joy of the fuzzy inside. "I learned that I need to go back to school."

8

*J*oy chased away the last vestiges of Ghost Amelia's funk as Laylea ducked in the back door of Common Electronics. This was where she had first met her best friend, KC, known to her parents as Karly Carlotta Delcampo. Her parents owned Common Electronics, and KC had worked here before she ran away to LPSS. Her parents had wanted her to go to her great-grandfather's school out west like all of her brothers had.

Laylea normally arrived as a dog and had to wait in the alley to shift, but she hadn't shifted once since the scare in the sleep lab. She could have used the front door, but then the bells would jangle and draw Mr. Delcampo out of the back office, and then he would follow her as she browsed. To avoid all that, she snuck in the alley door, as usual.

An unfamiliar male voice echoed through the back office as Laylea dashed past the doorway. "You have no idea where your daughter is, and you don't care." It was a rich voice, shaking with anger.

It was followed by Mrs. Delcampo's strident voice. "DJ Delcampo, you will address us with respect."

"My sister is missing, ma'am."

Laylea grinned. Clearly, KC's brother had a temper to match his sister's.

The "ma'am" in question sounded unimpressed. "You do not have a sister anymore."

Laylea's heart sank. Granted, one of her four parents was the evil scientist she had to hide from for fear he would do deadly experiments on her, but even he wanted her. The other three had sacrificed everything to keep her safe. How awful that KC's mother could even think such a horrible thing, much less say it.

"I have a sister. And I'm going to find her." DJ clearly agreed with Laylea.

The office door slammed as best it could, being a hollow-core door that hadn't been closed in the three years Laylea had been shopping there. She ducked behind the sales counter.

"Hi, there."

The rich voice sounded lovely when it wasn't grating through frustration.

She peeked up to see a copper-skinned guy about her brother's age pushing a stray lock of thick, black hair out of his eyes. He sighed, and she tried not to stare at the well-muscled chest straining his t-shirt.

He offered a wry little grin. "Didn't know there was anybody in the store."

Laylea gestured at her ear and shrugged as if she couldn't hear him. She almost tried signing something, but since the only ASL signs she knew were for barf and sea turtle, she refrained.

"Uh huh." DJ raised one eyebrow at her in an expression so reminiscent of KC that Laylea couldn't help but grin. "But you being deaf doesn't explain why we didn't hear the bells on the front door."

Laylea pulled herself up by the counter. She leaned over the glass top and whispered, "I sneak in the back because I don't like it when your dad watches me."

KC's big brother leaned in and lowered his voice. "It's not just you. He thinks everyone is going to steal something. And yet, he does not see forcing my brothers, sister, and I to work here for free as stealing from us."

"I thought he considered the things you learned while working here to be your payment." That's what KC had said.

"The only one of us to learn anything was my sister, and the best thing *she* ever learned was how to hack into an armpadd."

"Yeah. Tap, Tap, Cross Slide, Tap. Who knew it was so easy?" Laylea laughed, demonstrating on DJ's armpadd. The padd chimed, and DJ's settings screen opened. When she realized that he wasn't laughing with her, Laylea looked up to see a hopeful gleam in his eyes. It took several seconds before she realized that she had just admitted to knowing KC. DJ wanted to know where she was. KC didn't want anybody to know. She added, "Or so I hear."

He blinked a few times. She held her breath.

"Have you seen the fabulous new Dibs ID bands, all the way on the other side of the store?" He pushed himself off the counter and padded coolly to the shelves as far from the sales counter as they could get.

Laylea, hoping curiosity wouldn't kill the canine, followed. With a quick glance at the mirrors overhead, DJ bent to the boxes on the lowest level. Laylea was familiar with the security mirrors. DJ had crouched in one of the two blind spots. She saw movement in the mirror and spotted Mr. Delcampo coming out of the office, calling for DJ. She pretended to examine a twofer cable on the shelf in front of her, then casually lowered herself to DJ's height.

"These are not the latest and greatest." DJ pulled a bracelet out of a sliced-open package. It was a simple piece with a circular locket made of what looked like brass. "But you slip it on your wrist, tighten the straps." He matched action to words and secured the band around Laylea's wrist. "And forget about it."

Laylea glanced around as the bells on the front door rang dully against the glass. Mr. Delcampo's uninspired greeting followed close after. "Good afternoon. Welcome to Common Electronics."

DJ pulled a quarter-sized data transport device known as a dibs drive from his jeans pocket. "You can fit a dibs drive in each side of this center case." He demonstrated. "If there's room on the drive, you can copy files through the case, like this." He swiped and typed on his armpadd and took Laylea's arm to lay the drive on his screen. He leaned in as he did so. "Is she safe?"

Laylea thought about it. Any answer gave very little away. He'd already figured out she knew KC. She nodded.

"Is she where she wants—" His armpadd buzzed. DJ released her arm. "No. It's better if I don't know. Tell her DJ loves her." He pulled the sleeve of her sweatshirt down over the Dibs Band and bolted out of the aisle to offer help to the customer who had come in. "Ma'am, you need a replacement for those cables?"

Laylea stared down at her wrist. He'd put KC's happiness ahead of his own. KC hadn't talked much about her brothers, but from what she had said, Laylea had assumed they were just like her parents: self-centered jerks. It made her psychic tail wag to know she had happy news to deliver when she got back to school.

She stood from the shelf, shaking her head as if she hadn't found what she was looking for, and strolled the few steps to the front door. A glance over her shoulder showed DJ leading a woman to his father at the sales counter. Mr. Delcampo was well occupied as Laylea slipped out the front so carefully the bells barely tinkled overhead.

"Lee Woodford." Dr. Brock stood just outside, clutching an antique briefcase with two leather straps holding it closed and smoking an old-fashioned roll up cigarette.

Laylea inhaled to respond and broke into a coughing fit. Her lungs burned. She sprinted away from her client as fast as she could, terrified that she was about to shift. Her body did revolt when she reached the alley, but just to drag up all the morning kibble from her stomach and paint the brick wall with the half-digested mush.

"Ms. Woodford?" Dr. Brock called out. It sounded like he hadn't moved an inch from where he'd been.

Laylea wiped her mouth, took a deep breath, and returned to the doctor with a smile. The sickening smoke wafted everywhere around the man. She stopped far enough away to keep her stomach. "Hi. You startled me."

"Sensitive to smoke, are you?" He smirked before dropping the butt. He didn't even grind the embers out with his foot, just left it burning as he walked away, his case bouncing off his bum leg.

Laylea stepped on it. She considered picking it up and throwing it in a trash can, but her mouth already tasted like bile. She wasn't sure she could handle her fingers smelling like tobacco until she could get away from Brock and shift. She hustled after the limping man, thinking of all the things she needed to do before she could get DJ's message and Sanna's papers to KC and Oscar back at school.

She had to make arrangements with Fan and Madame Hu to make sure Bailey ate. She had to contact all the people who sent clients her way and let them know that she'd be unavailable for a while. She should check in with Tori at Northeve Labs about blood delivery for Kyle. She definitely needed to stop in to see Marcos at the assessor's office, so he wouldn't think she'd just disappeared. Morioka would have to be warned to expect letters from her at the station. It would make the cop super happy to see Laylea going away again. She wouldn't pose any more danger to the team. Only, Laylea hadn't endangered them. None of them got electrocuted, so what was the problem?

She was deep in these thoughts as Dr. Brock led her to the crumbling steps of a single-story shack that belonged on a horror movie poster. Deep beneath the warped wood and ivy-covered windows, the home's original charm scrabbled to keep its place in the overall first impression. Laylea considered maybe it was the ghost of the home's charm that was haunting Dr. Brock.

"Please, please, come in. Just let me set these things down, and then I will show you the specific bedroom that is a problem." The doctor let the screen door slam behind him but left the wooden door wide open.

The stairs creaked and groaned as Laylea climbed up, smelling a crispness inside the house that was at odds with the various molds growing on the outside. Stepping over the threshold was like entering another world. As much as the outside was a study in chaos, the inside was a monument to the precise.

The bungalow had been constructed with built-in shelves and elaborate lintels. To her left, a carved archway led to a space just large enough to hold a gleaming dining room table and six chairs alongside an antique sideboard and tall curio cabinet. Another archway in front of her led to a hallway with three doors. Laylea peered around a Tuscan column of highly polished walnut to find Brock taking items from his unbuckled leather case and placing them precisely in the pigeonholes of a rolltop desk. He drew a long-handled flashlight out of the front pocket of the case and slid it into the lowest right-hand recess. He tossed a collection of three tubes onto the green blotter. Each tube appeared to be the length and width of her pinkie finger and was topped with a tiny aerosol spray lid.

To her surprise, he peeled his armpadd off and placed it in the center drawer before he lifted the final item out of his briefcase and set it on the desk. Pink fluid sloshed inside the off-white plastic canister. Brock unscrewed the lid and smelled the concoction before closing it again and sliding it back into the farthest recesses of the old desk.

The man turned to see her standing at his elbow. He let out a shriek.

"What kind of medicine do you practice, Dr. Brock?" Laylea threw the question out to calm him. People typically liked to talk about themselves.

Dr. Brock took a deep breath before ushering her out to the hallway. "You could say I am a research scientist. This way. This bedroom here."

He led the way to the first doorway on the right. She followed. As he opened the door, he gestured for her to go ahead of him.

The "bedroom" had no bed in it. It was too thin a room to fit any human bed. It looked more like a coat closet that was missing its hanging bars. Light filtered in from the windows in the front of the house, but the room itself had no lights.

"What do you use this bedroom for, Dr. Br—"

Laylea turned to find the door closing. She leapt for it but was too slow to even get a foot in the crack. Several clicks and a metal susurration assured her that it had been no accident. Dr. Brock had just lured Laylea in and locked the door behind her.

9

---

*P*anic is almost never a useful response. Sure, adrenaline can be useful if you need to run or fight. Totally not helpful for hiding or thinking, though. Anger is also particularly distracting. Anger at yourself for getting trapped in a closet. Anger at the person who locked you in there. Anger at the former client or friend who told the person how to trick you. Anger blinded a person to the details of a situation and muddied their thoughts, making it super difficult to figure a way out.

Laylea wasted several minutes sniffing the air for any trace of the nauseating licorice-and-liver scent of her arch-enemy, Walter. She wasted a few more racing through why her parents would have reassured her and Bailey that they were safe if her father had found them. Then she considered if this was retribution for her having questioned Mr. Luke in public about his place on the super-secret Shifter Council. Or maybe one of the drug dealers had followed her home after she destroyed their taco truck?

She paced the narrow room, dragging her hands along the walls on both sides as she did, running through everyone she'd encountered in the course of the last week, including her friends, and one by one deciding each person was the one who had wanted to trap her. Then her brain started zipping through what they were going to do to her next. Her heart raced. She could hear her pulse pounding against her eardrums. It took effort to suck in air, and her soaking palms left streaks where she wiped them on her sweatpants.

A door slammed.

Laylea ran the three steps to the closet door and pounded on the wood, screaming for help. The only response she got was laughter. Two voices laughing and then leaving. Leaving out the front door.

Brock's voice lowered to a whisper as he shut the front door. Laylea's preternatural hearing caught every word. "Tell him it's handled. No one will ever hear from her again. And we're going to have a little playtime."

She sank to the floor, squeezing her eyes against the tears and whimpering apologies to her mother. "I'm sorry, Mom. I'm sorry. You sacrificed everything to keep me safe, and here I've gone and gotten myself killed. Please forgive me. I love you."

And then, somewhere deep in the wooly thoughts filling her panicking mind, Laylea heard her mother's voice. *If you address the problem, you won't have time to stress over it.*

She hugged her knees to her chest and gave her father's response, "Hello, Problem. What's up?"

"Well," Laylea responded to herself, "you've been locked in a super small room by a very likely mad scientist."

"How did that happen?" she asked.

"You wanted money, so you could go back to school and not worry about Bailey."

"Bailey, your grown-up brother, who said he doesn't need you?"

"Yeah, but focus." She banged her head back against the door. "Why did you go into a stranger's house?"

"Because he was a client. He knew my name." She sighed. "I assumed he'd been referred by another client.

"But you didn't ask who."

"No. Look, blame isn't going to get us out of here."

"Right, sorry."

She needed some advice. But she was alone. So, she searched through her memories for anything that would help in this situation.

Wood creaked elsewhere in the house. The break in silence allowed a hint of panic to roll back up her spine. She spoke out loud again, hoping to summon his advice with his name. "Clark—"

She immediately corrected herself. "The Dad."

A smile chased away the panic. *The Dad* was a title, an honorific Clark had earned many times over. He couldn't remember his dad. He couldn't remember anything from before the Consortium turned him into a weapon. His memory remained glitchy all through Laylea's puppyhood. Sometimes he couldn't remember what he'd just said. It was all very weird and scary. He told her that all he could do was keep walking. If he came out of a fugue while he was walking, he kept walking in that direction in hopes that he'd eventually remember why. Just keep going until it all made sense again.

She'd come into the closet to talk to a ghost. That's what she'd do.

She pushed herself to her feet and moved to the middle of the closet, shoving the panic down as best she could. Memories of Amelia's sadness threatened to cloud her thoughts, but Laylea shut those memories down. She focused on reaching out to the invisible world, the forgotten, the fringes of reality. Strange new scents filtered in as she drew a deep breath and let it out.

She faced east and murmured, "This is what I smell."

She turned south. "This is what I see."

She turned west. "This is what I hear."

She turned north. "This is what I feel."

Another deep breath started her back in the other direction, stopping between the points of the compass.

"Here is what I know."

Turn.

"Here is what I think."

Turn.

"Here is what I want."

Turn.

"Here is all I am."

She reversed, opening her awareness. "Trust me. See me. Hear me. Show me."

Other voices, all young, all girls', came fast and grew louder as she turned, until she was surrounded by the filmy, emotional figures of ghosts. A cold susurration of prayers and pleas and warnings filled the room like a stormy ocean threatening a life raft.

"Get out!"

"Help me!"

"Run away!"

"Mommy! Where are you, Mommy?"

"He's going to kill you!"

Some growls and hissing joined the voices as more ghosts discovered that she could hear them. Girls and animals huddled against the walls and against each other. A pig, a cow, a horse, and a lion all watched her, along with the human ghosts. Several less-solid ghosts floated through everyone like they thought they were alone. A large cat prowled the room, yowling and leaping at a grate high in the wall opposite the door.

"Shhhhhh." A skinny ghost with big hair calmed the rest. She couldn't have been more than ten or twelve when she died. "She can hear us."

Laylea focused on this leader. "I can see you, too."

"But, you're not dead yet." The girl looked up at the grate. "He hasn't sent the smoke."

Laylea followed her gaze. "He's going to kill me with smoke?"

"He might nearly kill you and revive you with the pink smoke a few times first, if you're good. If you're bad, he'll kill you right away."

Several voices from around the small room intoned, "If Papa ain't happy, nobody's happy."

A shiver ran down Laylea's spine.

The skinny ghost finished, "But, eventually you'll die. We all do."

"And there's no way out?"

"No," a dozen girls answered. A lion cub roared from the floor near the door.

"Are you all shifters?"

First, they looked at each other, fear painting their transparent faces. Laylea reworded her question, "Are we all shifters?"

One by one, they nodded.

Laylea breathed a little easier. That meant Brock wasn't working for Walter. Walter wanted to tear her apart to figure out how to create shifters, not just kill her. She couldn't think who would want to kill shifters. Other than the N kingpin. N, and lack of N, was killing shifters, wyrdos, and humans alike.

If she could just figure out who Brock was working for, Team Wyrdos could chase down the why. Not that it would matter if she couldn't reach them to let them know. Or if she was dead. Step one, don't get killed. She assessed her resources and attempted to gather information.

"My name is Laylea." She held a hand out to the lead girl. It was nice to offer her real name, for once.

"I was Isa." The girl gave Laylea's hand an odd look. "I'm dead. I can't shake your hand."

That's what Laylea had suspected her answer would be. "Sure you can. If you want to."

Isa placed her hand in Laylea's. At first, Laylea could barely feel a chill. Then it solidified as she curled her fingers around Isa's. Isa, and several others, gasped.

Laylea looked around at them. "Why are you all still here?"

Isa scoffed, "We died here."

"You know you're dead," Laylea pointed out. "That means you're free. You can go wherever you like. Move on to the next world or visit your family or swim with the selkies. You get to shape your own reality now."

The unceasing susurration of sound changed tone. A couple of the girls stood and moved closer to Laylea and Isa. Most of them backed away from the door. Footsteps sounded outside the closet, and all of the ghosts fell dead silent.

Laylea ran to the door and banged on it. "Let me out. I've met your ghosts. I can help you."

A small flap, about the size of Kyle in his bat form, bumped into

Laylea's foot. She stumbled backwards as a ceramic bowl half-full with oatmeal slid through the opening. The lion cub batted at it with a paw. Her paw passed through the bowl. The flap fell closed and thwapped back and forth a few times before sealing against the door. The pass-through was nearly imperceptible when it was closed.

Brock, or whomever had slid the food in through the escape hatch, tapped the door gently like there was a wounded kitten inside and went away without a word. Laylea looked down at the hatch, around at the silent ghosts, and back at the hatch.

"Right," she said. "So, it's a trap?"

"The food is fine," Isa replied. She shuddered. "It's not good. But it's not poisoned. He'll kill you with the smoke."

Laylea looked around to see if anyone else was on her page. The ones who could see her stared back, blankly.

"The hatch," she clarified. "Is the hatch a trap? Is there something, someone waiting outside?"

Isa shook her head. "No. It's just the food hatch. Nobody could fit through that."

Laylea grinned. "I can."

But only if she could shift. A quick glance around confirmed no conveniently exposed electrical wires and no stack of books to drop, not that she expected dropping them herself would startle her enough. She reached into her gut and felt nothing other than some residual grumbling from the many shots of adrenaline she'd given her system in the last twenty-four hours.

It was time to get the ghosts fired up.

"My name is Laylea, and I know a little something about being dead," she declared. "My friend Dee is a banshee, and I have seen her help people cross over, so I know, for absolute certain, that there is somewhere to cross over to. I also know that you can stick around if you want to. But you *do not* have to stay here. And Isa is going to prove it."

Isa's hand hadn't frozen her. It had burned. Isa wasn't sad or helpless. Isa was angry.

"Isa, Brock is out there. All of Brock's pretty ceramic figurines are out there in the dining room. I saw them. They're all arranged perfectly under twinkly lights that show off how he dusts them and arranges them and fawns over them. He was probably out there, polishing them with special creams, while you were in here choking to death on pink smoke."

"The pink smoke is the good smoke," Isa corrected her automatically. The ghost's gaze, however, remained on the door. The other girls hissed and cursed Brock. The lion cub growled low in her throat. It was more adorable than fierce.

"You want to go break one?" Laylea asked.

Isa nodded.

"So, go."

Not a heartbeat later, Isa disappeared. She didn't float through the door or slide under it. She flat out disappeared. Laylea readied herself, hoping that one tiny ceramic figurine would be enough. She needn't have worried.

A delicate, tinkly hurricane exploded outside the closet. The crowd of ghosts went wild.

Laylea shifted, her jaw dropped in a canine grin, and she wasted no time wriggling out of her sweatsuit. She slammed through the heavier-than-expected wooden flap, bounded down the hall, leapt through all the glass and wood and ceramic flying over the perfectly polished dining table, and launched herself up to the open rolltop desk. It took some maneuvering with her awkward paws, but she got the top center drawer open and snatched up Dr. Maurice Brock's armpadd with her teeth. Three leaps and bounds had her skittering back through the food hatch and into the haunted closet.

"What are you doing back in here?" Isa's shout was echoed by the others.

Laylea glanced up at the ghost who had just decimated Brock's curio cabinet in her first outing as a poltergeist. She tilted her head and raised her eyebrows at the ghost, thinking the very same thing.

She wiped her nose dry on her clothes and then tap, tap, cross swipe, tapped on the screen. The settings screen blossomed. The phone app had a dedicated icon pinned to the bottom of the screen. A circular number pad glowed in 3D when she opened it. She had to dry her nose twice while dialing Dee's number.

"Detective Dee Morton. How can I help you?"

Laylea barked bloody murder. The lion joined her with an absolutely adorable chittering. The pig and cow and tiger and some of the girls all raised their voices as well.

The cacophony sent a spark of joy into Laylea's fickle shifting trigger, and she grunted through an unusually painful shift. She attempted to calm herself enough to be able to work her fancy human tongue and heard Dee growling, "I have your location, Lee. I'm on my way. Morioka!"

The last was yelled just before the screen went black. A message popped up in red letters surrounded by triangles and exclamation points: *Service has been disconnected at the request of the customer.*

"Shit."

Dee couldn't track the GPS if the padd was disconnected. Laylea scrambled into her clothes as she desperately searched for a way to block the door. Brock knew she'd called someone. He'd be coming for her.

The ghosts were staring at her. The tiger yowled when Laylea caught the cat's eye.

She asked, "Anyone else feel like breaking stuff?"

Icy wind blew her hair back at the exodus of ghosts swarming around her and through the door. It took a moment for her to understand that the gray haze filling the room and filling her lungs wasn't the dead.

It was smoke.

Brock wasn't coming in. He was making sure she never got out.

10

An hour after Brock thought he'd killed her, Laylea sat cross-legged on Brock's rolltop desk, free and alive, waiting as Dee put Brock into the back of a squad car. She had shoved Brock's delicate antique briefcase onto the floor where the lion ghost's attempts at chewing on it had resulted in some pretty interesting ectoplasmic damage. Most of the ghosts who had trashed the dining room left the house after they'd expended their anger. Laylea couldn't say if they'd "traversed the veil and gauntlet" as Dee put it, or if they'd gone to see their family or explore the world as she'd suggested, but they had moved on. Other ghosts, like the lion, were sticking around to see Brock get arrested, or tased, as one girl hoped. And there were still more stuck in the room, unaware that they were free.

"Like Amelia," Laylea murmured to herself.

She leaned forward to glance out the one window with the shades up. Dusk was creeping in fast. Three police cars idled at the curb with their wig-wag lights flashing red and blue on the surrounding houses. Brock sat in the back of one of the cars. The door was open and the man wasn't handcuffed, but he wasn't getting back into the house. He didn't bother trying to hide his face from the gaggle of neighbors who had gathered with their evening cocktails to watch the drama. A tall figure in all black hovered at the edge of one of these gossip circles. He'd obscured his face with the hood of his sweatshirt but Laylea reflexively looked down to spot Kyle's Fox sandals, worn with black socks.

"Hide, you dumbass," Laylea muttered out loud. "You don't want Dee to see you're not dead."

"Bad news, Lee." Dee walked into the front room, and Laylea nearly fell off the desk. Dee had her head down over her armpadd. She didn't notice either Laylea's fright or Kyle outside in the street. "We can't book Brock for unlawfully imprisoning you."

"How about attempted murder?"

Dee glanced up at her. "That either."

Laylea crouched on her knees so she could look Dee in the eyes. "The only reason I survived Brock's smoke is because, when my lungs started shutting down, I shifted."

She'd busted through the food hatch so hard she'd rammed her head into the opposite wall and shifted right back to human. Then, she'd hidden under the desk until Dee rang the doorbell, and Brock denied having any little girl in his house. The backup cops standing beyond Dee had stormed in and thrown Brock face-first onto his spotless floor when Laylea ran out of the office stark naked.

"I know, kid," Dee said. "You're like a cat the way you keep escaping death."

The lion cub purred.

"You're one to talk," Laylea scolded the cat.

Dee looked in the general direction of the ghost lion and back at Laylea. "That wasn't for me, right?"

Laylea futzed with the mini aerosol canisters on the desk, rolling them back and forth in frustration. "He killed dozens of girls."

Dee sighed. "I know. But, the only one we have proof of him taking is you. And you don't exist, Lee Woodford. Not on paper."

Little noises echoed around the room with the ghosts' frustrations. A stool beside the desk swiveled. The curtains rustled. Couch springs creaked. And in the dining area, a wooden chair shattered against a wall. Hot air shifted the papers on the desk, though Dee couldn't hear the lion's little roar.

"Fingerprint the room," Laylea said. "You'll find prints belonging to Isa Owens, Kenda Moran, Olivia Schwermin, Leslie Corgana." She kept repeating the names as the girls around her shouted them out.

"I'm Ginger Havanish." A golden-haired eight-year-old stood where the lion had been. She played with the fuzzy unicorn on her shirt. Tears glistened on her eyelashes. "I was in the Northside Foster Center. Hemmendinger woke me up to tell me I had been chosen. I think I was in the basement for a while before he moved me to the closet."

"There's a basement?" Laylea asked.

Before she reported Ginger's nod, Dee had tapped the audio disc behind her ear. "Add 'basement' to that search warrant. The house has a basement." She listened for a minute, then barked, "I am working on probable cause. Just type up the warrant and get it to a judge."

Laylea could tell Dee wanted to swear. She might have, if it had just been them in the room.

"Lee. I need a clue. Something that ties these girls to this house or this guy. At the very least, I need some excuse for why we're here." She shivered and, for an instant, her wild red curls flashed white, like when her banshee powers took control.

Isa walked through the detective from the hallway. She wrapped ghostly arms around little Ginger. Laylea felt heat pouring off Isa and wondered, with the way Dee was looking in exactly the right place, if everyone could see the steam.

"Laylea, translate for me." Isa turned to face Dee. Laylea repeated her every word. "My name is Isa Owens. My family lives in Evanston. I struggled when Brock brought me inside." She led them out to the hallway, to a classic cast-iron radiator.

One of the two uniformed officers guarding the front door wandered over to see what was going on.

Isa patted at her big hair. "One of my brand-new pom-pom barrettes fell behind this thing. It matches this one." Isa pointed to the right side of her hair, but there was no barrette there.

"Don't move it." Laylea stopped translating to keep Isa from attempting to tear the radiator out of the floor.

"I'm not going to." The officer crouched beside it, pushing his cheek into the floral wallpaper. "I see something pink."

Dee rolled her eyes. "I need a legal reason for why we entered the house."

"How about this, Detective?" The other uniformed officer hollered from the porch.

"What is it, Garcia?" Dee waved the man over.

He came inside, holding out a bedraggled ball of something that might once have been pink attached to a rusty metal clip. Purple plastic letters sparkled as Garcia brushed the pinkish material back. "ISA. You told me, Detective, that we were coming here on a tip about a missing girl, Isa Owens. Do you think this could be her barrette?"

Dee smirked at the officer's suggestion but looked unconvinced. Isa looked like she was going to cry.

"Isa, do you know your parents' numbers?" Laylea asked. "Would they confirm they told Detective Morton to look here?"

The ghost spun into the air, whooping. "Yes! Yes! Can they come here?"

Laylea confirmed the answer to Dee.

The first cop, who was still crouching by the radiator, looked at Laylea, confused, "I thought you were Isa. Who are you talking to?"

Dee pulled the cop to his feet and shoved him toward the door. "Never mind that. Get outside until the warrant comes through." She held an evidence bag out for the other officer. "Nice work, Garcia."

"Thank you, ma'am." Officer Garcia dropped the bedraggled barrette into the plastic bag, but his eyes followed Isa as the girl danced back into the front room.

Laylea started to ask how long he'd been able to see ghosts, but Dee shooed her away with a jerk of her head. "Give us a minute, Lee."

Laylea winked at Garcia. He winked back. Then she hurried into the front room, where Isa was smacking each of the blinds until they rolled up, flooding the room with cool evening light and showing Captain Morioka getting out of her sedan in the street.

"They can bring my parents here, can't they?" she asked Laylea.

"Sure." Laylea nodded. "But it would be much faster for you to just go to them. Reach out. Can't you feel where they are?"

Isa froze where she was puffing up the lion-girl's long hair. Her eyes went unfocused, and then her whole face lit up. "They're at the cottage."

"You can go there."

"Okay." She practically cried the word. "But first, I'm just gonna go break all of the windows in the house."

Laylea snorted and then thought again. "There are a lot of people outside who are here to help. They could get hurt. Maybe skip the windows. Brock isn't going to be living here anymore, anyway."

Isa jumped from where she floated behind Ginger to reappear about an inch from Laylea's nose. All glee was gone from her voice. "Do you promise?" Hot air blew Laylea's hair back.

A familiar icy presence sidled up behind Laylea at the same moment. She fought the adrenaline bump that made her want to shift and curl her tail into her belly. Instead, she pointed out the windows to where Morioka was stomping up the porch steps. "That's Captain Yaksha Morioka. She promises."

Isa spun to see out the window. The grin she turned back made Laylea think the ghost could see Morioka's true demon form. She kissed the top of Ginger's head and disappeared.

"I don't have any family." Ginger's huge eyes glinted wetly. "I heard of this place in Africa where lions can run anywhere they want. Can I go there?"

"Sure, you can go to Africa, if you want," Laylea said. "I think, if we find a map or a picture, that'll help you get there." She hurried away from the icy zone at her back and started going through the desk drawers, looking for a padd or atlas that might show Africa. An umbrella stand beside the desk held a variety of canes, as well as several long document tubes. She grabbed one and dumped the contents onto the desk. The paper was cobalt blue, and when she unrolled the stack, she found a series of architectural designs. Something about them caught her attention.

"Is that Africa?" Ginger's awed tone spun Laylea around.

Officer Garcia knelt at Ginger's side. He was showing Ginger an image on his armpadd. "Yep. Close your eyes and see it."

Ginger laid one tiny, nearly transparent hand on Officer Garcia's arm. The hairs all around that spot stood up like he'd been electrocuted, but the man didn't flinch. "You see it?" he asked.

Despite her human form, Ginger purred.

"On the count of three: one, two, three, go!"

The ghostly little girl flashed back into a lion cub before she faded from the room.

Garcia looked up at Laylea. "Don't worry. She's probably not going to the real Africa."

"She's going to the one she's dreamed of?"

"I hope so. Anyplace is better than here."

Laylea thought about the early weeks of her puppyhood, spent being pinned down under the Eye and getting poked with needles and the shocker stick. Garcia wasn't right. But she was happy he'd lived a life where he thought this was the worst that could happen to a kid. "Can you help me help the girls stuck in the closet?"

"Sure." Garcia stood and immediately straightened to attention, nearly saluting. "Captain Morioka. Detective Morton."

Yaksha Morioka looked like a petite Japanese-American woman in mirrored sunglasses and a trench coat. She aimed her reflective gaze on Laylea.

Dee held her armpadd out to Garcia. "Here's the search warrant. I want you and Parkson to clear the basement before the nerd squad goes in. Take Brock with you."

"Yes, ma'am." Garcia tapped the screen of her padd with his, nodded sharply at Morioka, winked at Laylea, and then hurried out of the room.

Dee crossed to the desk and spread the blueprints wider. "Shit. This indicates an entire underground facility beneath this house. What's the date on these plans? Maybe it hasn't been built."

Laylea's eyes shot to the legend in the lower right corner of the front page. There was no date listed, just a version number, the name of the designer, and the words "Authorized: B. Gorshkov."

Dee pounded a finger on the name. "Gorshkov, again." She turned on Laylea. "What are you doing here? Were you chasing down a lead by yourself? Right after we ordered you to stand down?"

"A lead on what? Brock said he had a ghost." Laylea leaped to the obvious question. "Who's Gorshkov?"

"Gorshkov is the money." Dr. Brock lurched through the doorway. His hands were cuffed behind him and held by Officer Garcia. "I'm the genius."

Dee reached to close the pocket doors. "Get him out of here."

"Wait." Morioka didn't move. The cops stayed where they were. "Perhaps he can confirm a rumor I unearthed."

Laylea winced. Morioka was a demon, which meant she needed to feed on human souls to live. She generally "unearthed rumors" by consuming the gossip's brain. As far as Laylea knew, she had joined the police force, perhaps created it, so that she could have access to humans who did not benefit the world. She followed a strict moral code, for a demon.

"What rumor?" Laylea asked. Maybe now she could find out what they'd been hiding from her.

Morioka slipped the blueprints from the desk and rolled them as she said, "Every corporation we've run up against in our search for the origins of N leads back to one name."

"Captain," Dee interrupted. "Let's do this elsewhere. Lee is too young."

"I wasn't too young to go on the stakeout," she pointed out.

"Yes, you obviously were." Dee glared. "It was a mistake to take you. Gather your things. You're leaving."

Laylea turned to the desk. She had all of her things in her collar. But a familiar, freezing panic creeping up her backside made her reach for the aerosol vials. She pulled her hand back as Morioka reached over to take the records tube.

The captain tucked the rolled blueprints into the tube and tossed it back onto the desk. She turned her mirrored gaze on Brock. "Where can we find Gorshkov?"

"I am never going to tell you." Brock smirked.

Dee warned, "Morioka."

"Morioka?" Brock repeated the name. His voice shook.

"Lee, let's go." Dee crossed to her. Her hair flashed white again as she closed in on Laylea. Her pupils blew wide as well, and she retreated a step. Laylea took a slow breath to calm her racing heart. Amelia had walked through her to stand between her and Dee. The ghost watched Morioka approach Brock.

Morioka lowered her sunglasses. Her black gaze made the doctor stumble. He might have run if he weren't handcuffed and held by a much bigger man.

"I am Captain Morioka, Dr. Brock. I don't suffer demons in my city."

Brock choked out a half-hearted chuckle. "I'm not a demon."

Amelia's freezing aura swept through the room. Dee shivered. She repeated, "Lee, let's go."

Morioka spoke in a deadly quiet voice. "I've eaten demons less evil than you."

Brock whimpered, "I have a son."

Amelia hissed, for Laylea's ears only, "I have a daughter."

She burned with an icy flame that Laylea felt spike up her arm as the ghost grabbed her hand and set it on the tiny aerosol canisters Brock had left out on the desk. Laylea gathered them up and put them in her collar. She zipped the pocket. Then, in a blast, Laylea remembered Amelia's daughter's name: Deanna Amelia Gorshkov.

Morioka said, "Tell me where we find Albert Gorshkov."

Brock whimpered, "He'll kill me."

Laylea's mind raced with questions. Was Amelia Albert's mother, too? Could Albert be the "him" Amelia blamed for Deanna's coma? Laylea had to find birth records. Where would the city keep that information? Distracted by these thoughts, Laylea pushed away from the desk and headed for the hallway. She gave Morioka, Brock, and Garcia a wide berth.

Brock looked around like there was some escape available that he just hadn't seen up to this point while Dee shifted her gaze between Morioka's not so patient glare and Brock's panic.

She raised a hand to grip Brock's sweaty neck. "Garcia, can you give us a moment? Lee, go with him."

"Yes, ma'am." Garcia made sure Dee had a grip on Brock's hand-cuffed arms, as well, before he walked away.

"No, don't leave me here," Brock cried out.

Garcia ignored the man. Laylea slumped after him. It wasn't fair. She wasn't too young.

Dee said, "He's all yours, Captain."

Laylea couldn't see what Morioka did. Whatever it was, Brock cried out, "He's hidden. He's hidden in a secret school for shifter kids."

Laylea stopped. She spun around. Albert Gorshkov was hidden in the shifter school, was he? And every piece of the N mystery led back to him. Who was too young now?

She strolled back and leaned against the column. "Hey, Dee."

"I told you to get out of here."

"Yeah, but before I go, I just wanted to let you know that last year, when Captain Morioka arrested me, I didn't go to Juvie. She sent me to a special school under the Lincoln Park Zoo." She shot a glance at Brock. "A secret school for shifter kids."

"The zoo, huh?" was all Dee said.

"Oh, and now she has to condemn me there again because I'm not allowed to tell you about it." Laylea held her arms out to Morioka as if asking for handcuffs.

Dee released Brock's neck and tapped her armpadd against the dibs bracelet DJ had strapped around Laylea's wrist. "Here are the patient files from the sleep labs. If you have time between classes, review them. See if you can find a connection. We'll keep an eye on Bailey for you. When you find Gorshkov, send word to me." She turned her gaze back to Morioka. "The four four have been watching Morioka's correspondence."

The merest twitch of Morioka's head revealed her shock that Dee had discovered the cop code for shifter issues.

Laylea dashed over to Brock's desk to steal his heavy, black flashlight. She remembered the dark entrance to LPSS. She also remembered meeting her friends KC and Oscar there. She would see them again! A grin wriggled down into her belly, wanting to wag her tail. She tamped it down but grabbed the flashlight and ran out of the room anyway. "Meet you in the car, Morioka!"

She barely made it there before she shifted.

11

The east entrance of the Lincoln Park Zoo featured an iconic bronze lion statue that was installed in 2013. Tourists from all over the world took pictures with the lion. Few of them knew how to make it rotate off its plinth to reveal the student entrance to the Lincoln Park Shifter School. Few even knew there was a school under the zoo.

Laylea's butt froze through her sweatpants as she lounged on the stone plinth at the foot of the lion. Her mind fixated on poor Ginger. The girl would have found family at LPSS if she had only lived long enough to attend. Laylea assumed she'd have been pressed. It was unlikely an orphan could afford the tuition. *Pressed* was what they called the students attending either under duress or as part of a work/study program. KC and Laylea were both pressed. Oscar should have been pressed, but his family was rich enough and famous enough to bribe his way out of a shoplifting charge and into LPSS instead.

The other waiting kids skulked around the fancy archway entrance to the zoo. Laylea was the only one waiting by the lion. She'd have expected that legacy students would know how to get in, but not one of the eleven others seemed to have a clue. She could barely control herself, she was so eager to stroke the statue's nose three times and race down to see her friends. Some of the other waiting kids looked like they wanted to run away. Morioka's brief appearance may have convinced them to be more scared of her than of school.

The dragon demon, in human form, had driven to the school at her usual top speed and squealed up to the entrance, spinning the car to park flush against the curb. She popped the rear door at just the right moment and Laylea, her paws still tangled in her clothes, flew out onto the sidewalk. The flashlight bounced out after her and hit her hard enough to force a shift. Morioka had a particular driving style born of being a cop since long before horse-and-buggies were invented. Nobody was ever going to give her a ticket, much less demand her insurance information.

Laylea got her clothes sorted out in time for Morioka to drop her boots beside her. The tiny woman turned her back to the other kids. "Gorshkov is dangerous. Find him, quietly. Notify Dee." She lowered her voice even more. "Do not misunderstand. You are still off the team until we decide you are responsible enough to follow orders. If you get into trouble, we will not come to save you. Do not get caught."

Laylea listened. It was best to give a demon your focused attention when she chose to address you. Though, the tiny black bat swooping through the trees and playing peek-a-boo through the iron animals of the entrance archway was hard to ignore. Morioka said she was on her own. Kyle was making it very clear that she wasn't. Once she'd gotten her boots on, Morioka led her to the scattered group waiting under the archway. The kids gathered closer, assuming Captain Morioka was their guide.

All she said to them was, "Paids, pressers, you're all being tested. Strive to be worthy of graduating. Strive to never meet me again."

One muscled girl with bottle-blonde hair barked a short laugh. She looked like the oldest of the bunch. The kids near her took a quiet step away when Morioka's gaze, hidden behind her mirrored shades even in the darkness, turned to pin the girl.

"Jagger deRio." Morioka let the words land before she spread her wings. She adjusted her leather gloves, her only concession to the late winter weather, as she stood there, a tiny Japanese-American lady in a couture pantsuit and belted trench coat with fifty-foot-wide leathery wings gleaming green and gold in the moonlight. "I'll see you soon."

It seemed to Laylea that nobody breathed until the captain's tail lights disappeared onto Fullerton Avenue. Moments later, they all held them again as a black and white cop car pulled into the zoo parking lot and rolled to a stop where the kids were waiting. A uniform got out of the front passenger side and opened the rear door. A boy fell out with more grace, if less momentum, than Laylea had. Lank blond hair hid half his pale face. Dried blood flaked off the half Laylea could see. Blood also stained the puffy coat that cushioned his fall.

The cop kicked the kid a little farther from the car, so he wouldn't roll under the tires. She didn't even spare a glance for the dozen kids loitering on zoo grounds after dark. The police car was gone, turning onto Fullerton, before the kid stopped rolling.

When he did stop rolling, he burst out in hysterical laughter, fell silent, and started rolling again, gently rocking back and forth with a broad grin on his face. Laylea pulled herself together and hustled over to help him. "Hi." She stopped well clear of his reach. "You got a name?"

With the hair mostly clear of his face, she could see where the blood had come from. His nose was broken and his lip split top and bottom. It took him several blinks to focus his eyes on her face. He got lost examining her features.

"Your name," she repeated. "What's your name?"

The boy sucked in a breath so hard he almost choked. "Jimmy! My name is Jimmy." He said his name like he'd forgotten it for a while. He sat up and rubbed his face with both hands. It had to hurt. Jimmy didn't flinch.

"What's wrong with him?" A lanky kid sporting home-knit gloves and a matching hat with bobbles dangling from the side peered over Laylea's head.

Another boy answered, "N. He's coming down." This boy stood perfectly balanced on one foot atop one of the posts designed to keep cars from driving over the curb.

"I heard N made you feel like a shifter," Home-knit said. "But if he's here, he *is* a shifter, right?"

"Naw, he's prey." The blonde Morioka had called Jagger spat the word like an insult. "N is for the thumpers, to control them."

Laylea knelt by the still-rocking Jimmy while the others argued. "Easy there. Don't hurt yourself."

"He's on N." The flamingo-boy hopped to his other foot like the Karate Kid in the old movie. "He's definitely coming down from N."

A small girl playing with her elaborate blue braids back by the archway called, "It's not to control them. N is going to eliminate the thumpers." She couldn't have been more than twelve years old.

"No." Another super young girl wearing a puffy coat that was at least two sizes too big crossed over to her. "It's just to educate them, let them know what it's like to be a shifter. Hi, I'm Riva."

"I'm Leda." The blue-haired girl held out her hand. "Did you know that, like, thirty percent of thumpers who try N die within a week of taking it?"

"How do you know that?" Laylea asked.

"I overheard these cops talking after my parents died." Leda blushed when everyone stared at her. She added, "They were both thumpers."

"Whatever." Home-knit circled around Laylea and Jimmy. "Why's he taking it?"

"It feels good." The flamingo kid sounded like he knew from experience.

"And it will kill you." Laylea led Jimmy over to the plinth where she'd left Brock's flashlight. She laid him against the lion. He coughed and blood splattered the arm of his coat. Jimmy grinned at the blood and then wiped it onto his fingers. "Thumper or shifter," Laylea said. She added *or wyrdo* only in her mind, since shifter kids didn't believe in fairy tales like the boogeyman. "It's killing everyone."

Jagger smirked. "Not wolves."

It seemed to take a lot of effort, but Jimmy dragged his head up from where he'd been staring at his bloody hand and aimed his manic grin at Jagger. The air around him shimmered with an electrical glow before a brown-gray wolf circled to lay with its head in Laylea's lap.

Jagger's smirk fell. She stormed over, sucking in a breath to say something.

"Eager to enter?"

All the kids turned at the sound of the quiet voice.

Laylea hooked her elbow over the bronze lion's knee and twisted to see where the voice was coming from. A broad-shouldered man in green coveralls approached from the zoo. The zoo logo was printed over his breast pocket, along with a patch reading "Etienne."

He counted them twice. "Twelve. I was expecting thirteen."

"Oh." Laylea waved at him. "Jimmy's here. He's...napping."

"Passed out," Flamingo kid corrected.

Laylea stroked the wolf's ears. She didn't want him to wake up suddenly. Some people didn't like to be woken, and Jimmy had a serious set of teeth on him. He blinked, his deep brown eyes glazed over and confused.

"Hey, Jimmy, we've got to move so Etienne can open the lion." Hearing herself out loud, Laylea realized how little sense that made. But Jimmy stretched over her lap and dragged himself off the plinth to weave around Jagger's legs and collapse beside the flamingo kid's post.

Laylea gathered her flashlight and stood to find Etienne watching her. She grinned as she hopped off the plinth, away from Jagger. Etienne released a big sigh after waiting a full minute for the taller girl to move away.

"Wolf?" he asked her.

"Jagger deRio." She tossed her hair.

Etienne offered a half bow and swept his arm in a gesture inviting her to get off the plinth. "Your majesty."

She joined the other kids at the base. Several of them patted her on the back like she'd won some kind of showdown. Etienne waited for them to settle. The man looked over them all. His body tensed when he looked at Jimmy's wolf-form, and a wetness glinted in his eyes. Before tears fell, he turned to run a hand down the statue's nose.

"Once for pride, twice for pack, thrice so the phoenix will never come back."

Most of the kids stumbled backwards as the ground beneath their feet trembled.

"The lion!" The blue-braided Leda pointed pointlessly, as everyone was already watching the statue pivot aside, revealing an entrance in the middle of the plinth.

Etienne glanced down into the void and shuddered. If Laylea didn't know about the magical world down there, she might be tempted to run away. Several of the kids wobbled on their feet like they wanted to.

Etienne intoned, "Welcome to Lincoln Park Shifter School. Your last chance."

"Last chance for pressers, maybe," Jagger sneered.

Etienne laughed at her. One low, guttural scoff. He went on as if she hadn't spoken. "Learn how to shift. Learn how to please every-body. Don't screw up, and maybe you'll get to leave the zoo." He took a step away from the hole in the ground and focused on the dark waters of Lake Michigan. "Pressers, it has been determined that you are a danger to Chicago," he glanced at his armpadd, "and Michigan. If you can change, you could be a benefit to our city. You are being given another chance. If you fail, you'll meet the enforcer." Some life came into his face as he looked up to finish with, "The choice is yours, to take the chance or not."

Snow started to fall as Etienne shuffled off the plinth and ran for the parking lot. He hadn't gone ten yards before sparks flew from his armpadd. He clutched it to his chest and stomped back through the gathered kids and under the archway of iron animals into the zoo.

He hadn't reached the gift shop before Leda sniffled, "I'm leaving."

"Where you gonna go, Leda? Back to that foster family that dropped you off?" Flamingo boy smoothed his mohawk with both hands and hopped off the post. "You're better off here."

Tears poured down her face as she shot back, "How would you know, Karate Kid?"

"Name's Rehyan. I know because I pay attention," Rehyan replied, unruffled. "I hear you get fed every day down there."

"You're pressed." Jagger had to put in her two cents. "If you don't go down, you'll have to answer to the Council."

"Only if they catch her," Rehyan said.

"You're so hot to go to school, Jagger, why don't you lead the way?" The boy in the bobble hat challenged the werewolf but kept his distance.

Jagger asked, "What's your name?"

"Griff." The lanky boy wrapped his arms around himself.

"You're a paid, obvi." Jagger backed Griff up to the edge of the plinth. "Why aren't you rushing down, Griff?"

Laylea hefted her flashlight and scooted past them to the entrance. "Come on, guys. These stairs are treacherous enough already. They're only going to get worse with snow falling on them." She stepped down onto the first cobblestone stair and offered a hand to Leda. "It's not a big deal if we work together."

The little girl blinked, and the air shifted around her. Where she'd been standing, a beautiful egret blinked its beady eyes and leapt into the air. She soared over the gaping entrance hole and then flapped her way back to hide behind Rehyan.

"Guess you're gonna have to lead the way, dog." Jagger laughed. A few of the others laughed with her. Laylea sighed. She turned to head down just as Jagger added, "Mush," and pushed her.

The flashlight flew out of her hand, the beam flashing across her face once before spinning into the darkness. Flailing wildly, Laylea caught the curve of the bronze lion's tail. For a second, she thought she could find her balance and drop safely to the stairs, but bronze is slick, and Laylea's hand was just a little too small.

The distant clatter of the flashlight echoed up the stairs as Laylea's fingers slipped from the lion's tail.

12

lackness was the lion entrance's primary feature. Complete and utter blackness. And depth. Laylea was familiar with the depth. She and KC had depended on Oscar's superior night vision to get them down the skinny, uneven stone steps last year. The steps had been built against a wall on one side and not a thing on the other. There was no handrail, no barrier to falling all the way down to the stone floor of the cavern.

Cat luck, she might have, but Laylea doubted she would come back from this death. She instinctively kicked out as her hands slipped from the lion's tail. The momentum flung her too far, sending her soaring over the stairs to the open blackness beside them. Her adrenal glands reached deep and kicked one last shot through her system. Fire burned in every cell of her body. Fear suddenly stood her hackles on end instead of the hairs on the back of her neck. The sweatpants fell off and her very real tail tucked up hard against her belly. Tangled inside the White Sux sweatshirt, her claws extended. It was the claws that saved her.

The momentum of her kick slammed her tiny canine body against the far wall, several meters beyond the treacherous staircase. The rough cotton of the sweatshirt latched onto the stone enough that

Laylea fell out of it, her claws tearing the cheap fabric as she scrabbled at the uneven stone to slow her plunge. The sweatshirt was still tangled around her head when her butt hit some kind of outcropping, a ledge in the wall just big enough to give a twelve-pound terrier a fighting chance. The shirt tried to drag her down but she flung her head back and forth as she dug all four sets of claws into crevices and prayed to physics that she'd slowed her momentum enough to counteract gravity. The sweatshirt slipped off of her. It plummeted into the darkness. Every muscle in Laylea's body strained to stay on that ledge.

She lay sprawled on the stone, her muzzle pressed up against the wall until her instincts told her claws they could relax. Dog instincts were to be trusted. Still, she continued to lay there like a sunbathing pug until her heart stopped trying to pound its way out of her rib cage.

Other kids had braved the entrance by then. None of them seemed all that concerned for her. She heard someone declare, "It's a school. They can't harm us."

She didn't know who said it, but she knew how wrong they were.

Griff sounded like he had stopped only a few steps down. "Damn, it is dark."

A tiny voice, possibly Riva's, asked, "Where did that girl go?"

"She's probably already at the bottom," Jagger's voice moved away quickly. "Waiting for us."

Laylea heard the echo of pebbles falling from her perch as she wiggled herself around to face the steps. How did none of them hear her?

Several of the kids were using the lights from their armpadds to see the stairs.

"It's a long way down." Rehyan shone his light over the side. "I can't even see the bottom."

Jimmy wove around the others, nose to the ground, trotting far too quickly for Laylea's comfort. Leda soared over them. Her delicate wings glowed when they caught the light from the armpadds.

"Hey." Griff stood on a step level with Laylea's nook. He pulled off his mittens, shoved them into his back pocket, and held his arms out to her. "I'll catch you."

The ledge was not big. Laylea peered over the edge into the darkness.

"Yeah," Griff whispered, "not too many ways down."

He was right. But she considered that she could probably survive a good several days there on that ledge. Just until her hackles went down.

Then Griff echoed her words to Leda. "It's not a big deal if we work together."

Sure, she'd said it, but she wasn't referring to launching herself over a fatal drop into the arms of a complete stranger. Possibly into his arms. There was no guarantee that she could jump that far. She sighed. If she wanted to tell Oscar that his mother loved him and KC that her brother was worried, she'd have to get off the ledge. If she wanted to rescue the city from N, she'd have to jump.

Laylea didn't so much back up as scrunch her body until she was sitting up in the crevice. There was a neat little trough at the back edge, perfect for her tail. With no room for a running start, she'd have to launch cold, using only the strength in her hind legs. Luckily, thanks to her inability to control her shift, she couldn't take public transportation. Since she had to run everywhere she wanted to go, Laylea had super strong legs.

Griff tested his balance with one foot each on two different steps. "I'm ready."

"And I've got your back if he misses." Rehyan, the boy who had already proven his balancing skills, hustled back up the steps to join Griff.

Laylea barked.

The boys nodded.

She coiled her strength and imagined herself as one of those flying squirrels with extra skin on her sides to catch the air. With one last deep breath, she pushed off the shelf with all her might, reaching for the boy who was so loved by someone that they knitted him ugly clothing. He probably had sweaters as bad as Junior's. Eternity passed as she flew over the drop. Not quite as long an eternity as being trapped in Amelia's panic, but still, a lifetime. Then the flying turned into falling, and she fought her own panic.

Suddenly, a caw echoed through the chamber and cool air blew up at her belly, flapping the skin at her sides and giving her the extra hint of lift she needed to brush Griff's hands. Fingers grabbed her fur and pulled. Long arms wrapped around her, and an extra pair of hands slammed into Griff's chest above her, pulling him back from the edge.

For a moment, Rehyan and Griff panted, pinned up against the stairwell wall with her squeezed between them. Time froze again, just as it had while she waited in the nook to see if she had survived. Then it melted back into reality, and the boys set her down on the stairs. Two pairs of hands made sure she had her balance before they let go to high five each other.

"Oh, yeah!"

"You're a hero, man!"

"No, you are!"

Laylea lay on the uneven stones, watching her old raven friend, Dizzy, coast down into the darkness. Her wings had provided the final, extra lift to keep Laylea from slamming into the side of the steps.

Laylea's tail popped out and slapped her saviors' ankles. As far as she was concerned, they were both heroes. She bumped each of them with her head in thank you and then chased Dizzy down the steps.

The raven soared up to coast along beside her. Two kids tripped off the last step as Laylea leapt past them. She bumped into Jimmy, who appeared to have curled up on the packed dirt floor and fallen asleep. The other kids all milled at the bottom, unsure of what to do. The darkness was barely softened by the light of their armpadds.

Laylea remembered the corridor that led to the school. She peered into the black until she spotted a warm light sputtering against the stones. Laylea bounded toward it with Dizzy flitting overhead. Spitting, crackling sounds echoed down the long passageway, punctuated by Ms. Crow's anxious voice saying, "Come now. We're quite late."

Laylea sang out a greeting.

"Lee?" The school librarian lowered the flaming torch. It illuminated a worried smile in Ms. Crow's sculpted face. As usual, she wore her dark hair in a messy braid over one shoulder. Her loose linen jumpsuit was tied at the waist with a blue ribbon and topped with a lighter blue cardigan that matched her eyes. She adjusted her glasses and reached out to caress Laylea's ears. "So, you're surprise number thirteen."

A familiar face stepped into the light behind Ms. Crow. Brenda, a werepython from Mer dorm, ran a hand along her shaved head like she was slicking her hair back. "Knew you'd be back, Fido."

Ms. Crow stood. "Now, now, Brenda. We are the *welcoming* crew. Be welcoming."

"Welcome back to LPSS, Fido." Brenda crossed her bare arms in a way that accentuated her biceps. She had impressive biceps.

Ms. Crow raised the torch and looked over the small crowd of kids and animals. She held a hand up in warning to Griff and Rehyan. "Be careful, boys. The last step's a doozy."

They solved the problem by stopping before they reached the bottom.

"I'll need you all to shut down your armpadds." Ms. Crow waited as, one by one, devices chimed and went dark. "My name is Ms. Crow. I am your intake coordinator."

"Are you the person responsible for making paid students use the same entrance as pressers?" Jagger curled a strand of her unnaturally blonde hair around a finger.

Ms. Crow adjusted her blue sweater. "Every student makes their choice at Adelor."

A bright flash blinded everyone for an instant. Leda wobbled on her human feet. "Sorry. Where's Adelor?"

Rehyan hissed, "Adelor is the lion."

"He was the dean before Gorse," Brenda put in. "Spent a lot of time upstairs, apparently."

Ms. Crow cleared her throat. All eyes turned back to her. "Entering at Adelor and descending the stairs shows that you want to be here. We need every student to choose to come to LPSS. Yes?"

Laylea turned to see Rehyan holding his hand up.

He lowered it and gestured at her with his chin. "The dog didn't choose," he said.

"Watch it, freak." Jagger puffed her chest out like she was a gorilla rather than a wolf.

Rehyan wasn't cowed. "Or what?"

Laylea barked and bowed to show her wagging tail, trying to indicate that she wanted to be there and held no ill will against Jagger. The school's wolf pack hated her enough already.

"You shut it, dog." Jagger was going to fit right in with the pack.

Laylea barked again. She should have kept her mouth shut.

The air shimmered around Jagger for just an instant before the blonde thirteen-year-old disappeared, replaced by a fifty-pound wolf with fur so black it nearly blended in with the darkness. It would have been impossible to spot if not for the bright white bared teeth and low growl that showed them all she was stalking toward Laylea.

13

"Ms. deRio, this is not acceptable behavior." Ms. Crow moved to put herself between Laylea and Jagger. She had to weave through half a dozen kids to get there.

A canine whimper echoed off the stone walls a moment before an electric glow lit up the darkness at the bottom of the stairs. Human Jimmy wrapped himself in his puffy jacket and cowered in the corner. Another growl from Jagger, and he flashed back into wolf form.

Laylea's heart beat a mile a minute. She reminded herself that she had faced far more lethal dangers than one hormonal, wolf-supremacist snob. In the moment, her overworked endocrine system didn't care. It saw drool plop onto the dirt floor in the light of Ms. Crow's torch and wanted to flat out run away. Her brain knew that running from a hunter was a super bad idea.

Before her various organs had to fight it out, Dizzy flew out of the darkness and landed on the black wolf's head. The shadow of her wings stood out on the walls as if they were coming out of Ms. Crow.

Jagger growled.

Ms. Crow stomped a foot. "Bad wolf."

Dizzy opened her beak and snapped it closed on Jagger's sensitive nose.

Jagger deRio shrieked. She shifted to human in a sprawl at Ms. Crow's feet, one hand on her bleeding nose. Apparently, Jagger didn't heal when she shifted. Dizzy flapped up to a ledge in the wall. The rest of the kids stared at Ms. Crow with a mix of fear and awe.

Ms. Crow took it right in stride. She continued her introduction as she herded Laylea back over to where Brenda waited in a crouch, ready to tackle anyone she needed to. The kids' eyes stayed glued to the librarian, which gave Jagger the privacy to pull herself together.

"I am your intake coordinator. That means I'm here to help you get settled in. If you need something in the future and don't know where to go, come see me. You can usually find me in the library, but I also help out maintaining the gardens. If you ever hear bells ringing, report immediately to your dorm." She gestured for them to join her as she headed down the musty tunnel. Despite the low overhead, Dizzy flew above her. "Come, come. Follow closely now. This is not a good place to get lost. We don't use this section of the school anymore."

The new students followed quietly. Leda and Riva stayed on Ms. Crow's heels. Laylea bounded ahead, unable to contain her glee at seeing Oscar and KC again. Dizzy circled overhead, flying between Laylea and Ms. Crow. In her joy, Laylea raced ahead of the torchlight and ran into a wall.

"Lee! Come back, Lee," Ms. Crow called out from quite a ways back. "There's a turn here."

Dizzy poked Laylea with her beak and harried her until she retraced her steps out of the hallway she'd wandered down. She didn't remember there being any branching corridors the first time she'd come this way. But it was dark, and she'd been pretty scared that time. She'd thought the school was a prison.

"Aren't dogs supposed to have a good sense of direction?" Brenda muttered the insult low to keep Ms. Crow from hearing. Somebody else heard her just fine.

"Aren't pythons supposed to know when to slither away?"

"No." Brenda smirked at Oscar and dropped into a martial arts stance. "Pythons never back away from a fight."

Oscar Luke stood in the open doorway leading to the holding room antechamber with his mother's long neck and his father's enormous brown eyes and all his own lanky limbs. He'd grown taller but hadn't filled out. Flames flickered from torches set in the walls inside the room, limning Oscar with an unearned halo.

Laylea howled all the joy in her heart. She grabbed the bursting feeling and imagined it making her grow. Filling her mind with the image of her squeezing the breath out of Oscar with the hug to end all hugs, she didn't fight the burning pain that shot through her body. She soared to her feet and barreled into Oscar, slamming him into the ornate cabinet that nearly filled the velvet-carpeted room.

Dizzy circled around them and settled on one of the doors of the cabinet. Opened nearly as far as they could go, the doors doubled the cabinet's width. The inside was segmented into dozens of cubbies, each holding piles of blue jumpsuits like the ones worn by Brenda and Oscar.

"Ah, thank you, Lee, for demonstrating why we have these clothes closets situated throughout the school." Ms. Crow pulled a pale blue jumpsuit from the lowest, rightmost cubby. She tossed it to Laylea.

Laylea released Oscar to pull on the outfit while Ms. Crow addressed the new students. "We have a few legacy students here, but many of you may be new to shifter customs. Some shifters keep their clothing through the transition, some do not. Thus, we have clothes closets situated throughout the facility. If you are one of the unlucky ones—"

"Like Lee," Oscar put in. Laylea punched him. He rubbed at the spot. "Ow."

"Sorry. Hi."

"Hi."

"Yes. Like Lee." Ms. Crow shot a quelling glance in their direction. "You'll either learn to control your shift quickly, or you'll learn where all of the closets are located. The occasional nudity may be awkward for you at first, but please exercise the same respect you'd appreciate for yourself."

She ran through the organization of the closet and directed them each to select a jumpsuit or two. While the new kids looked through the options, Laylea reached into her collar and pulled out the paper bracelet she'd had Bailey charm. She dragged Oscar away from the scrum and slipped it on his wrist. "I come bearing gifts."

He ran his fingers over the red paper. "Is this my mom's note?" His eyes misted, but then his gaze shot to the swoopy decorations on the top of the cabinet. "Dizzy!"

Ms. Crow and several of the new students looked his way. His dark skin grew a shade darker. He turned to Griff, who had five jump-suits in his arms. "It's a dizzying selection. Just focus on sizing, for now. You'll figure out what style you like later."

Laylea snorted. Oscar kicked at her, but he couldn't hide the grin lighting up his face.

"Gentlemen, this is Oscar Luke. He is a second-year student who will be helping you in the changing room." Ms. Crow either didn't notice or ignored the gushing chatter from the girls.

Laylea noticed and looked her friend over. He was pretty good looking, with that smooth, dark skin and his kind eyes. He'd grown his hair out and twisted it into spikes. It looked good. His arms and legs were still far too long for his body, though, like he was a mari-onette with no strings.

Ms. Crow continued, "He'll also be collecting some information on your background and species. It is purely for school records. You can trust his discretion.

"Go, go. Oscar, you will see Laylea at Testing tomorrow, I believe."

"Yes, ma'am. I'll be there." He barked at Laylea.

She barked back and wagged her butt.

Ms. Crow turned from the boys as Oscar herded them through a door to the left of the closet. "Ladies, this is Brenda Samborsky. She is a sixth year and will be helping me in the ladies' changing room."

Samborsky. The middle-aged white guy in the sleep lab with great karma and the white tattoo was named Samborsky. Laylea wondered if they were related. Brenda took offense at anyone breathing in her direction. Laylea wasn't going to risk asking her a personal question.

At least, not tonight. She'd risked her life too many times today already.

The girls traipsed into the changing room and put all of their belongings into lockers. Only Leda and one other girl had brought any kind of luggage. Laylea guessed the bags held everything they owned in the world, and they had nowhere to leave it behind. She stuck with them as the girls scattered throughout the several rows of old, wooden lockers.

Laylea only had her collar. She checked the zippered pockets. The left one held her house key and KC's charmed crane. The right pocket held the three small aerosol containers Amelia had made her steal from Brock. That reminded her that she hadn't retrieved his flashlight when she got to the bottom of the hell stairs. It was still lying in wait in the darkness for some future student to trip over. As were her clothes.

A couple of voices in the next row of lockers caught her attention.

"... really Oscar Luke?" That was unmistakably Jagger's voice.

"Yep," Brenda responded. "The great Oscar Luke is now a presser."

A voice Laylea thought might be Riva's asked, "Why?"

"He tried to leave school without authorization." There was an admiration in Brenda's voice that made Laylea like her a bit more.

"No, why is he here at all?" Riva clarified. "I can't believe his family would send him here after what happened to his sister."

Leda tripped past Laylea and headed around the bank of lockers as if drawn by the gossip. "What happened to his sister?" She left her locker standing open.

Jagger answered, "Tishala Luke was here for a week when she went exploring on her own. She got lost in one of the old pre-phoenix dorms."

"I heard she fell from a tree," Riva said.

"Well, that's stupid." Jagger scoffed. "We're underground. There are no trees here."

Brenda laughed, but she didn't correct the werewolf. "Just stuff your clothes in the lockers and head out that door. We'll all gather in Holding."

Laylea closed Leda's locker and helped the other girl who'd brought luggage squeeze her camping-style backpack farther into her locker so the door could shut. She escorted her to the doorway and caught Brenda before she could leave the room. "Why wouldn't the Lukes want Oscar to come just because his sister got lost?"

Brenda pulled a face at Laylea. "She didn't get—" She interrupted herself to step back and let Ms. Crow and the last few girls go out into the room lined with rows of cots where they would all sleep that night.

Laylea could see Oscar out there, comforting Griff who, of course, had to leave his knit cap in the locker room. The boy's head was covered in feathers rather than hair, and Griff kept running his hand over his head, like he was trying to hide them. Whatever Oscar said made the kid blush, but he smiled, too.

"So, what happened?" Laylea pressed when the new students had passed them.

Brenda waited until the girls were out of earshot before she answered. "Tishala Luke didn't get lost. She died."

14

"We were told that Special Testing was born out of a desire to help the survivors of the Phoenix Event deal with the psychological fallout. Why the blood draws and invasive physical exams under hypnosis?" Laylea asked as she sat on Dr. Fenn's exam table. After a long night in Holding, she was ready to begin her search for answers. She figured there was no reason to wait until after her first-day physical.

Fenn may have held the instruments, but Laylea was the one asking the questions. Her health hadn't changed since last year. Her health never changed. If she ever got sick or injured or electrocuted by a taco truck, all she had to do was shift to heal herself.

The short, rugged man sighed as he peered into her ear. "I wrote to the Council about that. Many times."

"Did the Council ever respond to your letters?"

"What's Special Testing?" One of the new kids asked.

They were lined up for the exams in the front room, with the kids who'd already been looked at sitting around the edges. Fenn hadn't bothered to pull the privacy curtain around the table. He was clearly regretting that decision.

"Like I said, it's been cancelled." Fenn set the otoscope aside and plopped the headphones part of his stethoscope in his ears. "It doesn't matter because it doesn't exist."

"But, don't you want to know where all that blood went?" Laylea pushed.

"I want you to breathe in for me now, Ms. Woodford."

She breathed for him. When he dropped the earpieces around his neck again, she asked, "What happened to the teachers who let Oscar get electrocuted?"

Fenn sighed. "That unfortunate incident was handled five months ago. You are done, Lee. It looks like all the chairs are taken." He didn't look around at the available seating. "So, feel free to wait in the hall."

Laylea hopped off the table. She hadn't been expecting many answers. Her goal was to get him thinking, so she'd get better answers later. She'd corner him again when there weren't so many witnesses.

Laylea patted Jimmy's knee on her way by. He'd been first on the exam table. He hadn't been able to voluntarily shift to human to put his things away in the locker room. When he did shift upon entering the Holding room, as every normal kid did, he'd fallen to the ground in the fetal position, a strange whimper leaking from his clenched jaw. Dr. Fenn had helped Oscar change the addict into a jumpsuit and lift him on to a bed.

Laylea shifted to dog when she entered Holding, just as she had last year. Dr. Fenn was too busy with Jimmy to freak out about it this time, but Ms. Crow took note. Knowing Laylea wouldn't be able to reach the handle to the bathroom, the librarian had given her the opportunity to dash in and use it before running through the schedule for the next day.

It had been quite the day for Laylea. After the long night on stake-out, being electrocuted, excommunicated from the Wyrdos, haunted by Amelia, smoked by Brock, and kinda-sorta-definitely not not un-excommunicated to hunt for Albert Gorshkov, not to mention being kicked down the stairs by a wolf with a grudge, Laylea was tired.

She hopped onto a cot for Ms. Crow's lecture. She mussed up the blanket, circled left twice, and passed out while Ms. Crow was telling the kids about the school's mission to form students into thoughtful, well-educated citizens who would be a benefit to both human and shifter society.

In the morning, each new student got to pick the one item they wanted to keep. Since Laylea was still in dog form, Ms. Crow put her collar back on her, minus its contents. She brought a little cigar box decorated with cherubs to hold the rest of Laylea's eclectic collection of belongings and carried it to the infirmary to place it with all of the other students' things in the alcove between the doors to the infirmary and Special Testing, which had, apparently, been canceled.

The clothes closet featured in the Medical Wing alcove took up the entire wall behind a stiff couch and an over-stuffed chair. It was really just a line of black-brown Ikea bookcase towers with opaque doors. While everyone else set their belongings down in front of the sofa, Laylea had nosed open the door to the leftmost bookcase. She dragged a jumpsuit out with her teeth. For a doctor, Fenn was super uncomfortable with nudity, and Laylea fully intended to be human for her meeting with Dr. Fenn.

She hauled the super pale, super soft, armless jumpsuit into the infirmary with her and avoided the temptation to curl up in it while she waited. That would not encourage her body to go human. She reached for the burn, but her shift remained elusive as she stood in the line, watching the others get their cursory examinations. Riva shifted, on Fenn's request, into a fuzzy, gray-and-brown sloth with an infectious grin.

On her turn, Laylea hopped up onto a chair and from there to the exam table. Before her paws hit the paper sheet, the familiar burn flared through her body, and human-shaped Laylea hopped back off the table to pull on the jumpsuit. From the instant she could speak, she started questioning the good doctor who'd almost killed her last year.

She'd been counting on Dr. Fenn's heavy hand with the reflex hammer to make her shift, but she had shifted because she needed a voice. It was something to note.

Once he exiled her to the hall, Laylea beelined for the palm lock that operated the secret opening in the Ikea shelves. As expected, the kids' belongings were no longer sitting where they had left them. They'd been spirited away to storage through a tunnel behind the closet. The tunnel led to a cavern where student belongings were stored until they left.

It had opened for Oscar last October. It did not open for Laylea. Maybe Laylea's handprint had been excised from the school's system when she left. Or, maybe, the lock required a faculty print. KC had inserted Oscar's print into the faculty system.

There had to be another way in. Laylea opened the door to the tower that should rotate out when unlocked and searched for a manual lever or even a crack she could use to pull the hidden door open.

Ms. Crow's gentle voice stopped her. "Lee?"

"Yes, Ms. Crow?" Laylea spun around and dashed away from the shelves.

The librarian shut the infirmary door behind her before she strode over to the alcove, fussing with the buttons on her blue cardigan and keeping her voice low. "She may have avoided direct punishment, but Jagger deRio is going to test into a special sociology private study. It will appear to be an honor, like the musical private study Mr. Bianchi has insisted on for you." She leaned against the clothes closet, standing right over the palm lock that Laylea had been struggling to make work. "But Jagger's course is veiled counseling to help her work through her issues. I wanted you to know."

"Thanks, Ms. Crow." Laylea plopped down on the couch, sitting sideways with her back against the armrest, so she could see the librarian. Since they were alone, she asked, "Hey, do you know where I could find a listing of all the current students?"

"I can help you with that." Ms. Crow took a small vial from a pocket in her loose jumpsuit. She worried at it while she spoke. "Are you looking for someone in particular?"

Laylea trusted Ms. Crow. But she would want to know why Laylea was looking for Albert Gorshkov. Plus, Laylea couldn't take the chance that kind Ms. Crow would tell him that Laylea was looking for him. Better to err on the side of caution. She lied. "No, just wondering who has left since I've been gone and who's new. You know."

"You're very smart to stay aware of your surroundings. I'm afraid the best I can suggest is that you look around at dinner."

Laylea laughed. "You're funny." There was no way she could find one person in that chaos.

Ms. Crow laughed too, almost slipping the blue plastic vial back into her pocket. "You don't need to wait for the tour, Lee. Despite your successful shifting test last October, we're going to keep you in Mer dorm."

"Because I shifted in Holding?" Laylea asked.

Mer dorm took all the shifters who had trouble holding their form or deliberately shifting. Plus, you weren't supposed to be able to be anything but human in Holding. Dr. Fenn had wanted to do tests on Laylea last year because she went dog in the room.

Ms. Crow coughed and looked up the empty hallway before she replied. "You have friends there. It will be less stressful for you. Whoops." The plastic vial bounced on the stone floor. Ms. Crow bent to retrieve it, disappearing behind the couch for a moment as she said, "Friends can be very helpful when it comes to being able to shift."

Laylea wondered if Ms. Crow had figured out that Laylea's friends had helped her cheat on the shifting test that got her out of school. If she had, it didn't show in her eyes as she stood and joined Laylea on the couch. "We're hopeful your friendship with KC will help her. You know, she still has never shifted in front of anybody but you."

KC didn't shift in front of anybody because she had told them she was a coyote. She wasn't. KC was a wolf. She came from a famous wolf pack and her great-grandfather was the most feared, or respected, werewolf in the country. She had perfect control of her shift.

"Well, I'd be happy to teach her everything I know." Laylea managed to say this with a straight face.

Ms. Crow nodded. She patted Laylea on one knee. "I'm sure." She stood again and headed back to the infirmary door. "I've got to get back. Feel free to gather some breakfast and meet us at Testing. Do you remember how to get there?"

"Yes, ma'am."

"Very well." The librarian slipped back into the infirmary.

Laylea waited until the door clicked shut before she scuttled back to the shelves. She still had to figure out how to bypass the palm lock if she wanted to get her stuff. She reached the tower to find the secret doorway had cracked open. She looked down at the dark square of the palm lock. It hadn't changed in any way except that a blue plastic vial now lay beside it. Laylea picked up the vial. White letters printed on the side spelled out *Drink Me*. It was the general antidote Ms. Crow had given her once before, the one that had saved her life and KC's when they were poisoned with sligh nut.

She gasped. Ms. Crow had opened the secret door for her. Laylea hurried to make use of the gift. She palmed the vial and inched the tower of shelves open just far enough for her to slip through. Pulling it shut, she immediately wished she still had the flashlight she'd stolen from Brock, or an armpadd light, or a torch. She knew she was standing at the mouth of a thin tunnel, but with none of the light troughs that lined the walls in the rest of the school, she couldn't see a thing. Nor could she open the secret door from the inside, she realized. She couldn't get back out of the storage caves this way. The thought of the other exit chilled her heart. But that worry was for later. For now, she had to find her stuff.

She took a moment to tuck the vial into her collar and then dragged one hand along the cold wall as she crept down the rapidly shrinking tunnel. After only a minute, she stubbed her toe on the lip of a small opening at the back. From there, the tunnel widened into a massive cavern shrouded in deeper darkness. She knew there were gas lamps posted at intervals around the room. She could smell their faint scent in the air. But she didn't need light to find the cigar box of her belongings.

The magical pull of her house key led her directly to the newest pile of student belongings. Ms. Crow's cigar box had been placed in a cubby carved right into the wall. Laylea had to work her way around ancient trunks, suitcases, and a few stacks of cardboard boxes. By the time she'd fit Brock's tiny aerosol tubes, Sanna's crane, and DJ's dibs band into the zippered pockets of her collar with the house key and Ms. Crow's antidote, her eyes had adjusted enough that she could see around her. Without the key drawing her as it had the last time she'd found her way out of this cave, Laylea had to search for a good while before she found the alley leading deeper into the cavern.

The opening was blocked by one of the gas lamps. Being a skinny kid, Laylea easily squeezed between the brass upright and the stone wall. Beyond the lamp, the walls closed in on either side. No normal-sized adult could fit through here. She followed the tight alley all the way to a bend. The path turned left and went on for as far as she could see. But there, at the bend, was the low door she was looking for. It would only be considered a door to a dog or a dog's human, and only something smaller than a golden retriever could fit through it. Laylea, the human, wouldn't have much trouble.

Still, she couldn't bring herself to crawl through the rubber flap. The outer room of Special Testing lay on the other side of that flap. Her heart pounded in her chest. The last time she'd been in that room, a man had used magic and drugs to make her compliant. She'd poisoned herself to get out of there. Dizzy, the raven, had reminded her to take the antidote later. She owed her life to that bird. A giggle brightened her face as she realized that her thoughts of Dizzy were so strong, she could smell the raven.

Then a beak poked through the dog door and cawed at her.

15

"*D*izzy!" Laylea held the rubber flap open so she could run a finger along the raven's feathers. The sound of many muffled voices floated through the little door, but the space beyond was nearly as black as the storage cave.

Dizzy cawed again and hopped backwards. Laylea crawled through. She had to stay low as she entered the room because someone had positioned a metal platform so that it created a roof only a couple of feet off the ground. It continued about a meter beyond the doggy door. The metal vibrated with a low hum that filled the back of Laylea's brain. She was under some kind of machine.

Light and voices filtered in through a drape hanging from the edge of the platform. When she pushed the drape aside, the voices didn't become any clearer. Half a dozen students were working at different stations around the room. All of them wore tall rubber boots and gas masks. A small pair of those boots stood not a foot from where Laylea poked her head out.

Dizzy cawed at her, and Laylea ducked back in. Not fast enough. The boots moved, and in their place appeared a tragically pock-marked face half covered by a gas mask. Benny McBride Greene's blue eyes shot wide at the sight of Laylea. He glanced behind himself so quickly he couldn't have seen anything.

"Lee, you're back!" he whispered at almost the volume of a normal speaking voice. "Are you back? Does anyone know you're here?"

"Hi, Benny. I'm back." Laylea kept her voice low. "Spent last night in Holding, so someone knows I'm here."

A second pair of boots hurried over.

Laylea shrank into the shadows, but Dizzy hopped aside to give the new student space. This figure wore deep blue coveralls rolled up above the top of the boots. Laylea knew who it was as soon as she placed a hand on the floor. Deep black tribal tattoos covered the hand and arm. Ali's silky black hair draped over her tats as she leaned low enough to see under the platform.

"Hey!" Ali's whisper couldn't have been heard by a ghost. Laylea could barely hear her through her gas mask. "What are you doing under there? You are so weird."

Laylea ignored the insult. "What is all this?"

Benny explained, "Dean Gorse turned this into Fire Suppression Central when Special Testing was discontinued."

Ali added, "He gave this contractor asshole permission to use students to outfit the school."

"We manufacture the suppression gas in here. Next door, they're building the delivery compon—"

A high-pitched mechanical tone echoed in the space around Laylea. It buzzed through the metal over her head.

Light streamed in from a few feet to Laylea's left as another figure raised the drape at that end of the machine. Harper Pemberton's funny face blocked the light. He waved even as he hissed, "You better get out of there. Robby's gonna come back any second."

As if magically summoned, an unfamiliar male voice yelled, "Who has broken the Central Distributor?"

"Shit." Harper dropped his drape and disappeared.

Benny squeaked, and the drape he was holding dropped as light flashed around his form. A hard plastic knob hit the floor with a crack and rolled into the dark under the machine's platform. Laylea lifted the drape to see a turtle trapped at the neckline of a blue jumpsuit. Another flash had human Benny battling with his clothes. He whispered at her as he put his gas mask on upside down, "Only upper-level Chem students are allowed in here, Lee. You have to get out, or you'll be in serious trouble."

Ali rolled her eyes. "She might get detention and have to work for Robby in the next room over."

"Yeah," Benny retorted, "and she might never return from detention, like Cal."

Ali sighed. "Point."

Laylea asked, "Who's Cal? Who's Robby?"

Benny said, "Cal Christopherson was—" He stopped cold when a voice yelled from the far side of the room.

"I'm not going to ask again." The voice grew closer. It wasn't a kind voice or a pretty one. And it sounded angry.

"Cal was a cool first year. Great hair. That's Robby." Ali gestured for Laylea to crawl out.

"Oh no." Benny searched the floor with one boot on, one boot off. "I dropped the bypass." He hissed this at Ali, but Ali didn't reply. She just reached through the drape and dragged Laylea out with a grip on the back of her coverall.

"This way. Stay down." She hauled Laylea over to the nearest worktable and shoved her under it. Three sets of legs crowded close, between her and the machine. But not so close that Laylea couldn't see. She watched Dizzy drop the plastic knob onto Benny's newly rebooted foot.

"Who's broken my machine?" asked the voice that had said he wouldn't ask again.

"Me, sir." Benny's voice cracked. "I was just reviewing the procedure for changing hoses, and I dropped the reagent release valve."

Benny bent to pull on his second boot and discovered the knob there at his feet. Dizzy stood near him, making sure it didn't roll away again, but, of course, Benny couldn't see her. He plucked up the knob and held it out to Robby. Laylea couldn't see the man's face from under the table and behind Ali's legs, but she saw his throwback cargo pants and flannel shirt. Instead of the tall, ugly rubber boots all the students had, this guy wore hiking boots with a tweed pattern. He snatched the knob out of Benny's hand like a kitten who'd found the hand responsible for the red light she couldn't catch.

Dizzy circled the guy's head as he turned to face the machine. It looked, essentially, like a series of pumps connected to a hose that led to a gigantic white plastic reservoir that took up the entire length of the east wall. A clear tube ran along the top of the same wall. It caught Laylea's attention because the liquid filling this tube was the exact same shade of pink as the liquid in the container Dr. Brock had taken out of his briefcase.

"Do not take initiative, kid." Robby replaced the knob that Benny had removed. "You do as I instruct, no more, no less. We will only change the hoses if and after the system ever has to be activated. Do you expect the system to be activated?"

"No, sir." Benny's voice was quieter than when he'd been trying to whisper at Laylea. He kept his head tucked down and looked like he'd very much like to disappear into his shell.

Dizzy flew over and poked at Laylea. She hopped to the far end of the work table. Laylea followed, feeling like a coward for leaving Benny.

"Robby." Ali's voice froze Laylea in her tracks. Could Robby see under the table from where he was? "Could you just show Benny how to switch between the suppressant and cleaning agents? He's been stressing out about it, and he's stressing all of us out about it. I mean," Ali put on a simpering tone, "you're so smart. It wouldn't take you any time at all."

"Don't want you to be stressed, gorgeous." Robby took a step toward the table and Laylea tensed. She prepped to run.

A clattering sound drew everyone's attention to the machine where Benny held both hands to his mouth. "Whoops." Was there a hint of a giggle in Benny's voice? "Sorry, sir."

Robby's precious hiking boots spun in place and hurried away to the far corner of the machine. Laylea took the opportunity to race to the privacy curtain hung across the doorway to the lobby. She tried to slide under the curtain and misjudged how long it was. She hit it, making the chains at the top of the curtain jangle in their track.

"What now?" Robby growled.

Laylea's heart sank and then soared as the lobby door opened, and KC peered through. Laylea could make it out the door, but everyone else in the room would have to suffer this guy's bad temper if he didn't get an explanation for the unexpected noise. Laylea stood up.

"Hi." She smiled her client smile at the only adult in the room. Robby had a round face with a poorly fit gas mask crushing his thin beard. He glared daggers at Laylea. She searched for a reason she might be there. Had she been sent to fetch someone for a teacher or something? No. He could easily check that.

He raised his eyebrows and shook his head. She realized she'd been smiling at him for too long. "Is this the infirmary?"

Sniggers spread through the room. She spotted several kids she knew. In addition to Ali and Harper, she remembered Chloe, a moose shifter from Sphinx dorm, and Big Mo, the werewolf whose injury during weightlifting practice had taught her that not all shifters healed like she did. None of the kids dared catch her eye. Instead, they bent over their work with renewed industry.

Robby tilted his head at her. "Are you serious?"

Ali turned her back on Laylea. She raised her hand as she said, "Sir, that's just Fido. She's an idiot."

Inside, Laylea rolled her eyes. Externally, she kept her smile wide and nodded a little, laughing like it was a joke she didn't get.

Robby dismissed her. "Across the hall."

"Oh! Thanks!" Laylea spun and launched herself into KC's silently giggling form.

Dizzy swooped through the door to the lobby just before it fell shut.

"I knew you couldn't resist getting your stuff out of storage." KC kept her voice low as she led the way to the hallway door.

"Whoa." Last year, the lobby had featured a glass wall isolating the main computer system of the school. Now, the IsoTower that KC had hacked was walled off with bald plywood.

KC dragged her past the plywood and out into the hall. "They had to break the glass to get in after we sealed it last year. The tower and stacks are still in there. Welcome back. How's the real world?"

"Your brother misses you." Laylea hustled to keep up with KC racing down the hall and out of the Medical Wing.

"Yeah, right. Which one?"

Laylea pulled the ID band from her collar. "DJ. Here. This is from him. I got you the charm bracelet version, but it's at home." She slipped the ID band on KC's arm.

"Daniel Joaquin Delcampo does not care if I am alive."

"He does." Laylea pulled the straps tight around her friend's arm. "I overheard him fighting with your parents about where you are."

KC stopped walking. "You didn't tell him, did you?"

"No."

KC looked up the corridor toward the fancy double doors that led into the Executive Wing. She lowered her voice. "He'd tell my parents, and they'd come get me and send me to the Montana Shifter Collective."

"He wouldn't tell them."

"I'm not going to MSC." Her voice shook with a mix of fear and anger.

"I didn't tell him you're here, and he didn't want to know." Laylea remembered how DJ had asked but then reversed himself. "He was just glad to hear that you're safe."

KC made a barfing noise and continued down the hall.

Laylea shouted, "He wanted me to tell you he loves you."

"Whatever."

Laylea would have liked to convince her, but she could see that wasn't going to be an easy task. She changed the subject instead. "Did you know that Oscar had a sister?"

"Yeah, Tishala. Don't mention her." KC stopped in front of the E-wing doors and flipped her backpack around to dig through it. "He's been kind of obsessed with finding out what happened to her ever since he was electrocuted. He swears he saw ghosts."

"I did see ghosts." Oscar's voice echoed in the empty hall.

Laylea spun to find him jogging toward them from a connecting corridor. "Hi!"

"Hey, Lee." Oscar peered over KC's shoulder as she marked some numbers from a compass onto graph paper. He laughed. "More NavTech homework?"

KC blushed at his tone. "Yeah. I have to map five points in the school in relation to our classroom."

"Ooh." Laylea grinned. "Is this to keep you from getting lost?"

Oscar doubled over laughing. He was careful to keep the box he was holding from tipping. "Exactly. Vronumraju and Bianchi got sick of her being late to class, so they made her take Navigational Techniques." He snorted on the last word.

KC turned away from Oscar as she returned her supplies to her backpack, muttering, "We can't all be born cats."

Laylea tried to keep the laughter out of her voice as she commiserated with her friend. "Sorry, KC. I might be able to help. I learned lots about navigation flying with my dad."

"Before he died." KC said this in a loud voice.

Laylea hadn't noticed Reggie Betts coming down the hall.

"Yeah." She nodded her head, sighing. "Sucks to be an orphan."

They all waved awkwardly as Reggie passed them. He bumped fists with Oscar and ignored the girls, turning his head to yawn instead. Suddenly, the air wrinkled around him until he was a tiger, his mouth still open in an enormous yawn as he slunk down the hallway.

"Why isn't he in Mer?" Laylea wondered. That wasn't the behavior of a competent shifter.

KC said, "Cuz Dove's in Mer. They don't like siblings in the same dorm."

"Hey, I bet you're hungry." Oscar held out his box. It held a bunch of pressed food bars. "Chef Tod made these especially for you."

"Yes! I'm starving." KC grabbed one and tore into it. Almost instantly, her grin turned to a grimace, and she spat the food out into her hand. "What the phoenix is that?"

"Peanut butter, banana, oatmeal, and tuna fish."

Laylea beamed. The banana was a strange addition, but otherwise, those were the ingredients of her annual adoptionversary muffin. She took the bar from KC and the box from Oscar. She'd have to think of a big way to thank the Shetland pony shifter who ran the kitchen. "Aren't we going to the cafeteria, anyway?"

"No. KC and I both requested retesting last night. We're going with you, and as soon as we're all done, we have to get ready for the seance tonight."

"What?" Laylea stopped walking. She shivered as the memory of Amelia's panic washed over her.

"We tried one in Caves during Yule, but no ghosts showed up. Emerald thinks it'll work better if we're up in the open air."

KC grabbed Oscar by both arms and shook him. "No ghosts showed up because ghosts aren't real."

"Uhhhh, actually..." Laylea could have sworn she'd told her friends before.

KC stopped shaking Oscar. "You can see ghosts?"

"Yeah." She added, "if I want to."

"Let me get this straight." KC twisted the ID bracelet for a moment before looking Laylea in the eyes. "You can do magic, condition people to do well in Biology, are besties with a vampire, and can talk to ghosts."

Laylea grinned. "I can also shake, roll over, and sit pretty." She took a huge bite of Chef Tod's breakfast bar so she wouldn't have to answer any more questions.

16

Testing was the most fun experience Laylea had ever had. You hunkered down with a deskpadd and answered trivia questions until you reached a level where you got more wrong than right. Then you got to sit and talk about music and physics and art and biology and books with teachers. The testing didn't take as long as it had her first year, since the program had a better idea of her educational level.

She finished the digital questionnaire shortly after lunch and then sat for two moderator interviews. Technically, she had three. But her third interview was with Mr. Bianchi. He led her through a practical exam in musical theory and let her try her hand at a whole array of musical instruments. It was more like a lesson than a test. She'd never made music before, only enjoyed it. Mr. Bianchi promised her she would learn to play an instrument. He insisted she learn piano and then had her pick another. She was tempted by the xylophone, so she could play in dog form too. But she chose the guitar for her private study because it sounded so beautiful when he played. Even if she never got good, she'd get to listen to him play for a couple hours every week.

She was the last of the trio to finish Testing and barely had time to thank Mr. Bianchi before Oscar was dragging her and KC off to meet with Emerald, who sent them to gather candles, salt, and a gas burner. Ms. Muldoon caught them trying to take the burner from the Chem lab. She asked what it was for. Oscar said to heat up water, and she loaned them a battery-powered kettle without any more questions. Oscar stashed the items in his pod in Sphinx dorm while Laylea and KC went ahead to the dining hall.

Laylea had expected dinner to go on for ages as they introduced each of the dozen new students, plus her, but they were spared the ignominy. Mr. Bianchi merely listed which kids were joining which dorms and sent them on their way.

"They forego the public introductions when there are more than five new kids," Caliban explained as they headed back to Mer dorm. The linden tree shifter was taller than Laylea remembered. She had twisted her thick, dark hair into a Dutch braid that hung halfway down her back.

As Laylea remembered, the post-dinner scrum to the dorms felt like being swept along by white water; loud, gossipy white water. Her dorm, the Mers, had gotten three of the newbies. One of them was the boy with incredible balance, Rehyan. She swam over to him as the crowd swept around the final turning to their private section of the school.

"Hi." She held out a fist. "We never officially met. I'm Lee. This is KC."

"Rehyan." He bumped her fist and then KC's. "What's with the yelling about the sun?"

"The Mer war cry?" Laylea asked.

Ali overheard her and shouted, "Mers desperately want to see the sun!"

The responding cheer echoed off the walls.

"Yeah, what's with that?" Rehyan asked.

"Mers get the crappy shifters," KC explained. "So we're mostly not allowed upstairs."

"Upstairs?" Jimmy, the kid who'd been on N, ducked through a pack of roughhousing girls to join them just as they reached the double doors that led to the Mer's corridor. Laylea had never seen them closed. The Mers tended to make friends in both other dorms and welcomed anyone to visit while the Sphinxes required all visitors to have a Sphinx escort and the Centaurs kept their gate closed but generally told everyone how to get past it.

"Upstairs is what we call outside," Squirt answered, leaning down to hug Laylea from behind. "Welcome back, Lee." The Samoan kid had definitely grown another inch or two since she'd last seen him.

Conner Stone shoved his slim form sideways through the sea of bodies to knock into Jimmy. "But, you're a wolf. Me too. We have to go out once a month at the full moon. I'm Conner. You, me, and Carrie are the only wolves left in Mer."

They had no idea about KC.

"Th… they d… d… don't usually ho… hold it against us!" Carrie's little voice piped up from somewhere ahead of them. "Hey, what. . . wh…wh. . . wh—"

Conner finished her sentence. "What's he doing in our dorm?"

Just ahead of them, the corridor closed in tight. Beyond the fantastically carved double doors that hugged the walls, the corridor led to a low-ceilinged courtyard with real grass, two ponds, and a mix of couches, comfy chairs, and trees. A man stood on a ladder that leaned against the wall beside the entrance to the girls' podroom. He was futzing with a contraption set on top of the light trough.

Laylea recognized the tweed hiking boots and cargo pants. Even if she hadn't, several voices around her hissed his name. "Robby."

"What are you doing in our dorm?" Brenda Samborsky shoved through the pack of Mers. She stormed across the courtyard, ignoring the crushed gravel path they were supposed to use when they had shoes on. "It's after hours. Go away."

"I'm just making sure you're all safe, sweetie."

Even though she couldn't see Brenda's face, Laylea knew that if looks could kill, Robby would have crumbled into dust right there beside his ladder.

Several of the more temperate Mers jogged over to prevent Brenda from killing the man with her fists, as she very likely could. Laylea was surprised to see shy Carrie heading after them. The other eighty or so Mers spread out in the courtyard. Whether directly or not, everyone kept their eyes on the unwelcome visitor. Caliban, the linden shifter and oldest student in the dorm, possibly the school, took the lead.

"Thank you, Mr. Robby," she began.

"It's not Mister. It's not Doctor. It's just Robby." The sentence started out harshly, but by the end, Robby had turned on a thousand-watt smile. He rubbed a hand along Caliban's bare shoulder. His pasty skin looked unhealthy against her glowing olive tone.

Carrie tripped as she finally caught up to the small diplomatic corps. She barreled into Caliban, knocking her away from Robby's touch.

The man spun and caught Carrie, dipping her as if they'd been dancing. "Got you, little lady. Wouldn't want anything to happen to that beautiful face." He ran a hand down Carrie's frizzy brown braids.

Carrie squeaked. When he set her back on her feet, she dashed away into the girls' podroom. Robby tried to follow her. He found his way blocked by a tree, two wolves, and a bird with a wingspan wider than Robby was tall. Thunder rolled as the bird flapped its wings once and then hovered.

Ali, the only human in the living wall, played with the five piercings lining her left ear and examined the nails on her tattooed hand. She took her time catching Robby's eyes. When she did, a sweet, false smile warmed her face. Ali had spent the first twelve years of her life having the devil beaten out of her any time she shifted to a hawk. She was practiced at pretending to be harmless.

Before she could say anything, a new visitor drew everyone's attention to the corridor. This time, a couple dozen kids disappeared into hidden alcoves and the private boys' and girls' sides of the dorm. KC fell on her butt trying to hide behind Laylea.

The gorgeous stranger paid no attention to any of this. He straightened the deep blue vest that accentuated his muscled chest as he ducked in through the low entryway. His voice came out smooth and confident as he murmured, "Robby. I have news about your father. Come."

The contractor left his tools and his ladder. Kids scattered to get out of his way. It was like the students had become invisible to him. "What's wrong?" He sounded much as Laylea thought she'd sound if someone told her Bailey had died.

"Your father was taken by thumper police last night." The stranger turned as he talked. He spoke so quietly that he'd only gone three paces before Laylea could no longer hear him.

Instead of walking at his side, Robby fell into pace directly behind the well-dressed man as they left the dorm.

Ali sucked in a breath. It felt like the cue for everybody else to start breathing. "That was Denier, wasn't it?"

"Who's Denier?" Rehyan asked.

"Adrien Denier," KC murmured. "He's the Council's enforcer. You do not want to ever meet him."

Thunder clapped again as the bird folded his red-tipped wings and set down as a seventeen-year-old boy with blue-green eyes the same shade his wings had been. "They say be wary of the pretty ones."

"Then you should be fucking terrified of me, Ahanu." Brenda feinted a punch at the boy.

Ahanu dove out of the way. He addressed the room at large, "Any Mers worried about the phoenix coming out of deep freeze and torching the school again?"

A murmured chorus of denials sounded around the cave. Peter, a fox who'd never been able to talk to Laylea without blushing, put words to the murmurs. "If y'all have to wear gas masks so you're not poisoned by the retardant while you're making it, I sure don't want it pumped into the dorm. Let it burn."

Others echoed, some laughing, some serious, "Let it burn!"

"Cool." Ahanu spun as he leapt into the air. A third crack echoed off the stone, and then the great thunderbird snapped his beak through the flexible rubber hose running from Robby's equipment out into the corridor. Ahanu landed on two human feet and continued on out into the hallway. "Seance time. Let's go, before any other adults decide to invade."

"Seance?" Jimmy asked.

Conner put an arm around him and led him away to the boys' podroom. "Nah, you don't want to get expelled your second night here."

"Expelled, nothing. Denier is clearly busy." Ali strode over. She hooked her arms in KC's and Laylea's and nudged them toward the corridor. "With no enforcer around and all the faculty either up at Gorse's horse farm or deciding our fates in the auditorium, I don't think we'll ever see a safer time to get some fresh air and watch Em make a fool of herself again."

"Well, I'm in for that." Squirt joined them.

"You're in because you know Brian is in," Ali corrected him. Squirt blushed.

"C. . . c… can I come?" Carrie tripped out of the podroom and squeaked when she fell into Brenda. She immediately flash-shifted into a scrawny wolf with her yellow-brown tail tucked tight to her belly.

"Come on. You can protect me from the poltergeists." Squirt waved for Carrie to trot ahead of him.

"You're gonna need a lookout." Merrilynne tossed her purple hair in KC's face as she pushed past her to join Squirt.

Merrilynne liked to stick with other water species when she had a choice. The fact that Squirt was a saltwater dweller and she, as a koi, required freshwater, apparently didn't matter. Laylea would have thought the fact that he was being kind to a wolf would have made him persona non grata to Merri. Perhaps she'd opened her mind a little.

"You have four legs, Carrie." Merri's musical voice grated. "Move them faster and get out of my way."

Laylea sighed. Or not.

17

*L*aylea wasn't convinced that going upstairs was a good idea. She definitely didn't expect Emerald would seduce any ghosts to reveal themselves with her salt and candles. Plus, if Oscar, a rich boy with a father on the Council, got presser duties for trying to leave the school without permission, wouldn't they have put extra security at the Sphinx exit tunnel?

The question was answered when Ali led them left out of their corridor instead of right.

"The Sphinx tunnel is a no-go for getting out anymore." KC kept her voice low. "But Brenda heard there was a way out through the old Gryphon dorm."

Ali did not bother to whisper. "It took us a while to find it, but just you wait."

"Big Mo found it," Squirt added. "All by himself."

"Dudes." Ahanu called for them to hurry. When they caught up to him at a bend in the hallway, he ran a hand through Carrie's fur. "You better shift, Carrie. We're not hauling you all the way up."

Carrie dropped her head until Squirt squatted beside her and said, "I've never been here before. I don't know where I'm going. If I carry you, you can show me, right?"

The skinny wolf licked his face.

"Cool."

Several yards down the hallway, another half dozen kids and animals waited beside an old wardrobe-style clothes closet. Laylea recognized many faces from Sphinx, including the top dog in the school's werewolf pack, Patrick DelValle. He stood with Jase Batka, the worst example of wolfdom and meanest member of the LPSS pack. Jase had added a mustache to the tuft of fur on his chin masquerading as a goatee. The upper lip fuzz did not help his attempt to look tough.

Beyond them, Brian chatted quietly with Emerald, who never looked entirely comfortable out of her seal skin. She ran one hand absently along her bestie Chloe's muzzle whenever the moose nudged her.

Big Mo, the wolf from Centaur who'd broken his leg last year, nodded at Laylea. "Did you find the infirmary?"

Everyone who'd been in the Special Testing room when she met Robby laughed.

Oscar, his sleek black leopard form nearly invisible in the darkness, paced the corridor, weaving through all the kids and Chloe's moose legs. His skin rippled as he turned, the classic leopard spots standing out as blacker patches on his black fur. He rubbed himself against Carrie before knocking his head into Laylea's shins like she'd done to him at Holding.

"Everybody ready?" Patrick DelValle leaned against the wall directly opposite the clothes closet. He rested a hand on one of the ancient torch holders that still dotted the walls around the older parts of the school. "We need to get through quickly. The Gryphons weren't a trusting bunch."

Oscar loped down the hall a few paces and came back carrying dark blue coveralls in his jaws. KC grabbed them from him. Everyone moved in close to the closet.

"Three," Patrick said. "Two. One." He slowly twisted the sconce. Four quiet clicks sounded from the base. And then, nothing. Laylea jumped when muted gears ground behind the walls. The stone around them shook as various mechanical elements whirred and spun and dropped into place.

The antique walnut wardrobe split down the center, each side drawing away. Blue student jumpsuits shuddered on their shelves as the closet opened to reveal a courtyard of wood and iron, girded 'round with trees and roofed with a ceiling of stained glass. The kids raced through with Carrie loping ahead. Chloe shifted to fit through. At the last second before the clothes closet slammed shut, Oscar bounded into the hidden dorm.

The Gryphon dorm hadn't been in use since the population of the school was decimated by the Phoenix Event. It was creepy to traipse through their empty, echoing courtyard, especially considering they were heading upstairs in hopes of meeting some of the victims of that disaster.

Laylea would have held the seance right there.

One by one, they crossed the rotting rope bridge over a pond at the base of a circular arena vaguely reminiscent of the acropolis or an Incan ruin except with steel and glass frames and trees creating separate lounging areas.

Beyond the amphitheater, as Big Mo named it, near the rear of the courtyard, a ladder of branches led up through the canopies of five trees. Everybody scaled it in human form except the birds and Brian, who shifted to gorilla for his extra strength. He took Carrie from Squirt and climbed the ladder with her wolf form draped across his shoulders. Up beyond the canopy of leaves, they clambered onto one of the iron beams crisscrossing the wrought-iron and stained-glass ceiling. Crumbling nests rested in the circular designs of the ceiling's support beams. Ali explored, peering into each of the nests. Laylea wondered how many birds had lived in Gryphon Dorm and how many of them slept in animal form. It was a practice frowned upon by everyone except the Mers.

At a point where three of the beams crisscrossed, Big Mo helped each of the non-avian kids transfer from the first enormous beam to another. Big Mo, it turned out, had been the one to discover the dorm's upstairs access while he was rehabilitating from his weightlifting injury last October. Patrick retook the lead when they reached a wall of stone at the end of the second beam, because wolves.

The birds looped around and folded their wings to dive at the wall. Laylea gasped when each disappeared right through it. Echoes of their cries floated out to the others. As each person passed through the wall, the air shimmered or flashed or popped behind them. Just ahead of her, Big Mo took a single step left on the thin outcropping in front of the wall. Then he, too, walked through solid stone. When her turn came, she stepped to the left and saw the entrance to a tunnel. It had been so cleverly carved into the stone face that it was all but invisible until you stood directly in front of it.

She turned back to grin at Oscar and KC, the only ones left behind her.

"When you get to the stairs, run ahead of everyone. Distract them," Oscar said, unzipping his jumpsuit.

Laylea tilted her head. "Why?"

KC looked up from where she was twisting her ID dibs around her wrist. "Just go. Let's get this over with."

Oscar echoed her with a look that said *trust me.*

Laylea turned back to the tunnel and took a step forward. Instantly, her body burned with the pain of her shift. As she dropped to the ground, she understood why KC was nervous and Oscar was taking his jumpsuit off. The passage forced them to shift. She wriggled out of her own loose suit and dragged it with her along the short passageway.

At the end, Big Mo held a door open. He gestured for her to hurry. "Come on."

As soon as Laylea was clear, he slammed the door behind her and laughed.

Jase, Laylea's arch enemy, shifted from wolf to human to laugh with him. "Dude! Does he have any idea how to open it?"

Big Mo raised his hands in a shrug. "I figured it out. A genius from the famous Luke family shouldn't have any problem. Let's go! Maybe we can get to the top before he finds the trick." Big Mo took off, racing up the stairs.

Jase chased after him. "You're such a bastard. He's gonna be pissed at you."

Everyone's eyes were on the roughhousing werewolves ahead. Nobody else saw when the door opened and Oscar came out. KC followed, helping him into his jumpsuit.

"The cave makes everyone shift to animal form," he explained quietly. "But you have to be human to work the locking mechanism on the door. Big Mo told me about it."

Once again, KC had managed a forced shift without anybody seeing the beautiful white wolf she really was. Big Mo had made sure nobody would be there to see her as a wolf. It made Laylea wonder if Big Mo knew KC's secret.

Moonlight streamed impossibly through the wrought-iron skylight overhead. Everyone traipsing up the endless circular staircase ahead of Laylea kept peering up as if wondering how the light could be so clear. Laylea skittered up the wooden steps, which were smooth as marble and smelled like thousands of shoes and paws and hooves. She sang out a trilling bark. She wanted to ask in wonder, "Where are we?"

The others understood. Eight humans replied, "Gryphon's Dorm."

Ahanu and Ali spread their wings and swooped over the brass handrail, Ali's hawk voice screeching in counterpoint to Ahanu's deep song.

Brian climbed the outside of the intricate wrought iron railing in his gorilla form, his massive fingers looped through the designs. He swung over to crouch on the steps beside Laylea. Instead of bellowing as a triumphant gorilla would, he attempted a howl. Laylea threw her head back to join him. Three of the Sphinx wolves shifted and showed what true howling sounded like. Carrie kept her furry head down and focused on the slippery steps with Squirt guarding her from behind.

The very top of the staircase ended in a low arch which led to a dark, dank room. The plasterboard wall to their left held a crumbling door with a grate centered at the bottom. Ali and Ahanu folded their wings and pushed through an identical grate high in the right-hand wall. It swung open like a doggy door.

Merrilynne raced for what Laylea thought was an old drinking fountain sticking out of the third wall, saying, "Later, losers. I'm going for a swim." She leapt and performed her graceful transformation into an iridescent koi in midair. She landed in the fountain with the tiniest of splashes and disappeared.

Laylea trotted over to the door. She tried the low grate with her head. It moved. She pushed through with Carrie on her heels. They found themselves in another dark foyer underneath a set of metal stairs. The door on the opposite wall read *Ladies.* The door they'd come through had a chain across it at waist height. Its label said *Staff Only.*

Carrie scrambled up the stairs. Laylea followed while the human kids opened the door and ducked under the chain to join them. At the top of the stairs, a short ramp led into the open air. Stars offered plenty of light for their animal eyes. Laylea stuck close to Carrie's tail as the little wolf galloped around a copse of trees into the children's area of the zoo. Laylea recognized it when they ran past a pack of bronze wolves, the sculptures of KC's uncles. She sang out, remembered they were trying to be stealthy, and wuffled more quietly. Then she put on speed and raced down the path to the depressed bear's enclosure.

She took the final turn in a dead sprint. Ahead, she spotted the giant hollow log that lay on its side, bisected by the plexiglass cage. Kids could climb into the log and watch the bear napping in the log on the other side.

Only, the depressed black bear wasn't napping in the log inside his cage. He was sitting on top of the log. On the public side of the plexiglass.

18

---

he Children's Zoo's Bear Hollow offered goat petting and animal encounters during the day. Kids could run around the little alcove created between the plexiglass and chain link bear enclosure on one side and a man-made forest on the other. They could climb in and on the hollow log, wend their way through the maze of wooden arches, play tag around the circle of benches, or picnic in the clearing in the middle. But at night, the goats and petting zoo animals were put inside and Toby, the depressed bear, ruled Bear Hollow.

As Laylea and Carrie approached the alcove, they saw him perched atop the log like a king. He stared at the stars, one paw lazily scratching his white ear. For the moment, he seemed at peace with the world. Laylea's heart lightened to see him happy. It was a rare sight.

The moment ended the instant Toby spotted the two shifters. He dropped his casual posture and leapt for a tree standing nearby. In the space of a breath, he was up the branchless trunk, over the barbed wires topping his cage, and dropping silently onto the hollow trunk inside the enclosure.

A shadow followed the bear, not as a shadow should beneath the pale moon and bright stars, but as a person walking through the fence.

Laylea blinked. Was she seeing a ghost without consciously opening her mind?

"Fido, put some clothes on, you loser." Jase traipsed into Bear Hollow. He crossed directly to the plexiglass near Toby and pounded on the cage. "Hey, Toby, my man, how's it hanging?"

The bear lowered himself from the trunk and slunk off into the copse. He stopped just beyond the tree line and sat, his shoulders slumped and head hanging low, his usual posture.

Laylea wouldn't have known where he was if it weren't for Toby's bright white left ear. It reminded her of her long-lost brother, Rhemy, who also had one bright white left ear. A sad cry went up from the others just reaching the clearing.

"Aw, Toby, don't be like that," Chloe shouted as she started pulling candles from her backpack and setting them in a circle in the very middle of the seating area. Carrie tried to leap onto the hollow log, but her little wolf legs weren't strong enough. She bounced off the side and fell to the ground, landing in human form. Toby looked up at the thump she made when she rolled into his wall.

"Hey, Lee, here." KC handed Laylea the jumpsuit she'd abandoned at the bottom of the stairs. "I'm worried about Oscar."

Laylea was so stunned to see Toby free, she hadn't noticed herself shift. Hadn't even noticed the cold winter night on her skin. She followed KC's eyes and spotted Oscar getting instructions from Emerald. He set the borrowed kettle in the middle of Chloe's candle circle and turned it on to heat up the water that Jase and Patrick poured in.

"Ali!" Emerald called from where she knelt on the ground, pulling multi-colored crystals from the bag that held her selkie skin. She set the bag on a bench. "Ali, I've got your suit. Get down here."

"You go ahead, Em." Chloe pulled a modern jumpsuit out of Em's bag.

It was rare for a selkie to let someone else touch her bag. Without her skin, a selkie could never shift again. It said a lot that Em let Ali store her suit there and that she let Chloe handle it.

The hawk touched down on the bench. Chloe held the jumpsuit

out, but Ali just ruffled her feathers. She hopped around, off the bench and back on. She leaped into the air and spread her wings, then folded them and let herself fall to the ground. She landed hard but didn't shift. Ali cawed her displeasure when Chloe dumped the suit over her feathery head and went to wash her hands in salt.

Emerald called to everyone, "The water's warm. Take a little salt and scrub it on your hands. Then let Oscar rinse your hands with the water." She turned to Oscar, holding her hands out to him. "Think about Tishala. Keep her in your mind."

The selkie was using a show voice. Normally, the pale, delicate-looking girl could be heard across the dining hall in casual conversation. Now, she'd put a whisper in her tone and crooned in that way that was supposed to be soothing but really put everyone on edge.

Laylea stopped KC before she crossed over to take her portion of salt. She took Sanna's crane out of her collar. "Here. A gift from Sanna, Bailey, and me."

"What?" KC looked dumbstruck.

Laylea had to set the crane into her open palm. "Oscar's mother made it. Bailey charmed it. I…well, I'm giving it to you."

"This'll let me see Dizzy, like Oscar's bracelet?" she asked, her eyes glittering.

"Yeah. Among other things."

KC laughed. "Do they protect us from ghosts, as well as magic?" She started toward the hand washing line. Laylea walked with her, but her eyes kept returning to the shadow watching the kids from the bear's side of the fence.

"Ghosts *are* magic," Laylea explained. "Life animates living souls. Magic animates souls with no body. I need to talk to that ghost hanging with Toby. I'll catch up."

She felt KC watching her as she trotted over to the fence. The unmistakable scent of sage wafted over to her on a freezing breeze, and Laylea realized for the first time how cold it was. No wonder frail Emerald was rushing things.

Laylea turned in a circle once she'd reached the fence. Instead of chanting her usual mantra, she quickly addressed each major point of the compass before whispering at the shadow on the far side of the fence, "I saw you. Can you see me?"

Darkness turned. The shadow solidified just enough that she could pick out a Black face wrinkled with age and laugh lines and a body in green coveralls with a name tag. The name glowed when she peered at it, seeming to grow more real because she was taking an interest. *Guillaume.*

Guillaume's deep, southern-accented voice sounded exactly as a shadow should, amorphous and smoky. "I see you."

She could have circled again, respected the places in between and probably been able to see him better, but she cut to the chase. "My friends are putting on a seance. Are there dangerous spirits here?"

"Open your eyes and see."

"I think I'd rather not." The words surprised Laylea, but as soon as she said them, she knew she'd been afraid since before she saw Guillaume. She'd been afraid since Amelia had held her hostage in the sleep lab.

Guillaume nodded as if she'd said something wise. He stepped through the fence and looked around the clearing with its children's climbing toys. But he did not look at the dozen shifter students circling up around Em's candles. He looked at other figures, figures Laylea could not see. Finally, he whispered. "All spirits are dangerous, cherie."

Laylea knew she was holding back her sight. She kept her eyes on the real, living people in front of her as Ali finally shifted and shivered as she pulled on her jumpsuit. She ignored her sneaking suspicion that the freezing breeze that kept blowing through her hair was not winter but Amelia.

"Circle up, everybody!" Emerald called as she dribbled a thin circle of salt around the candles she'd lit in the center of the clearing. "We must combine our energy to reach out to the other side."

Another canister of salt sat on the bench beside Em's skin-bag. Laylea grabbed the dispenser and let it spill while she casually walked around the circle of kids as if looking for a place in it.

"On your knees," Em directed. "Spread your fingers out and set them palm down in front of you. You want your thumbs touching, and make sure that your pinkies are touching your neighbors'. We want a complete, unbroken circle. Lee, hurry up, scoot in there beside Ahanu. Everyone, close your eyes."

Laylea dashed a couple more steps to complete a circle of salt around all of the students. She muttered a final line of her father's self-protection song, *"Their lives are in my hands, and I will not throw them away."* A spark rose as the final spray of salt closed her circle. The spark illuminated Amelia and Guillaume before it spread into a shimmering golden curtain between the kids and the ghosts.

"Sorry, Ahanu. Can you scootch?" She carefully stepped over the salt line and dropped to her knees, spreading her hands in front of her.

"It's about time, Fido." Jase set his hand in place on Ahanu's far side.

"Close your eyes." Emerald intoned, "Come to us, spirits! Come share your pain with us."

Laylea felt the icy wind surge up her neck and stand her hair on end. Amelia had moved behind her, safely on the far side of the magical wall. Then, Jase kicked out behind himself like a wolf gearing up for a fight. "Bring it!" His kick sent salt flying into the air.

A pop sounded in Laylea's soul as her circle of protection was broken.

Except for KC, who shot her eyes to Laylea, the kids felt nothing of the change that swirled through the icy air. Amelia floated closer, draping her panic across Laylea's shoulders. A rich, cheroot-scented breath tickled her ear.

"Open your eyes," Guillaume hissed. "Before everyone dies."

Laylea's eyes shot open. Her psychic eye shot open an instant later, showing her the dozens upon dozens of ghosts closing in around them.

19

Flying had always been a special time for Laylea and her dad. Just the two of them, far from the earth and all its troubles. Sometimes, the Dad would raise the plane into a blanket of clouds, and they wouldn't know which way was up or which was down except by trusting gravity. The longer you sailed through the clouds, the less trusting you became. Cold seeped into the cockpit. Doubt seeped into your mind. If they coasted there for too long, Laylea would crawl into the Dad's lap and bury her nose under her tail.

The storm of ghosts—human and animal—descending on the seance felt like days of cloud flying. All the kids felt the danger; few of them understood how fatal it could be. Most blamed each other.

A ghostly eel swam through the air as though it were water. It slithered between Patrick and Jase. Both boys shivered. Jase giggled nervously. Then the ghost eel spotted something about Brian and dove into his chest.

Brian sucked in a breath. The hairs on his arms stood on end. "Jase, I swear to phoenix." He tried to sit back and pull his hands out of the circle. He couldn't. "That's not funny."

An electrical shock zipped through Laylea from the pinkie that overlapped Brian's to the pinkie that rested against Ahanu's. Each of them jerked as the electrical connection continued around the circle. Laylea couldn't pull her hands away, either.

"No, please," KC begged as a semi-transparent girl in a zoo employee uniform ran through her. Tears started pouring down KC's face.

The zoo girl slashed a hand through Big Mo's head as she ran on, disappearing when she hit Toby's fence.

Three lines of blood welled on Big Mo's neck. He kept his eyes shut but turned his head toward Em's best friend. "That really hurt, Chloe."

"I didn't do anything." Chloe opened her eyes to glare at Big Mo. "My hands are on fire."

They weren't. They were being held by a male ghost whose lips moved as if he were trying to speak.

"Hey," Ahanu laughed, but it sounded strained. "Who's putting ice down my back?"

An older woman wearing a full-length skirt and short jacket lay against him, her arms wrapped around his chest.

Laylea's heart broke at the sound of Oscar's whispered plea. "Tishala?"

Emerald continued her schtick as if nothing were wrong, as if she hadn't already called all the ghosts to their unprotected circle. As if she couldn't feel the trio of ghosts draped across her body, pushing her down over her knees.

"We call on those who have come before us, those who have paved the way. Those who have studied at the altar of LPSS yet never left. Shift now into the world of living and touch us with your truth!"

"What are you doing, Mo?" Chloe screeched, "My hands are really on fire!"

"I can't move. I can't pull my hands away." Patrick tried to sound stern. His voice cracked when a goat lowered his spectral horns and impaled the Alpha's thigh. "Emerald, this isn't funny anymore!"

"Shala, are you here?" Oscar cried out.

Carrie wailed, "I wa... want to g... go downstairs."

In a stroke of sheer random luck, Emerald finally happened upon a repetition that connected with the magical spirits. She cried out, "See us! Hear us! Touch us!"

A Clydesdale horse with hooves shod in iron galloped out of the darkness, ahead of a destructive wind that flashed across the circle and tore through the trees, spinning new leaves and dead twigs over the kids. The candles sputtered and went out. They fell into Em's circle of salt, breaking their last small protection.

KC screamed.

The Clydesdale shook its mane, whinnying a deathly cry. It leapt over the crouching kids to touch down behind Emerald. Ghosts scattered. Emerald sat up as her trio released her. She threw her head back, chanting nonsense into the freezing air while starlight lit her face in a manic glow. The angry spirits zipped around the circle as the horse spun and danced, its flaming eyes focused on pale Emerald.

"Please, Shala, speak to me," Oscar yelled into the rising storm.

"Love and joy!" Laylea screamed. "Love and joy is the way to win through!"

She surged to her feet. Because they were still electrically connected, Ahanu and Brian had to stand as well.

Jase swore as he was forced to rise. "Shut it, Fido."

The Clydesdale pawed the dirt behind Emerald. Every head turned her way as the ground shook.

Oscar opened his eyes. He saw the horse and shouted, "Emerald, look out!"

Emerald peeked his way and scoffed. The ghosts did not like that.

"Chloe, Ali," Laylea pleaded with Em's best friends. "Hug Emerald! Protect her!"

"What is wrong with you?" Big Mo shouted to be heard over the wind.

Patrick added, "It's just a little thunderstorm."

"That isn't thunder." Ahanu's voice was so quiet, nobody heard but Laylea and Jase.

Laylea's attention spun to Brian. Instead of trying to pull his hand away like everybody else, Brian grasped Squirt's hand more fully and helped him to his feet. "Love and joy, huh?"

Squirt's deep brown skin darkened with a sweet blush. He held tightly to Brian's hand, staring into his eyes as if they stood alone against the storm. The slimy electric eel shuddered and fell from Brian's body. It hit the dirt, sending a cloud of dust into the air as everyone stumbled about, finally released from each other. Laylea crashed to the ground. She inhaled a lungful of dirt.

Squirt and Brian helped each other off the ground and ran from the clearing. Carrie tumbled ass over teakettle into one of the wooden benches. She whacked her head so hard Laylea could hear it over the storm.

Big Mo crawled through the outer salt circle, trying to get to his feet. "It's freezing out here. Screw talking to phoenix failures. Let's get back downstairs!" Ghosts surrounded him, keeping him from standing.

"Em, stop this!" Ali hollered, the glowing tattoos wrapping her left arm holding the ghosts away from her somehow.

Laylea turned to the hawk shifter. "Hug her, Ali. Hold Em."

KC screamed again as the ghost horse reared up over Emerald. Its massive hooves bicycled over the thin girl's white hair. Laylea lurched back to grab a handful of salt and dirt. She wrapped herself in the imaginary green sweater knit of her father's love as she sent the salt flying at the horse. "You cannot touch her! She is loved! Chloe—"

Her words were cut off when a green-blue wing smacked her to the ground. Ahanu stood, half shifted, his wings spread wide. He darted across the circle on human legs and wrapped his arms around Emerald. He gave one mighty beat of those wings and thunder deafened them all. He and Em shot up into the sky just as the horse stomped down, sending dirt flying from the impression of Emerald's knees.

Sparks blasted through the ghosts closing in on Ali. Her hair snapped in the wind of the swirling ghosts one instant, and the next, her feathers fluttered and settled as she rose above the melee, chased by ghostly wrens, an owl, and a crane. They followed her as she followed Ahanu and Emerald. Chloe dashed through a half dozen ghosts to snatch Emerald's skin-bag from the bench.

A dark shadow solidified from the mist of bodies. A woman so beautiful that Laylea wanted to cry reached one thin hand out to steal the bag from Chloe.

Chloe's eyes teared up in fear and awe as she suddenly saw the ghost trying to take her friend's sealskin. Her body melted as if she were going to faint. But she didn't. Chloe screamed and yanked the bag back against her chest. The ghost beauty dove through the bench at Chloe, but Emerald's bestie shifted into a thousand-pound moose and ran like her tail was on fire.

"Go," Laylea shouted at Big Mo. "Go with her. Make sure she gets the bag downstairs."

Big Mo rubbed a hand on his neck where the girl in the zoo uniform had scratched him. He looked down at Carrie crouched where she fell, wailing and gasping for breath. KC pulled the little werewolf to her feet and helped Big Mo haul her to his shoulder. "You coming?" he asked KC.

KC said, "Right behind you," but she stumbled to Laylea's side instead, holding Sanna's red crane out like a shield between her and the army of dead. "Are they real? No one else can see them. Is it this? Is this why I can see?"

"You can see because they want you to feel them, but you are protected." Laylea knew this wasn't really true. Her lizard foot wasn't protecting her from Amelia. "Take Oscar downstairs."

"We are not leaving without you." KC grabbed her hand and pulled Laylea to her feet. "Love and joy, right?"

Oscar stood alone. His eyes darted through the ethereal faces. When he caught a ghost's gaze, he begged, "Do you know Shala? Tishala? Where can I find Tishala Luke? Have you seen a leopard, a black leopard?"

"Oscar, dude." Patrick dusted himself off. He brushed at the snake slithering around his neck and then looked at his hand as if expecting to see some residue. He sounded bored, but his eyes flashed with fear. "We're going down the tunnel. Come on."

Jase let out a whoop that was carried away on the spectral wind. "I ain't afraid of no ghosts." He threw his arms to the sides and stepped forward into the transparent form of a man in a modern zookeeper uniform. "Shit, it is cold. I'm out."

It saddened Laylea to know that Jase, too, liked Ghostbusters. They had something in common. The moment of despair was enough for Amelia. While Jase dropped into his wolf and trampled through the man-made forest with Patrick hard on his tail, Laylea's muscles seized up. She froze, overwhelmed by panic that her daughter would die without having really lived, and sheer terror that Bert would never be punished.

20

"Oscar!" KC's scream sliced through Amelia's deadly hold on Laylea's senses. "Lee, we love you. You help people. You help ghosts." KC's voice receded, but Laylea could still feel her hand squeezing tight. "She helps ghosts. She can help you. She can hear you." A muffled roar sounded in the distance. "Oh, shit! Oscar, help us!"

Laylea sucked a small breath into her paralyzed lungs. She whispered into the great void of death, "I can see you. My name is Lee."

The white-out blindness that came with Amelia's embrace cleared just enough for her to see the dark face of an old man in green coveralls. Guillaume held a hand out to her. "Toby is safe in his cage. But not out here."

Laylea's vision cleared enough that she could see through Guillaume to where Toby's claws poked through the chain link section of his cage. He was halfway to the barbed wire top. The roaring sound was coming from him. And from the whirlwind of ghosts surrounding Oscar.

He knelt in the midst of the scattered candles, his arms out in supplication, crying his sister's name.

KC screamed for him but refused to release Laylea's hand.

"There is no Tishala here." Guillaume said it simply.

Laylea reached down into her gut, not for the burning of her shift but for the giggly joy of the love she felt for Oscar, who so loved his sister he risked his very soul to find her, for KC, who had never known loyalty from her family but shone with it in the face of terror like she'd never felt before, and even for Toby, the depressed bear who had saved her life when he'd been meant to kill her. She tore her free arm from her side and reached out to grab Guillaume's cold hand.

"I am looking for Albert Gorshkov." It was a statement to Amelia and a request to Guillaume. The panic subsided a touch. "I'm trying to save Deanna and everyone else in the sleep labs, everyone taking N."

Guillaume tugged. Laylea stumbled forward, out of Amelia's embrace. "I remember Bert," he said. "He woulda loved N."

"I'm okay, Toby!" Laylea hollered to the bear. He was tearing at the barbed wire. Blood dripped from one paw. "Get down."

Toby looked over at her. Better still, Oscar did too.

Guillaume grinned at her as Toby moved down the fence. "Merci."

A baboon abandoned the scrum around Oscar to hoot at Laylea. A pretty young man with long hair pulled into a high bun followed him. His voice hissed with static. "Berty loved all the drugs. It made him popular."

"And he was rich enough to get away with it," a woman added.

KC's voice shook. She pulled Laylea close. "Albert's a drug dealer?"

Several voices laughed. The Clydesdale who had tried to kill Emerald brayed. The wind raised again as many half-formed voices spoke.

Guillaume interpreted. "Bert gave them away. He just wanted to be popular."

"Is he still in school?" she asked.

The temperature dropped a degree. Guillaume laid his other hand on top of hers. "We don't go downstairs no more. We're trapped in the zoo."

"But…" She looked around at the dozens of human and furry spectral faces. "You're not."

"We are," the pretty young man insisted. "If you cannot shift, you cannot leave."

Laylea took a breath. She led KC through a half dozen ghosts, as creepy as that was, to pull Oscar to his feet. "We're alive, the three of us and Toby," she said, carefully.

Guillaume rescued her from the other half of that sentence. "And we're dead. We know."

"Then..." She tripped alongside KC as she pulled them toward the path away from the clearing. "Then, you should know that you can be anything you want. You can shift. You can grow wings and fly. You can swim underwater for as long as you like. You can go downstairs."

KC pulled her arm sharply. "Maybe not that."

Laylea looked at her friend. "I'm not gonna lie to them." She turned back to find all of the figures watching her. There was a commonality to the humans that she couldn't quite put her finger on. "You can go anywhere. You can traverse the veil and gauntlet and cross over if you want."

"What does that mean?" the pretty man asked.

Laylea spurted out a giggle. "I have no idea. It's a dead thing."

A light suddenly glowed in the pretty ghost's eyes. His whole body reflected light as he rotated to stare at something Laylea could not see.

"It's true," the man murmured. He turned in a circle, looking around at all of the dead. "She's right."

He turned into the light, and then he wasn't there anymore. A dozen ghosts disappeared. Some animals shifted into humans, and some of the humans shifted into animals. Some of the ghosts grew more solid and colder. Not all of them reacted well to the news.

"You're good." Oscar whispered this in Laylea's ear, his voice thick with grief. Laylea worried that he didn't seem to notice the angry ghosts. Laylea backed slowly away from the spectral crowd, pushing her friends behind her.

Guillaume gave her the side-eye. "Can it be true, ma petite chienne?"

She offered him a slight nod, and with the next blink of his eyes, the old man flashed into a pure white dove. The bird fluttered over to swoop around the depressed bear's head. Toby watched the bird flying around with no hint of his usual malaise.

Without Guillaume's calming presence between them, the other ghosts approached Laylea. She tried to find one kind face to focus on. She found mostly glowing eyes, raised hackles, and fangs. She backed away more quickly.

They were all startled when a figure crashed through the trees. Some of the feline ghosts ran away before the girl delivered her message.

"Run!" Merrilynne bent over her knees, gasping for breath, water dripping from her hair. "Where is everyone?"

"They already ran," KC said, speeding their progress down the path, away from the ghosts.

Merrilynne jogged along with them. "But I *just* saw Gorse and the wolves coming out of the cafe."

"He's supposed to be at the placement meeting." KC glanced back at the following phalanx of dead shifters. "It's being held at his horse farm."

"Duh." Merrilynne turned and flat out ran down the path. She called over her shoulder, "But he's not there."

Laylea jogged backwards, keeping her eyes on the ghosts and trying to help them find peace. "You are spirits. You are pure magic, and you get to choose your own adventure now. Amelia." She stopped to face the angriest spirit of them all, despite the danger of being caught up again and despite Oscar and KC tugging on her arms. Amelia tore a path through the others to hover an inch from Laylea's nose. Laylea couldn't think why the ghost was following her, except that maybe she wanted Laylea to find Bert Gorshkov as much as Morioka did. "I'll find him."

Deanna Gorshkov's mother flared with brilliant fury and then dissolved into air.

The remaining dozen ghosts surged forward. Laylea had no more words. She turned tail and ran with her friends. A white figure zipped by overhead. Guillaume flew ahead of them down the path. They'd just reached the bronze wolves when he flashed back into human form. "Dean Gorse is just around the bend. Shift and cut through this way."

He ushered them ahead of him to the side where thick trees would slow them down if they weren't four-legged. They'd have to shift. He kept himself between them and the alternately dissipating and flaring ectoplasmic figures who had chosen not to go into the light.

Oscar stripped down and handed his jumpsuit to KC before he slipped into his sleek leopard form. KC tied the suit around her waist and turned to take Laylea's. She wrapped Laylea's thin suit around her neck and, with the slightest wave in reality, dropped into a beautiful white wolf. Laylea reached for the burn in her gut. She felt nothing but the ice left from Amelia's panic. Her own panic rose.

A voice surfed to them on the clear winter air. "You're filthy rich, Bertram. You can afford it."

When all the ghosts turned to face the voice, Laylea had a moment of hope. Then she realized being caught upstairs by the dean might be worse than being swept up in a dozen personal hells.

Oscar and KC paced between the grass and the path. Laylea bent to see if she could crawl through the low space. It was dark, and she couldn't see far. The trees were too tightly packed. She would slow them too much. She reached for her shift again, but it was hopeless. She couldn't do it. Oscar pawed at her. KC butted her with her furry head.

"I can't shift," she whispered. "You go without me."

Dean Gorse's voice was suddenly much closer than she expected. "Is there any way to help her without him?"

Laylea searched around for a place to hide.

"Lee," Guillaume murmured. Laylea spun. The man grinned and then leaped into a flash shift.

She hissed at the bird, "That doesn't help."

The dove cooed and then darted at her face. He scratched her so hard, she felt hot blood pouring down her cheek in the instant before her body did its healing thing and shifted. KC and Oscar waited for her to dash past them. Then all three raced through the trees and made their way to Adelor the lion and his deadly stairs. The ghosts didn't even come close to the entrance.

21

*A*hanu had been Testing every month since he arrived, hoping to gain an early graduation. The two things holding him back had been his utter lack of math skills and the ubiquitous Mer challenge with shifting at will. Whatever the motivation, once he'd spread his wings in human form during the seance, he found it easy to repeat. Still, come the next Testing, Ahanu skipped.

He'd planned to go. He'd gotten up early and put on his lucky coveralls and strolled out of the dorm for a quick breakfast. A few hours later, Laylea found him in the infirmary.

"Hey, Ahanu. Did the math section break you again?" She hopped up on a chair beside him and slipped.

Ahanu dove forward, but by the time he caught her, she was a twelve-pound bundle of fur and blue fabric.

He dug through the clothing to find her muzzle and helped her out, letting her stay on his lap. "Just between you and me," he said, "I didn't go."

Laylea tilted her head in the universal gesture for *huh?* and then, because she was a dog and had standards, nosed at his hand to make him pet her. He complied.

"I thought it was because Emerald knows I exist now. But she's there. She's at Testing. We were supposed to meet there. I came here instead because I was sick-to-my-stomach nervous." He looked over at the closed door to the private exam room, then hoisted Laylea up, so she was closer to his face. He kept scratching her fur. "I'm afraid to go upstairs."

He was about to say more, but the door opened, and Jimmy came out, followed by Dr. Fenn.

Jimmy perked up when he saw them. "Hey, guys. Are you my escort?"

Laylea barked. She was. Ahanu set her down before he stood up to fist bump with Jimmy. "Yeah," he joked. "We're mentoring you through your first full moon. The wolves were all busy."

Dr. Fenn looked concerned, but Jimmy cracked a smile.

"I'm here! I'm here!" Carrie burst through the door, dropped into a tawny, irresistibly cuddly wolf, and then immediately back into her slightly chubby, blond girl self. She picked herself up off the ground, ignoring the blush that lit up her face. "S... sorry. I'm h... here. Thanks, Lee."

"You're Jimmy's mentor?" Dr. Fenn's tone made it clear he thought that was a bad idea.

Laylea shifted out of sheer indignation. She pulled her jumpsuit on. "Jimmy needs someone he can trust to walk him through his first wilding. Everyone trusts Carrie."

"Of course." Dr. Fenn backed away from the four Mers.

Carrie ruined their dramatic exit when she walked into the opening door. Big Mo came through with a kid Laylea had never met.

She stuck her hand out. "Hi, I'm Lee. What's your name?" She'd found you had to ask for their name. Most kids hadn't been taught how to properly greet someone for the first time. Laylea had only learned because her parents spent a lot of time teaching Bailey how to naturally converse with strangers without giving them any truths.

The kid automatically shook her hand, though his brown eyes sought reassurance from Big Mo. He was a lanky kid with a tiny head. He'd probably hurt himself if he had to look down at little Laylea for too long. His voice was ridiculously high pitched when he finally answered, "Murph."

So, not Bert Gorshkov. She released his hand.

Big Mo crossed straight to the doctor. "Dr. Fenn, can you look at this scratch?"

Murph followed him. "Ms. Correnti yelled at Big Mo for bleeding in class."

"Uh, M… M… Mo. Ahanu's b… been wait… waiting." Carrie said it quietly.

"For Jimmy. I'm good." Ahanu yanked the door open and gestured for the other Mers to precede him out. "We've got to get to class."

Laylea followed the others out. She goggled at the little waiting area. A dozen kids sat there. A few on the couch and chairs, but mostly they lounged against the walls and on the floor. Every single one of them wore a gas mask. None of them had been there when she went in to the infirmary. They must all be on break from working in ST on the fire suppression system. The thing was, she didn't recognize any of the kids.

"Hi, I'm Lee. Who are you?" She stuck her hand out, but some instinct kept her feet glued in place.

Jimmy didn't pay any attention to the kids. His wide eyes were focused on Carrie. He whimpered, the whine coming out with the rough edge of a wolf's growl. "I don't want to do the wilding."

"B…But, you're a w… werewolf." Carrie crinkled her brow. "You have to."

"Naw. I hide during full moons. I don't like it." He played with a strand of his long hair.

"All the w… wolves in LPSS will be there. It k… keeps us safe."

A couple of the gas masked kids hopped up from the couch and approached. Laylea stumbled back. If they were wolves, they wouldn't like it that Carrie was talking about wilding in front of her and Ahanu.

Ahanu rubbed at the back of his neck. Laylea noticed that hair was standing up all along his arm.

He said, "I used to be jealous that y'all got to go upstairs every month. But now, I don't know if it's safe. The wolf pack is pretty powerful."

"No no no." Jimmy shook his head. He backed away from Ahanu. "It's not safe. I was changed on a full moon. I'm never gonna do that to anybody else."

Laylea kept one eye on the crowd of kids, especially the ones approaching. They were moving...crookedly. But she had to ask, "What do you mean you were 'changed'?"

"I was bitten and left for dead. Only, I didn't die. I went furry."

Carrie and a few of the gas mask kids stood straighter at his words. Carrie looked away toward the bend in the corridor. She didn't seem to notice the crowd in the sitting nook because she didn't lower her voice. She just leaned into Jimmy a little. "Y... you're not supposed to t... tell non-wolves about that, remember?"

"Why not?"

"I don't... I don't know." She thought about it for a moment. "I don't know. It's just safer to f... follow the rules."

A hot breeze wafted from the approaching kids. Laylea held her hands up in a placating gesture. "Sorry, we'll get out of your way. Come on, guys. Don't want to be late for class. You coming, Ahanu?"

The taller boy was brushing down the hair on his arms. His breath came a little faster as he squinted at the seating area. "Who are you talking to, Lee?"

Carrie led Jimmy away, reassuring him. "I'll stay with you the wh... whole time."

"Lee?"

The breeze turned into a wind, a biting hot wind that charred the hair on Laylea's exposed arms. Ahanu's long, black hair blew off his shoulders. One of the gas mask kids, a tall girl with long box braids wearing a deep gray jumpsuit with the collar popped, walked through him to face Laylea. That was the moment Laylea realized that all dozen or so kids were wearing gray jumpsuits, had gray hair and faces, and that none of them were alive.

She swallowed against a sudden lump in her throat and sucked in a breath to respond to Ahanu. She could barely see him through the ghost girl. Her voice shook. "We've got to get to class." She tried to walk away and found her body frozen in place.

"Lee?" Ahanu's voice came from far away. The edge of panic in it slapped her out of her own.

"So," she asked, "You and Emerald?"

As she had hoped, a grin lit up Ahanu's face. That infectious joy freed her to move. It caught the ghost's attention as well. She shrank away from it. Laylea grabbed Ahanu's hand and walked at a semi-normal pace after Carrie and Jimmy.

"She's amazing. She wants to go to the Boston Conservatory, you know, for music. That's why her parents transferred her here from the New England Shifter School. They want her to do something practical. But, have you heard her sing?"

Laylea could practically feel a shield forming around them from the strength of Ahanu's love. Even Jimmy perked up as Ahanu's gushing monologue continued. Laylea was able to push them to walk just a little faster than was casual. Carrie noticed and shot Laylea a look. She grabbed the younger girl's hand and skipped a few steps. They'd gotten halfway to Ms. Syperek's shifting classroom before she felt safe enough to glance over her shoulder.

The ghost was there. Three less-solid figures hovered there with her. When Laylea caught her hollow eyes, the tall girl threw back her head. A scream echoed off the stone walls, even muffled behind the mask. The trough lighting, a bright yellow to imitate late morning, blinked off, then flashed through a series of unnatural colors. Green. The ghosts dashed closer. Blue. They grabbed Laylea's arms, her hair, her jumpsuit. Red. Tall Ghost slammed a hand on either side of Laylea's face. She lifted her off the ground. Her eyes glowed green behind her gas mask as her thumbs closed in on Laylea's eyes.

The ghost screamed, "DON'T LOOK AT ME!" And plunged her thumbs into Laylea's eyes.

The world exploded into shades of blue. Thousands of kids swarmed through the halls everywhere in the school. Laughing, monkeying around, smaller kids getting hassled, books scattered on the cold floor, clothes closets opened and closed over and over, kids shifted and animals raced through the corridors, into classrooms, into dorms, into the dining hall, up through the triple tunnel and the winding staircase, climbing up on a ladder and a crumbling wooden fence and through a maze of tall bushes and trees. Time melded into one world, and Laylea saw it all, shivering and trapped.

KC's voice cut through the din of dead voices. "Lee!"

Some combination of love for her friend, joy at hearing her voice, and pain from burning ghostly fingers in her eyeballs sparked the fire in Laylea's belly. The fire racing through Laylea's body reached the tall girl's fingers.

The ghost shattered.

Laylea blinked and tumbled to the ground. Ahanu tried to catch her. Carrie tried to catch her. Jimmy threw himself down so she landed on him. Her tiny puppy body bounced off of him, and she landed on the cold stone a human, tangled in a light blue jumpsuit.

"What was that?" Ahanu helped her to her feet.

"Just practicing for class." She managed to make the tremor in her voice sound like embarrassment rather than terror.

A shades-of-gray tiger with green eyes prowled beside Ahanu. Saliva dripped from her bared fangs. A growl that shook the walls emanated from deep in the ghost's guts. It took a single step toward Laylea. The three human-shaped spirits behind her all followed.

"Race you!" Laylea shot a smile at Ahanu. From his reaction, she didn't do it well. But she didn't stay to be certain. She tore down the hallway, followed by four angry ghosts.

She turned the final corner with them right on her heels. Robby, the fire suppression guy, perched on a ladder just outside Ms. Syper-ek's classroom. Dean Gorse stood at the base of the ladder.

"You are in everybody's way. Why aren't you even done yet?" The dean's face was red, as if he'd been complaining for a while.

"I could be done already if I had skilled help that didn't have to run off to class." Robby was not impressed with the dean's frustration.

Laylea ignored them. Burning fear raced up her body from a single ghostly fang piercing her bare heel. An unknown reserve of adrenaline spurred her down the hall. She aimed for the classroom door, betting her soul on the thin hope that if the ghosts were still running across the ground, they didn't know they couldn't be stopped by doors. Her speed would save her. She was there, just a yard from the doorway. Her fingers tickled the knob.

Suddenly, a hand grabbed her upper arm in a grip so fierce it made her fingers go numb. She came up short, her shoulder wrenched out of the socket.

22

*F*ear froze Laylea until she realized it was her own fear. Not the ghost-generated fear, panic, anger, or sorrow she had expected to overwhelm her. All she felt was physical pain in her arm and her shoulder.

She dared to look behind her. The ghosts, all human again, hovered far down the hall, the shortest protected by the other three. Light gray hair stood tall in a mohawk between the straps of his mask as a gash on his head dripped bright red blood on the stone floor. Their eyes sparked with anger, yes, but also fear now. And they pinned their gazes on Dean Gorse.

It was Dean Gorse holding her arm.

"There is no running in the halls." The dean didn't even look at her. He kept his eyes on Robby as he squeezed her upper arm from Caucasian to actually white. "Shall I speak with Enforcer Denier about getting outside assistance?"

He said it like it was a threat. Robby took no notice. He kept his eyes on his work attaching tubing above the light troughs. His voice was tight, as though he didn't like Dean Gorse and wasn't afraid to let the man know. "That would be great. In the meantime, why haven't you sent Lee Woodford to detention?"

Laylea's eyes shot from the ghosts to the contractor. Did he really just say her name? The man wasn't looking at her. He didn't seem to know that she was Lee Woodford. The dean's grip, impossibly, grew tighter.

"Lee Woodford hasn't been sent to detention because she is a good student."

The crisp, accented voice of Ms. Lagat made Laylea want to cry with relief. Dean Gorse dropped his grip at the sound and folded his arms as if he hadn't just been physically assaulting a student.

Adele Lagat taught a variety of classes in addition to advanced shifting. She was the oldest-looking person in the school and, considering many shifters lived for centuries, it was anybody's guess how old she really was. Laylea had never had her for class. But she liked the woman because the woman cared for Toby. Just like Laylea, Ms. Lagat had a particular fondness for the depressed bear. Unlike Laylea, she was able to go upstairs at will to take care of him.

"You have a short memory, Adele." The ghosts fell back farther at the ice in Dean Gorse's tone. Tiger girl put an arm in front of the bleeding boy, pushing him back. "She endangered your precious black bear, didn't she?"

The ghosts were afraid of him. They'd given up catching her because of the dean. If she could show them that she didn't like him either, maybe they'd leave her alone. But how could she do that without getting in actual trouble that would send her to detention?

She had to take a chance. Better to make Dean Gorse hate her more than let the ghosts steal her soul.

"I didn't endanger the bear." Laylea gathered courage at the sight of her friends rounding the corner into the corridor. "Captain Morioka herself cleared me of all wrongdoing, Dean Gorse. Maybe you didn't hear about that because you were in prison at the time?"

The ghosts moved closer, looking between Laylea and Gorse. She'd drawn Robby's attention as well. He leaned forward on his ladder, trying to see her around Gorse's imposing figure.

KC dashed through the spirits, completely unaware of them. "Hey, there you are. We're late for class. Come on."

With Carrie, Jimmy, and Ahanu close on her heels, KC pushed Laylea ahead of her to the classroom. Ms. Lagat opened the door. Laylea got one last look at the ghosts. They scattered, fading away to avoid him as Dean Gorse stomped away from the shifting classroom. The puddle of impossibly red ghostly blood remained until the Dean's shoe splattered it. Robby skittered down his ladder, racing for the door.

Ms. Lagat shoved her inside with one wrinkled, black hand. With the other, she stopped Robby. "Students and staff only in the classrooms. You remember."

She locked the door as she shut it behind her.

"Adele?" Ms. Syperek sat in a comfortable chair looking over the array of couches and chairs scattered about the room. Her chair was raised on a platform which also held an impressive cat tree with several bird perches on each level so that Ms. Syperek could command the room even in her long-haired Nillu rat form. Ms. Lagat was famous for soaring around the room in pigeon form when she was pleased with her students. With bad students, she'd perch on the highest branch, preening her pink chest.

As the kids settled around the classroom, Ms. Lagat brushed her nails against her chest. "I'm bored with my cocky shifters, Carolyne. Do you mind if I observe your class today?"

"I welcome the company. Make yourself comfortable anywhere." Ms. Syperek's thin lips disappeared as she smiled.

Ms. Lagat slipped into a chair set right beside the door. "Merci."

The wrinkles around Ms. Syperek's eyes crinkled up behind her square glasses. She smoothed down some flyaways in her gray-speckled red hair as she turned to the students lounging in groups around the open central area where they stood to try shifting on purpose. "A reminder, class. Tonight is the full moon. Ms. Davies will be coming to collect you wolves. You'll have no problems shifting tonight, so let's start... with... our—" She looked around and landed on KC. "With our coyote. KC?"

KC dragged herself off the couch and slunk to the center. Kids all around the room settled in. Milly, a mouse shifter from

Mer, rolled over from the other side of the couch to pull a book out of KC's backpack. Before she could roll back to her side, she cried out and then squeaked. The book fell to the floor. In response to her spontaneous shift, Carrie, Chloe, and Brian all shifted as well.

"All right, calm down everybody. Brian, could you move that couch so Chloe can have a little extra room?"

KC relaxed a little when the attention shifted from her to the gorilla and moose in the room. She shot a grin at Laylea. They'd talked about how the phenomenon of some kids shifting whenever they saw someone else shift being like some people throwing up when they saw someone else barf. It was called sympathy vomiting. The doctors had actually given it a name.

Early on, Ms. Syperek had tried to use sympathy shifting to get KC to change. She'd brought in her advanced students and bombarded KC with shifting. Every other Beginner Shifting student had shifted except for KC. She'd later admitted to Laylea that she'd had to work pretty hard to stay human.

"Now, KC. I want you to take some deep breaths. We're going to try something new today." Ms. Syperek sat back in her chair, as convinced as the others that nothing would work. "I want you to visualize. Shut your eyes." She closed her own.

Around the room, kids shut their eyes. Jimmy groaned, but he didn't shift. KC kept her eyes open and fixed on Laylea. Laylea grinned back at her.

"Okay. Now I want you to visualize life as a thumper."

Ms. Lagat opened her eyes. Thumper wasn't a word you heard from the teachers very often. It was not a polite term.

"A life," Ms. Syperek continued, "where you are always human. You can never again run with the wind, your paws pounding over the ground. You'll never feel a breeze through your fur or the intense smell of your friends. Imagine your coyote dead in a ditch, never to be seen again."

Milly popped back to human and swore quietly beside Laylea. Rehyan's mouth dropped open in shock. Ms. Lagat clasped her hands together as if she were physically holding herself back. A tear rolled down KC's face.

Laylea shot a glance over at Carrie. The wolf lay curled up in a fat chair beside Jimmy. Ahanu crouched on a stool behind them, hugging his knees to his chest. Carrie mouthed a silent howl at Laylea. Laylea grimaced and mouthed a howl back. Ms. Syperek was describing the nightmare they all had. Laylea tried to break the spell.

"Is that possible, Ms. Syperek?" she asked in the kind of voice that could be heard over a plane's engine. "Is it possible to cure wereism?"

Clearly, her question hadn't been obnoxious enough because Ms. Syperek didn't even open her eyes. "Shh, Lee. We're focused on KC now and feeling what it would be like to shame all her ancestors by abandoning her coyote to die a bloody death in the ditch of neglect."

Eyes popped open around the room to stare in shock at the teacher. Laylea pushed. "I mean, since you can catch werewolfism by being bitten, surely we should be able to cure it."

That worked. Ms. Syperek looked too appalled to find words. Ms. Lagat simply raised one questioning brow. Nobody was staring at KC anymore.

"The movies are true?" Britny, a goat from Centaur, turned to ask Conner, another wolf from Mer, but he looked just as freaked.

"No," he stuttered, unsure. "I don't think so."

Looking at Jimmy, another question occurred to Laylea. She posed it to the class. "And if werewolfism is a disease, then is N like a mild infection?"

"N is a drug, not a disease," Milly said, sounding super confused.

A clatter of hooves turned into footsteps. Chloe approached Laylea and Milly's couch from behind. She kept her voice low. "Wolves aren't a disease."

Rehyan laughed. "Yeah, N's a club drug, Lee."

Laylea nodded. "Sure. But maybe the high they get is just what we all feel when we shift."

Too many kids responded to pick out any one thought. They all seemed to agree that shifting was better than any drug. Jimmy kept his mouth shut and his head down. He buried his fingers in Carrie's fur.

"Lee. Stop this right now." Ms. Syperek sat up in her chair. "I cannot allow you to insult your classmates."

"Yeah," Conner sputtered. "I'm not a disease."

Jimmy looked up. "I'm not insulted. That is kinda what N is like, but without all the fear and pain."

There was a murmur of agreement and condolences. Other kids kept arguing the disease question. They shot furtive glances at the three werewolves in the room.

Ms. Syperek tried to regain control of the class. "It should not be painful for a wolf to shift, Jimmy. That's one thing you're here to learn. Would you like to take the center?"

KC started to hop out of the center circle, but she stopped after glancing at Jimmy. Jimmy tried to hide behind tiny Carrie's fluffy wolf. He did not want to take center.

"Lee, why do you think N is like a weres...wereism infection?" KC stuttered over Laylea's newly invented disease.

Laylea looked around. She wondered how many of these kids had tried N. "N is made with shifter blood."

The room lost it.

"What?"

"No!"

"Ew."

"Well, we know it's made with blood," she amended. "I'm just guessing it's shifter blood, *our* blood, because N supplies kinda dried up after Dr. Durrah was arrested."

"Oh my phoenix!" Dove sat up on the back of her chair. "I always came out of Special Testing with rashes around my elbows like I get from the wrap Dr. Fenn puts on to keep pressure on the vein after he takes blood."

"Holy crap, and we were always weak." Brenda moved in from the corner where she'd been stretching instead of paying attention. "Was he taking blood from us? For N?"

"That rumor has been proven false," Ms. Syperek shouted over the uproar. "Dr. Durrah was convicted of animal endangerment, nothing more."

"Are you calling us animals?!" Brenda brought her hands up like she was ready to fight.

"That was a human conviction." Laylea wasn't sure if Ms. Syperek was just spouting the party line or truly believed in Durrah's innocence. "They don't even know LPSS exists."

Ahanu asked, "Why else would N become so scarce just after Captain Morioka shut down ST?"

Spittle dropped on Laylea as Chloe spat out, "The enforcer would never allow it."

"Are you kidding?" Ahanu echoed a popular Mer opinion. "Denier was probably in on it."

Laylea knew that he was.

As the other kids took up the argument, KC strolled out of the shifting circle and curled up on the couch beside Laylea. Whatever else happened, Laylea had made sure Ms. Syperek had forgotten all about her.

KC rested her hands on her face and whispered behind them, "The wolves are gonna find out you called them a disease."

Laylea coughed into a hand and murmured back, "You think Carrie or Jimmy is gonna tell?"

"'Course not. Conner, either. But," she glanced behind them to see the moose shifter focused on screaming at Ahanu. "Chloe is definitely throwing your ass under the bus."

Laylea giggled. "As far as the wolves are concerned, I'm a bus mechanic. I live under there."

"What do you want to bet this Bert Gorshkov kid is a wolf?"

Laylea sat up a bit. "Hey. You know how we find him? We put the word out we want to buy drugs."

"Nobody—" KC ducked as a pillow flew over her head at Chloe. "Nobody is going to believe you and I want drugs."

"They'd believe Rehyan, though." Laylea caught KC's eyes.

KC looked at Rehyan, who seemed pretty high already, standing on one leg on a stool and lobbing shots on both sides of the argument. "Yes," KC agreed. "Yes, they would."

23

It was a dark and stormy night. But the weather had little effect deep under the zoo. The trough lighting brightened and darkened and changed color through the circadian rhythm of the day, as it always did. Teachers and classmates continued to be appalled at Laylea's scholastic genius and complete ignorance of shifter matters.

Rehyan had eagerly agreed to ask around for drugs in search of Bert. But, three weeks on and he hadn't gotten back to them. Laylea told KC about Robby wanting her to get detention, and they tried to figure out why but couldn't come up with anything. On the bright side, the wolves had yet to confront her about her suggestion that they had a disease, though Conner confirmed that Chloe had, indeed, spilled to the Sphinx pack. He had pointed out to several fellow wolves that Laylea had suggested that *all* shifters had a disease. It didn't seem to help.

Most kids, other than the wolves of Sphinx dorm, had given up calling Laylea, "Fido." The new thing was to yell "Love and joy" whenever she entered a room, passed in the hall, asked a question in class, or reminded people that she existed. It was super not fun. She hoped it would die down in time, but it had been nearly two months since the seance, and the cry was still going strong.

Honestly, Laylea would have been more bothered if she weren't faced with her permanent entourage of young ghosts in gas masks. They followed her nearly everywhere. She was safe from them in the dorm, and they continued to avoid shifting class as well. The only place she could avoid both mocking catcalls and ghostly glares was in the library. If she hadn't already believed Ms. Crow's haven filled with books was magical, this solidified the fact.

She took the corner from the Music Wing at a dead sprint, so to speak, pushed off the clothes closet for extra speed, and barreled for the library's double doors, each with its grid of smoky glass panes. Their deep gray shade echoed the color of the semi-transparent figures following her.

Bursting through the doors should have welcomed her to the peace of the library. Only she stumbled right into Jase Batka and a crew of werewolves, including Julia Jimenez, who cracked each of her knuckles while staring at Laylea with death in her eyes. Big Mo hung to the back, looking anywhere but at Laylea.

Jase stroked his wannabe goatee. "Watch it, Fido." He looked around to be sure his sycophants were paying attention before he added, "You running from some scary ghosties?"

They all laughed.

Laylea automatically replied, "No, I'm running from your mom."

The wolves found that even funnier, which annoyed Jase, making the whole encounter just a little awesome. But the pack still shoved her around on their way out. Julia got her with an elbow, though not hard enough that she needed to shift. It was all for show. It was sad, the way they picked on the easiest prey.

"Hey, Rehyan." Jase's obnoxious voice floated back through the closing door. "You ready for a good time, bird boy?"

Laylea looked, but the door closed on Jase handing Rehyan something, the two surrounded by semi-transparent ghost-masked kids glaring at her. She hurried away to the circulation desk. She pulled a folded letter out of her collar while Ms. Crow checked in some books from little Leda, the crane who had started school the same day Laylea came back. She was the girl who had said that N was designed to kill thumpers.

"Uh, Lee?" Big Mo whispered and then turned to be sure the Craftsman-style doors had shut behind his pack.

"Yeah?" She peered at the doors as well, wondering what she was going to do about the ghosts waiting outside.

"You okay?"

"Hm?" Laylea turned back to find Big Mo staring at her. "I'm fine. Did you need the bio homew—" She got a good look at his face. His dark skin had turned an ashen gray, and his deep brown eyes were glassy. He was an athlete. Even with his injury last year, he'd swum every day and did upper body workouts until he was able to walk again. Now, his shoulders slumped, and she could see a bandage gently seeping blood on his neck. "Are *you* okay?"

He thought about lying and then shook his head. "I got scratched that night we—" he paused as Leda flashed into her crane form and flew over the study tables to the back of the library. She settled on one of the few high windowsills with moonlight dribbling in from the Fields next door.

"Your neck still bothering you, Mo?" Ms. Crow turned to take a first aid kit from her desk. She gestured for Mo to show her the wound.

"Yes, ma'am. Lee was with me when I got scratched. I was hoping she might have a suggestion about how to make it heal."

"Since Lee heals when she shifts, I'm guessing she is not well versed in first aid?" Ms. Crow aimed the question in Laylea's direction as she peeled the bandage from Mo's skin.

Laylea set her letter down, pushing it toward Ms. Crow as she climbed the steps that allowed shifted kids to see over the check-in desk. "Actually, my mother was a vet. So, I picked up a few things."

Ms. Crow picked up the letter, glanced at the address, *Detective Dee Morton ℅ The Office*, and slipped it into a pocket of her blue cardigan. She slid Leda's books aside and tapped the counter. "Well, hop up, then. Where did this happen?" She caught the look Mo shot Laylea and revised her question. "How did this happen?"

For the hell of it, Laylea opted for the truth. "A ghost scratched him during a seance."

Mo laughed uncomfortably. Ms. Crow merely nodded. "Did you see the ghost, Mo?"

"She's joking."

"She's not." Ms. Crow drew in her breath when she got a good look at the three inflamed scratches along Big Mo's neck.

Laylea answered, "It was a woman, but she had claws like she was partially shifted."

The library door opened. Oscar pushed in and nearly rushed right by the front desk.

Ms. Crow stopped him. "Oscar?" She slipped a red envelope from under a typewriter-style keyboard and held it out.

His voice was strained as he said, "Thank you." He caught Laylea's eye and jerked his head toward their nook.

"Did you find him?" she asked.

"No." His eyes said he had more he couldn't share in front of Ms. Crow.

"Be right there," Laylea assured him.

"Go on, Lee," Ms. Crow said. "This isn't a wound you can help with."

Laylea hopped off the desk. Oscar offered her a hand, but she leaned over the counter to whisper to Ms. Crow first. "Ms. Crow? Can you see ghosts, too?"

The librarian lowered her eyes. She fished through her first aid kit for a fresh bandage. "I could when I was younger." Her breath came in short spurts, like she was holding back a sigh. When she looked up, her eyes glistened. "Did you see anybody familiar?"

"No, ma'am."

"Good," she breathed. "That's good. Come, Mo. You and I must visit the farm for what you need."

Mo tried to stutter something. The hair was standing up on his arms and sweat beaded on his forehead.

Laylea put her hand on his. She lowered her voice, as her mother had taught her, and caught Mo's eyes before she intoned, "You are going to heal."

"I'm going to heal." Big Mo didn't sound too sure, but he said it.

With Oscar's help, Laylea hopped off the steps. He started to pull her away, saying, "There is no student file for Bert or Albert Gorshkov. Or for my sister."

"What? Hold on." Laylea turned back to the counter as Ms. Crow came around to meet Mo. "Ms. Crow?"

"Yes?"

"How did you stop seeing ghosts?"

Ms. Crow looked carefully at Laylea. Her brow crinkled. "Are you seeing them now?"

"No. Not in the library."

The woman let her breath go in a rush then reset as she saw her relief wasn't shared. "I can't help you. Once upon a time, I could have helped you close your third eye. But, now. . . I'm sorry. I can't." She put an arm on Big Mo's broad back and ushered him ahead of her to the door. Laylea barely heard her last words, "Not without Delilah."

Oscar whispered, "Who's Delilah?"

"No idea." Laylea shook her head, watching the blood welling out of Mo's two-month-old cut.

"Come on." Oscar drew her through the study tables and between two of the massive shelves to the nook KC preferred. Dizzy flew out to greet them. She touched down on the French chair that blocked the entrance to the little alcove. Laylea scratched the raven's neck just where she liked it.

"Finally." KC stood up from where she was typing and swiping on a deskpadd. She'd set the corduroy cushions from the bench against the wall and had stacked up a pile of pillows as a chair. "We have to be more careful."

"Why?" Oscar and Laylea echoed each other.

"I've been lurking in the wolf encrypted message boards, especially on the Edict site." She shut down the deskpadd and stuffed it into her backpack. "Parents are warning their kids to behave."

Laylea raised an eyebrow. "And that's unusual in the shifter world?" Her parents were *always* telling Bailey to behave.

"Not in my house," Oscar said. He tilted the chair to get by. Dizzy chittered at him and spread her wings to keep her balance.

KC rolled her eyes at the two of them. "After the little incident last October when thumper authorities invaded the zoo, the Midwest Shifter Council gave Dean Gorse expanded authority to dole out punishment."

"What does that mean?" Laylea looked up from Dizzy.

"Did you hear about that kid who never came back from detention?" KC asked.

"Cal," Oscar said. "He was a Centaur dorm wolf. Had a white mohawk that matched his wolf's fur markings. Super cool."

"Nobody knows what happened to him. His aunt is demanding answers, and the dean is insisting Cal ran away. The Council is backing him."

Laylea said, "Oscar, you should look to see if his record is missing, too."

"What do you mean 'too'?" KC looked up from where she was shoving stacks of books into her bag.

"There are no student records for either Bert or my sister," Oscar said. "But Brenda told me that there are secret files somewhere. She doesn't know where, exactly, but she knows they're in the Executive Wing."

"Okay, so we break in and search the place."

"Lee!" KC threw her hands up. "You are the last person who should be drawing attention from Dean Gorse. He will definitely kill you if he gets the chance. Besides, what did the dragon shifter of Chicago tell you?"

Laylea scowled. "Don't get caught."

"Right. Look, we've got two strikes. Rehyan was directed to Jase in his search for drugs. No one he spoke to has ever heard of a Bert. Oscar can't find Bert's records in the Wing. So, we go with your original secondary plan."

"Kitchen duty." Laylea sat on the bolster. She'd gotten the idea to work the line at dinner from Ms. Crow's suggestion that she could meet everyone in school in the dining hall. "I'll have to put in for it through the presser request system, and it'll be a whole week after that before I could even get assigned."

"Orrrrrr," KC grinned. "I hack in to the system, swap you with Brian."

Laylea tilted her head at her friend. There was something extra in her grin. She guessed. "You already did it, didn't you?"

"You start tomorrow."

"Thanks, KC."

"Thank me after you've worked the shift. I have to run. Madrigal auditions." She slung her backpack over her shoulders and headed for the shelves. "You coming, Oscar?"

"No, you go ahead."

"Oscar Luke. Do not break into the Wing after hours and get your ass kicked out of school, or worse. We'll find out what happened to Shala." She bounced on her toes as she begged, "Come sing with me."

"I should go make nice with the wolves." He couldn't even get through the sentence without choking. "Nah, I'll come tralala. It'll entertain Bianchi, if nothing else."

"How about you, Lee? It'll be fun."

Laylea thought about it. "You know, maybe my singing would scare off the ghosts."

"It would," Oscar said without a beat.

KC looked worried. "You're still being followed?"

She nodded.

"Help me out here, Oscar." KC threw her arms around Laylea. Oscar threw his arms around both of them. KC whispered, "Love and joy."

When they let her go, Oscar held out the red letter from his mom. "Here. This should, no doubt, keep you safe."

Laylea took the paper. It was blank. She flipped it over. Blank.

"But," she risked, "There's nothing on it."

He shrugged a shoulder and lowered his eyes. "Nothing but love."

"Awwwww."

Both girls tried to hug him, but Oscar scrambled over the chair and ran from their giggled pronouncements of how sweet he was. Dizzy followed him, cawing. KC turned back to grab one last book from the stack on the bolster. "Hey, maybe you need to do your circling thing in reverse? Would that get rid of the ghosts?"

Laylea nodded. "Yeah, maybe."

She'd already tried that. It didn't work. Maybe because she knew that even if she couldn't see them, the ghosts would still be there.

"Lee?" Ms. Crow peeked around the bookcase. Apparently, it hadn't taken very long to show Big Mo how to get rid of his spectral scratches. She pulled her orange sweater close, sort of hugging herself with it.

"Yes, Ms. Crow?"

The librarian pulled the French chair aside and crossed to the bolster. She redistributed the pillows that KC had stacked as she spoke. "I don't know how much you know about those spirits who can't find their way on from this world. But, if you're seeing the same ghosts over and over, it means they need something, and they believe that you can help them."

Laylea and KC shot each other a look and sat on the bolster bench together. The bench was hollow. It was a secret place for Dizzy to hide little things she collected. Ms. Crow was cleaning fairly aggressively, and they didn't want her to accidentally find the raven's small treasures.

Laylea asked, "What if what they need is revenge on me?"

KC grabbed her hand.

"What could you have done to them that they would want revenge for?" Ms. Crow stopped fussing and sat down on Laylea's other side.

Laylea looked at her feet. "I shut down Special Testing. That cut off the blood supply for the N producers, which made N less available, which is why addicts are dying."

"Oh, Lee," KC murmured.

Ms. Crow let a tiny laugh burst through her mask of authority. "And all of those addicts just happened to be wearing gas masks when they died and hunted you down in a secret underground school to haunt you as revenge?" Ms. Crow's face crinkled with doubt.

KC laughed outright. Then she blinked. "Hey, how do you know they're wearing gas masks?"

Ms. Crow's mouth dropped open. After a minute, she raised one eyebrow and said, "A little birdie told me." It wasn't really an explanation, but she didn't give them time to think about it. "I don't think you've perfected your mind reading skills quite yet, Lee. And I know that you are not responsible for what Dr. Durrah did with Special Testing." Ms. Crow pushed off of the bench and stepped around the French chair. She caressed the wood where Dizzy usually perched. "I wonder how you could figure out what they really want?"

Laylea looked up and rolled her eyes. It was easy for Ms. Crow to tell her to ask them when the librarian wasn't going to be the one risking another viewing of the school through all time.

She was saved from considering it by Oscar yelling, "I am not doing this alone."

"Thanks, Ms. Crow. I'll think about that."

KC and Laylea ran out of the nook.

24

Kitchen duty was about as much fun as spring cleaning back home. Laylea, being the newest on the kitchen crew, was stuck in dishwashing. A month in and she hadn't met any new students beyond Audra, a sailfish shifter from Centaur dorm, who taught her how to scrape the plates into a slop bucket and rinse them before putting them into the huge, hot dishwashing machine. Audra didn't know anybody named Bert. The whole plan was a wash.

Mr. Bianchi wanted her to swap out of kitchen duty because the extended soaking her fingers got every day was preventing her from building up any good calluses. Even though she'd chosen guitar for her private study mainly so she'd get to listen to him play, once she'd gotten over the pain, she'd found she really liked playing herself. It was fun to apply all the theory she'd learned from books. Mr. Bianchi seemed convinced she couldn't become really good until she'd worked up some calluses.

Laylea met with Mr. Bianchi four times a week. Officially, her lessons were scheduled for an hour and a half. In reality, they could last upwards of three hours if neither had any pressing engagements. They met in a small room off to one side of the Music Wing. Bright tapestries hung from the ceiling, which had also been covered with thick drapes. Hooks hung in front of the tapestries holding instruments that varied from session to session.

Dizzy always joined Laylea for her lessons. She liked to perch on Mr. Bianchi's hand-carved walnut music stand and peer at his fingers as he played. Typically, four chairs and stands were set up facing each other with more chairs folded in one corner. Since he only set up two chairs and two stands this time, Laylea's ghostly company had to sprawl on the thickly carpeted floor. The tiger curled around the reason the other chairs had been moved aside. She worried about the ghost's angry heat warping the wood.

"What is that, again?" Laylea asked. She'd been too distracted at the start of her lesson when she'd first seen the beautifully carved instrument. It was the size and relative shape of a concert harp laid on its side, like a piece of art with strings running through the middle.

"It's a floor harp," Mr. Bianchi said as he strummed the classical guitar in his hands.

Laylea ran through a scale on her own guitar, though stumbled might be a more accurate description. "That's a logical name."

"Are you still worried about N addicts, Lee?"

Laylea looked up from her fingers. The conversations she had with Mr. Bianchi covered more than music. She'd told him about her theories and the Wyrdos and the work they'd been doing. He didn't question the existence of brownies and banshees like the other faculty, so she told him a lot of things she'd never tell another teacher. She hadn't told him about the ghosts.

"You shouldn't worry about things like that, Lee. You're a kid. Enjoy it. Let adults handle it. It sounds like Captain Morioka and your friends are on it."

He didn't know they were counting on her to find Bert Gorshkov. If she found him, then sure, she could hand it off to them. They could shut down the whole N operation if they had Bert Gorshkov. And she had not delivered. The best info she'd gotten so far had been from a crowd of angry ghosts. If they were dead and they knew who Bert was, then he'd been around for a while.

She strummed the bar chord she'd just learned and adjusted one of the tuning pegs. "Did you go to school here, Mr. B?"

He chuckled a bit before he answered. It wasn't out of line. He talked about himself plenty. He said it was only fair if he was going to ask her personal questions. "I did. I graduated in the 1980s. Got a job at a high school out in Ohio." He looked down to tune up his own instrument. "I didn't like having to hide who I really am. Never found anywhere particularly safe to live upstairs. And I like the school. Down here, I'm not limited to choir or band or orchestra. I can teach everything. And I can spend real time with each of my students." He struck a dramatic chord, then modulated into a goofy arpeggio.

"Cocaine was the problem in those days, right?" she guessed, based on *Die Hard* and other movies her parents had from the eighties.

"Yeah." He sighed. "There's always a variety. And shifter-specific chemicals, too. Just before I was pressed, there was one rich kid helping everyone find whatever drug they wanted."

Laylea thought of what the ghosts had said. She took a risk. "Bert?"

Mr. Bianchi raised a perfect brow. "Wow. Kids still talk about him, huh? Do they call Jase *Bert*?"

Laylea's jaw dropped. Mr. Bianchi knew that Jase was the school's current supplier?

"Yes." He read her mind. "We know. All of his mail is thoroughly checked now."

"You read our mail?"

"I do not. Ms. Crow does not. Dean Gorse..." He sighed. "Since it's just you and I in here..."

He looked over at the door, not seeing Dizzy perched on the music stand, or Amelia hovering behind him, or any of the gas masks lounging on the carpet. Four more gas mask ghosts had shifted into their animal forms. One of them was a small wolf with a stripe running down his back that matched Laylea's fur. He wasn't any angrier than the rest, but the fact that he was a wolf put her on edge.

"You should avoid the dean. He's not a fan." Mr. Bianchi's forehead glistened. He slid forward on his seat and hung the guitar on its hook.

He reached for hers, leaning in to whisper, "He's dangerous, Lee. And he's losing his grip."

The tension around his eyes scared Laylea more than his words. He held the neck of her guitar but didn't hang it up until she nodded.

A knock echoed dully in the padded room. Dizzy launched from the music stand. Laylea hopped off the chair and tucked her new pick into her collar.

"Be careful out there, Lee."

"Always."

She pulled the door open just as Jimmy knocked again. He tripped into her and caught himself with a hand on the doorjamb. The ghost wolf leapt toward the door as if he would catch him. Jimmy shivered as the wolf wove around his legs.

"Sorry about that." Jimmy sounded awful and looked worse. His cheeks were sunken in like food was a last season fad. His blond hair hung limply against his shoulders. The scar above his nose glowed white and red against his pasty skin. "I was hoping I could play for a bit, Mr. B?"

"Of course, Jimmy." Mr. Bianchi's smile drooped when Jimmy groaned through his shift. His eyes glistened behind his spectacles.

The tiger-shaped ghost sat up as Jimmy the wolf climbed onto the Floor Harp. He plucked some strings with his claws and used his teeth to adjust the pegs. Dizzy circled the boy a few times and then settled on one edge of the sounding board, well out of his way.

Mr. Bianchi's mournful expression gave Laylea the guts to push him for more information. "Do you know if there's a record somewhere of all the students who've gone to Dr. Fenn for N related issues?"

The music teacher didn't hide his despair. He straightened his vest and moved closer, keeping his voice low. "None that the Council will ever see, I'm sure. But I'd bet my bowties Dean Gorse's comprehensive file makes mention of all those he heard of, and all those who died." His eyes turned back to Jimmy, who stood poised with three paws on the frame of the floor harp. The ghosts and Dizzy flanked the wolf.

"Ms. Lagat mentioned that file. Where is it?"

Mr. Bianchi turned back to his music stand. Every creature in the room, living and dead, watched as he released the pendulum arm on the metronome. It ticked back and forth four times.

Jimmy plucked a single string that rang for four more beats. Then, waving his tail for balance, he used all four paws to set up a bass line and pick a complicated melody and harmony from the harp. He kept time with the metronome, creating a percussive rhythm with his paws landing on the carved wood. The haunting tune filled the room and Laylea's heart. She wanted to cry.

"The Dean's private records are kept on the Dean's private server in his office. Nobody has access."

Laylea didn't think before she said, "You really think he cleans his own office?"

A grin flashed across Mr. Bianchi's sharp features so quickly, she might have imagined it if he'd been able to hide it from his voice. "Thank you, Lee. Keep up the good work." He said this with a glance at Jimmy, and Laylea was sure he meant her work fighting N and not her musical education.

"Later, Mr. B." She held the door open for a moment, inviting Dizzy to go with her. Her ghosts stood, caught between following her and listening to the music. The raven looked over and shook her head. Laylea asked, "You'll keep an eye on Jimmy?"

Dizzy cawed.

Mr. Bianchi nodded, thinking she was speaking to him. "Of course."

Laylea turned to Jimmy. "That's the most beautiful song I've ever heard, Jimmy."

The wolf howled. His sorrowful tone echoed off the cold walls of the corridor.

25

"Who you torturing in there, Fido?" Jagger deRio lay sprawled on the first row of chairs in the chorus room, across the hall from Mr. Bianchi's private lesson room.

Laylea did not want to get into it with Jagger. KC might still be furious at the girl for kicking Laylea down Adelor's stairs their first day at school, but Laylea reasoned that Jagger didn't know how dangerous the stairs were. She didn't mean to threaten Laylea's life, just her ego. And Laylea's ego could handle anything Jagger deRio threw at her. It wasn't hard to avoid her, thanks to the girl's unrelenting prejudice against any and all non-wolves.

She didn't respond. Just kept her eyes down and headed out of the Music Wing, focusing on how they could get into Dean Gorse's *comprehensive file*. She was caught so deep in her own thoughts, she didn't notice Brenda rushing down the hall after her until the python shifter was right on her tail.

"Slow down, will ya? You walk like someone's chasing you."

"Aren't *you* chasing me?" She slowed enough for Brenda to catch up and walk beside her.

Brenda blinked. "Yeah, but it's not like I'm a wolf or anything."

"You still call me Fido," Laylea pointed out.

"Alright, Lee." Brenda put emphasis on the name. "I'm here because Oscar won't listen to me."

Laylea stopped walking. "What's going on? Is he okay?"

"He's searching for his sister."

"Yeah, I know. Her file is missing from the student records, so he's looking for the secret files."

"There are no secret files." Brenda started walking again.

It was Laylea's turn to catch up to her. "You're the one who told him about them."

Brenda cracked her knuckles. "Yeah, I know. I just wanted to give him some hope. And maybe trick him into cleaning the grosser old rooms." She examined her nails with more care than was really needed. "And now he won't believe me when I tell him I lied. He's obsessed. And it's freaking me out."

Laylea felt a burn surge up from her gut that had nothing to do with shifting. She took a deep breath to calm herself. Getting mad at Brenda for being selfish wasn't going to help Jimmy or the other N addicts out there who were counting on her. She wanted to grab Brenda's arm to stop her walking, but since touching Brenda was guaranteed to land anybody in the infirmary, she appealed to her ego instead. "You know everything about the Executive Wing. How can there be no proof that a student was ever here?"

"Shala was here. I remember her. We did Intake together." Brenda shadow boxed the wall before she added, her voice tight, "She was here for a week, and then she was gone. I don't remember hearing about any accident. There are no records of an accident in the infirmary. There is no record of her at all in the Wing. Maybe she wasn't here long enough to get a file."

"You checked the infirmary records?"

Brenda shrugged one shoulder. "Yeah. Oscar was freaking me out. Here." Brenda dug a hand into her jumpsuit pocket. "I know you're looking for some kid named Bert Gorshkov."

Laylea must have gasped because Brenda laughed. "Yeah, your boy Oscar isn't the most elite spy. I found this in the bottom of a file drawer." She shoved a hanging file tag at Laylea.

The rectangular piece of green plastic held a printed card. In block letters, the card read GORSHKOV, ALBERT.

Proof. He had been a student at the school at some point, and somebody had removed his file from the records.

"Thanks, Brenda." Laylea stumbled. She felt wrong-footed moving so quickly between anger and gratitude.

The printed name reminded her of the names on the patient charts in the sleep lab. She figured, as long as she was in Brenda's good graces, she might as well push her luck. "Your name is Samborsky, right? Brenda Samborsky."

Brenda's shoulders stiffened. "Yeah, why?"

Laylea had been wanting to ask ever since Ms. Crow announced Brenda's last name at Holding. Brenda was as pale as the white guy lying in the sleep lab. Her hair was the same shade of brown. In a town as Polish as Chicago, it was still a long shot. But, if there was any truth to Laylea's suspicion that the sleep lab was filled with shifters, that would increase the odds significantly. "Are you related to someone named Brian?"

Brenda stopped dead in the corridor just steps from a turning.

Laylea ran into her before she could stop herself. As pale as Brenda was from being Polish and living underground for however long she had been, Laylea watched her face go even whiter.

"Whatcha doing, Mers? Crying cuz you're never gonna leave this school?" Jagger strolled down the corridor. She'd followed them from the Music Wing, now accompanied by a half dozen other Sphinx wolves. A part of Laylea noted she'd met them all. None of them were Bert.

"Come on, Jagger, be smart." A voice from around the bend in the corridor shot an unwanted spike of adrenaline through Laylea's body. Jase Batka. Her instincts feared the boy who'd poisoned her with sligh nut fudge in front of the whole school, even if she wanted to forget it had ever happened. Jase rounded the corner with Julia, Dustin, and Vaughn. "Why would Brenda want to leave? She's been here since she was ten."

"And the puppy dog is an orphan," Jagger said. "She's got nowhere to go."

Laylea hadn't told Jagger her cover story. That meant the wolves had been talking about her. Great. Laylea caught Jagger's double meaning when she realized the wolves had her and Brenda hemmed in on both sides.

Before Laylea could come up with something self-deprecating to de-escalate the situation, Brenda squared off with Jagger and said, "Lee was just telling me that you're starting school so late because your applications to MSC were rejected four semesters in a row."

Jagger's upper lip rose on one side without any other movement on her face. It was impressive. And frightening.

"You're late for the Wing, aren't you, Brenda?" Jase stepped back to open a space between him and Julia.

Brenda didn't spare a glance for Laylea. She smirked at Jase and took the offered escape. Laylea sighed. She planted her feet facing Jase. Sure, Jagger hated her, but her attempt to kill Laylea had been accidental. Jase's attempt had been deliberate. Plus, he was friends with Oscar. She could use that.

"Actually," she laughed a little, keeping her tone light and not pants-wettingly-terrified, "Brenda and I were just talking about Oscar. You guys are tight. How's his search for his sister going?"

Julia responded, "His sister is dead, and your play-acting at the seance was cruel, Fido. That's what I know."

It was easy to smile in response to anything Julia said, no matter how vicious. Ali had made sure that Laylea couldn't think of Julia Jimenez' name without hearing Ali's mocking voice asking if the wolf came from La Jolla and only ate Jicamas. "We missed you at the seance, Julia." She giggled a little saying her name. "But I guess you get plenty of upstairs time, since you're in all the upper-level classes."

"Are you calling me old, Fido?"

Laylea was flabbergasted. She'd been super proud she was able to find a compliment. "I'm saying you're smart."

"I'll show you smart." Vaughn Howe had built his arm muscles up so much that he couldn't rest his hands at his sides. He always looked like he was wearing a kid's snowsuit. To call Vaughn Howe dumb would be an insult to morons. Laylea kept all these thoughts inside. Instead, she searched for the right thing to say, the thing that would get her past the wolves. She wondered if she'd be safer heading back to the Music Wing.

Then Jase stepped in. "Easy, Vaughn. We're all friends here."

"No, we're not." Dustin Huono moved in on Laylea. "Oscar's a friend. Fido made fun of him."

"Wait." Laylea turned back to Jase, the clear leader. "This is about Oscar?"

"This? This is just some friends running into each other in the halls."

"And finding out someone is spreading lies about me," Jagger growled.

"You've screwed up Oscar's head," Dustin said. "He never hangs with us anymore."

Jase let his smarmy smile drop. "Leave the drug business alone. N isn't any of your concern."

"Hey, y'all. I've been waiting for you in the band room." Patrick DelValle approached from the direction of the Music Wing. He carried a covered tray from the dining hall. "Not much of a birthday surprise if nobody shows up."

"Oh, hey, whose birthday is it?" Laylea grasped at the happy interruption.

"Mine." Patrick removed the tray's lid with a flourish. The tray was filled with mini-cupcakes. "I made cupcakes."

Jase snickered. "You should have one, Fido."

Patrick pushed through the wolves around Jagger. He selected a cupcake frosted in orange icing with a P drawn on it in sprinkles. "Here you go, Lee."

Laylea laughed. She was not going to be fooled again. "I don't think so."

Patrick frowned. "You don't want a cupcake I made with my own hands?"

"No." She said it firmly. A bit too firmly. The memory of the sligh nut hallucinations was too bright in her mind. She added, a bit late, "Thank you very much, though."

"That's really insulting." Patrick's joviality had disappeared.

"He offered you a cupcake before anybody in his pack, Fido." Jase stepped to his alpha's side.

Jagger growled, "Eat the damn cupcake."

Eugene, a rabies-mad werewolf who lurked like a champion, just growled.

Patrick sighed and tilted his head just so. It was all the signal the pack needed.

Someone wrapped a large hand around the back of her neck. Jagger snatched the cupcake out of Patrick's hand. Dustin Huono shoved his fingers in Laylea's mouth to pry it open. She didn't dare bite him. The effort made her gag. That made Dustin retreat in fear.

Eugene darted in. He grabbed her ear and a huge chunk of hair. Laylea scrabbled fruitlessly at his hand.

"Don't make her shift," Jase warned him.

"Not gonna." Eugene twisted her ear. "Open your mouth."

It hurt. But not enough. She focused on the pain, leaned into it, searching for that feeling in her gut. A different feeling came when Dustin punched her.

Not only did it dissipate the gathering heat of Laylea's shift, it forced her mouth open. Jagger shoved the orange cupcake in so far that Laylea gagged again. That made Dustin, at least, stumble back to get out of the way. His huge muscles and utter lack of grace forced most of the other wolves to fall back or be crushed by him.

Laylea didn't care about anything except not swallowing that cupcake. She dug in her mouth with both hands, throwing cake and frosting everywhere. She suffered Eugene yanking on her ear to pull her back and Jase kicking her feet out from under her. None of it registered against her fear of being poisoned with sligh nut again.

The food had pumped her saliva glands into high gear, and she used it to spit the cake out. Glittery frosting dribbled down her chin. She almost sighed in relief, until Eugene punched her in the ribs. After losing all the air in her lungs, she swallowed against the pain. A lump of cake slid down her esophagus.

The punch had been too hard. Jase knew it, and he yelled at Eugene. But it was too late.

Laylea had swallowed. The sligh was in her system, and she wouldn't be able to shift. She finally accepted that she wasn't going to walk away from the wolves without help, and she threw her head back and yelped.

26

*L*aylea yelped. She tried to scream, but she yelped because a dog can't scream. She'd swallowed the cupcake, but she'd still shifted. Laylea took stock of her surroundings. The smell of bitter adrenaline came to her first, followed by the musty odor of her own fear. She had shifted. Which meant that the cupcake wasn't poisoned with sligh nut.

Realizing that she was a dog took longer than it should have, but as soon as she got it, she wriggled out of her jumpsuit, dashed for the turn in the corridor, and ran smack into a pair of legs that kicked her right back to the wolfpack.

"Ms. Woodford." It was a teacher's voice.

Laylea rolled to her feet and looked up, sniffing the bitter scent of someone who was angry a lot and didn't shower often. Ms. Davies. A werewolf, and one of the staff who had allowed Oscar to continue being electrocuted last year. Laylea's hackles shot up. It wasn't polite, and it wasn't a reaction that a werewolf was likely to miss.

"Ms. Woodford, you will lower your hackles immediately. I am a staff member at this school and your superior in every way."

The wolf pack had followed her, and they froze in their pursuit when they saw Ms. Davies. Patrick slipped to the front of the wolf pack. He may not have started the business, but he was Alpha to Sphinx and thus, to all the underage wolves. If he let Jase take the blame, he'd be admitting a weakness. "Ms. Davies, would you care for a birthday cupcake?"

"My birthday isn't for another week. Has anybody been injured?"

There was an awkward pause. She wasn't asking Laylea. Were any of the wolves dumb enough to admit to being hurt by a domesticated dog? Yes.

Dustin held his hand up. It was covered in cake and saliva. "She bit me."

The awkward silence resumed as the other wolves tried to figure out how they could reasonably pretend he wasn't with them. Laylea wondered if Ms. Davies would ask the logical question, *how did he get cake all over his hand?* She didn't.

"Mr. Huono, report to the infirmary. We don't know where Ms. Woodford came from. It would be a shame if she gave you rabies."

"That's a highly communicable disease, isn't it?" Jase asked, reminding Laylea that they were not okay with her *wereism* theory.

"Ms. Woodford, fighting is not permitted within this school. I will report this infraction to your presser supervisor. Mr. Vronumraju will, I'm certain, adjust your work schedule so that you aren't as free to roam the halls causing trouble."

Mr. Vronumraju was a good teacher, and he had killer facial hair. Laylea had him for Physics, and KC had him for her private coding lessons. They were shocked when he'd been one of the teachers to watch Oscar fry. It wasn't like him. He wouldn't be hard on her. He'd believe her when she told him the whole story. But he'd definitely give her extra duties in a way that the wolves would see.

"On your way, Ms. Woodford. Keep your nose clean. The next time you're found messing in wolf business, you will be referred to the enforcer." She stepped aside. "What do you have to say for yourself?"

"Lee!" KC's voice rang down the corridor.

The pack had relaxed, some of them jostling each other as Ms. Davies dressed Laylea down. Now they returned to full alert.

"Oh, hi, Ms. Davies, Patrick." KC struggled to catch her breath. "Are you done with Lee? She's late for meal prep, and Chef Tod is furious. He's galloping around the dining hall, trying to set everything straight himself. It's just awful."

Laylea put everything she had into tamping down her tail. She could not let it give away her internal giggles. Chef Tod had the temperament of a kids' party pony. He never got mad. His attitude was that losing was learning and screw-ups were opportunities.

"Hm," Ms. Davies snorted. "Ms. Dells, *you* are supposed to be leading the study group in the dining hall. I know because I took the chance of leaving you in charge. Ms. Woodford will attend to her duties when I am done with her. Go."

KC's entire body shrank in on itself. If she'd had a tail, it would have been tucked hard. She took a breath to argue. Laylea shook her head. Ms. Davies knew that Laylea was expected somewhere, she wouldn't hurt her.

Ms. Davies noticed the brief rebellion. "Mr. Howe, escort Ms. Dells back to the dining hall."

"Yes, Ms. Davies." Howe grinned. He kicked Laylea as he ran by her, hard enough to knock her over. She scrambled upright and tamped down hard on the burning shift, trying to ignore the sharp pain in her ribs. Ms. Davies said nothing.

KC yelled over her shoulder as she hopped away, avoiding Vaughn Howe's reaching grasp, "I'll tell Chef Tod you're on your way."

Laylea barked. It hurt. She hung on tight to her tail though, and her fur and her superior sense of smell. She did not shift.

"You deliberately stand there in your secondary form so that you cannot answer my questions. It is rude, Ms. Woodford, and I am taking notice." Ms. Davies went on this way so long the wolf pack lost interest and started shuffling their feet rather than murmuring agreement. Laylea kept her butt on the floor, her eyes on Ms. Davies. It was the closest she could get to *yes ma'aming* in her dog form.

Eventually, the lecture ran down, and Ms. Davies released her to report to Chef Tod, warning that she would be checking to be sure that Lee went there directly. Laylea would have to warn the chef. She stood and walked away slowly. It was not safe to run from predators, ever. The second she turned the corner, though, she bolted.

Once she had put several corridors between herself and the Music Wing, she allowed the pain in her ribs and, after all the running, her lungs too, to blossom into a shift, right beside a clothes closet. She sat there for a moment, taking stock. No ghosts chilled the corridor. The wolves had failed to hurt her. Greatest of all, Ms. Davies hadn't given her detention. Laylea had not forgotten that the creepy Fire Suppression System installer guy, Robby, wanted to get her in detention. A shiver ran down her spine at the memory of his cold voice saying her name. She knew why the wolves wanted her dead. What did this stranger want with her? Why should he hate her so much when they'd never met?

She dragged herself to her feet using the silver handles of the converted, turn-of-the-century pantry. The softest jumpsuit she'd ever found lay alone on the far right of the lowest shelf. She pulled it on and rolled the legs up once. Otherwise, it fit perfectly. She did up the buttons on her chest as she continued, more sedately, toward the dining hall.

She had her head down, working the upper buttons as she reached the T-junction that led to either the Science Wing or farther in toward the dining hall.

"Oh, that's plenty of buttons." A voice that had crawled out of the gutter stopped her cold.

Laylea looked up.

The slimy voice came from Robby, standing high on a ladder propped against the wall of the Science Wing hall. "In fact, it's way too many."

Two older girls crouched at the base of his ladder with stacks of tubing. The one who could have been a line-backer sniggered. The smaller, paler girl looked vaguely sickened by Robby's words. Laylea didn't recognize either one of them. If they'd been boys, she would have been tempted to ask their names. As it was, she didn't even pause. She turned to the right and barreled into a second ladder. It toppled.

The boy standing on it shifted into a white wolf with sable ears and muzzle as he fell. He landed with the grace of a cat and bounced up, shifting again as he did. He caught the ladder before it could hit the ground and righted it.

Laylea blushed to her toes. "I am so sorry."

"Meh, we're in the way. We should have warning signs." The boy flipped a loose strand of black hair out of his face.

She recognized him. It took her a moment to place the sparkling eyes and cleft chin.

She'd met this boy at Common Electronics the day Dr. Brock kidnapped her. This was DJ Delcampo. KC's brother. What was he doing here?

"Hi." She smiled and looked up again, just in time to catch the moment his deep brown eyes remembered her.

He shot a glance over her shoulder and then bent to wipe an imaginary mote of dirt off his pant leg. It brought his mouth close to her ear. He spoke quietly and quickly. "If you know a girl named Lee, tell her Robby's out for her blood."

Either DJ Delcampo was psychic, or her terror was printed all over her face. She was guessing, from the sudden cold running down her spine despite a lack of ghosts in the vicinity, that it was the second.

His copper skin paled, and all the breath expelled from him on one word, "Shit."

As if reinflating, DJ sucked in a breath and straightened. He put a hand on each of her shoulders, keeping her facing him. "Sorry to make you late. Just doing my job. Gotta make sure the 'fire suppression' system is installed to Robby's satisfaction."

Laylea tilted her head. DJ said "fire suppression" as if it were in quotes. Was it not a fire suppression system? Before she could think how to ask, her human hackles rose. A body stood far too close behind her.

"That's right," Robby crowed. "If Papa ain't happy, nobody's happy."

Despite herself, Laylea spun around. She searched Robby's face. Was that a common shifter saying? She'd heard it somewhere else, recently. And it made the hair on her arms join the hair on her neck in standing up. DJ stepped aside, leaving her free to get away.

Before she could, Robby asked, "You know what makes Papa happy?" He reached a hand for her face. The heat from his palm turned bitingly cold the instant he made contact. He snatched his hand back and stared at it.

Laylea stared at the blackness of Amelia's bobbed hair. The ghost faced Robby, though her icy sorrow flowed out from her in all directions. Laylea stumbled backwards a few steps. "I'm sure good little kids who get to class on time make Papa happy. Bye." She spun on her heel and darted sideways to get past DJ.

Unfortunately, that path ran her into the ladder again. Robby laughed, as did the girls helping him. DJ ducked around but failed to catch the ladder this time. It clattered to the floor. Robby didn't help. He, too, backed away from the cold and turned his ugly flirting on the broad-shouldered blonde waiting by his ladder.

"Sorry." Laylea struggled to right the ladder herself, shooting glances at Amelia, who stalked Robby.

DJ stood staring down the hall at a pair of figures heading their way. Laylea turned to see KC and Oscar hustling toward them, their heads down over a notebook.

DJ breathed, "Is that—?"

Laylea stopped breathing. KC's brother was about to reveal KC's real identity.

27

"KC." Laylea left the ladder where it lay. She stood. "That's my friend, KC. She's a coyote."

"Right." He tore his eyes away from his sister. "Of course." He lowered his voice. "She good?"

He started to look back, but KC looked up at that moment and saw Laylea.

Laylea grabbed DJ's bicep to keep him facing away. "You should get back to work." She snorted. "Make Papa happy."

DJ chuckled, but the laugh didn't reach his eyes. "Be careful."

Laylea nodded and hurried to catch her friends. "Hey guys, let's go to Mer. The wolf pack was headed to the library."

They didn't object. She got them turned around and heading away from DJ, Robby, and Amelia while they fussed over her.

Oscar asked, "Are you okay?"

"Yeah." Laylea turned to KC. "How'd you know to come get me?"

KC closed the notebook she was holding, using a finger to mark her page. "Brenda came into the dining hall shouting about someone being hurt in the band room. Ms. Davies rushed out. I knew you were at your guitar lesson, so I followed. Were you hurt?"

"Not that Brenda saw. I thought she'd abandoned me to them."

Before they turned the corner leading to Mer dorm, Laylea looked back. DJ was watching. He lifted his fingers in the tiniest wave. She took a deep breath and turned back to her friends. "KC, you're not gonna like this, but I need to tell you—"

KC wasn't listening. "Did you know there were already files on this drive my asshole brother gave you?" KC held her wrist up.

Laylea stared at it. "What?"

KC said, "Pictures of patients and their records?"

"That wasn't DJ. Dee put those on there before I came to school." Laylea remembered in a flash. "I was supposed to see if there's any connection between them. But KC, DJ—"

Oscar interrupted her. "There is a connection. They're all shifters. One patient is referred to only as Kitty Kitty. I recognize most of the names from the files I've been searching through in the Wing."

"The names you don't recognize might be in Gorse's private comprehensive files." Laylea said it almost to herself and then realized they didn't know yet. "Mr. Bianchi confirmed the dean has a comprehensive student file in his office."

Oscar jumped on the info. "So, I just have to steal the key to his office?"

"And then KC has to hack his computer," Laylea added.

"Hold on. I don't know if we can blame the dean for all of these sleepers. A lot of them are adults, plus—" KC opened her notebook. The page was covered with a list of names and notes. "Some of these people have been there for a very long time. Brian Samborsky—"

Oscar interrupted KC to say, "I wonder if he's any relation to Brenda?"

"If so, I feel bad for her. He's been there five years." KC ran her finger down to the next name. "The little girl, Deanna?"

Laylea had told them about her. "Yeah, Bert's sister, or whatever. Amelia's kid." She glanced behind them, looking for the chilly ghost.

The woman wasn't there, but her gas mask friends had returned.

KC didn't notice her distraction. "She's been in the sleep lab since she was eight years old. This lab is way older than the N epidemic."

"It looks like it's part of it though, right?" As they walked, Laylea looked over her shoulder again at the gas mask ghosts.

"Based on the extensive blood analysis," KC said, "Yeah."

"Maybe it took them that long experimenting to find a drug that worked the way they wanted it to." Oscar pulled Laylea out of the way before she ran into the wall at a turning. "Are you sure they didn't hurt you, Lee?"

Laylea dragged her gaze from the ghosts. "What?" Her friends stared at her, concern writ large on their faces. She took a breath and tried to focus on how much she loved them. Her friends were amazing. The sleepers weren't their problem. N wasn't their problem. But the two of them were searching through records Dee had asked Laylea to examine, in their free time. "It's the gas mask ghosts."

"They're here?" KC asked.

"With Amelia?" Oscar added.

Laylea smiled. "No. Amelia seemed more interested in Robby than in me."

KC spun, looking around in all directions. "Why can't we see them? We could see the ghosts upstairs."

"The ghosts upstairs wanted you to see them. They wanted everyone to see them." Laylea wasn't sure why her friends had been able to see the zoo ghosts, but it seemed to make sense. "The gas mask kids want something from me."

"What?!" KC yelled down the apparently empty corridor. "What do you want from my friend?"

Oscar snorted, and KC giggled at herself. Laylea tried to laugh along, but it came out flat as she remembered the tiger girl's thumbs pushing against her eyeballs and all of history flashing through her mind.

A cheer rose from the courtyard of Mer dorm. All three friends hurried forward to find Peter and Rehyan high-fiving over a sizzling mound of broken furniture, crumpled papers, and blue jumpsuits.

"What the hell, Ali?" KC grabbed at the hawk shifter's tattooed arm as she backed away from the growing flames.

Ali grinned. "Robby announced that Mer dorm's suppression

system is complete and operational. We're just testing it." She turned back to the wild courtyard and yelled, "Mers make fire!"

All around the courtyard, kids, even the ones hiding far from the fire, pounded their chests and grunted. Ahanu leapt into the air, spreading wings from his human back. He flapped them once, and a clap of thunder echoed off the stone walls. Emerald wrapped her arms around him as he landed, her head thrown back in a laugh.

"Mers are crazy." Oscar muttered this even as he ran over to help Peter, Conner, and Rehyan fan the flames.

Laylea started to follow, but KC stopped her. She turned away from the courtyard and kept her voice low. "Hey, in the patient files, there's a picture with no name."

Laylea focused on KC's face rather than the gas masks hovering inches behind her. "No name? No medical records?"

"No. She's got medical records. She's called Kitty Kitty, and she's been there since September 2033." KC glanced over her shoulder at Oscar and the other boys dancing around their fire. "Shala died in September 2033."

Laylea put it together. She remembered seeing the girl the day she met Amelia. She had compared her to Sanna, Oscar's mother. "Is it the emaciated girl with a black tattoo on her arm?"

"Yeah. You think...?" She tilted her chin in Oscar's direction.

Her breath escaped Laylea in a rush. If the sleeper was Shala, it would change everything. How had Shala gone from LPSS to Gorshkov's sleep lab? The answer was obvious. Denier had taken her. But why? If she was injured in the fall and not killed, why lie to her family? Was Shala the reason someone was keeping Sanna addicted?

She looked over to where Oscar and the fire starters were racing around, trying to control the growing flames. Would he be happy to hear that his sister was alive but had been kept in a coma for the last seven years?

KC murmured, "Yeah, I don't know if I want it to be her, either."

Ali swooped around the perimeter of the room at the same height as the hose Robby had strung up. She folded her wings and settled on the arm of a couch, shifting more smoothly than any Mer should be able to. "Anybody feel any rain coming down?"

"Anybody feel any fire extinguisher goo?" Emerald asked in a similar tone.

"Hey, KC! Lee!" Rehyan, standing, as usual, on one leg, paused as a chorus of voices yelled, *Love and joy!* "You guys see anybody running in with wool blankets?"

"We do not see a brace of firefighters bolting down the hallway," KC hollered to the room at large.

"And that confirms my hypothesis." Ahanu executed a neat little bow with one arm still around Emerald's waist.

The Mers and their visitors applauded. Those closest to the impromptu bonfire coughed as they cheered. Oscar doubled over.

"I wish your honor guard could loan me a gas mask." KC looked down the corridor, clearly not seeing the tall ghost girl standing at her back.

Laylea tried a joke to slow her racing heart. "I wish they could put out a fire."

"We all knew it wasn't a fire suppression system. Did nobody plan on another way to put out this fire?" Dove Betts spoke up from where she lounged in one of the comfy chairs.

"There are blankets in the podroom antechambers." Caliban shifted lazily from her linden tree form, yawning the words out. Carrie bounded over to the girls' side and pushed through the door with her furry head. Ali followed her. Squirt and Peter ran for the boys' side. Peter shifted into fox form as he hit the door.

KC spun to Laylea, an idea bright in her eyes. "Hey, you think Amelia would know if the sleeper is Shala Luke?"

"I don't know if Amelia knows anything but guilt and panic."

"It's worth asking, though, right?"

Laylea took a deep breath and let it out slowly. She kept her eyes on the fire, away from the hot breath of the ghosts at her back. Hell, Amelia's freezing panic might help contain the blaze on both sides. "Yeah. Um, Amelia?"

The icy chill preceded the grief-stricken mother, chilling Laylea before she could see Amelia's drawn features inches from her face.

"Have you found him?"

Laylea knew her answer was the wrong one. "We've got a new lead."

The temperature plummeted. KC shivered.

Laylea continued, "We're going to find Bert, Amelia. And we're going to get Deanna out of that sleep lab."

Laylea cringed. It was not a good idea to make promises you might not be able to keep. Especially to an angry dead person. "We're trying to find out more about the sleep lab. Do you know the other patients? Is one of them named Shala Luke?"

Laylea was deafened by Amelia's reply. "There is no one but Deanna!"

Leaves blew off the trees in the courtyard. Caliban's willowy hair swirled around her. She shifted into the more rooted form of her tree and rocked with the wind. The fire blazed and then died, leaving a ring of white frost around the ashy leftovers of the Mers' makeshift fuel. The kids who had been trying to tamp down the fire with towels and blankets stood shivering just outside the white ring. Oscar dropped his towel. He held his hands to his face and breathed on them as if he were on the Lake Michigan shore in winter.

"Soooooooooo," KC said. "She'll look into it?"

Laylea rolled her eyes at her friend. Amelia and the gas mask ghosts had disappeared after the grieving mother made her pronouncement, but she'd left icicles on Laylea's eyelashes. The burn raced through her body and shifted her.

Oscar jogged over to them. "Hey, what got you, Lee? Fire or ice?"

KC answered, "Amelia."

"Wow." He shivered and then shrugged. "At least she put the fire out."

Laylea barked. She wanted to crawl into her pod and skip the rest of the day. She was sad about Jimmy, mad at herself for failing the food gift test again, confused by how fiercely KC hated her brother when he seemed like a very nice guy, and exhausted from the gas masks' anger and Amelia's grief. She was grateful she couldn't speak and didn't have to tell Oscar his sister might be in Denier's sleep lab.

"Do all ghosts have that kind of power?" Oscar crouched at her side.

It was another issue that couldn't be answered in dog form, so Laylea stood up on his knees and nosed his hand for scratches instead. She was grateful he hadn't asked what had made Amelia freeze the courtyard. Oscar scratched behind her ears and then worked his way down her neck. His eyes got that glazed over, pained look they got when he was thinking really hard. It worried Laylea.

Ahanu's voice cut over the din in the courtyard. He stood with Ali, Rehyan, and Merrilynne under the "fire suppression" contraption Robby had installed near the girls' door. Dove, in her tiger form, wove through their legs. "He'll just fix it. I've tried twice. He just replaces the tubing. We have to hack the device so it won't do whatever it is designed to do."

Everyone in earshot turned to look at KC.

She sighed. "I am good with computers, not general technology."

Laylea sang out a series of barks that were as close as she could get to laughing. KC had spent her entire childhood working at Common Electronics for her parents. She knew more than computers.

Ali wasn't buying it, either, "What she said. Get over here and look at this thing. Squirt, some help!"

The large Samoan male jogged over, ready to lift KC up so she could reach the device. Caliban shifted and strode over at the same time. "Perhaps I can provide a steadier platform."

She planted herself below the device and raised her arms, shifting as she did to grow two branches parallel to the ground. KC collected a hand-sized toolkit from her backpack and hopped into Squirt's arms. He lifted her onto Caliban's rough platform. The linden shifter then grew taller until KC was at the height of the light trough with easy access to Robby's device.

"It doesn't matter what you do to the system." Brenda strolled in, cracking her knuckles. "It doesn't change the fact that the teachers are all lying to us."

"Dean Gorse is lying to us," Peter said. "Just like he was with the Special Testing bullshit."

"I think it's time we all run away." Emerald earned a worried look from Ahanu for that suggestion. She didn't notice. "You ever find out where your big sister ran away to, Dove?"

Dove's jaw cracked as she spread her tiger maw to yowl a response. A second later, with a barely perceptible waving of the air around her, she shifted into a beautiful girl with curly black hair and emerald eyes. "Never heard from Riley again after she left school. But I'm not running. This is our school. Dean Gorse should run away and never be heard from again."

There were some cheers for that. And some arguments for leaving. As with all Mer discussions, it got loud. Laylea couldn't make sense of anybody's words. Oscar had folded her ears down and was scratching them with some vigor. She licked his nose.

"Step one," Oscar said, "we have to find out where Gorse keeps his key. Your ghosts have access to everywhere. Could you ask them to find it?"

Laylea hung her head. She had no interest in talking to ghosts for a good, long while. Amelia had nearly frozen her to death. She could imagine what the gas masks would do to her. They burned with their anger.

Luckily, before Laylea had to give Oscar an answer, a spark flashed in front of KC on her perch. A cry of horror went up around her. She quickly reassured everybody, "I'm okay. Just a little blinded."

The shocked cries didn't lessen a bit. They weren't worried about KC so much as the fact that Caliban's upper leaves had caught on fire. The new blaze scorched the low ceiling above Robby's fire suppression device.

"Hmm," Dove observed. "You know what would be really helpful right now?"

Ali casually responded, "A fire suppression system?"

"Yeah."

"Too bad we don't have one." Rehyan raced over with a bucket of water from one of the pools. He tossed it over Caliban and KC.

KC dripped, but her voice was dry as sand. "Thanks, Rehyan."

28

There were days when Laylea felt the weight of the stone walls and ceiling pressing her down, when icy Amelia and the burning gas mask ghosts felt like a chain dragging from her heels. Upstairs, July Fourth was a time of celebration: food, family, and fireworks. The school threw a feast to celebrate. It wasn't the same without sunlight.

Laylea got to eat with her friends. Then she got to clean up after everybody. Sure, she was only one of many pressers assigned to the kitchen, but Ms. Davies had put the word out that she was to get extra chores, and the werewolves took that to mean that they could give her theirs. One by one, the others cut out for the dorm parties and their pods until only Laylea and Chef Tod remained in the kitchen. The chef offered to finish up himself, but Laylea stayed.

Amelia floated quietly in one corner. Something about the chef calmed her. The gas mask ghosts had multiplied over the course of dinner as more and more faculty left for their own party upstairs. In the end-of-dinner announcements, Mr. Bianchi had explained there was an all-staff meeting at Dean Gorse's horse farm down the shore. But it was July the fourth. Everyone knew it was just an excuse for the faculty and staff to go see the fireworks over the lake.

When Ms. Davies and Mr. Barret departed together, the gas mask ghost contingent grew to more than three dozen silent, burning specters hovering in small packs all around the dining hall. They hadn't spoken since the first day Laylea saw them. They hadn't touched her again, either.

She shivered when she remembered seeing the school through all time. She hadn't told KC and Oscar about that vision. They'd tell her to let the lead girl touch her again and look for Bert. And Shala. KC and Laylea had decided not to tell Oscar about their suspicion that Kitty Kitty was Shala until they had proof, or a way to get her out. Laylea had written to Dee asking her to look into it.

The usual kids were heading up through Gryphon to watch the fireworks with the depressed bear. She'd said she'd join them upstairs when she finished kitchen duty. She had meant to. She wanted to see Toby again, and Guillaume might help her figure out how to get rid of the gas masks.

But while they were mopping the floor, Chef Tod had told her how LPSS used to do yearbooks. The kids didn't get a copy like they did at Bailey's school. The school printed a single copy and kept it on file in the library. They had names and photographs of the human kids with sketches of their furry selves. He wasn't sure if they were still kept there, but he'd found them on the highest shelves in the far southwest corner of the library, near the wall with the Arachne tapestry.

So, once they'd prepped the kitchen for the breakfast crew and said goodnight, Laylea pushed through her exhaustion and prepared to race to the library. Amelia watched as she dropped her jumpsuit in the bins just outside the enormous doors of the dining hall.

Laylea moved closer to the ghost to use her cold panic. Frosty air streamed from the grieving mother's translucent form to chill Laylea until she shifted into her fur coat. The air became more bearable still when Amelia faded away into a mist. Though, without her panic, the gas masks' anger quickly heated not only the air but the stones beneath Laylea's paws as she raced through the corridors. The tiger girl and the wolf with the blond stripe shifted and burned Laylea's tail all the way to the double doors of the library.

Inside, Laylea resisted the urge to keep running straight to their nook, curl up in the pillows, and nap. She needed to find Bert Gorshkov to save Jimmy and Sanna and Deanna and all the other sleepers. A vision of the emaciated young woman with the black tattoo flashed in her mind, and she wondered if she'd find Shala Luke's picture in the yearbooks. Although, was it likely they'd include a student who died in the first three weeks she was there?

Laylea was familiar with the Arachne tapestry. It was the pride and joy of the spider shifters. Early in the school's history, a lone golden orb-weaver shifter had spun her own silk into thread, dyed it with plants found along the lake and in the botanical garden, then wove a portrait of Arachne, the Greek weaver turned into a spider by Athena, weaving an azure egg. Laylea trotted under the tables and chairs, taking the most direct route to the aisle she needed.

She read the titles all along the bottom shelves until her eye caught on an empty space on the second shelf. A wolfhound-shaped bookend held the books up on either side of the space. With all the books in the library, it shocked Laylea that Ms. Crow would leave shelf space empty where she could cram in at least two dozen more books. Then she saw the note. A triangle of tented cardstock held a hand-written note that read "LPSS yearbooks have been removed for security at the order of the Shifter Council."

What security concerns could yearbooks pose, hidden away underground in a school that only permitted shifters entry? Laylea was pondering possibilities when she heard voices coming from the next row.

"Lizzy Crow, do you really think more time will change anything?" Ms. Lagat's barely audible voice echoed and grew louder as though she were drawing closer.

Ms. Crow's answer was obscured by creaking and a click like when you shut one of the clothes closets in the older sections of the school.

"That prophecy is a myth." Ms. Lagat sighed, the echoing quality gone. "There is no chosen one. We cannot live our lives around a story."

Laylea padded to the end of her row, closer to the voices. She peered around the shelves. With the library carpeted in multiple layers of rugs, there was no danger she would be heard. The adults stood in the middle of the aisle, brushing dust from their clothing.

Ms. Crow pulled her blue sweater closed and held it like she was cold. "I can and do. That's why I chose the library when I had to make my choice."

"Guy chose the library, too, Liz. So that he could search for proof of that story. He found nothing. We are on our own."

A caw broke the sacred stillness of the library. Laylea fell over and saw Dizzy hovering over her head. The sight startled her into shifting, and she banged into the shelf, knocking some books onto the ground.

"Lee." Ms. Crow released her hold on her sweater and rushed over to help her collect the fallen books. "You should be in bed."

"She should be at a party, Elizabeth."

"Oh, shush, Adele. What are you doing here, Lee?"

Dizzy cawed as if echoing the question. She hovered over Ms. Crow's head.

"I..." Laylea started to say she'd fallen asleep studying, but she trusted these two teachers. She didn't want to lie to them. "I was looking for some yearbooks Chef Tod told me about, then I heard voices. You scared me."

"You scared us. We didn't think there was anybody here." Ms. Crow ran a hand along the spines to even the books before she stood up, brushing gray dust off her slacks. "But it is serendipitous, running into you here, without anybody else around." She directed this observation to Ms. Lagat.

Dizzy gurgled a croak and swooped around Ms. Lagat and out of the stacks.

"Is it?" Ms. Lagat shot Ms. Crow a meaningful look before she led the way out into the corral of study tables. "You care for Toby, Ms. Woodford. Yes?"

Laylea nodded.

Ms. Lagat walked to the front desk, where Dizzy perched on the *Recommended Reading* display. Ms. Crow stepped around to her usual side of the counter. She reached under and pulled out a buttery-soft jumpsuit that she tossed at Laylea, who put it on as Ms. Lagat stuttered her way through a speech about the safety of the animals in the zoo being paramount and how students should show them more respect.

Ms. Crow interrupted her after a minute. "Lee has shown respect for the animals and cares for Toby, Adele."

Dizzy snapped her beak at the shifting teacher and chattered at Laylea. It was hard for Laylea to keep from laughing at the bird.

Ms. Lagat sighed again and took a deep breath. "I am worried about the bear. There is a bat that has been flitting about in Toby's enclosure. It wears a collar similar to yours."

Laylea glowed inside. Kyle was looking in on her. "Oh, you don't have to worry. He knows I like Toby. He'd never hurt him."

Ms. Lagat raised one eyebrow. "And does the bat know your feelings about werewolves?"

"Adele." Ms. Crow sounded shocked. "Lee has done nothing to harm the pack. The offenses have all been on their side."

Laylea laughed. "It's okay. Kyle has his own feelings about werewolves."

"Kyle?" Ms. Lagat asked.

"The bat. He's a friend of mine."

Ms. Crow hid a grin behind one hand. Dizzy leaned toward her as if wanting to move that hand. She tilted her head, and Laylea did laugh.

Ms. Lagat glared at the librarian. "I thought as much." She plucked up a card that Ms. Crow had slid across the counter and handed it to Laylea. "He dropped this."

The thin rectangle of plastic had her fake name, Lee Woodford, embossed below the title People's Credit Union. A chip glinted silver on the reverse side. She grinned. He'd fixed it. Somehow, Kyle the vampire had gotten Lee the minor a bank account.

"Thanks." She spotted the concern behind Ms. Lagat's well-schooled expression. "Kyle's a good guy. He can be a bad guy to people who hurt...anybody. Toby's safer with Kyle hanging around."

"This came for you as well, just tonight." Ms. Crow handed her a piece of paper folded into an envelope and addressed only with her name.

She figured out how to unfold it and read it immediately, hoping for news about the sleep labs.

> Lee,
>
> Dr. Maurice Brock was killed in custody the day after he was arrested. Before Captain Morioka could question him. His personal notes indicate he feared he would be murdered by Lee Woodford or Bert Gorshkov. These personal notes were posted on a public website and have been making the rounds on social media. I fear for your safety. Stop looking for him. Keep your head down.
>
> Stop searching for Bert Gorshkov, or I will tell Bailey about the rawhides Junior gives you in secret.
> Dee

Laylea's breath caught in her chest. She tried to suck in air but couldn't get her throat to work. If Brock was a ghost, he could find her here. He wouldn't harass her like Amelia or even just terrify her like the gas masks. He knew death when he was alive. Dead, he'd know it even better. And he would kill her.

Distantly, she heard the two teachers calling her name. Dizzy sang out a deep, rasping call. Their voices sounded muted in velvet.

"Breathe, Lee. You have to breathe," Ms. Crow urged.

"It's okay, Lizzy. She'll shift before she passes out."

"What's in that note?"

The world was going black around the edges. Gentle hands sat her on the carpets. Claws gripped her shoulder, and a beak poked at her cheek.

There was the crinkle of paper, then Ms. Lagat reported, "It says that a Dr. Brock was killed. . . blames her. . . she's to stop looking for Bert Gorshkov."

"But Bertie died years ago, didn't he?"

Bert Gorshkov was dead? Laylea suddenly felt her chest loosen. She gasped for a lungful of air. Her hearing improved, colors dimmed, and smells brought the library to life in her canine brain. Ms. Crow and Ms. Lagat were sitting on the floor with her. Ms. Lagat folded the note. Ms. Crow smoothed the fur back on Laylea's hackles. Dizzy hopped around, dipping her head and trying to catch Laylea's eye.

"You're okay, now, Lee," Ms. Crow murmured. "You're safe here. We made the library safe."

Dizzy croaked as if confirming her words.

"And you don't have to worry about Bert Gorshkov," the librarian added. "He OD'd years ago, not long after he graduated. He was driving at the time. It was a horrible accident."

Ms. Lagat tucked the note into Laylea's collar and zipped it up. "Didn't Grandpa Delcampo fly out from Montana to help cover up the mess?"

"He did. It was quite the to-do." Ms. Crow wrapped Laylea's ears around her fingers and rubbed. "So, there, you've found him. You don't have anyone to search for. You can keep your head down and stay safe."

Sure. She'd "found" Bert Gorshkov. But how was she going to ever get Amelia off her back now? And what could she possibly do to protect herself from the ghost of Dr. Brock, the gas man and killer of little girls?

29

A lot could change in seven days. Not much did, though, in the week after Dee called off Laylea's mission. She kept going to class and to kitchen duty. She hid in the library whenever she could and avoided the wolves at all times. Her gas-masked escorts grew and shrank in number in a pattern she couldn't figure out. Amelia came and went on an equally unfathomable schedule.

She saw Dizzy so little that she wondered if the raven had gone invisible to her. She never saw Oscar, and since the madrigal choir was busy gearing up for the summer concert, she only caught up with KC in the podroom as they collapsed into their beds.

The only class the three of them had together was a once-a-week, combined-levels Phys Ed class. It met in the Fields, and they could generally sneak off somewhere in the guise of playing whatever game Ms. McCobb, the new head Phys Ed teacher, chose to torture them with.

Laylea had planned to tell them about Dee's note as soon as they could get away. But then Ms. McCobb sent them on the obstacle course run she thought encouraged the unskilled shifters in the group. It only frustrated them. The athletes would race through the Fields to the finish line at the Caves, the kids who could shift at will but didn't like to put themselves out would stroll through, and those who couldn't shift were forced to struggle their way through, rarely reaching the Caves before the end of class. The birds laughed at all of them.

Before Laylea could tell her friends she had news, Ms. McCobb blew her whistle, and Oscar took off after Reggie Betts. The tiger shifter from Centaur dorm got picked first for every sports team, and the straight girls of Mer dorm, all excepting his twin sister, Dove, drooled over him. Dove generally shifted and hissed whenever the drooling started up in front of her.

So, instead of telling both of them at once, Laylea told KC everything as they slogged through the course, followed by nearly a dozen gas-masked ghosts in varying degrees of solidity. The tall-girl ghost took on her tiger form to dive in the river when Laylea went in to fetch the first ribbon, tied to a rock in a meadow of stonewort.

The first thing KC asked, after digesting the information for a long while, was, "Where did Ms. Lagat and Ms. Crow come from?"

"What?" Laylea froze halfway up a gnarly tree, one foot still pushing off of KC's shoulder, the other's toes gripping a knot in the trunk. The ghost tiger lounged on a branch one up from Laylea's goal.

"Get the ribbons first," KC growled.

They had to collect ribbons along the course, which was another thing that was easier for certain kinds of shifters. As a wolf, KC could have bounced from trunk to trunk in the tight grove, snatched a ribbon from the high branches, and then shifted to put it in her pocket. Since wolves got to keep their clothing when they shifted, they could collect all the ribbons and carry them easily.

Even if Laylea could shift at will, she couldn't exactly fit all of the ribbons they had to collect in her collar. And some of the kids didn't have a collar like hers. She didn't know any other shifter who would voluntarily wear a collar. It was not a fair course.

Laylea snatched two ribbons and slid down the trunk. KC added the ribbons to her pocketed collection. She continued, "If you were in the library all alone and then you heard them in the middle of a conversation, one row over, where did they come from?"

Laylea had completely forgotten about that mystery in her fear of Brock's ghost. She thought about it as she hopped from rock to rock across the first whitewater pool where the racing river flowed into the Lakes section of Fields. "Their voices were drowned out for a moment by a loud noise that I thought was a clothes closet closing."

"But there aren't any closets in the library. Otherwise, your friend the boogeyman would have access to the school."

Laylea waited for KC to catch up to her on one of the islands to clarify, "Junior can only travel through closets in rooms where people sleep."

KC raised her eyebrows in disbelief. "You've never fallen asleep studying in the library?"

"Good point," she conceded, remembering drooling all over her Shifter Studies homework just a week ago.

They hopscotched across another line of rocks, KC leading this time. KC stopped halfway to the next islet. "Hey, you know somebody has to have slept on that couch in front of the closet in the Medical Wing."

Laylea shook her head and hopped to the next rock, taking the lead. "If anybody had, Junior would be here. He worries about me. And with Brock blaming me for his death, he'd be here." She reached out to help KC across the last gap, ignoring the ghosts behind her who still didn't get that they didn't need to use the rocks.

Once she'd gotten her balance, KC asked, "Do you remember what aisle they were in?"

"Yeah." Laylea nodded. "It's the one right under the Arachne tapestry."

"Okay, let's get through this course and go check it out."

They had to stop talking as they wove their way through the many lakes. KC swam to an island for the next ribbon. She squeezed her hair out as they made their way over some particularly intrusive willow roots and through the brambles. "Lee. If Gorshkov died so long ago…"

Laylea finished for her, "Why is he still listed as the owner of all those buildings?"

"Yeah." KC counted the ribbons in her pockets. "I mean, I get big corporations do all sorts of weird things to avoid taxes."

"Does having a dead guy as your CEO give you a tax break?" Laylea glanced around at the ghosts surrounding them. "Maybe my friends have an in with high finance and that's why they're sticking around."

"And they're haunting you just for fun?" KC turned to Laylea as they reached the final challenge in the Caves room. The last ribbon of the course was tucked in a nest on a ledge halfway up a small mountain. They had to climb to the top, find the giant blue flag that would mark the finish line, and make their way there. "I'll get the ribbons. You just get all the way up. Don't want you having flashbacks to the ledge at Adelor's entrance."

"Ha!" Laylea laughed at her friend. "You don't think I'm gonna have flashbacks the whole way up this face? Who is this obstacle supposed to prefer, the mountain goat shifters?"

"Actually, it's pretty fun to watch Theresa, the lion, run around in here. Feed her too much sugar, lead her here, and watch her go." While KC talked, the ghost tiger leapt halfway up the rocky face in one bound.

"The gas mask tiger is having fun."

KC grinned. "That's good. Is she less hot?"

"She's too far up to tell. The others aren't any less scary." Laylea sighed and gripped the highest outcropping she could reach. "Brock may be in luck. If I fall off this mountain, he won't have to come haunt me to death."

"You get the feeling we're missing something?" KC asked.

"Yeah," Laylea replied. "Ropes."

They climbed. Laylea reached the ledge first. It was more of a cave, but a cave too small for even her dog form to fit into. Milly, the mouse, would find this obstacle easy, if she could drag the ribbon up the rest of the hillside. Laylea grabbed both ribbons and rushed to summit before KC. It took every ounce of her strength to drag herself over the lip to the ridgetop. Mist from the great waterfall cooled her. She rolled over to help KC up.

When Laylea had caught her breath, she said, "Thing is, I came back to help stop the distribution of N."

KC looked up from where she was marking compass coordinates on her crowded graph paper. She asked, "Hm?" though Laylea couldn't hear her over the rush of the waterfall.

Off the look on KC's face, Laylea yelled, "I came back to stop N."

"And to help the sleepers." KC stuffed the compass and paper into a thick plastic bag that already held Sanna's red crane and shoved it all into a pocket.

"And to help the sleepers." Laylea hopped to her feet. "So, who did Amelia mean when she said *he* was here? Bert made sense. Bert had the same last name as her daughter. If not Bert, who's *he*?"

KC climbed up Laylea's body to standing. "You may just have to ask her."

Laylea blanched at the idea.

"Look!" KC pointed over to the fancy Southern mansion doors leading out of the Lakes.

Oscar and Reggie stood holding the blue finish line flag amongst a small crowd of kids, not all of them from the class.

"Let's go find out what's going on. Maybe we can get your mind off Gorshkov and Brock and Dee and the Wyrdos."

As KC grabbed her hand to lead her under the waterfall along a shortcut to the doorway, Laylea looked around herself and added, "And Amelia and…whatever your names are."

The roar of the waterfall precluded any further conversation. But, as they drew away from the falls and closer to the door, Oscar's voice carried over the muttered conversation of the crowd. "But are you really sure your sister ran away? What if they just told you that?"

Reggie laughed. "Dude. Riley hated us. She couldn't wait to get away from the fuss everyone made over me and Dove."

"Because you're twins?" Oscar asked.

"Because we're a litter."

It was Oscar's turn to laugh. "Two is hardly a litter."

"Do you have any idea how few litters are born to shifters these days?"

Laylea looked to KC. KC nodded. That was something to think about. Laylea was one of five. What would the shifter community do if they knew that?

KC must have read her mind. She whispered, "Yeah, it's best that Lee Woodford only has one, non-related, brother."

Laylea wanted to ask more questions, but Reggie's next words struck a chord in her memory.

"Riley felt invisible at home. She just wanted to be seen."

Laylea rubbed at her eyes. She remembered two burning thumbs pushing into her eyeballs, opening her vision to the space where all time existed at once. She turned to see a full dozen gas mask ghosts standing between her and the tall tiger girl. She wondered.

She must have wondered for too long, because KC danced back to drag her around the copse of willows to the finish line flag. She waved two handfuls of ribbons in the air. "Are we last?"

Reggie faced them with his thousand-watt smile. "You are the last to bother finishing the course after McCobb was summoned away by Dean Gorse." He took the ribbons and dropped them in a box at the foot of the flag. His eyes fell on Laylea as he folded the long pole and rolled the flag around it. "Hey, you're Lee, right?"

Laylea raised an eyebrow. They'd been in Phys Ed together for four months. Plus, last year. And he'd been in the dining hall when Jase poisoned her with sligh nut. No one could forget that shining moment. Surely, he knew who she was. But all she did was nod.

"You're the ghost girl, the one who upstaged Emerald at her seance," Reggie asked.

She stuttered. "I...I guess so, yeah."

"She saved Emerald from being stomped by a Clydesdale," KC corrected him.

"Oscar thinks my big sister's dead. Would you give a look around for a tiger shifter: tall, green eyes, totally aggro." A faraway look came into his eyes, and he grinned at a private memory. "A scar on her collarbone."

"Sure." Laylea blushed. She really didn't want everyone in school to start calling her "ghost girl." She agreed just to get out of the conversation. She didn't want her suspicion to be true. "I'll look for her. Her name was Riley?"

The grin fled Reggie's face. "It *is* Riley."

"What the hell, Lee?" Sparks flew from Oscar's eyes. "You'll ask the ghosts about his sister but not mine?"

30

Oscar glared at Laylea like she was the one who'd taken his sister from him. She'd only agreed to look for Reggie's sister because Oscar had put the idea in his head.

"I..." Laylea couldn't think of what to say. She *had* asked Amelia about Shala. Amelia had blasted Mer dorm with cold. Didn't he remember that? No, he didn't, because she had never told him. "Oscar. I asked—"

"Listen up, you shifty and shiftless lice hotels!" Ali burst into Lakes so violently that both doors slammed into the clothing cubbies on either side. Brenda, Emerald, Chloe, and Squirt followed on her heels with Dove and Harper bringing up the rear. Reggie crossed to speak to his sister as he tossed the rolled-up flag and basket of ribbons into one of the cubbies.

Ali shoved through the kids to the center. She waited a brief moment to be sure she had everyone's attention. When all eyes were on her, she announced, "The wolves have been herded into a special meeting of the pack. It's time for a . . ." She tilted her head expectantly, and a dozen voices cried out, "Wilding!"

"Here, Captain." She tossed an orange cardigan at Laylea. "First one since you got back, you have to be an Alpha. Oscar." She turned to

Oscar, totally missing the tension radiating from him. "Brenda says you got detention for breaking into Gorse's office. That earns you Blue Alpha. Pick your teams."

Ali danced back into the crowd of kids jostling to one side or the other, vying to be picked first. Oscar crushed the sweater in his hand, breathing like he'd just finished the obstacle course. Laylea felt sweat trickling down her face as the gas mask ghosts fed off of Oscar's anger.

KC stepped between them. She turned her back to everyone else. "Let's have some fun. Forget about ghosts and siblings and Gorshkov. You're friends. We'll work it out."

Oscar did not look mollified. He didn't even glance at Laylea. "Ahanu, you're my Beta."

Ahanu dragged his hand out of Emerald's and dashed to Oscar's side.

Laylea's heart wasn't really in it, but if KC wanted to play, then she'd let her play. The Betas didn't get to play as much, so she picked the first person she saw. "I pick Emerald for my Beta."

"Ooooooh!" The kids reacted like she'd picked Ahanu's girlfriend to taunt him.

Though he said it quietly, everybody heard, and everybody laughed when Squirt said, "Damn, they'll have all the ghosts on Orange team."

Oscar went for the obvious choice and picked Reggie next. Laylea picked Caliban, who waved a branch to acknowledge her selection.

"In that case, I pick—" Nobody heard who Oscar picked because the double doors opened again, though only a crack. An underfed tawny wolf squeezed through, barking and growling with an almost ear-splitting whine under it all. She ran to Ali and stood her front paws on the tattooed girl's chest.

Ali stumbled back, letting Carrie fall. "What's up, you freak?"

"Carrie." KC ran to kneel by the Mer wolf. "Why aren't you at the pack meeting?"

Carrie spun around and barked at KC. She whimpered a series of vocalizations that sounded like she was trying to speak.

KC shook her head. "I don't know what you're saying."

Carrie howled and bent herself in half to snap at her tail.

"No!" KC grabbed the scruff at the nape of Carrie's neck. "You are a good wolf."

From the middle of the crowd, a baritone voice sang out a tune Laylea had heard in the school before. She didn't know it, but all the shifters raised by shifters knew it. Brian made his way through the kids to kneel with KC. He took Carrie's muzzle in his hands and gently held it closed as he sang at her. Her whimpering chatter quieted and died away. Emerald stepped out from behind Oscar and sang out a high harmony to Brian's song. Carrie howled a note through her closed lips. The note vibrated Carrie's whole body. It seemed to vibrate out into the air around her, and then the girl lay there, her face in Brian's hands, KC's hand on her back, a clear note ringing out from her throat.

She cut herself off, the note swerving into a jarring dissonance to Brian and Emerald's song. "Th... th... th—" Carrie looked like she was going to cry. She sucked in a breath and sang on the melody of Brian and Emerald's song, "The pack is coming. Jimmy didn't know. He told them." Carrie struggled to make herself understood through her tears and her stutter. "He... he d... didn't know it was a secret."

Ali dragged Carrie to her feet. "Did Jimmy tell the wolf pack we're wilding?"

Carrie nodded. She couldn't force any more words out. Dove, Harper, Reggie, and all of the Centaurs present rushed out the doors. Other kids took tentative steps toward the door, their eyes still on Carrie and Ali.

"Why didn't you deny it?" Ali asked. Rather stupidly, Laylea thought.

Carrie's words tumbled out. "I tried. I th... thought up an ex... excuse why he misunderstood. But be... be... before I could speak, I... I shifted. So, I j... jus... ran here."

"Were you followed?" Squirt asked.

"N... n... no. Jimmy said you'd b... be in the Fields. He... he d... didn't say where."

Laylea stepped forward. Everyone was acting like the wolf pack was going to win. Like the only safe thing to do was to run away and hide. And that wasn't dumb. Laylea just didn't want the wolves to be in charge of whether anybody else had fun. "So, let's go Wild in Gryphon dorm. Added bonus: whatever that fire suppression system is, it's not in Gryphon."

"What?" Brian's panic attracted Amelia. She hovered near him, not helping. "No. We have to drop it."

"Yeah." Oscar spat the words at Laylea. "You need to get out of here."

"Do we, though?" Squirt looked around at the remaining kids. "I mean, are they gonna spend all night hunting us down, or will they just assume Jimmy's done too much N?"

Ali raised one eyebrow. "They will hunt us down all night. These are wolves."

Squirt raised his eyebrow back at her.

Ali pursed her lips, rubbed a hand along her tatts, and stood tall. "So, let's go to Gryphon dorm and seal the door. Let them waste their night hunting." She threw her head back and howled, quietly. Most of the kids joined in.

Laylea echoed with her own quiet howl and followed Ali.

"No." Oscar swatted Laylea with the blue sweater. "You don't go with us. Get out of here, Lee. Go the other way, hide in the library."

"What are you doing?" Laylea snatched the sweater out of his hands. "This is Ms. Crow's sweater. Show her a little respect, even if you're mad at me. It's not her fault."

"You want to—"

"What is going on in here?" Kids who'd been on their way out the door backed up as Ms. Davies shoved her way into the Lakes. She would have hit some of the kids if Caliban hadn't stopped the doors from swinging wide with her branches. Laylea goggled at the sight of a tree growing so quickly.

She should have been paying more attention to Ms. Davies.

"Lee Woodford." Ms. Davies stalked over to her as if there weren't half a dozen kids between them. "Lee Woodford, why am I not surprised to see you standing here holding contraband as though nothing can ever touch you. You are not getting away with it, this time."

Around the small entryway, kids shivered. Amelia fed on their panic, sending her cold anger out from her amorphous form in waves. Emerald, who lived two steps from fury at all times, straightened as the wave washed through her. Laylea sought Ali's eye. She tried to tell her to get everybody out before the rest of the wolf pack showed up. Ali didn't need to be told. Though she had to pull Emerald with her. Squirt had to drag Brian away, but not because of Amelia's intoxicating anger. Brian was not one to ever abandon his friends. Oscar and KC stayed by her. And Caliban stayed by the door. She grew a root along the base, effectively locking the door from the inside.

"I asked you a question, Lee Woodford."

"What was. . . what was that, Ms. Davies, ma'am?" Laylea hadn't been listening. Did it really matter why Ms. Davies was yelling at her?

"Did you break into Ms. Crow's quarters and steal her sweaters? She never even wears the orange ones. I haven't seen an orange cardigan since her sister died. They are precious to her, and you thought, 'well, she's just an evil old teacher, she doesn't need these sweaters as much as I do,' did you?"

Laylea looked down. She was holding the blue and orange sweaters, one in each hand. It was going to be a hard charge to deny. "I didn't take them. I don't even know where her quarters are. Does she sleep down here?"

"How dare you ask personal questions about a teacher. Did you steal those sweaters?"

"No."

"She did," Oscar suddenly said. "She wanted the sweaters, and she took them. She belongs in detention. You should take her directly to the Special Testing rooms."

Laylea's jaw dropped. Literally. She gaped at Oscar.

"Well, young lady, that is exactly where I am taking you."

Neither Oscar nor KC objected. KC caught Oscar's eyes for a moment, and then she ran away, deeper into the Lakes.

Laylea turned to watch her dash along the shores, shoving willow fronds out of her way until she gave up on going around and dove into one of the largest lakes. Oscar ran for the door.

While Caliban retracted her roots, Oscar looked back to ask, "Are you going to do the paperwork first or take her straight to ST?"

"I'll be taking Woodford to ST and opening an investigation into what other crimes she has committed before filing the paperwork in the Wing. It's good to see you taking an interest. Your father will be proud to hear of it."

Mention of his father made Oscar pause for just an instant, but then he was out the door. Whether it was the crow in Ms. Davies' voice or just the lack of other targets, Laylea didn't know, but Amelia suddenly soared out of her frozen form and dove into the teacher. Ms. Davies wrapped an ice-cold hand around Laylea's bare upper arm and pulled her so hard, Laylea lost her feet. Laylea cried out as her knees slammed into the floor. Ms. Davies let her fall before grabbing her in the same spot on her arm and dragging her up and toward the door. Ms. Davies did not need Amelia's encouragement.

"Stop it!" Laylea cried out, trying to reach the ghost. "Deanna needs you."

Amelia screamed. Ms. Davies shook Laylea, her words barely audible under Amelia's soul-splitting wails. "What did you say?"

"Go to Deanna. Deanna needs you!"

Amelia's tantrum ended in a flash of ice. Then she was gone.

"You're telling me to go to hell? How dare you?" Ms. Davies shook her again, but it didn't have the same force, and her hand sweated around Laylea's arm. "I don't know what you've heard, but I am not Dean Gorse's mare."

Before she could parse that, Laylea's attention was drawn to a deep, slow creaking sound by the door.

Caliban stood there, slowly shifting, her trunk shrinking and her branches sucking in while other twigs grew out of her head, transforming into strands of hair that cascaded down her back. Her voice sounded far away, like wind through a grove. "It's hard to remember all the rules. Have a care, Ms. Davies."

"Stealing is not a rule that might be hard to remember."

"I was referring to the school's decade-long rule against corporal punishment." Caliban's gentle tone camouflaged the rebuke so well that it took Laylea a bit to realize she was talking about Ms. Davies' throwing her around. It took Ms. Davies a minute longer.

The teacher tightened her grip, and her voice shook as she finally got it. "Young lady—"

"I'm at least seventy-nine years old, Ms. Davies. Hardly young. Lee and Ms. Crow are quite close. You should go by the library and verify that Ms. Crow didn't simply loan Lee the sweaters."

Ms. Davies' anger translated into pain for Laylea. But the teacher squeezed too hard. Laylea felt the burn and relaxed, anticipating relief from the pain. Ms. Davies was squeezing as hard as she could. When Laylea's arm turned into a furry leg, Ms. Davies' grip simply tightened, leaving Laylea's puppy body to fall. The sweaters fell to the ground.

Laylea did not immediately follow. Her weight first wrenched her leg from its socket before dragging her from Ms. Davies' hand at the same moment the injury shifted her back to human. She landed hard. Her hip slammed into a protruding root, and she shifted yet again. Ms. Davies merely reached down and lifted her by the fur at the nape of her neck. She snatched the sweaters up in her other hand. Laylea whimpered.

There was nothing mother-comforting in the teacher's grip, or her voice. "Get out of the doorway, Meilissene. You are treading on thin ice here."

"Interesting." Caliban's roots pulled up, making a mess of the packed dirt in front of the door. "You have no proof against Lee, but you're physically harming her in your efforts to get her to detention. While I am clearly and flagrantly breaking the rule against talking back to teachers, and you're just giving me a warning. Is there a chance you know of the wolf pack's prejudice against her and are trying to curry favor?" Caliban smiled in the face of Ms. Davies' shock. Her roots finally transformed into legs, and she stepped aside, clearing the way to the door. "You are a jackal. In the end, wolves only protect wolves. I'll let Dr. Fenn know that you're going to be late for Biology, Lee."

Laylea barked her appreciation. She didn't have biology with Caliban. But Ms. Davies didn't know that.

Ms. Davies shook her. But she also tucked Laylea under her arm, so she wasn't dangling from loose fur anymore. "She won't be in class at all."

"As I'm sure you know, according to the school charter, detention cannot be served at times when it would interfere with classes or presser duties." Caliban leaned against the doors, ostensibly kicking the displaced dirt out of the way. "I'll let him know you're processing and scheduling, and that Lee will arrive in time for our quiz."

"Get out of the way, Meilissene. When I have situated Woodford in Special Testing—"

"Detention, you mean?" Caliban asked.

"I will arrange for a suitability hearing, and you will be found a detriment to LPSS. Pack your bags. You'll be going back to that weevil-infested orchard you came from. You need counseling."

Caliban grinned as she opened the door for Ms. Davies. "I do. I have deep-rooted issues."

Laylea shook with the giggles her canine form couldn't produce. She shot Caliban a grateful look as Ms. Davies stormed out of the Fields. But the worry on Caliban's face made her temporary glee congeal like bad kibble in her gut.

Ms. Davies was taking her to Robby.

Robby wanted to hurt her.

31

*T*he cold corridors of LPSS echoed with Ms. Davies' footsteps as she stormed through them with Laylea under her arm. There was nothing Laylea could do. Her tail kept tucking up under herself in fear, but it would touch Ms. Davies' arm and retreat. She tried to focus on how to save herself but couldn't pull her mind from her tail. Base canine terror took over. She cringed and couldn't keep back a whimper when Ms. Davies slammed the outer door to ST open.

"Stop shivering. It's just detention." Ms. Davies shook her. "And be quiet. Do you want the other kids to know what a coward you are?"

Laylea sucked in her breath and squeezed her eyes closed. But she couldn't stop. Her best friends had abandoned her, and they knew that creepy Robby wanted her in detention for his own purposes. Dee had taken her assignment away, renewing her suspension from Team Wyrdos. Plus, Brock was dead and wanted her the same.

Ms. Davies shook her again. She removed the hand supporting Laylea's haunches and dangled her as she shook. Laylea flailed, adrenaline flooding her body. She flashed back to when Walter, her evil scientist father, had carried her like this. Remembered anger chased away her fear, and she opened her eyes, a growl unwisely escaping her control.

From wisps of ectoplasm to solid, burning figures, ghosts in gas masks filled the lobby of ST. The tall girl and her three constant companions blocked the doorway to the first room of ST. Ms. Davies didn't see them. She held Laylea dangling in front of her as she walked into them to push through the door into the inner room. Laylea squeezed her eyes shut again and held her breath. Still, her nose wrinkled at the stinging smell of all the different chemicals that killed these kids. One scent rose above the others, creeping through her sinus cavities and deep into the memory centers of her brain. She recalled a gray haze filling a tiny closet which was also filled with dead children. It was the smell of the smoke that Dr. Brock had used to try to kill her. Her eyes popped open just as Ms. Davies reached through the amorphous figure of the tiger girl to sweep aside the privacy curtain.

A deafening cry went up from the ghosts. Laylea thought she might shift from the pain in her head. The noise stood in stark contrast to the calm students arranged quietly around tall tables fitting together pieces of tubing. They were assembling the pieces for devices similar to the one Robby had installed over the girls' podroom door in Mer dorm.

Ms. Davies barely glanced around the room before demanding, of no one in particular, "Where is Robby?"

Nearly all the kids stopped their work and looked over. Nobody responded.

"I asked a question. Who is in charge here?" Ms. Davies shook Laylea to emphasize her question.

Another moment of stunned confusion swept through the ranks as the kids looked at each other for direction. A clatter sounded from near the doorway to the inner sanctum of ST. Then Big Mo stepped away from the machine on the opposite side of the room that Robby had called the central distributor. "Robby isn't here, Ms. Davies. He left me in charge while he's gone."

"Where did he go?"

"Uh, I'm not sure, Ms. Davies. He generally doesn't tell us things like that. Would you like to set Lee down?" Big Mo jogged over to a table near the curtained entrance and shoved kids out of the way to clear a spot. When Ms. Davies didn't move, he physically took Laylea from the teacher and set her on the table. Laylea wanted to breathe a sigh of relief, but she didn't dare suck air into her lungs. Ghosts surrounded the kids, enveloped them. Some lay midair, as if still reclined on the medical chairs that used to fill this space. Some shot through the air, fighting demons Laylea couldn't see. Some attacked Laylea herself, trying to shove her off the table or spirit her away to join them. None had moved her yet, but that didn't mean that one of them wouldn't figure out how to interact with the living world. All of the ghosts wailed. She pinned her ears back, crouched low on the table, and held her breath.

One living kid Laylea couldn't see asked, "Didn't Robby say he was going to the Fields?"

"No. I thought it was a dorm, to fix some system malfunction." Theresa contradicted the other kid.

"He went to the kitchen to get some ginger ale for Benny." Griff didn't sound like he was making fun of Benny, but everyone in detention laughed and turned to look at Benny, awkwardly holding a piece of fabric up against one of the tables.

The turtle shifter blushed, but he responded with his own suggestion. "Didn't he go to see Dean Gorse?"

"No," Rehyan, standing, as usual, with one leg propped up against the other, shouted too loudly from the other side of the room. "Gorse is meeting with teachers today to give out their bonuses. Robby isn't a teacher."

Ms. Davies' pinched frown melted as one eyebrow rose. "It doesn't matter. I'll leave Woodford with you." She slammed the sweaters onto the table beside Laylea. "Tell Robby that she is to serve one hundred hours of detention. If he needs clarification, I'll be in the Wing. Filling out paperwork."

That last bit was too much detail. When adults gave too much detail, especially an adult who had as much disdain for kids as Ms. Davies, it meant they were lying. She was going to see if she was getting a bonus.

"Yes, ma'am." Big Mo nodded crisply, nearly saluting, the very model of a perfect student.

As Ms. Davies swept back through the privacy curtain and the army of too-young ghosts, the werewolf scooped Laylea from the table and headed for the inner door. "We'll just have you wait for Robby inside."

Dozens of ghosts swarmed Big Mo. A dozen more attempted to block the inner door. The werewolf cried out and slapped a hand to his neck so quickly that Laylea nearly fell.

Ms. Davies half-turned in the doorway. "Is there a problem?"

Big Mo laughed, but it was a strained sound. "No, ma'am. Stubbed my toe."

"Very well."

The teacher left. Big Mo backed away from the inner door. Despite the crush of ghosts, the pressure in the room released like someone opening a soda bottle. Kids slumped. Benny dropped his fabric. Big Mo loosened his grip on Laylea to wipe blood from his neck. His ghost wound had reopened. Laylea wanted to help him, but she wasn't going to stay and find out what Robby wanted with her. She had to get away from the gas masks before they figured out how to touch her. And even though she liked Big Mo, he was a werewolf, and a Sphinx werewolf at that. She couldn't trust that he wouldn't turn her over to the pack for inventing non-wolf wilding.

She leapt from his arms to the nearest table, dashed through the mess of tools and tubing and electronics, hopped to a tall chair and from there to the floor. The curtained platform holding Robby's central distributor and hiding the secret passageway into the storage caves lay two strides away when an unexpected voice stopped her in her tracks.

"Hold on. We have to take these with us."

Laylea spun to see KC grab the sweaters from where Ms. Davies had tossed them. "Can't leave proof for Robby to find when he comes back from the dining hall."

Laylea barked.

The ghosts still swirled around the tables, but they gave KC space to pass. Laylea wanted to ask how she'd gotten there. KC dropped to her belly and began backing under the machine platform, stuffing one sweater into the top of her jumpsuit.

"Thanks, guys. Big Mo, you were great. And that was genius, Benny. Come on, Lee. Let's go." KC's head disappeared behind the curtains.

KC was too big to fit through the doggy door into the caves. What was her plan? Laylea looked around the room. Dozens of kids, dead and alive, urged her to follow KC. So, she did. She skittered under the platform to find a fluffy white wolf with black markings holding Ms. Crow's blue sweater in her teeth. Laylea's tail popped up and wagged against the curtain.

Big Mo's voice drew closer. "Fido, get going." A hand shoved her farther under the platform, and KC swiped at Laylea with a paw, sliding her even closer to the hidden doggy door.

It was the thought of Big Mo, a wolf, peering under the platform and seeing that KC wasn't a coyote that got Laylea moving. She galloped through the flap and turned to see KC squeezing through right behind her. The small passageway fluffed the orange fur behind her ears, making her look crazy. The sweater in her teeth didn't help. But Laylea sang out a quiet trill of joy at seeing her friend in wolf form. It was only the second time she had.

And with barely a shiver of disruption to the universe, KC the girl sat there in the darkness on her butt, the sweater still hanging from her human teeth. She yanked it out. "I told Robby there were kids messing with his installation in the kitchen. If we hurry, we can get the sweaters back to Ms. Crow and hide in Mer dorm without him or the wolves finding us. Come on."

KC rolled to her feet and led the way, not toward the storage cave holding all the students' belongings but farther down the thin alleyway. Laylea barked. When KC looked, Laylea trotted a few steps in the right direction.

"No, we're not going out that way. Trust me."

Laylea tilted her head.

"Hey," KC pulled her compass from her pocket and grinned. "Turns out I've learned something in NavTech."

Without another word, she turned and continued jogging deeper into the dark alley. Laylea followed.

32

Most of the people that Laylea knew lived in darkness. The kids at LPSS knew nothing of magic or the wyrdos in the world that weren't shifters. Most of the wyrdos didn't know about Chicago's complex shifter society and their deadly politics. Neither group was aware that there was an evil Consortium building super soldiers and torturing humans and animals to do it. Average, ungifted humans had no idea about any of it.

As she followed KC through the deep structural underground beneath the Lincoln Park Shifter School, navigating around the ten-foot-round columns and pools and roots, Laylea considered whether she was cursed or lucky to be aware of all the madness in the world. What made it visible to her? Her enchanted lizard and KC's crane allowed them to see the sparkling static of residual magic coating every surface of this dark, low-ceilinged sub-sub-basement. Did she carry some lizard in her genes that allowed her to see brownies and shifters and boogeymen and super soldiers and ghosts while the rest of the world stumbled around in darkness?

"Okay, we're past the Fields now." KC looked up from her compass to grin back at Laylea. "Start looking around for stairs. You just know there has to be a way up into the library."

She'd thought KC had abandoned her. While Laylea was being dragged off to detention, where Robby wanted her, KC had run away and leapt into a pool, just so she could race through this magic-soaked underworld and chase Robby out of ST before Ms. Davies and Laylea got there. KC deserved to have all the knowledge Laylea was saddled with. She'd do some good with it, rather than repeatedly making herself a target for murderous madmen, ghosts, and wolves.

A spray of shimmering magic caught Laylea's eye off to the left ahead of them. It rose into the ceiling at an angle rather than straight up like the columns. She barked and trotted away in that direction. She hadn't gone far when something hit her in the head. It didn't hurt that badly. It didn't really hurt at all. But it was apparently the final straw for her frazzled nerves. The now familiar shifting burn exploded through her body and left her lying naked in a sprawl on the cold ground. The thing that had hit her skittered to a stop just out of her reach. It was the dibs drive ID bracelet DJ Delcampo had sent to his sister.

"Here." KC pulled a soft, 1930s-style jumpsuit from inside her own jumpsuit and held it out. She worked the ID bracelet back onto her wrist as Laylea pulled the clothes on, then picked both sweaters up from the ground and tossed one to Laylea. "We'll get Ms. Crow's sweaters back to her so Ms. Davies has no evidence and then go hide you in the dorm."

"Sure." Laylea pushed to her feet and headed for the glow, which was clearly stairs from this close. "As long as we don't run into Robby, Ms. Davies, Dean Gorse, or any of the wolves, we'll be fine."

KC laughed, jogging beside Laylea to reach the stairs faster. "Don't forget about the ghosts."

Laylea shivered. "I haven't seen Amelia since I sent her to Deanna to get her out of Ms. Davies. The gas masks were busy in ST. We might be safe from them for a little while."

"Do you think ST is where they all died?" KC climbed the rickety stairs with complete faith.

Laylea followed more delicately. "They are all wearing gas masks.

Durrah used gas masks in his medical experiments, and Robby uses them to protect kids from the chemicals they're using."

"Maybe." KC stopped when she reached the door in the ceiling at the top of the stairs. She grunted as she pushed against it. "Maybe they think that ST isn't over because there are still kids in gas masks in those rooms."

Laylea reached up and released a catch on one edge of the door. It flew open.

"Thanks." KC invited Laylea to climb up into a darkness that had no sparkling magic residue to light the way. "Maybe they want you to end ST."

Laylea had thought the same thing. But since she'd shut down ST by exposing Dr. Durrah last fall, she didn't know what else she was supposed to do. She let the question go and turned to help KC up into the dark tunnel. "Which way, now, navigator?"

Instead of answering, KC shifted. Reality folded around her until her intelligent brown eyes shone out of a furry face. She trotted over, licked Laylea's face, and then dashed away down the tunnel. A moment later, she returned and ran off in the other direction. A moment after that, she barked a deep woof and then called out, "There's a door over here."

Laylea hopped to her feet and jogged in that direction. She reached KC just as dim, late afternoon light flooded the tunnel from the opening door. The door screeched in protest and then went silent.

KC grimaced at Laylea. "Apparently, you have to lift as you open."

Laylea put her finger to her lips. They still didn't know what lay on the other side of this door. They held still and listened, but there was no reaction on the other side to the racket. KC shrugged at her and lifted the door open a little farther. Even as her eyes adjusted to the sudden brightness, Laylea could see layers of carpets outside the door. They'd found the library. She grinned at KC and gave her a thumbs up before peeking out to see if there was anybody in the aisle.

"It's clear," she whispered and slipped through the thin crack.

KC followed. It was harder to lift the door to close it from the outside. The latch was hidden under a chair rail that was also the only place to hold the door. The click of the latch connecting seemed to bounce off the bookshelves and echo into the library, but still, nobody came to see what was going on.

KC led the way out of the stacks. Laylea turned to see the expected Arachne tapestry hanging on the wall. Had Ms. Crow and Ms. Lagat been in the underground? Where else did that tunnel lead?

They rushed through the fairly empty library to the front desk. Ms. Crow stood behind the check-in counter watching Brenda scanning through three books on the archive desk back by the enclosed stacks. Laylea had to clear her throat to get Ms. Crow's attention.

"Hi, ladies. Aren't you supposed to be in Fields?"

"We've been studying." KC set the orange sweater on the counter without looking at it. Laylea shook a little dirt off of the blue one before she set it up beside the orange one.

Ms. Crow looked down at the sweaters and then back up at them. "Ali's not using them?"

"Ali?" KC asked, her eyes wide and innocent. "Using what? Hey, those are pretty sweaters. Where did they come from?"

Ms. Crow tilted her head just a little. Laylea almost laughed at the look on her face. After a moment, she murmured, "mm hm" and tossed the sweaters under the counter. "Don't be late for dinner."

KC started to drag Laylea away. Before she went, Laylea said, "You might need to look at Big Mo's neck again."

Brenda looked over from her books. "You talking to me?"

"No. We weren't here." KC put both her arms around Laylea and pushed her to the door.

Ms. Crow called after them, "I'll check on him."

The two tried to keep a casual pace in the halls. It was awkward with both of them listening for any sound of pursuit or the wolf pack. KC peered around turns and down side corridors before letting Laylea join her. They would have looked guilty to anybody they ran into. It was good they didn't run into anybody.

They reached the dining hall corridor which splintered out into the individual dorm passageways before they heard anything but their own footsteps.

"I delivered Lee Woodford to detention." Ms. Davies' voice floated out between the crack in the dining hall doors.

KC and Laylea froze, staring at each other.

"Good." Robby's barked response was followed by the sound of a hand slapping on the door. KC and Laylea tripped over each other trying to back away down the corridor to the last turning. They nearly ran into Ms. Crow. The librarian rushed past them with no apology or even a word of acknowledgment.

Ms. Davies' voice grew louder as one of the doors started to open. "You'll tell Enforcer Denier who delivered her." It wasn't quite a question.

They didn't hear Robby's answer because Ms. Crow had reached the magnificent doors. She planted one hand on each, pushing them closed. Sounds of protest were muffled by the thick wood. KC shot a desperate look at Laylea, and then the two of them reversed direction again and barreled past Ms. Crow, racing for the turning to Mer dorm. They'd just made it when they heard Ms. Crow's awkward apologies. They froze, pressed up against the stone, trying to hold their breaths, so Ms. Davies and Robby wouldn't hear them. Though neither responded to her, Ms. Crow continued apologizing over and over as their voices receded into the distance.

Laylea whispered, "What was that?"

"That was close," KC whispered back, "is what that was. Come on, let's not push our luck."

She turned, just as a voice farther down toward the junction between Mer and Gryphon called out, "Robby!"

They were caught. Laylea went to run past the voice. She could escape out through Gryphon to the zoo and disappear for a while, or just leave school altogether, since there was no reason for her to be there now that they knew B. Gorshkov wasn't there. But then she saw the speaker's face just as he saw them. It was DJ Delcampo.

33

"*R*obby, hold up. Oof." DJ Delcampo chuckled as he and KC ran into each other. Laylea imagined she could see KC's hackles shoot up. Certainly, every muscle in her friend's body tensed. KC sucked in a breath, and it was like she had taken all the air from the corridor.

It took KC's brother a moment longer to recognize his sister. When he did, DJ's pupils shot wide, and he barely breathed the word, "Shit" before he grabbed his sister in a hyper-masculine, two-handed handshake. He held onto her as he babbled, "So sorry about that. Nice to see someone concerned about getting to class on time. Don't worry about running into me. I'm not hurt. Don't want to get in your way."

KC wrenched her hand out of his. Her ID bracelet caught on DJ's armpadd and snapped back against her arm with a sharp slap. She spared an instant to glare at Laylea, nearly spitting at her, "You told him I'm here? How could you?" Then she was gone, tripping past Laylea and tearing down the corridor, away from the dorm. She took the corner so fast she nearly fell.

DJ's face crumpled in disappointment. For a moment, he looked like he might apologize to Laylea, but all he said was, "Go."

She hesitated. From just around the corner, they heard Robby's obsequious tones crooning, "It can't be all that bad, gorgeous. Come on, you know you'd be so much prettier if you smiled."

"Go." DJ shoved her toward the Mer tunnel.

Laylea ran.

The double doors loomed before her, making her feel small. The Mers had kept them closed ever since Denier's visit. Laylea had never had to open the way by herself before. The corridor stood only six feet high where the doors blocked the way. But there was something in the way the dark wood was carved that made them feel like a castle entrance. Laylea reached for the forged iron door handle on the left. Her hand shook so violently that she couldn't find the slots for her fingers. She pushed her head against the door and tried to peer down to see the smooth slots in the iron but found that her vision was blurred by tears.

"Hurry," DJ hissed at her from where he stood poised to head around the corner.

She gave up on the human latch and dropped to her knees to lift up on the iron kickplate at the base of the left door. A small panel popped out of the wood. Laylea pushed the tail of a carved mermaid at the bottom of the panel to release the secondary catch. Her sweaty fingers slipped on the panel, but she barely needed to open it any further to fit through. She made sure to push it fully closed from the inside of the Mer tunnel.

Once safely inside, Laylea slumped against the rough wood. Her knees gave way, and she found herself on the ground, sobbing. KC would never believe Laylea hadn't told DJ where to find her. KC hated her family, and now she hated Laylea, too.

Oscar hated Laylea so much he'd thrown her to Ms. Davies. She *had* asked about his sister. Amelia had nearly frozen the courtyard when she did. If it weren't for the fire, kids would have gotten hurt. Was Oscar really willing to sacrifice other people just so he could talk to his dead sister?

Laylea pushed herself to her feet, propelled by the anger coursing through her veins. She slammed a palm against the door, willing DJ and Robby on the other side to just go away. What did she ever do to Robby? What had she ever done to the wolves? They wanted her dead, that was more clear than ever. But Ms. Davies had said that she wanted credit with Denier for delivering Laylea. Denier was the reason Robby wanted her in detention. Denier was the reason the wolves were after her. What had she ever done to him?

Ice crushed her heart. Denier ran the sleep labs. Did he know that Laylea had found them and was investigating them? Did he know that she knew there was a connection between him and the labs and N? She had to get out. She had to hide. Her feet started moving as her head made plans. Laylea wasn't a hundred percent in charge of either.

The Wyrdos didn't need her here anymore since Gorshkov was dead. They'd told her to stand down, even expelled her from the team. She didn't need to stay for them. Hell, the Wyrdos were all grownups and gods. It was ridiculous that she had ever thought that she, a kid, a shifter who couldn't control herself, could help them stop a drug epidemic. She was ridiculous. She was stupid.

She'd pack her things, climb out through Gryphon dorm, and go say goodbye to her brother. Then she'd make her way back west to the family's deep woods cabin. Only, no, she couldn't risk going to see her brother. If Denier was having her followed, he'd find out about Bailey and kidnap him to get to her. And then Bailey's temper would set his magic free, and who knew what might happen then. She couldn't risk it. She couldn't see Bailey. She'd have to just get away, and then—

She froze at the small threshold separating their dorm from the tunnel. A bouncy tune played on the deadly still air of the courtyard. Laylea caught her breath. She'd been so deep in her thoughts she hadn't heard the music or the angry voices. She had to pay better attention, or she'd get herself killed.

"Like you're one to talk." Jimmy leaned against a willow at the back of the underground grove at the edge of the freshwater pool. His stringy blond hair obscured his face just like the willow fronds obscured him and his companion. Impossibly, he looked thinner than the last time she'd seen him. He held a ukulele, strumming a cheery tune at odds with his words. The courtyard was abandoned except for him and whoever he was arguing with. "At least I admit I do drugs because I'm too chicken to kill myself."

Laylea plastered her hands over her mouth to keep herself from crying out. She heard a perfunctory denial from a figure she couldn't see.

Jimmy didn't let the person finish their sentence. "Oh, listen to that. The little Mer wolf disagreed with something. Be still, my heart."

The short, pigtailed figure of Carrie stepped out of the shadows to face Jimmy. Her voice shook more than usual. "You d... don't know what you're t... t... talking about. It's the eh... N talking."

"No. N makes everything clear. I know you." Jimmy sobered for a moment. He pushed off the tree and backed Carrie out from under its draping branches. "You use your wolf — your 'inability' to shift — to avoid taking responsibility for anything. You don't agree with the pack any more than I do." He threw his head back in a laugh, strumming some sour chords before fingerpicking the same melody Brian sang at Carrie in the Lakes. He looked down at his fingers as if they belonged to someone else.

"Th. . . they're the p... p... pack. You have to d... do what they say."

Jimmy looked up. His hair fell clear of his face, revealing eyes that scared Laylea. He went on as if he hadn't heard Carrie. "Instead of standing up to them, you shift and oh no, boo hoo, poor little helpless Carrie who *would* say something if she only wasn't a wolf. You're not a wolf. You're chicken. Bawk bawk." After squawking at Carrie, Jimmy bent double in a fit of laughter, tripped forward a few steps, and fell sideways into the freshwater pool. The ukulele flew out of his hands and spun in the air before splashing down, itself.

Carrie waited until he surfaced. Her stutter wasn't helped by her sobs. "At least I would n... never rat on my fff... f... friends."

"No." Jimmy splashed water at the girl. "But you'd never rat on your enemies, either. You'd just shift, so no one can blame you." He slid under the surface with his last words.

Carrie didn't have anything to say to that. She let her tears win and ran off into the girls' podroom.

Laylea followed her friend, though she kept one eye on the pool.

Jimmy didn't resurface. The clacking of the beaded doorway in the podroom muffled Carrie's sobs. No sound came from the freshwater pond.

Another wave of ice raced through Laylea's veins. She changed her mind and dashed to the side of the pond. Ripples marred the surface, showing where Jimmy had gone under. Smaller circles expanded from the spot where the ukulele had taken its dive. They encountered the ripples from Jimmy and both were distorted.

Laylea shook her head clear. She tried to assess the situation. Jimmy had been under for half a minute. An average person could generally hold their breath for two minutes. Jimmy was high. He wanted to die. Laylea had no idea how deep the pond was. She'd never been in it. She'd never been in any body of water as a human. She didn't know how to swim.

A wave of panic scattered Laylea's assessment. She couldn't see clearly, couldn't think clearly, couldn't hear anything but her pounding heart. Tears poured, unbidden, down her cheeks as she tried to suck a breath into her tight lungs. Hair stood up all over her body and a shiver ran through her.

She felt like a girl made of ice. An instant later, she knew she was a mother getting revenge for her daughter. Her daughter. Her daughter she couldn't find in the shadow world, who wouldn't wake up in the solid world. Her daughter who was caught in limbo, alive but not living, because her father sold her away.

Laylea looked down at the pool but saw a hospital bed and Deanna Gorshkov's young face framed with white hair, tubes running under the sheets. Her heart monitor beat steadily, as it had since Gorshkov abandoned her.

34

No. This wasn't right. She was not Amelia. She was not at Deanna's bedside. Laylea pushed the smell of antiseptic from her, reaching for her therapeutic memory of airplane fuel and fresh dirt. Slowly, it came to her. Distantly, the sound of her father's voice clawed through the icy panic trapping her. To keep himself sane, her father sang a song her mother had written.

Laylea sang in a tiny voice.

"I will not kill another soul today.

"His life is in my hands, and I will not throw it away."

She felt her own heart beating, her own living heat surrounded her. She struggled to murmur, "I am Laylea."

Amelia threw her head back and screamed. Waves of ethereal ice soared through the lab and struck the technician adjusting settings on another sleeper's machines.

Another sleeper. The sounds were wrong. Laylea leaned into Amelia's hearing. She picked up the faint, arrhythmic cacophony of all the other heart monitors tolling their useless reports.

"Hear that, Amelia. You are not alone."

The panic receded, as did the vision of the sleep lab. Laylea pushed but couldn't free herself from the grieving ghost. She could see the pond growing smooth as the ripples faded.

She begged, "Please, let me go. Let me save my friend."

"Find Bert!" Amelia's order blew back the branches of the willow, its weeping fronds disturbing the water and sending ripples dancing across the surface again. The little waves cracked the ice forming on the water.

Laylea knew she couldn't lie. She was enveloped by Amelia. Amelia would know. She just wasn't sure Amelia would react any better to the truth, but she spoke it. "Bert is gone."

"He is here!" The dorm courtyard flashed into clarity. The sleep lab remained linked to them, but distantly.

Laylea offered a compromise. "If you let me save my friend, I will find Bert's ghost."

"Bert Gorshkov is alive."

"He's not." Laylea pushed against Amelia's hold. "He died years ago."

"Bert Gorshkov is alive and in this school." Leaves fell from the willow and other trees, shattering into ice crystals as they hit the grass. "Find him."

Fed up with this dead woman, fed up with the wolves and her friends and this whole mess, Laylea stomped her foot. "I am not going to find anyone unless you let me save my friend."

"Save my daughter." Leaves shattered around the courtyard.

"No."

"Save my daughter!" The pond flash froze, frost barring any chance of seeing into the water.

"No!" Laylea stomped again. Her foot came down at the edge of the water. "I will save Jimmy, who is, right now, drowning in this pond!"

"You came here to save Deanna!"

A rush of clarity fired all the sparks in Laylea's mind. Amelia was right. She had come to save Deanna and Oscar's N-addicted mother. She didn't come because the Wyrdos told her to. She came back to school to save everyone like Jimmy. That was why she was searching for Bert Gorshkov.

"I did." She stopped pushing and let her words sink in. When the cold winds calmed, she said, "And that boy down in the water has the answer."

Amelia heard her loud and clear. She released Laylea. With an ear-splitting screech and one last blast of arctic air, Amelia released Laylea right into the pond. The pressure of Amelia's push sent Laylea crashing through the ice and deep down into the water.

Laylea had an idea that shores descended into ponds gradually, but that was not the case with this one. The edge dropped precipitously into a pool of water that was larger than the width of the bank. Like everything else in the shifter school, there was more under the surface than a student could see just from looking. Laylea brushed past true fish and thick, underwater grasses as she fell deeper, her mind struggling to make sense of the swirling world around her. She spun and tossed through the water until she slammed into another person.

She struggled to grab any part of Jimmy, but her chaotic spinning dragged her away into the swirling wet. Whether down or up, she couldn't tell. Blackness closed in, tunneling her vision and confirming that her eyes were open and that there was a deeper black than the freezing, tumbling water.

Light burst through that blackness as pain shot through her scalp. Her head snapped forward. Water rushed by her in one direction. Her hair. It was her hair that hurt. Someone was pulling her by her hair. She tried to reach up and free herself. She got a heel to the back of her hand for her trouble.

When she finally broke the surface, instinct, more than anything else, sucked air into her lungs. Jimmy pulled himself out of the water and dragged her up over the sharp edge. She lay there, gasping, one hand clutching at Jimmy's arm to keep him from slipping back into the pond. His arm felt like it was on fire.

"You're burning up!" She turned to examine his face.

"You're frozen." He ran a hand through her hair. It crackled. Ice fell around Laylea.

Jimmy only felt hot because Amelia had frozen Laylea. And he wasn't breathing hard at all, whereas she was still struggling to get her fear under control. If she had inhaled water, as she almost did, her body would have shifted to save her. But a dog couldn't breathe underwater either. Shifting would not have saved her. She could have died.

"Your hair is so pretty." Jimmy ran his fingers through the sopping mess dripping on Laylea's shoulders. He didn't sound suicidal. He sounded giddy.

She reached up to help him sluice the sleet and ice from her short blond hair. They worked on it for a full minute before she found a way to ask if he was high without sounding judgmental. She went with a joke. "Does N allow you to breathe underwater?"

"Ha." Jimmy laughed quietly for a moment before he let her hair slip from his fingers, his hands dropping to lay limply in his lap. "I grew up in the ocean. Scuba diving is better than any drug." It seemed like Jimmy was disappearing into his memories, but then he sat up. His eyes flashed. The vague smile faded into a definite frown. "I didn't want the N. Jase made me take it. He hid it in a piece of fudge."

"Yeah, that sounds like Jase."

"Weren't you going to stop N?"

"I was trying. But all my leads are dead."

"But," Jimmy scrunched his face like he couldn't keep his thoughts in order. He shook his head. Laylea's eyes were caught by his fingers strumming an imaginary chord on an imaginary instrument. "You can talk to the dead."

"Yeah, but—" Laylea wasn't sure what she'd been about to say. Jimmy was right. She could talk to the dead. It wasn't fun, but what did that matter in the face of an epidemic? Ms. Crow knew something about ghosts. Maybe she could help Laylea find Bert Gorshkov.

She pushed herself to her feet and pulled Jimmy with her. "Come on. You're coming with me. I'm not leaving you alone."

"Can I go watch the spider-girl?"

"I don't know who that is. How's the library sound, instead?"

"That's where she is." Jimmy's morose features spread into a smile.

Laylea paused at the threshold to glance back at the doorway to the girls' podroom. She'd like to check on Carrie. What Jimmy said had hit the werewolf hard. What could Laylea tell her, though? Maybe this was one of those things the girl had to work out for herself.

"I'm gonna make Jase pay." Jimmy wrapped an arm around Laylea's back.

She wrapped an arm around him and dripped with him over the grass to the entrance. "Or just avoid him and never eat anything he offers you?"

"That sounds easier," he agreed.

They reached the magnificent double doors. Jimmy flicked a piece of molding around the handle, and the entire lower right panel slid aside like a pocket door. He climbed through first and then helped her, even though she was much smaller than him. Once they were both outside, he twisted a bolt on a hinge and the panel closed.

Laylea peeked around corners and kept her head down. Jimmy stumbled along beside her, giggling and sobbing in turns. They stopped only once, at a cupboard beside the fire door entrance to the Mod Tech corridor. Laylea grabbed a dry jumpsuit at random and changed, ordering Jimmy to do the same. Her jumpsuit was way too big for her tiny body, but she didn't take the time to find a better fit. She rolled up the legs as Jimmy tossed their wet uniforms into the used bin, and then they moved on.

Miraculously, they reached the library without running into anybody. The library itself held more students than Laylea had ever seen in there at once. A hundred heads turned their way as the door fell shut behind them. Jimmy took no notice. He took the lead from Laylea, pulling her to a trio of comfy chairs arranged in a loose semi-circle at the end of one row of shelves.

"Is the spider-girl here?" Laylea glanced at the three Centaur girls in the chairs. Leda and Theresa sat on either side of Riva, running their fingers through her fur and giggling. None of the three were spider shifters, or, as they called themselves, wereachnids.

Jimmy didn't respond. Laylea looked to see him staring across the room at the tapestry of Arachne and the azure egg. "Oh."

Riva shifted from her sloth and climbed out of the middle chair. "Hey, Jimmy, you want to sit here?"

Jimmy enfolded Riva in a hug that looked like it was going to last a while. The girl waved Laylea away, mouthing something she couldn't understand before she shifted back into her cuddly sloth.

Leda murmured at Laylea as she collected the pile of pillows from Riva's chair to make room, "We've got him. You should go hide."

"Somewhere else." Theresa said it so quietly a normal human wouldn't have been able hear her.

Laylea glanced around the unusually crowded and quiet library. Everyone was either openly or surreptitiously staring at her. She backed away. The rugs felt soft and safe on her bare feet. Changing uniforms had helped, but her wet hair gave her the shivers as she walked back to the front desk where Brenda stood, engrossed in her deskpadd.

"Hey, where's Ms. Crow?" she asked.

"Ms. Crow went to the Fields a while ago. You don't want to go there. You want to go to your precious little alcove and smooth KC's hackles down. She stormed in here and has been back there, muttering to herself and bothering everybody. Would you go get her and hide from the wolf pack somewhere else, please?"

"Thanks, Brenda." Laylea headed for the door.

"Your alcove is the other way," Brenda called out.

Laylea turned to shoot a grimace at her. Suddenly, the library door flew open and smacked her in the side of her head. As Laylea fell backwards in a tangle of too-big jumpsuit, she saw Jase Batka striding into the library. The one werewolf she knew might actually kill her.

35

*J*ase Batka glanced at the check-out counter. Apparently assuming there were no teachers around, or not caring if there were, he yelled in a voice too loud to be muffled by the carpets and tapestries and books, "Where's Fido?"

Laylea hit the carpet just as he yelled, so he didn't hear the tiny cry she yelped into the cotton suddenly draped over her furry face. And she didn't wait for anybody to answer the wolf. She wriggled out of the mess of blue fabric and dashed out the doors before they could close.

The corridor was empty. Taking no chances, she galloped along the cold stone floor, every sense alert for the next danger, be it wolf, ghost, or faculty.

She made it to the Fields door without seeing anybody at all. The doorknob loomed far over her head, taunting her. Shifting had probably saved her from a bloody nose, but if she just sat out here in the corridor, she was sure to be found by the wolves or Ms. Davies or Robby, and who knew what would happen to her then. Her heart pounded like she'd just swallowed sligh nut.

Her mind, too, raced as crazily as if she'd been poisoned. If the wolves didn't kill her, they'd hand her over to Denier, who would drag her out of the school. Walter would find her, and he would take her apart to see how she worked. She'd never see her parents again. There would be nobody to protect Bailey from himself, and he'd turn into the dark witch she'd feared every day since leaving Foothills. A dark Bailey could destroy the city. He'd burn it down more successfully than the phoenix had. Laylea whimpered, the noise squeezed out by a feeling of hopelessness that froze her colder than Amelia ever could.

Laylea spun around, searching the empty hallway. There was nothing she could use. Just stone walls and stone floor in all directions.

Cold, hard stone. It gave her an idea.

She sat and sucked in a breath, considering a plan. This was nuts. This was all nuts. But she was the only one who could talk to the ghosts, find Bert Gorshkov, and stop whatever he'd started that had caused the N epidemic in the city. She had no choice. She scooted back until her tail was squeezed against one wall, her claws digging into a crack in the floor.

She chanted her parents' song. *I will not kill another soul today.* Except she very well might. *My life is in my hands, and I will not throw it away.* She ran as hard as she could across the short distance and bashed her head into the wall.

A flash of pain burst in her head the instant before the familiar burn shot through her entire furry and then fleshy body. The hard stone felt blissfully cold beneath her bare skin. She didn't let herself revel in it. She shot for the doorknob and slipped inside the Fields.

Laylea's human senses were not quite up to canine par, but she still sucked in a deep breath as the smell of the rich, magically-built forest washed over her. Her toes curled in the mossy ground, and her whole body relaxed at the feeling of being outside, no matter how loudly her brain screamed that it was an illusion. She dashed from tree to tree, using extra caution when she had to cross the river. There was nowhere to hide on the earthen bridge. The Fields appeared to be abandoned. At least, Laylea didn't encounter anyone. She slipped through the little tunnel leading to the Farms and stopped cold when she spotted Ms. Crow.

Ms. Crow knelt by the river. She'd pushed up the sleeves of her blue sweater, but dirt still stained the fabric. Her eyes focused on a swirl in the water. Her lips moved as if she were speaking, but even Laylea's enhanced hearing couldn't catch the words. Tendrils of deep brown hair had escaped her bun and floated around her face. They tangled in the earpieces of her glasses. Smudges decorated the belly of her pale blue overalls like she'd wiped her hands there without thinking. Her feet were bare, bent toes white where she sat on her heels. Her shoes, sensible white canvas sneakers, sat on a bridge, safe from the dirt and grass and myriad stain risks in the rows of vegetables. The bottoms of Ms. Crow's feet blackened the butt of her outfit.

A necklace Laylea had never seen before dangled from Ms. Crow's neck. A single strand of gold chain descended from a choker. A rough blue-and-orange stone had been worked into the metal halfway to the matte black pendant at the end of the chain. The pendant swung as Ms. Crow swayed over the water. The ripples on the surface mimicked the jewelry's motion.

Laylea didn't mean to move. She felt like she was trespassing, like when she trotted in on her parents cuddling on the couch back home in Foothills. But her feet drew her forward to see the pendant more clearly. A leaf crackled beneath her just as Dizzy soared overhead, her caw echoing through the tunnel.

Ms. Crow looked up. She snatched her hands into herself as though the water had burned her. She stuffed the pendant back into hiding, but not before Laylea saw it was shaped like an hourglass.

"Laylea." Ms. Crow appeared to wipe loose hairs from her face as she stood. She left a smear of mud under one eye. "Do you need me?"

Laylea stepped forward. Dizzy circled Ms. Crow, cawing and swooping so close, Ms. Crow's hair fluttered in the wind from her wings. Ms. Crow swiped at her hair again, leaving another smear of mud on her forehead. She moved to pull her blue sweater closer around herself.

Laylea called out to stop her, "No." She sighed as a palm print of mud transferred to the sweater. "I mean, yes, I'm here to see you. You have mud on your hand, Ms. Crow."

The librarian looked down at her hands, still holding her sweater like a security blanket. "Oh, dear." She smiled vaguely and murmured, "I was washing my hands."

Laylea crossed to her and sat cross-legged on the bank. Ms. Crow knelt again. Dizzy perched on Laylea's knee, tilting her head at the water swirling around Ms. Crow's hands.

"You know ghosts are real." Laylea paused, almost as if waiting for Ms. Crow to confirm it. Nerves drew one hand up to futz with the lizard foot on her collar. They drew her eyes down to the raven's blue-black feathers. "You know how to treat injuries from ghosts, which I don't really have to worry about. I got scratched by a dove named Guillaume up in the zoo and shifted instantly." She took a breath. She was warming up for a serious babble, and she didn't have time for that. "I need to find a particular ghost. Do you know how I would do that?"

"Guillaume?" A hitch in Ms. Crow's voice drew Laylea's attention up from the equally agitated bird. Ms. Crow and Dizzy both watched her closely.

"Yeah." Laylea searched her memory for any reason the name should mean something. "He saved me from some of the angrier ghosts...and Dean Gorse. Did you know Guillaume?"

Ms. Crow shook her hands dry. "Guy was a good friend. He was Ms. Lagat's husband. You saw him as a dove?" A sad joy brightened her face.

Laylea nodded. "And as a man. A whole bunch of the ghosts seemed to think they had to stay in the zoo if they couldn't shift. I don't think they knew that death changes the rules."

Dizzy crowed and launched herself off of Laylea's foot. Ms. Crow pushed to her feet. "A lot of people don't know that." She sucked in a deep breath and let it all out in a rush. "You want to find a particular ghost. Tishala Luke?"

Laylea laughed. Of course Ms. Crow would know about Oscar's sister. "No. I mean, yeah, but...I've heard rumors that she's not dead. If she was expelled, though, why wasn't she sent back to her family?"

"She wasn't expelled." Ms. Crow stretched her neck, rotating it from one side to the other. Then she turned from the river and led Laylea into the fields. She picked at plants as she talked, pulling some bugs off vines or bending to work a weed from the soil. "There is a process for expelling students, a great deal of paperwork. It has been expedited, on occasion." She fell silent as they crossed an open space into the cornfield.

The stalks stood well over Laylea's head. Even Ms. Crow would have to stand on tiptoe to see over them. She strolled deeper into the field. Dizzy soared in and out of view overhead.

"But, Ms. Crow, if I want to speak to a particular ghost..."

Ms. Crow bent to examine an ear of corn. "There are many ghosts in the ST rooms, aren't there?"

Laylea glanced up as Dizzy buzzed by. Her breath came faster. Dozens of ghosts had filled the foyer and outer room of ST when Ms. Davies had dragged her there. She had gathered her original gas mask crew just outside ST. It took a moment before she realized Ms. Crow was waiting for her to answer. She breathed, "Yes."

Ms. Crow kept her eyes on the corn. She pulled the husk back on an ear and poked at the kernels. "Many kids have been expelled and escorted directly from ST to upstairs. We have no formal follow up, but Ms. Lagat tries to check on students after they leave school, as Guy did." She wrapped up the ear and moved on to another. Her voice was unsteady when she went on. "She rarely finds them. Did you know Cal Christopherson?"

Laylea shook her head, but Ms. Crow wasn't looking at her. "Cal, the Centaur wolf who never returned from detention? He left before I came back."

"Well, Cal, with his clever mohawk, was registered as an orphan, like many of the kids who were given expedited expulsions. But some weren't orphans, and they never reached home. People say some of them ran away because the shame was too great."

"Like Riley Betts?"

"Dove and Reggie's big sister? Yes. She was expelled after several contentious visits to Special Testing. She was a tough girl. A lot like

Brenda. They had to call in Mr. Denier, the enforcer himself, to escort her upstairs. So, I hear."

Despite herself, Laylea asked, "Why were so many kids expelled? Why was Cal expelled?"

"I don't know. Cal was like you, a small kid with an enormous brain. Like you, he read everything he could get his hands on. He adored chemistry. I know he got detention for possession of N."

"He was an addict?"

"No." Ms. Crow glanced at Laylea. "Ms. Muldoon said he was trying to break it down to its components. Dean Gorse dragged Cal to his office and then to detention. Nobody saw him again."

Ms. Crow held an ear of corn in her hands, but she didn't husk it. She breathed. Her body nearly shook, as if she were fiercely angry and barely able to hold it in. A flutter of black feathers flitted between Laylea and the librarian. Dizzy perched on Ms. Crow's knee and tilted her head. She leaned in as if willing the woman to see her and cried a low, mournful note.

Ms. Crow rasped, "Have you seen a small ghost with a mohawk in ST?"

She hadn't. She'd been too busy trying to escape ST to really look at any of the ghosts there. "No, ma'am." She let that rest a moment, watching Ms. Crow's shoulders relax. "I'm looking for—"

"The challenge in looking for a particular former person is that ghosts generally stick around because of someone else. They don't entirely exist as themselves anymore so much as a conduit of whatever emotion keeps them attached to a living person. If you meet a... a—" Ms. Crow stuttered and changed what she'd been about to say. "If you meet a mare, for example, I'd guess she's here haunting Dean Gorse."

Laylea snorted. Dizzy ruffled her feathers at the noise. "I can't imagine anyone sticking around for Dean Gorse."

"Dean Gorse is mean because he's an unhappy man. He wasn't so bad before his wife died, leaving him with an infant daughter. He loved that little girl more than life itself. She was a joy. She brightened these cold corridors."

Dizzy cawed into Ms. Crow's face. She flapped her feathers and must have dug her claws into the librarian's knee, because Ms. Crow slapped a hand there. Dizzy tumbled to the dirt and then launched herself into the air, soaring up, up over the corn and high into the late afternoon sunlight streaming in from the glass ceiling above.

Laylea asked, "He had a daughter?"

"Yes. When she was eight years old, she fell, leaving her unable to shift. Now, all of Dean Gorse's considerable income from his horse farm goes to pay for her care. And all he cares about is her. He resents all of you for not being her."

"But why? Where is she?"

"Deanna lives in a special hospital for broken shifters out in Lipizzaner, Colorado."

Laylea's blood froze with no help from Amelia. She found herself standing. "Dean Gorse's daughter is named Deanna?"

Dizzy's cry echoed off the glass roof far above. She soared down and circled the two, screaming and diving in so close Laylea's hair fluttered in the wind of her wings. Ms. Crow brushed the whipping tendrils from her eyes. She stood, searching for the source of the wind.

"Are there ghosts here now, Lee?" she asked.

Laylea caught her breath. The hair was standing up on her arms. Her mind raced through everything she'd discovered, slotting the facts into different places now that she knew that Deanna was Dean Gorse's daughter. "No, Ms. Crow. There are no ghosts here. I don't think I need to talk to them anymore. I need to go."

"Lee?" Ms. Crow called after her.

Laylea didn't slow. She yelled over her shoulder, "Thank you, Ms. Crow."

She rushed back down the row, not feeling the sharp leaves striking her hands and face as she pushed her way through the corn. She hadn't realized how deep they'd gone. Her chest tightened as the row seemed to grow longer with every step she took. When she heard the babbling of the river, she broke into a run.

She ran right into someone and bounced back, already apologizing. "Sorry. I'm in a rush."

"Lee." Ms. Crow stood before her. "You need to slow down. Whatever you're planning to do, think about it. Detective Morton told you to keep your head down. She said Dr. Brock died and blamed you. She ordered you to stop looking for Bert Gorshkov. Your life is in danger, Lee."

Laylea blinked. How did she go the wrong way in the corn? Ms. Crow must have come out the way they went in while she flailed through the field. Ms. Crow looked more put together than she had when they went in. Her orange sweater was buttoned up. Laylea could have sworn the librarian had been wearing her blue sweater. "I'm…" She meant to say *I'm fine.* But it wasn't true, and Ms. Crow had just told her secrets no other teacher would have shared. She owed her honesty. So, instead, she said, "I know. But Jimmy's life is in danger, too. And Oscar's mother's."

Her palms felt sweaty. She shouldn't have shared that. That wasn't her secret to share. "Everyone who's addicted to N is in danger. Humans are diving off buildings, thinking they can fly. Shifters are losing their ability to shift. wyrdos are forgetting their gifts."

"And you won't be able to help any of them if Brock gets his hands on you. Most all of the staff are at Gorse's party upstairs. There's nobody here to help you."

Laylea never expected the staff to help her. She did wish she had KC and Oscar by her side. But even without them, she had to do what she could to help the Wyrdos stop N. "Thanks, Ms. Crow. I just have to go."

A crinkling sound in the midst of the corn made them both turn to look. Laylea took the opportunity to run.

36

*L*aylea burst out into the corridor. She didn't stop to peek or think who might be out there. Her mind was too busy working through all the facts that had just fallen into place and why Ms. Crow had told her all those things and then tried to stop her from doing anything about them. So, she didn't see the wolves until she ran headlong into Jagger deRio. The tall girl stumbled back a single step before she lunged forward to grab Laylea's hair.

Another set of hands wrapped around her arms and threw her against the far wall. Clumps of hair ripped out of her skull. She saw them hanging from between Jagger's fingers before her gaze shifted to the boy who had thrown her. Oscar. He stood with five wolves. Five of the angriest, most out-of-control wolves glared at Laylea. Jagger growled. Eugene dropped into his deep brown and gray wolf self. His ears flattened against his skull and his tail stood straight out behind him, twitching like a cat.

Sweat beaded on Laylea's brow at even thinking the insult. But then, Oscar was a cat. Why was he standing with the wolves? Was he really so mad at her? Her facial muscles all flexed in the weird ways they do when you're trying to hold back tears. She didn't dare speak. What would she say anyway?

Jagger finally translated her growls into words. "So, you like wilding, do you?"

The other wolves howled and jeered, urging Jagger on. Laylea could feel the heat of their unreasonable anger rolling off of the pack.

"You know what we do in a wilding, right, Fido?" Eugene asked.

More jeering and hooting. They knew where this was going. Laylea knew where this was going. Her blood rushed to her extremities, urging her to run even as her intellect reminded her that running would be a very bad choice. Still, her muscles twitched.

"We h... h... hunt." Carrie's shaking voice came from behind Laylea. It echoed off the stone walls. The small girl walked past Laylea. Her whole body shook like her voice. She had one hand in a pocket, the other clenched in a fist at her side.

The pack howled. Julia Jimenez shifted into her wolf-form and bared her teeth.

Carrie stopped walking when she was just a few steps in front of Laylea. She stood between the pack and her fellow Mer. "We hunt—" Her words were cut off. In a flash, Carrie, the girl, disappeared and her fluffy puppy-wolf stood in her place. The wolf threw her head back and let out a cry that echoed off the walls, piercing Laylea's sensitive ears. Several of the human-shaped wolves flinched. The furry wolves all barked and backed away, their ears rotating away from the sound.

Before the echoes died away, Carrie, the girl, stood in front of Laylea again. One hand remained in her pocket. She raised her clenched fist over her head as if she were pulling herself up. She ground out, "We. H. . . hunt. Upstairs. D. . . Denier decreed we n... n... never hunt each other. We n... n... never hunt our cl... classmates."

The wolves rankled at this. Hackles raised down Eugene's and Julia's backs. Dustin flashed into his wolf.

Another familiar voice spoke up behind Laylea. "Code Edict three point one dash four. Y'all know how easy it is to hack your private wolf web?" KC's voice approached. Laylea didn't dare turn to look, afraid to see hate in her friend's face.

But then KC stepped up beside her and wove her fingers into

Laylea's. Laylea's heart leapt as KC stood up to the wolves. "So easy. It didn't take me five minutes to figure out how to message Enforcer Denier and let him know you were wilding inside the school."

The tone of the growling and grumbling shifted from murderous to worried.

"You're full of it," Vaughn Howe sneered.

"She's not. G… Gorse is coming b… back from the party to m… meet Denier here," Carrie added. "But they c… can't do a… anything if they can't p… prove anything."

"And they can't prove anything if the dog is dead." Jagger smirked, but Dustin and Eugene took subtle steps away from her.

"I d… didn't want to—" Carrie flashed into her wolf and immediately back to human. Her voice strained with the effort she was making. "I didn't want to d… d… do this. But Denier can't p… punish us if we were out of our minds." Without explaining her odd statement, Carrie pulled her hand from her pocket. She flung a rich purple powder into the air over the pack and blew the remnants from her hand into Jagger's face.

Jagger sneezed and shifted. She brushed a paw along her muzzle, like there was something she needed to get off. Then she rolled to her side, scratching at her fur with all four paws.

Oscar took a step toward Carrie, his hands out as if he could shield the wolves. "Is that wolfsbane?"

As the dark powder settled on them, the werewolves all clawed at their own skin. Every one of them shifted into wolf form.

"Run for the waterfalls!" Oscar put action to words and ran for the door Laylea had just burst out of. He pulled it open, urging the pack to hurry. "That stuff will burn through your skin in seconds. You have to get to the water. Go. Go. Go."

"Go." Carrie turned and whispered this at KC and Laylea before she, too, fell into her wolf form and bounded into the midst of the pack racing into the Fields.

Laylea and KC edged past the straggling wolves and ran.

Two turns later, Laylea panted, "I thought you were mad at me."

"I was. I'm sorry." KC shook her head. Her double ponytails

bounced off her shoulders. "I should have trusted you. I went to the library. I was planning to look through the patient files again, but then I found a note from DJ on the dibs drive from my bracelet." She held up her arm and snapped the bracelet as they ran. "He copied something onto it when he grabbed my arm."

They panted around a couple more turns before Laylea begged, "What did the note say?"

"Dean Gorse isn't who he says he is."

"Hey." Laylea tripped to a stop. She grabbed KC to stop her, too. "You're running for the Executive Wing."

KC looked confused for a moment. Then the dime dropped. "You are, too."

Laylea nodded.

"You know who Gorse is." KC wasn't asking a question.

Laylea laughed. "Ms. Crow told me Gorse has a daughter. Named Deanna."

"No!"

"Yes!"

"Holy phoenix! It's been under our noses the whole time. I hacked into the staff system and then wrote a program to search the wolf web, scanning for any mentions of him and found out the dean was hired as part of a deal to avoid prison."

"For drugs?"

"Yeah. Manufacture and distribution. They faked a car accident to kill him and gave him a totally new face. Guess who paid the bill?"

Laylea shook her head but started jogging for the Wing again. "Denier?"

KC jogged beside her. She kept her eyes forward. "No. My grandfather."

The wolves had put Gorse in charge of the school. Why? What was their endgame?

They reached the doorway to the Wing, and Laylea looked to KC.

KC stared back at her. "What?"

"You have a code, right?"

KC blanched. She shook her head.

"You hacked the staff database but didn't steal a code to get us into the Executive Wing?" Laylea asked.

KC swung her backpack to her front and started digging through it. "Hold on. Hold on. I can fix this."

"No need. I have a code."

Both girls turned to see Oscar jogging down the corridor.

"But…" Laylea had no idea what to say. He didn't seem mad at all. He had pushed her just a minute ago.

KC asked him, "Where are the wolves?"

"Bathing. It's well known cats don't like water, so I told them I was going to find the rest of the pack and tell them how Carrie saved the day. They are not happy with her." He said this as he stepped to the keypad beside the oak double-doors of the Executive Wing and punched in a sequence.

Nothing happened. He typed again. Again, nothing.

"Oscar, aren't you mad at me for not finding Shala?" Laylea had to know.

Oscar turned away from the keypad. "I was. I was really angry. But…" he looked down at his lanky fingers and scrunched his face up like he was literally chewing his words over. When he spoke, the words came pouring out from behind the dam. "I don't want you to find her. I want to believe you haven't found her because she's not dead." He pressed on before either girl could respond. "I pretended to fight with you so I could stay on the pack's good side. They're under orders to hurt you so bad you have to be taken out of school to the St. Francis Medical Center."

Laylea's face scrunched up. Surely the wolves had noticed her particular gift. They'd inspired it enough times. "Can't happen," she said. "I'll just shift and heal."

"Not if they slip you sligh nut first." Oscar turned to tap at the keypad again while Laylea shivered.

The keypad buzzed at them. KC dove for the door handle. It didn't budge.

"That buzz means you've frozen the system for three minutes." Brenda spoke quietly as she ran down the corridor toward them on her silent feet. Like Laylea, she shunned shoes most of the time. She pushed past Oscar to face Laylea. "You asked me if I knew a Brian Samborsky." She breathed heavily through her nose, reminding Laylea of a bull preparing to charge.

"Yeah. Are you related?"

Brenda's eyes shone. Her skin glowed, pink rising from the collar of her jumpsuit until it suffused her face. Her lips squeezed together in layers of wrinkles. When she spoke, her voice sounded as tight as her lips. "Is he one of your ghosts?"

It took Laylea a moment to understand what she was asking. Brenda looked angry, but she wasn't angry at Laylea.

The python-shifter sucked in another breath before Laylea could respond. Brenda said, "He's my father. He was sentenced to be a teacher here. They let me move into the dorms when he died. But he's not dead. Is he?" A single tear floated on the edge of Brenda's lashes.

Laylea's head shook before her tongue could catch up to blurt out, "No. He's not. He's in a sleep lab run by Denier. He's right upstairs, in the city."

The tear evaporated as Brenda blinked. Her shoulders fell and her head rose and she suddenly stood tall and strong, the Brenda they were all familiar with, but with the hint of a smile behind the fire in her eyes. Brenda pulled her hands from her pockets and stuck a key into the end of one of the door handles. She reached over to the keypad and typed in a code so quickly, Laylea couldn't catch it. The key turned. The handle turned. The door opened.

Brenda held the door for them. "Burn it to the ground, Fido."

Laylea could only nod. When Brenda extended her arm to push the door open, she'd revealed a white tattoo on her forearm of two triangles end to end. The same double delta tattoo that her father had. It disappeared under her sleeve as Brenda stepped back into the corridor. "If you get in trouble, ring the all-call."

"What's the all-call?" KC asked.

Oscar answered, "Emergency bells. Everyone is supposed to report to their dorms when you hear them."

KC's face scrunched up with doubt. "Does anybody know that?"

Laylea remembered Ms. Crow saying something about them during intake. "Yeah, Ms. Crow told us about them this year."

"Or just don't get in trouble. I'll distract the pack." Brenda's fierce grin frightened Laylea. She watched the girl as the door fell shut between them. She wanted to ask about the tattoo, about her father, and about why someone would be *sentenced* to teach here.

They didn't have time to talk about it now, though. They had to get to Gorse's office.

Laylea trotted along behind KC as Oscar led the way through the maze of carpeted halls and offices back to Dean Gorse's private office. What were they going to do there? She'd known that's where she needed to go as soon as she figured out who he was. KC had come to the same conclusion, as had Oscar. But what were they going to do?

She had returned to LPSS to find Bert Gorshkov and report his whereabouts to Captain Morioka. That's what she would do. They would get proof that the Dean was Bert Gorshkov and deliver it upstairs. Then she'd go back to keeping her head down, as ordered, and watch the fallout with everyone else.

KC's whispered shout brought her back to the present. "What do you mean you don't have the code?"

37

*A*nother door. Another lock. Another barrier between them and the truth. It made Laylea certain that proof lay inside the room on the other side of that door.

"He keeps the key on a chain around his neck. How was I supposed to make a copy of it?" Oscar complained.

KC hissed back, "Keep your voice down."

"There is nobody here." Oscar backed away and gestured wildly at the empty desks around them. His voice was sucked up by the thick carpet underfoot. He nearly fell as he ran into a chair pushed back from a desk. He spun and dragged the chair over to Gorse's office door. He ran his fingers along the ledge above the door.

"What are you doing?" KC stared at him.

"My dad says you can't count on anything except your enemies not being as bright as you think they are. And I think Gorse is pretty dumb. Maybe he hides a spare nearby."

"We're trusting your father, now?" KC murmured this so quietly Oscar could pretend he hadn't heard. He did shoot her a quick glare, but KC had her head down. She typed and swiped on her padd and peered at the keypad on the wall beside the door.

Laylea decided to look around for tools. Locks were complicated.

Wood could be broken. Or burned. The school had been beefing up its fire preparedness. Maybe there were fire axes around. She didn't see any on the walls in view, so she trotted farther down the hallway.

The cold came on so suddenly, she was blown back from the unexpected pain. Her skin burned with the icy air surrounding her. Amelia's voice followed an instant later. "Have you found him?" The ghost dropped to the ground to put her face on a level with her human contact, her nose inches from Laylea's.

"Yes." Laylea buried her fingers in the plush carpet, holding herself still. "We just have to get past that door, and we'll find the proof we need to free Deanna." She looked over her shoulder but couldn't see around the corner. She could hear Oscar and KC bickering over the lock.

"A door is no impediment," Amelia hissed.

"Not for you," Laylea muttered.

Amelia disappeared, and Laylea sucked in a breath of air that felt too warm after the bitter wind of the grieving mother. She flipped herself over and scrambled to get back to her friends. She'd just turned the corner when the unmistakable sound of a horse neighing echoed from inside Gorse's office. KC and Oscar fell back a step.

"Come here!" Laylea called to them.

They ran to her, clearing the doorway an instant before the door smashed outwards, sending dust plumes billowing from the ancient carpet. A silky white mare, her mane blowing in an icy wind, ducked out of the office. She pawed once at the door on the floor and then brought her hoof down on it with a powerful blow. A crack splintered the wood. The horse neighed again, shaking her head and baring her teeth at the three kids. Then she disappeared.

KC shivered. She wrapped her arms around herself. "Was that Amelia?"

Despite standing several feet behind them, Laylea nodded. They didn't really need her confirmation.

"I saw her." Vapor floated on the air with KC's awed words.

"Me too. Damn. And I thought leopard mamas were scary." Oscar shook himself, brushed dust from his overalls, and rushed into the dusty air. "Come on. I'd bet that set off some kind of alarm. We've got to hurry."

Once they got through the cloud, the air cleared quickly. Gorse's office was barely affected. His desk dominated the center of the small room. It was a much smaller room than Laylea would have expected a man with Gorse's ego to work in. Bookshelves lined the walls, alternating with tall, wooden file cabinets from different ages. The shelves didn't hold many books. Most of the eye level shelves held trophies shaped like rearing horses and ribbons and framed certificates from horse shows. A wrought-iron coat rack resembling a turn of the century streetlamp stood in the corner to the left of the door. It held a raincoat, a deep grey fedora, and a single ultra-modern gas mask. The gas mask sent Laylea's gaze up to where the walls met the ceiling. Even Gorse's office had been outfitted with Robby's tubes and a device smaller but similar to the device the Mers had dismantled in their dorm. Oddly, a traditional red fire extinguisher hung in the corner just beyond the coat rack.

The wall behind Gorse's desk featured a nine-by-twelve portrait of a little girl with brown braids posed on a white stallion's bare back. Lake Erie and the Navy Pier Ferris wheel filled the background. Laylea and Oscar stared at the painting while KC dove for the ancient desktop monitor on one side of Gorse's desk.

"He's a Lipizzaner," Oscar breathed.

"Can't be," KC murmured, not looking up from her typing and swiping. "The shifter Lipizzaners died out a decade ago. Left all their money to a wildlife refuge out in Colorado."

Laylea asked, "The shifter what?"

"Lipizzaners. It's a rare horse breed," Oscar explained. "White Lipizzaners are especially prized. There used to be a line of Lipizzaner shifters, but we thought they died out."

"You think that's Gorse?" Laylea asked.

"Yeah. Doesn't he seem like the kind of guy who would have a picture of himself dominating his office?" Oscar raised an eyebrow at her and then headed to open one of the filing cabinets.

"But who's the girl?" Laylea asked.

Both KC and Oscar looked at her. Oscar asked, "That's not Deanna?"

Laylea examined the little girl's face. She shook her head. "I only saw her briefly, but I know that little girl in the sleep lab had white hair."

KC held her dibs bracelet to the CPU beneath the monitor and pulled up a picture from the sleep lab records. "That's the same face. See the giant freckle under her left eye?" KC turned to point at the painting and sucked in a deep breath. "Oh, wow. No wonder Gorse is so upset about her not shifting."

"What do you mean?" Laylea almost wished Amelia were there to confirm what was going on.

Oscar slammed the drawer of the filing cabinet and moved to another. "Lipizzaners aren't born white. You don't know they're valuable until they turn."

"Wait." Laylea trotted to a filing cabinet on the far side of the room, remembering that they were looking for proof. "If Deanna's hair hadn't turned, she wouldn't be valuable? To her parents?"

She caught the look that KC and Oscar shot each other.

Oscar was the one who finally answered. "In my family, black is the coloring you want. We have panther genes, but not everyone shows them. I know it didn't matter to my mother. But I'm not sure my father would care about me as much if I hadn't turned all black. I remember Shala was worried about it."

"Cal Christopherson!" Laylea cried. She might have flicked right past the file if her eyes hadn't caught on the side-by-side pictures of a kid with a bleached mohawk and a wolf with a fawn stripe running the length of his spine. Ms. Crow had asked if she'd seen a small kid with a mohawk. She had. Just not in Special Testing.

Her eyes flicked up to the protective rubber face shield hanging on the coat rack in the corner. She'd seen Cal hanging out with her gas mask ghosts.

"The wolf who was expelled for having N?" KC asked. Then she slammed her hands down on the keyboard. "Can he help us find this secret database? Because there's nothing on Gorse's computer. Like, nothing except records of horse lineages and wins."

Laylea yanked the plain, brown manilla folder out of the drawer. She tossed it onto the desk. "I think he might. Ms. Crow told me that Dean Gorse dragged Cal to his office before expelling him. He's been in here before."

Oscar and KC shot another look at each other before Oscar said, "But, he's not here now, Lee. He's been expelled." He said it slowly, like she was an idiot.

Laylea sighed. Instead of telling them, she turned north, east, south, and west, muttering the words that always drew her closer to the spirit world.

Oscar recognized what she was doing. He breathed a thick, "Oh no."

KC whispered, "What?"

"Cal," Laylea called into the void. "Cal, I know you're here. Come talk to me. I promise I'll listen now."

She barely heard KC's hushed, "Oh," of understanding.

A rush of hot and stringent air blew back Laylea's short hair. The leader of the gas mask crew filled the open doorway of the dean's private office. Her eyes glowed green. Laylea's eyes dropped to the neckline of the tiger girl's jumpsuit. A pale scar traced the length of the ghost's collarbone, and Laylea's gut clenched with despair. "Riley?"

The overwhelming thickness of the air let up for an instant. The ghost flashed into her tiger form and back. When she stood again as a human, her gas mask was gone.

"I'm Riley." It was almost a question, but not quite.

Laylea said, "We know your little brother and sister, Reggie and Dove."

"Get them out!" Riley floated two steps into the room, shoving her force at Laylea so hard, Laylea's back slammed the filing cabinet drawer shut.

She needed to focus. They didn't have much time. "Is Cal with you?"

The striped wolf ghost stepped through the doorway, picking his way over the broken pieces as if his paws were actually touching the ground. The air around him shimmered, and suddenly a boy stood there. He reached up and unclasped the straps running alongside his light gray mohawk. Without the gas mask, Laylea could see how very young the boy was.

"My name is Cal." He looked around the room as if he were trying to remember something. When his eyes landed on Laylea, they filled with tears. He said, "I died here."

Laylea sucked in a deep breath and slowly let it out before she could control her voice enough to ask, "In this room?"

Cal shook his head. He raised one hand like the Ghost of Christmas Future and pointed at the giant painting of Deanna Gorshkov. "In that room."

"In the painting?" she asked.

Cal laughed. He let go of his earthly restraints and swooped through the dean's pristine desk, through KC, who shivered, to float through the painting and back out again. He gripped the frame and pulled, saying, "In the room on the other side of the painting."

The wood smoked at his touch, and it moved, ever so slightly. Oscar dashed over to grab the frame and then snatched his hands back and blew on his fingers.

"Sorry." Cal floated through the painting again to get out of Oscar's way.

Oscar gasped, he turned to Laylea, but his gaze swerved violently to the tall girl floating beside her. "I saw him— Riley?"

KC stood up from the desk, her eyes wide. "I see her, too, Oscar. Let's get into that room and find some proof against Dean Gorse."

She joined him at the painting, and together, they pulled on the frame. The entire wall shifted, revealing the dean's secret office.

38

The portrait of Deanna riding on her father rotated to the side, so it was still visible when the entrance it hid was opened. The border between the two rooms was accented by a bright area rug laid atop the faded berber carpet that added to the dreariness of the rest of the small room. The walls were lined with steel and wood filing cabinets, paint peeling from all of them. The center of the room featured a data tower like an older version of the one now boarded up in the anteroom to the Special Testing suite. This data tower supported four displays ringing the central processing unit.

The three living kids, and a sudden crowd of dead ones, poured through the opening into the dean's hidden office. Oscar reached the interface panel first. He folded down the keyboard and started searching around the old equipment.

"Where's the palm lock?"

KC reached the device an instant behind him. She went for the keyboard and started typing. "Ha! Finally, his ego is working for us. There's no security. I'm in. Ugh, but there's no master file either." She reached a hand up to the display screen and two-finger swiped a stack of files to the monitors on her left and right. "Here, I split the files, so we can scan them faster."

Oscar hustled to the left monitor and started flipping through the digital folders. Laylea did the same at the other station. She tried to focus but couldn't help glancing repeatedly over at the outer office. The hairs on the back of her neck expected a staff member to appear at any second.

"Betts!" Oscar called out. He read the names out as he flipped through files. "Dove. Reggie. Riley."

The tall ghost zipped through the power tower to Oscar's side. Others floated with her as if they had to follow. She tried to stab a finger at the monitor, but her hand went right through. Oscar spread his fingers to open the file.

The searing heat that characterized the tall ghost's aura faded as she said, "I died in Special Testing."

"There's a note here from Gorse to Denier," Oscar told them when Riley's voice trailed off. "'The trials of Project X version 3.2 have been concluded. Changes must be made to the formula. The casualty will be formally expelled. Please fetch the remains at your earliest. Yours, Dean Gorse.'"

"That's me?" Riley looked to Oscar for answers. "'The casualty?' 'The remains?'"

He nodded before he found his voice. Sweat dripped from his forehead. "Yes."

Riley floated back from Oscar, fading as she did. Cal stepped into the space she vacated. "Am I in there?"

"I'll look." Oscar swiped Riley's records from the screen and returned to swiping through the files.

Laylea did the same. She sped through, counting on her brain to catch the pattern of the letters she was looking for without her having to read every student's name. It worked. She had already flipped several files beyond when she realized that she'd seen the name *Gorshkov*. As she flipped back to it, Oscar found Cal's file.

"Calvin Christopherson?" He looked to the mohawked ghost for confirmation. Cal nodded. Riley stood beyond him, her spectral form glowing blue with heat though her face was as unreadable as if she wore her gas mask.

Oscar's face fell as he flipped through the documents in Cal's file. "Oh, no."

"Adrien," Cal read. "The problem has been eliminated. The kid was a fighter. He would have made the pack proud. His records, however were incomplete. An aunt has surfaced, questioning his expulsion. Your assistance with this woman would be appreciated, as would any assistance you can offer in cleaning blood out of carpet. Bert."

All eyes turned to the bright rug at the entrance.

"Guess Adrien wasn't much help." Cal's tone was dry, but his aura burned as hot as Riley's ever had. Sweat poured down Oscar's neck.

Laylea forced her attention back to her screen and the file in front of her. They were there to find proof that Gorse was really Gorshkov. That was her job. She would find Gorshkov. Morioka would threaten Gorshkov. Gorshkov would reveal all of his holdings, and Team Wyrdos would defeat N.

She splayed her fingers on the smartglass, and the items in the folder spread out around a white label reading *Albert Gorshkov Samira*. The sweat that dripped from her forehead had nothing to do with gas mask ghosts. Her heart pounded as she shuffled the items around to bring a picture to the fore. And then her heart skipped a beat.

It wasn't the dean. She didn't recognize the face at all. They'd been wrong. Dean Gorse wasn't Berty Gorshkov.

KC gave a sudden sharp stutter of breath. Her face blanched, and her fingers froze on the keyboard.

"Look. Another black panther." Cal floated behind KC, who stared at the screen before her in silence. The kid turned his haunted eyes to Oscar. "Like you."

Riley looked from Oscar to the screen. "I knew her."

Oscar reached KC in two strides. Ghosts scattered from his path.

KC spun her ID band until she had the dibs drive centered. She slammed her wrist against the power drive and used her left hand to copy files onto it. Oscar's face went blank. At the same time, Laylea saw a simmering pool of emotion ready to explode from his eyes. He looked much like Riley and Cal.

Laylea caught KC's eyes. KC swiped a copy of Tishala Luke's file over to her monitor.

Shala's file showed pictures of a sleek leopard with the same black on black patterns in her fur as Oscar's shifted self. Her human photo sent shivers down Laylea's spine. She recognized the girl with the bright eyes and eager expression, though when she'd seen her, Shala had been sleeping.

Oscar's whisper grated in the sudden silence. "They killed her."

"No," KC whispered, though her expression was hopeless.

Even as she kept swiping through Albert Gorshkov Samira's records, Laylea insisted, "They didn't."

"This is Dean Gorse's letterhead." Oscar's voice was flat as he read the letter. "Enforcer Denier, Ms. Luke was an excellent student. She was well behaved and a favorite with the teaching staff. Having been unable to find an excuse for expulsion that would be believed in the community, I feared I would be forced to disappoint you, sir. However, as you indicated that a formal exit of the school of any kind would be acceptable, I have applied a member of your pack to the problem, and he has succeeded admirably. I go now to inform the school of Ms. Luke's tragic mortal fall. I leave it to you to deliver what news you will to her family. Warmly, Dean Gorse."

"Oh my phoenix." KC murmured the curse even as she hurried to the monitor Oscar had been scanning. She slammed her dibs drive against the power drive and began copying documents. "Bert Gorshkov isn't just the key to the N epidemic. He's all-around evil. He covered up Riley's death in Special Testing, killed Cal for analyzing N, and had Shala killed just because Denier asked him to. The dean has to be stopped."

Laylea shook her head, murmuring, "No. She can't be dead." She looked up from her search to catch KC's eyes again. "Show him." She didn't wait for KC's response. Some good had to come out of this day. It was better that Oscar know his sister was alive than to see his grief so stark he looked more miserable than the ghosts.

She was desperate. The face on her screen was not the dean's.

She'd never seen this boy, this Albert Gorshkov Samira. Everything they'd been doing was a waste. And now she had to tell them.

The whisper rasped from her throat. "It's not him."

"What do you mean?" KC glanced over, her fingers never slowing on the keyboard.

"It's not him." The confession spilled out of her. "Bert Gorshkov isn't the dean. He doesn't look a thing like him. It isn't him."

"Yes, it is." A voice made of air and light caressed Laylea's ear.

She spun to see the transparent form of an old man in a zoo uniform floating beside her. Guillaume, Ms. Lagat's husband, reached out and splayed her hand on the display. The carefully organized files went into a spin.

One folder icon was red. "Open that one." Guillaume pointed with a transparent finger.

Laylea reached out and tapped it. The screen filled with a collage of newspaper articles, blog posts, and on-camera media. Many featured pictures of emergency vehicles with lights flashing surrounding a pile of too many crashed cars to count. Bodies thrown from the wrecks lay on hoods and the pavement. Some bloody survivors clung to these bodies. Others limped away from the crash, helping each other.

Headline after headline played with a grisly pun. *LSD fueled crash kills twenty-four on the LSD. The LSD on LSD, a deadly combination. Twenty-four dead in Lake Shore Drive tragedy. Rich kid causes carnage. Party boy Gorshkov faces manslaughter charges. Gorshkov, the LSD killer, declared DOA at St. Francis Hospital.*

Laylea swiped articles out of her way. Each picture was more grisly than the last. Obituaries documented a professor, a cancer researcher, an up-and-coming actor, three schoolchildren, a war veteran. Each of the twenty-four victims was represented. She shook her head, tears trembling in her eyes.

She murmured, "But this just shows that Bert Gorshkov died."

Guillaume pointed at a document at the very bottom of the screen, partially obscured by the multitude of news articles. The thumbnail preview showed rows of words and numbers. "Read that one, friend of Toby."

She tapped it. The clippings settled to the edges of the screen as an invoice opened in the center. The letterhead indicated a doctor's office; The West Loupe Reconstructive Surgery Center. The odd spelling twigged at her brain, but her eyes moved down to the list of medical items being billed. Words jumped out at her as she scanned: blepharoplasty, rhinoplasty, comprehensive rhytidectomy. This was a list of plastic surgery procedures. All of them done to the patient's face.

The second page of the invoice featured two pictures: one of a handsome, arrogant young man with a bloody cut over one white eyebrow. It was the boy from Gorshkov's student profile. The second picture was of Dean Bertram Gorse. A ghostly arm reached over her shoulder, perhaps a little through it, from the icy spike she felt, and pointed to the signature at the very bottom. Payment was verified as having been remitted in full by one Luis Delcampo.

Delcampo was KC's real last name. Was this her great grandfather, the head of the American wolf pack? If so, why had the top dog of the werewolves paid to change the Dean's appearance? Laylea looked up to verify KC's great grandfather's name, but the horror on KC's face stopped her. KC was looking over to where Oscar stood frozen in the middle of a throng of ghosts, some with gas masks, most without.

They all stared at the screen in front of him. Oscar sucked in a deep breath and slowly let it out in a rasp. He sounded so broken, Laylea ran through the ghosts to reach his side, ignoring the battling ice and flames. Files labeled with names rotated around the periphery of the screen. In the center of the screen, a spray of medical records surrounded a picture under the label *Kitty Kitty*. The picture was of the dark-skinned girl with the equally dark tattoo on her arm.

"Oscar?" KC's quiet voice drew all the ghosts' eyes to her. "Those records are from the sleep lab. She's just sleeping. She's alive."

Oscar's tears were enough confirmation. The girl in the sleep lab was undeniably his sister, Shala.

Three of the patients in the sleep lab had been transferred there from the school: a teacher, a student, and the dean's daughter. And none of their families knew.

"What is the meaning of this?"

Dean Gorse attempted to storm into the outer office. His rage was hampered by having to pick his way over the destroyed door. They all got a good look at his face when he saw them in the inner office. It went as pale as his horse form in the painting until the blood started creeping up, anger painting his face a glowing red.

"You three have gone too far." His voice was tight and fierce. "You can back away all you want. But you will not get away."

He clearly didn't see the ghosts or feel the heat of their anger sparking fires from thin air.

39

*B*erty Gorshkov stood on the bright area rug he'd laid down to hide Calvin Christopherson's blood. As dean of the Lincoln Park Shifter School, he'd allowed students to die. He'd lied to parents. He'd lied to the community. He deserved anything the gas mask ghosts did to him.

But he was also the key to stopping N. The key to preventing more deaths.

Laylea wrestled with her conscience as the dean rambled on about how he was going to punish them before he turned them over to the enforcer. He stood there, over Cal's blood, facing two dozen ghosts all, once again, wearing gas masks. He loosened his tie as he lectured. But that was the only indication that he was at all aware of the dead kids' presence. Cal floated at the very center of the crowd closing in on the dean. Laylea knew she should stop them.

The Wyrdos had given her a job. Her job was to find Bert Gorshkov and let Morioka know. That was it.

That, and not get caught.

She'd been caught. But she was fairly certain the proof that he was the Bert Gorshkov who had killed twenty-four people in one drug-involved car accident would keep his mouth shut. They'd have to promise not to tell anybody. And they were going to tell Morioka. But was it really wrong to renege on promises made to a liar?

Before Laylea could bring herself to stop the ghosts, KC interrupted the dean. "Yeah, yeah. You're buddies with Adrien Denier. We've got a buddy too, Mr. Gorshkov. We've got a direct line to Captain Yaksha Morioka, who was under the impression that you died fifteen years ago."

The dean stopped talking and started spluttering seconds after his real name crept through his ears to his brain.

Laylea didn't make any effort to understand his stuttered denials. She took advantage of his momentary confusion to address the dead kids. "Stop. We need him alive."

Some of the ghosts turned to look at her. From the back of the crowd, Riley growled, "He killed us."

"Under Denier's orders," Laylea snapped back. "We can use him to get Denier."

Gorshkov laughed. "You three aren't getting out of this room, much less getting anywhere near Denier." He ran a hand through his thick white hair, looking at his fingers curiously when they came out wet.

Oscar sounded like his jaw could not clench any tighter. "That heat you're feeling is anger. You're surrounded by the kids you killed by letting Denier run experiments on them."

The dean didn't notice the barely contained murder in Oscar's eyes. Again, he laughed. "Oh, did you find your sister?"

Cal Christopherson soared so close, his hot words blew the dean's hair back. "Shala lives!"

The other ghosts echoed his words. Gorshkov stumbled back from the heat. He searched the room for an explanation until Oscar repeated, "Shala lives."

"You know Shala lives," KC flicked three fingers at the screen in front of her, sending Shala's files flying onto the monitor facing Gorshkov. "We have proof you've been using Special Testing to experiment on kids, selling their data, selling their blood, and making N.

You've put Shala in a coma, along with Brenda's dad and your own daughter. Why?"

"My daughter is not—"

"Answer them!" Riley flew through the glowing crush of ectoplasm to scream in Gorshkov's face.

His eyes blew wide, and he stumbled from the bright carpet, one hand reaching out to brace himself. He screamed, "I'm just following orders. The enforcer cut me a deal. He saved me from prison under the condition that I run LPSS according to his orders. I am the last foundation stud of the Gorshkov Dynasty. I can't die." The carpet beneath his feet smoked. Steam rose from his hair.

"Riley!" Laylea pushed herself out of her shock and waded through the enraged ghosts. "Morioka has plans for him."

"What are her plans, Lee?" Oscar asked, his voice deceptively calm. "You know where the sleep lab is. What do we need this guy for? Why stop his victims from getting their revenge?"

"Yaksha Morioka plays a long game." Guillaume floated into the crush of kids. His cool form calmed some and pushed others away who were too hot to handle his presence. "Revenge may feel good in this moment. But this moment is fleeting."

Laylea repeated, in case the others couldn't hear, "Guillaume says revenge is fleeting."

Gorshkov paled even further, if that were possible.

Guillaume touched down, his ghostly feet crushing the bright carpet's pile and smothering the growing heat blackening the threads. He spoke to the kids, living and dead alike, as if the dean were of no consequence. "We have powers this little man cannot dream of. Yaksha Morioka has powers we cannot dream of. We must help Lee get her message to Captain Morioka. Then we keep this little man from following orders we don't like."

Bright blue light flashed through the room, cooling all the ghosts and drawing sparks from the power tower. Where Guillaume, the man, had stood, a pure white dove now hovered in the air beside the dean. The dove flapped his wings and darted at the man's face before soaring out into the main office.

Gorshkov slapped a hand to his ear with a cry. "What the hell?" His hand came away bloody.

"That's a taste, Gorshkov, of what my ghostly friends can do." Laylea stepped up. "Since you didn't get the hint from Cal burning the carpet you buried his blood under. Since you didn't catch the clue when Riley Betts singed your hair. If blood is the only thing that speaks to you, we'll show you blood."

Oscar added, "Your blood."

"I'm not responsible. I help them with their research, that's all."

KC sent more files to the front monitor, more pictures of dead students. "What are they researching in Special Testing?"

"Shifter biology."

"Is that what Robby's tubes are for, too?" Laylea asked.

Gorshkov scoffed. "That's a fire suppressant system. You were raised by thumpers, so you may not be familiar with the Phoenix Event, but fire is something we take very seriously."

"Riley?" Oscar searched for the tall ghost. "That painting looks flammable."

She swooped across the room and traced her fingers delicately on the top of the frame, close to the tube running along the ceiling of the room. The wood burst into flames.

"No! Not Deanna!" Gorshkov ran into the outer office, heading for the fire extinguisher behind the coat rack. He was driven back again when the ribbons on his shelves sizzled and burned. Ghosts smashed the glass from the frames and the certificates blackened to ash. "My legacy!"

Riley stood before him. Her form solidified. Laylea couldn't see Gorshkov's face, but she saw his back stiffen. Riley removed her mask and curled her lip at him. She murmured an altered echo of his words, "My life."

KC waited for a moment of calm before she asked, "Why isn't the fire being suppressed?"

"It... it's not active yet," Gorshkov stuttered, finally as scared as he should have been from the moment he interrupted them.

KC continued her typing and swiping as she mentioned, "I've

taken several of the devices apart. There is no sensor that could detect smoke or heat."

"Fine." Gorshkov removed his suit jacket and swung the fabric at the fire consuming Deanna's frame. "It's a data collection system to help Dr. Brock gather biomedical readings from shifting students to improve his process of fixing duds."

Guillaume launched from where he'd perched on the front monitor, shifting smoothly to land on his feet in front of Gorshkov. The flash of his shift sent a wave of blue light through the room. Laylea felt her heart calm. The adrenaline that had flooded her system at the doctor's name abated, until Guillaume repeated it, asking the dean, "Maury Brock?" Nobody heard him but Laylea.

"You keep lying, Dean *Gorse*, and you're not going to have much of an office left." KC stepped away from her keyboard, smoothing the dibs ID band. She pulled one of Robby's devices out of her backpack. KC tossed the canister to Gorshkov. "No drive or data transfer unit."

Laylea's heart leapt at the sight of the white plastic canister and the memory of where she'd seen one like it before. Dr. Brock had set one on his desk before he attempted to smoke her in his death closet. She reached a hand out to hold herself upright. "How is Dr. Brock involved?"

Guillaume turned to her with surprise on his old face.

Gorshkov sucked in a breath. "Put out the fires, and I'll tell you."

Guillaume shifted to bird and back. The blue flashes of his transformation doused the flames.

Laylea never took her eyes from the dean.

"The system *is* gathering biomedical readings. The data from ST, and much of my considerable wealth, goes to Dr. Brock's hospital for the care and rehabilitation of shifter duds. He is curing my daughter. Dr. Brock's techniques could even train you to shift." He still looked down his nose at her, despite her friends' demonstrations of how they could hurt him. It was a fascinating character study.

"How are they training Deanna to shift?" KC asked. "She's in a coma."

"No, she isn't." He turned his disdain on her. "She's running with the wolves on a hundred acres of wild land out west."

Oscar, KC, and Laylea looked at each other. Gorshkov didn't know. KC returned to the power tower. With just a few keystrokes, she flicked the picture of Deanna onto the front screen.

Many of the ghosts crowed at the sight of the sleeping, white-haired girl. They watched Gorshkov intently, waiting for the moment he recognized his daughter. The moment didn't come quickly. He didn't believe it was possible, and so he couldn't see what was right before his eyes.

"That's her, right? Deanna Amelia Gorshkov," Laylea whispered.

As she spoke, a chill raised the tiny hairs all over her human body. Any still smoldering heat had no chance. Half a dozen gas mask ghosts disappeared. Laylea didn't look around to see where Amelia had manifested. She kept her focus on the dean. "Deanna is in a coma in a sleep lab connected to the distribution of N. She's right upstairs, here in Chicago."

The dean stumbled when he finally saw. He stopped breathing. One of his hands reached up as if of its own accord. He stroked the hair of the girl on the screen. "White." He sucked in a breath and whispered, "Her hair turned white. She's a true Lipizzaner." There was joy in his stricken face. Amelia floated through the screen. Frost painted the glass. Then it shattered.

Gorshkov snatched his bleeding hand away. The gas mask ghosts moved in.

"We need him alive." Laylea hissed a warning.

Gorshkov's eyes darted between the three living kids, as if he could finally see the dozen or so less-solid figures between them. His ear bled. His hand bled. Heat and ice warred on his face as Riley and Amelia overlapped in front of him, each screaming threats unheard by any living creature but Laylea.

Guillaume laid a hand on each of their shoulders, murmuring in a reassuring drawl, "We'll keep an eye on him. We can keep him in line." He reached out and flicked the dean's bleeding ear.

Gorshkov slammed a hand against the side of his head to protect his ear. He backed away to the bright, burned carpet.

Oscar followed Gorshkov. "They're using your daughter and my sister..."

KC stepped up to Oscar's side, adding, "And Brenda's father and all the kids in this room."

Laylea moved to join them. "All the kids in this school."

Oscar growled, "To make N."

"And this system of Robby's is not a fire suppressant system and it is not gathering data," Laylea said. "So what is it for?"

A cackle of laughter interrupted any answer the dean might have offered. He spun around to see the man the rest of them could already see standing in the smashed doorway of the dean's outer office: Robby, himself.

"Dear phoenix, you are all so stupid."

40

*R*obby, the installer of tubes, leaned against the broken doorframe of the dean's office. His standard plaid shirt had come untucked from his cargo pants. He tried to straighten his clothing with one hand while he ran the fingers of the other through the sad attempt at a beard that looked patchier the more it grew in. He ran his gaze over the foursome as he caught his breath, staring hard at Laylea and KC, despite Gorshkov's burnt hair, bloody ear, and face twisted in a rictus from Amelia wrapping her ghostly arms around him.

Robby's usual grin was glued to his face, but there was something else there, too. Violence. And triumph. He darted his eyes between KC and Laylea a moment longer before dropping them to the scrap wood at his feet.

"Boo." He kicked a loose piece of the door so hard it slammed into the dean's desk. The sound popped Laylea's inconsistent shifter switch. She barely noticed the pain shooting through her as her point of view dropped. Her sensitive canine nose wrinkled from the burned wool of the rug, the fear and anger wafting off Gorshkov, and the cloying sweetness of Robby's not-so-subtle cologne. Guillaume popped, as well, the flash sending some more gas mask ghosts into the aether. The dove settled to the floor between Laylea and Robby.

He must have seen something in Robby that she had missed, because when she looked up, the installer's gaze had settled on her. Violence flashed across his face, and she recoiled from the stink of his adrenaline spike.

When he spoke, though, his voice was controlled. "At last we meet, Lee Woodford, the dog shifter of LPSS. I'm disappointed." He pushed up the sleeves of his flannel, revealing an armpadd on his left forearm and another slim device on his right.

Cal dashed through Gorshkov to get a closer look at the device. "I've seen this." He tried to grab it, but his hands slipped through Robby's arm. "It's some kind of kill switch. One of a kind." He looked over at the other ghosts, as if one of them could confirm it. Nobody answered.

Robby didn't even notice the kid. "I don't know why Denier is so fascinated by you, Lee Woodford. Any idiot could have figured it all out, but you think Gorse designed N. Dr. Maurice Brock designed N, you moron. He was a genius. And he would be alive now if it weren't for you."

Laylea tilted her head as any confused dog would. She wanted to slap herself.

KC stepped out from behind the tower. "Prison is a dangerous place. If he hadn't killed all those kids, maybe he wouldn't have been there."

"My father wasn't killed in prison," Robby growled.

Robby was Dr. Brock's kid? That explained why he was so interested in meeting her. And why DJ hid her from him.

"My father was assassinated in Captain Morioka's holding room, so she couldn't question him. He could have defended himself if this bitch hadn't stolen his Permashift spray."

"Permashift spray?" KC asked, because one of them had to.

"It's a weaponized version of the serum he created to force a were to shift and never shift back."

KC whispered to Oscar, "How would you use that, other than as a weapon?"

"Defensively!" Robby shrieked the answer before sucking in a deep breath and visibly calming himself. He strolled over to the coat rack.

The instant Robby looked away, Gorshkov stepped forward, out of Amelia's freezing aura. He found breath to sneer, "Brock. What did your father do with my daughter?"

Robby spun and pulled a gun from the pocket of his cargo pants. It was a gun, so it was scary. But, Laylea couldn't help but wonder what kind of doofus kept a pistol in his thigh pocket. Gorshkov stumbled back. Amelia gathered him into her arms before he could run into the shattered monitor. His face showed the pain he felt. Robby either didn't notice, or he took it as a reaction to his surprise cargo pocket weapon.

The installer answered with a cruel laugh. "Papa made use of Deanna. The wolves just needed her out of the way while they bled you of money. My father began designing N with her blood. You know why it's such a popular drug?"

"Because people feel invisible and helpless most of the time, like they're ghosts." KC answered the rhetorical question. She held Sanna's red crane up, stroking it with her thumb. When Robby just looked at her like she was crazy, she shot a desperate glance at Oscar.

Robby scoffed. "Shut up. My father made N so it works differently depending on the genetic makeup of the user. Where better to find the ingredients he needed than here? LPSS is a convenient collection of every genetic variant he needed, except for thumpers. And they're easy enough to hunt." His face wrinkled in an unpleasant grin and then he shuddered through a spate of different emotions. "N was phase one. There are too many goody-goodies like you lot for N to be the final solution. The Permashift spray came out of my father's work on phase two."

KC and Oscar shot each other looks and gestures throughout Robby's diatribe. Oscar wasn't getting the message that KC was trying to psychically send him. Neither of them tried to communicate with Laylea. She didn't know what KC was trying to express either, but it still made her feel rotten that they discounted her just because she was a dog. They weren't wrong to, though. She was useless. She couldn't even ask what phase two was.

Robby lifted the gas mask from the dean's coat rack. He examined it like he'd never seen one before.

KC grunted her frustration out loud. When Robby raised his eyebrows at her, she let out a huff and said, pointedly, "Your father made a lot of angry ghosts wearing gas masks like that. Aren't you afraid of them haunting you?"

"Ghosts aren't real. If they were, my father would have stuck around to finish his work. But he's not here. He's gone. Because you condemned him to death." Robby glared down at Laylea.

Guillaume ruffled his feathers and hopped forward, trilling little sounds that might have intimidated another bird. Or an insect.

Oscar suddenly blurted out, "Ghosts aren't helpless."

"No. They're science fiction."

Oscar turned to look at Riley. "I've seen ghosts move things to get revenge."

Robby tossed the gas mask in his hand and laughed. "I promise you, my father will get his revenge. If Papa ain't happy, nobody's happy. And he was not happy with phase two. The gas never quite worked right. Denier wanted it to freeze a shifter's abilities. Most of the time, it just killed them."

That got the ghosts' attention. Oscar and KC shook as if they couldn't find the words. Laylea had words, but she didn't have a voice.

Robby slipped the mask over his head. Masks appeared on ghosts around the room, imitating him. Guillaume shifted to human, but his blue flash couldn't bring down the temperature this time. And Laylea wasn't sure she wanted it to. KC had been trying to tell the ghosts they could disarm Robby. And, like Laylea, they seemed to finally be getting the message. Cal slapped at the gun. His ghostly hand slid right through it.

Robby's voice was muffled as he strode closer. "Papa is gone, and it's up to me to get his revenge. So, let's try phase two and see what happens. Maybe those final changes he made will work as Denier wanted them to." He hopped onto the dean's desk and rested his feet on his chair, oblivious to the ghosts swiping at him and the gun. He didn't notice the desk smoking as the wood burned from the ghosts' anger. "But it doesn't really matter. There's nobody to carry on his research, nobody brilliant enough to follow in his steps. So, there is no reason to maintain a collection of blood donors."

He tapped and swiped on the slim device on his right wrist. Laylea was close enough to see the small face pulse with red light. Smoke slithered out of the tubes overhead. Cal slammed his fist repeatedly through the device.

"I remember!" he cried. "Robby bragged to me while he was dragging me here. This switch is the only way to turn the system off!"

Somehow, Cal's words crossed the veil of life because Robby confirmed, "Yes, this is the only kill switch. And you'll never get to it. Also, there is no antiserum." He bent and hit a button under the dean's desk. Deanna's portrait creaked and started sliding on its track.

As the kid ghosts all slammed themselves into the same space to try to hit the kill switch on Robby's wrist, Amelia soared over and scrabbled at Laylea's throat. Guillaume stood in the doorway, between Robby and the rest of the humans. Oscar snatched a cloth from his pocket and covered his mouth and nose. KC roared and ran. She shifted into wolf mid-run and leapt. She was on a trajectory to soar right through Guillaume when Robby pulled the trigger.

The shot echoed in Laylea's ears

KC's yelping filled the air as Guillaume slammed backwards into her, solid enough to knock her to the ground. With effort, he stumbled forward and fell into Robby, knocking him over the desk.

Robby dropped the gun, rolled from the desk, and took off out the door. His terrified face looking back was the last thing Laylea saw before Deanna's portrait slammed shut, trapping them in the dean's secret inner office.

41

*L*aylea had one assignment. She was to find Bert Gorshkov, alert Dee, and not get caught. She'd found Bert Gorshkov. She'd found out he wasn't the answer to everything. But instead of alerting Dee, she'd gotten herself and her two best friends trapped in a small room with the creep and his dead wife while a likely deadly gas poured into the entire school. She was right back in Brock's closet. Though it was unlikely she would find a food door to escape through this time.

"You're a wolf!" Gorshkov stared at KC. His shocked voice cut through the buzz as Laylea's ears tried to recover from the blast of the pistol.

A howl rang from her throat as she bounded away from the icy panic of Amelia to help her friend. KC lay on the floor at the base of the wall-door with her tongue hanging out of her mouth and her eyes shut. Oscar landed at her side as Laylea licked KC's muzzle. He shook the wolf gently, almost begging, "Wake up. KC, wake up."

Laylea barked and sniffed her way down KC's chest and belly. She didn't smell any blood or spot any matted fur. Oscar saw what she was doing and rolled KC to her side to look for wounds. There was nothing obvious. KC had been directly in the line of fire. How was she unhurt?

"Open the door, Gorse." In his distraction, Oscar used the dean's false name. "We have to get out of here."

Gorshkov slammed a fist into the wall. "There is no way to open the door from the inside. And all signals are blocked. We can't even contact anybody to get us out."

"Not to mention, they're all out there dying from smoke, just like we are!" Oscar spat back.

A whimper drew their attention back to KC. She whimpered again and opened her eyes. An instant later, KC, the girl, lay there, feeling her gut and staring in amazement when her hands came away clean. "Guillaume," she whispered.

"Guillaume stopped the bullet?" Oscar asked as he put his handkerchief over her mouth and nose and tied it around her head.

"Guillaume who?" Gorshkov demanded before reverting to his standard self-centered focus. "Denier lied to me. Lee, take me to my daugh—"

Before he could finish the word, the dean started coughing.

KC sat up. "Open the door before you pass out, Berty." She pushed herself to her feet with Oscar's help, and the two started searching the outline of the door. Laylea sniffed along the bottom.

Gorshkov reiterated, "There is no way out."

"Then how is Lee supposed to take you to your daughter?" KC asked the man before turning to Oscar. "Grab Lee's uniform. Use it to cover your mouth and nose."

Laylea barked. Amelia was on her knees again, scrabbling at Laylea's neck. One icy cold ghostly manifestation reached into her throat, and Laylea shifted human to defend herself. "What? What?" She grasped her collar with both hands. "You want something I have?"

Laylea stood, backing away as Amelia followed her. She unzipped both pockets and pulled out her house key, the new bank card, Ms. Crow's blue vial, a guitar pick, and the three aerosol tubes from Dr. Brock's rolltop desk. Amelia's aura grew and encased Laylea for just a second. Just long enough for Laylea to feel her triumph. Laylea dumped everything else back in but one of the tubes. Before she could act, Amelia raised Laylea's hand, pointed the vial at Gorshkov, and sprayed.

"What the phoenix? What is—" Gorshkov's exclamation ended in a whinny as he shifted from a plump, middle-aged ex-playboy to a distressingly beautiful white stallion. He reared back and smacked the ceiling, sending plaster flying. His front hooves flailed, smashing the old wooden file cabinets along the north wall. Files and papers and kindling flew through the room.

Oscar backpedaled to cower against the south wall with KC and Laylea. Laylea held her arm up and breathed into the crook of her elbow. The horse, their dean, began to calm after smashing five or six cabinets of student records.

Before he fully settled, a second white horse appeared beside Gorshkov. The mare reared, whinnied, and bit Gorshkov's haunches. Gorshkov reared again in panic. He tried to gallop back and forth, but there was no room, and whichever way he went, Amelia was there, snapping at him with her long teeth and stomping her front hooves at him. He spun once, doing irreparable damage to the power tower and then reared in full attack against the north wall. The drywall flew. After that, the joists splintered, and Amelia drove him through and out into the open plan office beyond.

The kids scurried to follow. Smoke and drywall dust obscured the opening. Laylea couldn't cover her mouth while she picked her way through. She was climbing over a toppled filing cabinet that had nearly survived the rampage when she inhaled too harshly and was blinded by a coughing fit. Before she could secure her footing, the burn shot up from her gut, and her tiny canine form fell into a crevasse created by dead cabinets and the deconstructed wall. She yelped.

Her claws had barely touched down when a black paw swatted aside a two by four and hot breath warmed her head. It took him two tries to get a grip on the loose fur at Laylea's nape, but then she was up, and Oscar was off with her in his teeth. He slunk through the disaster as smoothly as one would expect a cat to navigate. His paws padded over precarious footholds without swaying them. He leapt lightly from one teetering stack to another without a thought. Safely away from the destruction, he set her on her paws and loped back into the mess, shifting into human to offer KC a hand.

She took his help and gave him his lost uniform. "It might do more good if you hold that up to your face to block the smoke."

Oscar laughed and pulled it on as he and KC joined Laylea in the aisle between four desks. KC wiped at the slobber on her fur. Laylea couldn't see her mouth, but her eyes were sparkling enough that she didn't need to. The giggle in her voice couldn't be hidden. "You've got a little something here on your fur."

Laylea growled deep in her throat. KC laughed outright.

Oscar crouched as he buttoned up his overalls. He grinned, "I won't tell anyone if you won't."

Laylea barked sharply at both of them and took off. They had to get to ST and figure out how to spread the antiserum. The others followed, making plans.

"We have to get everyone out of the school," KC said from behind her handkerchief.

"We can't send everyone upstairs." Oscar coughed.

"I don't know what else we can do." KC dodged a series of chairs Laylea had simply run under. "If they stay here, they're all gonna die."

Oscar nearly ran into a wall, but pushed himself away to keep chasing KC and Laylea. He coughed out directions. "The all-call bells are operated from that box on the wall beside the Executive Wing entrance."

Laylea reached the entrance well before the two-leggeds. She scratched at it and inhaled to howl. The smoke filled her lungs. It felt thicker than the smoke in Brock's closet, like the smoke was solidifying into cement in her chest. She coughed and shifted.

She started yelling before her body had settled enough for speaking, "The pink tube in ST is antiserum."

Her friends only caught the last word.

KC pulled tools from her backpack to pick the lock on the callbox cover. She didn't even glance over as she said, "There is no antiserum."

"Robby told us," Oscar added.

"Robby is a liar. The ghosts in Brock's closet told me he revived them with pink smoke."

"The reagent is pink." KC stared at Oscar.

"It's not reagent." Oscar pounded on his chest as if he could release some pressure. "We all knew it wasn't what he said it was."

KC yelled, "It's the antiserum."

Laylea nodded. "Yeah."

The cover popped open, nearly bopping KC in the face. She looked to Oscar to operate the equipment. "Send everyone to the dorms! We can reroute the hoses in ST to spread the antiserum. That way, no one has to explain to Chicago why three hundred kids suddenly appeared in the Lincoln Park Zoo."

Laylea wanted to ask why the secret mattered in the face of everyone dying, but Oscar suddenly bent double, hacking and scratching at his chest. Both girls turned to help him, but he pushed KC back toward the all-call box. He pointed repeatedly. There was nothing she could do to help him, so Laylea joined KC.

She opened the cover. Two dozen switches filled the box in two neat rows. Each switch was accompanied by a white label with areas of the school handwritten on them in different inks. The whole thing looked like an electrical panel, except with the addition of a big green button and a big red button at the top. KC looked at Laylea and hit the green button.

Nothing happened.

Laylea began flipping the switches all the way down the right column. KC did the same on the left. When they were all flipped, KC smashed the big green button again. This time, whirring sounds indicated some mechanical process stirring to action.

KC yelled at Oscar as they both wrestled him out of the Executive Wing, "Get up. We have to get to ST. You can do it!"

The hallway looked as though some kind of underground fog had rolled in off the lake. Laylea tried to crouch low where the air was more clear, but Oscar was leaning on her too much for her to be able to run that way. They got three steps from the Wing doors when KC bent over in a coughing fit. Oscar fell. Laylea reached him in time to cushion his head before it hit the ground, but he wouldn't rouse to her shaking.

"Where are the bells?" KC coughed through her question.

Laylea's eyes watered. She wasn't sure if it was from the smoke or despair. "I'll go back."

"No. We have to get Oscar to—" She bent over her knees, coughing despite the bandanna.

Laylea coughed in sympathy. When the spasms passed, she finished KC's thought. "To ST?" She hooked a hand in Oscar's armpit and tried to drag him. "Do you know how to switch the hoses?"

KC nodded.

"Then we need to get to ST."

KC nodded again. When she caught her breath, she rasped, "It's our best chance."

"Where are the bells?" Laylea had failed. She must have missed a step in her rush to get out of the Wing. How many kids would die because she hadn't made sure she'd done it right?

KC stumbled to Oscar's other side and helped Laylea. They hauled with everything they had, and Oscar's body moved a few inches. Laylea's chest felt like lead. Pulling in another breath was impossible. The pain from her gut was almost unnoticeable beneath the panic of not getting oxygen. One flash of burning and she could breathe again. Her paws rested on Oscar's shoulder, where she'd been gripping him. She jumped off and dug her teeth into his coveralls. She couldn't budge him. Oscar wasn't big, but KC was small and Laylea was a twelve-pound dog. They didn't have a chance.

A raven's caw echoed off the stone. As if in answer, deep bells tolled. A sleek black bird soared out of the smoke. Dizzy landed on Oscar's chest and screamed into his face. When he tossed his head, she nipped his nose. His eyes opened. She cawed again. His eyes fell shut again.

Laylea felt her lungs filling and focused on the terror of certain death. She shifted. "Come on, KC. We can do this."

Dizzy crowed and tried to grab at Oscar's clothes to help pull.

With the healing activated by Laylea's shift, and encouragement aimed at KC, they were able to drag Oscar several feet before KC dropped him in the throes of a coughing fit, and Laylea shifted back to dog. She howled. They needed help. KC needed to leave them and go swap the hoses. But KC collapsed beside Oscar.

Laylea and Dizzy dashed to her side, one licking her ear, the other pecking at her hair. KC waved them away.

"I'm okay," she whispered. "It's just hard to breathe." A whimper escaped her. Laylea echoed the wordless cry.

The hall rang with the doleful bells which did nothing to thin the gray smoke slowly thickening the air. Nobody was coming to help them. Nobody else knew how to save the school. It was up to them. Laylea licked KC's ear. She turned and licked Oscar's eyelids. He wasn't going to get up. She looked into Dizzy's beady eyes, sucked in a deep breath, and reached for the burn.

She shifted. Breathing as shallowly as possible, she grabbed KC by the shoulders and dragged her to her feet. "You know how to deliver the antidote. We need to get you to ST. We have to," she choked on the words. "We have to leave Oscar."

KC shook her head. Dizzy cawed a mournful cry that echoed in descant to the bells.

Laylea insisted, "He'll get the antiserum, same as everybody else. We have to leave him here."

But KC kept shaking her head. She held the handkerchief against her face and leaned in close, so she wouldn't have to shout. "I go to ST. You go after Robby. The smoke can't stop you. Get the kill switch."

Laylea started to argue, but a shimmer in the smoke startled her into silence. It was that barely perceptible wrinkle in the universe that accompanied the most subtle of shifters. The smoke billowed as Ms. Crow stepped out of the grayness close to the girls. She removed her orange sweater and tied it around her head, covering her mouth and nose.

The sight of the librarian reminded Laylea that she had a blue vial of magic potion in her collar that Ms. Crow had given her to counteract sligh nut poisoning. She reached for her collar. "Maybe this will work."

She pulled the vial out, but Ms. Crow stopped her with a shake of her head. "It won't help with inhaled poisons, only ingested ones. KC is right. You're our best hope, Lee. I saw Robby heading for the Sphinx tunnel. The first barrier will be down, thanks to the alarm. Go." Ms. Crow crouched and hauled Oscar into her arms. "Go, Lee. I'll follow when I can."

Ms. Crow didn't wait for arguments. She turned away and disappeared with Oscar into the smoke. KC grabbed Laylea to her in a hug and then ran after the librarian. Laylea stumbled three steps away before she shifted again and poured all the speed she had into her four powerful legs.

42

*L*aylea made it all the way to the library before she had to shift again. Her body wanted to shift earlier, but she managed to hold it off. As she stretched her human legs, she considered grabbing a uniform from any of the many closets she passed, since she was going upstairs. But she wouldn't be able to drag it along in her furry form, and it would only slow her down between shifts. So, she focused on running and yelling at any conscious kids she passed to get to a dorm and stay low.

She skidded into the turn from the dining hall foyer down the Sphinx dorm corridor. Her feet slipped out from under her, but she landed on four paws and picked up speed. She had to dodge and leap to avoid the bodies lying in her path. It seemed like the Sphinx kids had tried to obey the bells but didn't quite make it to the dorm. Laylea's instincts screamed for her to help. She ignored them until she saw Brian lying in his gorilla form, two other kids lying unconscious beside him like he'd been carrying them. She licked his face.

"I've got him." The voice was thin. Laylea looked up to see Cal Christopherson kneeling at Brian's side, his hands on her friend's chest. "You said we're magic. We'll give them our magic."

Laylea looked around. Now that she knew they were there, she could see ghosts hovering in the smoke over many of the other kids who had succumbed. Could they really keep the kids alive? She didn't know, and she didn't have time to think about it. Whatever magic they had would not last forever.

"Robby and Guillaume went that way." Cal and all of the ghosts turned and pointed down the corridor toward the tunnel where Oscar had first sneaked Laylea and KC upstairs into the zoo.

Laylea sang a trill of thanks at them and ran. Kids were dying. Ghosts were giving their life force. She had no time to waste.

One turn past the Sphinx's curtained archway, the illusory wall that hid the exit tunnel was gone. Praying the forcefield was also gone, Laylea put her head down and barreled for the exit. She allowed her lungs to suck in a breath of relief when she passed into the darkness of the tunnel. The breath brought Brock's poison into her lungs, and she shifted human just in time to leap through the second archway. *Second gate, second form.*

You must be in your natural state to get through the third gate. She chanted the third gate rule in her head and vowed to take up jogging in her human form as she pushed through the darkness toward the third archway. The deep core burn eluded her. She tried to think of all the bodies lying along the hallways, kids who would die unless she could stop Robby. It didn't help. She thought of Robby, out in the zoo, taking their only hope farther away by the second.

Running as fast as her legs could pump, Laylea ran full speed into the magical forcefield that was the third gate. The air sparked, and Laylea flew back, landing hard enough on the stone floor to crack her skull in the instant before the beautiful burn flooded her body, and she shifted. She froze a moment in the remembered pain. The sound of her cracking skull still echoing in floppy ears. Then she rolled to her paws and was off again, through the gate and weaving through the kiddie-sized tunnel around a molded-cement tree and out into the Regenstein Center for African Apes.

Her claws caught purchase on the carpet, and she turned for the double set of doors leading to the outside path. They were closed. She huffed in frustration and noticed that the air was clean. She sucked in a deep, cool breath of fresh air. Her head cleared. Movement at the doors had her running again. A broad-shouldered man in deep green coveralls yanked the far door open. Laylea would have to be quick.

She huddled in the shadows by the inner doors, waiting for the right moment. Dogs weren't appreciated in the zoo. If the employee caught her or put out the alert, she would never be able to catch Robby and turn off the gas.

The guy looked over his shoulder at something down the path as he passed through the outer door. He strolled too slowly through the airlock, muttering to himself. Laylea despaired as the first door floated closed. She'd need the luck of a golden retriever to catch it. The inner door cracked. Laylea made a break for it, caution be damned. If he saw her, it was too bad. She had to get through that outer door.

His muttering became audible as he pulled the door wider. "Get out of your way? You get out of *my* way, asshole. Whoa!" The zoo employee staggered as she dashed between his legs. He kicked her without meaning to, and she sprawled into the glass of the outer door just as it clicked shut.

Unable to hold it in, Laylea howled her frustration. She leapt to her feet and threw herself at the outer door.

"Hey, there." The disgruntled guy in green talked to her like she was a real human being. "You're gonna hurt yourself."

The tone shocked her enough that she looked up. His ruddy face was familiar, as was his voice. Her eyes shot to his name tag even as his flashed to the path outside. The man was Etienne, the same guy who opened Adelor back in March when she returned to school. She didn't have to pretend to be a dumb animal around him. She howled and scratched at the door.

"Are you chasing that guy? You're after Robby?" he asked.

She barked and threw herself at the door again.

With a few select words her parents would not approve of, Etienne moved to the outer door in two enormous strides. He pushed it open, swearing again when the closing mechanism resisted. "Go get him. Bite him in the ass for me."

Laylea scraped her sides getting through the door. It hurt badly enough that she shifted. Gravel scraped her knees. She rolled through it and tore down the path, human, buck naked, and upstairs. Dee was not going to be happy with her.

Etienne called after her, "He's headed for the party. Just follow the noise."

She flipped him a thumbs up and kept running. Voices and music carried through the zoo. Laylea worried she wouldn't be able to tell where it was coming from with her wimpy human ears, but after passing the gorillas' expansive outdoor enclosure, she spotted some guests. Her feet stumbled to a stop. People in fancy clothes gathered in groups ahead and down the path to her right. Someone threw popcorn into the air like confetti. Others laughed and danced. She couldn't see any sign of which way Robby had gone. She swiveled her head from path to path, searching the crowds, aware that someone could spot her at any moment, and people didn't tend to overlook stark naked teenagers hanging out at a rich people party.

A sound drew her attention to the right-hand path. It wasn't music or voices, and it had seemed to be right in her ear. The coo warbled again, so close the bird would have to be on her shoulder. Her cheek was brushed and a breeze tousled her hair from the beat of a pair of wings.

She whispered, "Guillaume?"

Then she caught sight of Robby's flannel shirt flashing dully between glittering dresses far down the right path. His plaid stood out against the sea of couture just long enough for her to catch a glimpse.

"Merci," she whispered and then dashed forward, preparing to sprint.

A scattering of popcorn took her out. She slipped and skidded along the paved walkway, flensing a horrid amount of skin from her right thigh. She automatically took a moment to be grateful she hadn't landed on her left side. That hip was already messed up in her dog form, she didn't need it as a human weakness as well. The thought and the pain translated into that familiar body burn, and Laylea was prepared. She shifted mid-leap and landed with her paws pumping.

The DeGee Pavilion was just ahead on the south lawn. It looked like that was where Robby was headed. Did he think he'd be safe in a crowd? Maybe if Laylea had been raised with the shifter strictures of staying hidden, she'd care more about being seen. But she'd been raised by the thumpers he had such disdain for. And she was really kinda over hiding.

As it turned out, she caught him before he reached the pavilion. He had no clue she was behind him. A few of the guests noticed the fawn dog dodging around their legs, but only one teenaged girl verbalized her surprise with a laugh. Laylea bit into Robby's pant leg and darted to one side, taking that leg out from under him. He fell, hard. She bounded over his body and latched her teeth onto the kill switch on his wrist. The blinking red of the device blinded her, but Robby offered no resistance until her teeth scratched him while she pulled it over his thumb. He woke and shoved her away.

She tumbled through the sea of legs, bumping to a stop in a cloud of chiffon. By the time she got extricated from it, Robby was scrambling up and pushing through the crowd, the kill switch in his hand. She launched herself off the legs under the chiffon and buried her teeth in the leather of Robby's pristine hiking boot.

Robby stopped cold in the midst of the crowd. They were curious now, wondering about the scuffle. A few of the guests gasped as Robby kicked Laylea. The toe of his boot caught her in the ribs. She rolled off the path and into the grass, struggling to breathe. Blood spurted out of her nose, spattering a pair of lovely lavender wing tips. She offered an apology—half bark, half choke—as the blessed burn shot through her, and she found herself lying naked at the feet of a distinguished older gentleman. Mr. Vronumraju would have admired the man's double-rung handlebar mustache. In the instant she lay there, the man caught her eyes and winked. It was not the response she had expected. But she didn't have time to wonder.

Party guests started yelling. Somewhere, musicians played on, unaware, as yet, of the commotion. Laylea rolled to her knees, searching for Robby as she pushed off the grass. A cry went up, farther down the path, and then she heard Robby's voice shouting the same rude words Etienne had used. She darted through the crowd, keeping low and alternating between "pardon me" and "excuse me."

"Whoa, Robby. What's going on?" DJ Delcampo's voice cut through the commotion because it was the only voice Laylea recognized. Her heart leapt. DJ would help. "Denier sent us to help. He said someone hacked the deep cold databanks."

Laylea hurtled toward a trio of older women in crepe pantsuits. She couldn't control her body any more than her mind. Did DJ work for Adrien Denier? Was she wrong about him? A figure slipped out of the crowd, and she slammed into the warm, velvety mass of a lion instead of barreling into the ladies. The lion shifted as she righted herself, trying to see DJ and Robby through the mass of formal wear. Strong hands lifted her into the air as she spotted the two men crouching just on the other side of the pantsuit brigade.

A voice so deep it felt like a purr brushed her ear as the lion shifter set her on her feet again. "How can I help?"

She glanced at his shoes, spattered with her blood, and looked up to see the distinguished gentleman who had winked at her. She stuttered, "I... I have to get the device that guy is holding."

"Brock?" he asked.

She nodded, too shocked for words.

"I'll have to be tricksy. Can't have anyone know we're working against Denier." He winked at the ladies as he said this, not being secretive at all. "You go that way, and be ready."

He strode around the far side of the women. Laylea ducked around them on the near side to find Robby struggling to get past DJ while they argued. DJ's eyes searched the crowd. He didn't see Laylea. Then the lion man was there, stumbling like a drunk and falling into the pair. Robby and DJ both went to the ground. The device tumbled from Robby's grip.

The red light pulsed like blood from an arterial wound. Laylea dashed for it. So did DJ.

43

*P*anic gripped Laylea so hard she almost looked around for Amelia. Her lungs seized up, and she flashed back to the feeling of inhaling Brock's gray smoke. How long could anyone survive that smoke, even with the ghosts' help? How long had she been chasing Robby? She was their only chance. Everyone in the school would die if she didn't get that device.

The trio of ladies behind her tittered like a flock of rare birds. The crowd at large complained or marveled at the unexpected excitement. The lion man gripped Robby, drunkenly helping him from the ground as he apologized for his inelegance. Brock was an honorable gentleman and should expect better treatment. Whoops, slipped again. Ha ha, grass stains would be hell to get out of his tux. Would young Brock like a drink?

The kill switch skittered through the sea of feet, its red light illuminating shoes like they'd tiptoed through blood. Laylea sucked in fresh air and pushed herself hard, racing DJ as he scrambled away from Robby and her lion friend. KC's brother tripped as his feet caught in the loose fabric of his slacks. He flew forward, landing hard and skidding along the pavement. He didn't even try to stop himself, reaching forward instead. His fingers brushed the flashing face. Laylea's hooked the wrist band.

She continued stumbling through the crowd even as she swiped the screen live and tapped the enormous red DEACTIVATE icon. Nothing happened. It kept flashing red.

DJ hissed, "You need to be downstairs for it to work."

She looked back. He was right behind her, clothes bloody and torn, his head on a swivel, searching the people surrounding them. She stared at him, still confused about whose side he was on.

He held his armpadd up to his mouth and said, "Message Beta: I spotted the dog heading toward the seal pool."

The seal pool was in the other direction.

DJ gasped for air, his face a mess of emotions. "Get downstairs. Save them." Laylea goggled at him for an instant. That was too long for DJ. He shoved her. "Go!"

She turned and raced north through the thinning crowd. Adelor was the closest entrance. A laugh bubbled up, bursting her panic. One lion had already helped her. Now, she needed to reach another. Cats were earning big win points today.

The partygoers parted for her. Many of them were heading toward the zoo entrance, themselves. She wondered why, because it hadn't looked like the party was ending. Then she saw the stone lion. Adelor was swung aside on his plinth. A dozen kids ran and stumbled off the steps. Most were coughing. Many hung on to each other, barely able to walk. The guests converged on the kids to help them.

Laylea had just reached the first of the three steps up the plinth when a wolf plowed into her. Her face slammed into the stone. Before she could fully grasp the shooting pains exploding behind her eyes, she shifted. The kill switch skittered away from her thumbless paws toward the open stairwell. Laylea pulled those paws under her and faced the wolf. All teeth and growl, the brown wolf with white ears and splotches stalked forward. Laylea didn't bother snarling back. Her coward tail tucked under, negating any tough-guy show she might have offered.

The wolf stopped advancing. Its face scrunched up, and it

suddenly jerked to nip at its own butt. A tiny speck burst from the rumpled fur. The air boiled. That was the only way Laylea could think to describe the shift. A deep, lung-thumping note rolled out of the boiling air, and suddenly Robby was standing beside the wolf, struggling to catch his breath and his balance.

He didn't look at the wolf baring its teeth at him. He glued his gaze to Laylea. "Thanks for the ride, Sierra. Go fetch the rest of the pack."

The wolf growled at Robby. He didn't pay her any mind, but Laylea inched backwards, distancing herself. When Sierra followed, Robby kicked the wolf's hind leg.

"Back off," he spat. "She's mine. Denier promised I could kill her."

A shimmer in reality accompanied Sierra's easy shift. One moment, she hunkered over Laylea, slobbering, and the next, she stood stroking her blond ponytail where it lay over one shoulder. The expression on her face didn't really change. "Denier ordered you to catch her, Robby. You're not supposed to hurt her."

Both of them turned at the sound of roaring in the distance. It sounded like a bear, an unhappy bear.

"Go take care of that, Sierra."

"Whatever." Sierra flipped her ponytail over her shoulder and ambled off into the zoo. "You're still a loser, tick."

At odds to the werewolf's languid pace, Laylea's mind raced. She would need fingers to operate the kill switch. She and the switch needed to be downstairs. As Robby watched Sierra strolling away, Laylea moved sideways, up one step.

He saw her. "You're done for, Lee Woodford. You killed my father, and now I will have my revenge on you, your friends, and every lousy kid in that pit who ever made fun of me." He strode past her to the statue. "You're not going to die quickly, either. I am going to hurt you." He stroked the lion's nose, and Adelor trembled into motion, slowly closing off any chance of getting back into the school in time.

The plinth rumbled beneath her paws. Her heart rumbled in her chest. Everyone was going to die, but Robby couldn't blame it on her. His father chose to be evil. It caught up with him.

He grunted, "Where is the Permashift? Give it to me."

Laylea bared her teeth. She planted her paws on the stone. She would never show him. She would die first.

Adelor hit a sticky bit, and the vibration knocked her to her butt. In that instant, light flashed in her brain as bright and cool as if Guillaume were shifting in front of her. Her anger evaporated as two things became clear to her. One: She knew where the Permashift was. Two: He couldn't hurt her. No one could really harm Laylea, not for long.

Robby had just told her how to save the school.

Laylea sucked in a breath, steeled herself, and buried her teeth into her bum hip hard enough to taste blood.

She shifted.

Adelor was nearly closed. The kill switch lay just behind Robby, mere steps from the stairwell. Laylea's human fingers found the tube in her collar as she came to her feet.

Fear ghosted the sneer on Robby's face, and he stepped back from her. His heel sent the kill switch spinning for Adelor's rapidly closing entrance. Her heart stopped, and her feet moved. She shot Robby with a spritz of the Permashift as she pushed past him, leaping at Adelor.

His hand closed around her arm before his daddy's serum activated, forcing him to shift. The tug sent her spinning and falling toward the flashing red device. Her outstretched arm hit the ground first, followed by her chest. She heard and felt her ribs crack and tamped down on the burning she knew would follow.

Don't shift. Don't shift.

The hard corner of the device dug into her palm as she followed it through the open sliver of space beneath Adelor's paws. She clenched her fingers around the kill switch and rolled to get her other hand into position. The screen felt slimy under her fingers. A stripe of red smeared the screen as she swiped it awake. Red light flashed in the darkness of the stairwell, complimenting the shattering agony of her spine hitting the stairs. Electricity shot down her arm, and her hand went numb. Her fingers fell open, releasing the kill switch. Laylea jammed the flashing red DEACTIVATE icon just before the device fell from her grip.

Pain flared through her body as she soared beyond the stairs and rammed into the stone wall beyond. Outside, she heard the bear. Was it Toby? Its cry rumbled in her eardrums as if it were right there above her, beyond the stone lion still sliding home. A distant part of her brain, a part that wasn't flooded with adrenaline, hoped it stepped on Robby.

Every other part of her brain screamed in fear as she fell, following the kill switch. The lion shifted a final inch, drenching the stairwell in darkness. There was no light but for the cool, green glow spinning down the walls of Adelor's stairwell.

44

$\mathcal{V}$oices drifted through the spinning green haze into Laylea's woozy brain.

Familiar, friendly voices.

"If she'd stayed a dog, I wouldn't have found her," KC argued.

Oscar retorted, "But when she shifted human, you couldn't move her."

There was a moment of heavy silence. Laylea blinked her eyes open. It took another moment for the view to come into focus. KC sat cross-legged, working on something in her lap that looked like the kind of bag an EMT would use to pump oxygen. Her mouth worked at trying to come up with a response to Oscar, who sat with his back to Laylea.

KC huffed out a breath. "Are you suggesting that if I had kicked her really hard in the head, she would have shifted, and I could have carried her?"

"It's worked in the past."

Laylea grinned. It might have worked. She stared at the scene beyond KC, trying to figure out where she was. Even with her dull human senses, the room smelled green, outdoors green. The three of them were on a patch of soft, thick grass separated by several trees from the small steel, glass, and stone amphitheater.

A dozen kids lounged on the many levels of the circular gathering spot surrounding a pond. Other kids moved among them with water, food, and more oxygen bags. She saw Emerald, Ali, Squirt, and the other kids who had been wilding among them. The stone wall beyond them featured a wooden section that could have been a door except it lacked any handles or visible hinges. Pink smoke trickled out of an open archway on the right wall. Ms. Crow came through the archway, a satchel with a red cross on it hanging at her hip.

KC shook her head at Oscar. "We should have kicked you really hard."

He shook his head back at her. "My leopard form weighs even more than my human form. You couldn't have carried me either way."

Laylea inhaled a deep lungful of fresh air. "How about we kick him now and find out?" She caught KC's eyes.

"Hey there, sleepyhead." KC spoke casually, but Laylea didn't miss the look of relief she shot Oscar.

Oscar didn't hold back. He spun around and dove down to hug her. When he'd squeezed her sufficiently, he held her at arm's length. "How're you feeling?"

She took a moment to decide and responded, "I don't feel like I fell down a stone stairway."

"Or inhaled a whole bunch of poison and then got crushed by a bear?" he asked.

KC smacked him with the squeeze part of the manual respirator. "Toby didn't crush her. It looked like he set her down before he passed out."

"Toby?" Laylea asked, pushing up to sitting.

"I found Toby lying unconscious in the corridor outside Mod Tech. I was about to run for help when you shifted human underneath him. Big Mo brought you here."

"*Here* is the Gryphons' dorm?" Sitting, she could see that they were in the middle of the five trees whose branches formed a ladder up into the rafters.

"Yeah." KC sighed. "The reagent system in Mer dorm didn't work."

"Because y'all broke it every time Robby fixed it," Oscar said.

"So we relocated everyone here, where there is no install at all, gray or pink."

Oscar handed Laylea a bottle of water. "KC and Benny rigged up a smoker in the girls' podroom. The bad cases go in there. Everyone else is hanging out in the nest." He looked over at the area around the pond, so Laylea assumed that's what he meant by nest.

She swallowed and asked, "Why are we over here?"

KC shrugged. "This is where Big Mo dumped you. You're really breathing okay?"

Laylea nodded. "How's Toby? How's everyone?"

Oscar and KC gave each other a long look, as if debating who had to tell her the bad news.

"What?"

KC shrugged. "We don't know."

Oscar jumped in with, "Toby is fine. Word got to Ms. Lagat, and she hijacked Brian to help her get him somewhere safe."

"We've been focused on Mers and anyone Big Mo and Brian find in the halls. It's been a few hours since the gray smoke stopped, but it was still pretty thick last time I was out there. Ms. Crow says there's a way to flush the air."

"Ms. Crow has been amazing." Oscar looked over to where the librarian was setting oxygen bags beside the students giving first aid. "She stole these manual oxygen bags—"

"Ambu bags," KC corrected.

"Ambu bags," Oscar mocked her, "with pink agent heaters attached from Dr. Fenn's office and saved my life while KC and Mo bypassed the center distribution."

KC rolled her eyes. "We used the central distributor bypass to transfer the backup hoses to the pink agent. Once Benny came to, he figured out how to siphon agent from the vats into these manual gassers." She held up the ambu bag she'd been fiddling with.

The floor rumbled. Laylea leapt to her feet, ready to run. Oscar and KC merely looked over at the wooden section of the wall beyond the amphitheater nest. It split in half, each side sliding along the wall to reveal a stone corridor and an ancient iron torch holder. The wood was the backside of the clothes closet entrance to Gryphon.

A couple of students stumbled through as soon as the opening was wide enough to admit them. They were followed by a familiar tiny Asian lady in a trench coat and dark glasses. Another student lurched in behind her, hanging off Ms. Crow.

How did Ms. Crow get out of the dorm without using the doors or the ladder above them? Laylea looked over to see only students in the nest. Milly's ankle rested on top of the first aid bag that Ms. Crow had been carrying out of the podroom earlier.

Ahanu hustled over to help the kids with Morioka into the nest. Squirt scooped Ms. Crow's companion into his arms and rushed around the nest and through the archway into the podroom.

"Is Lee here?" Ms. Crow's question carried over the tense quiet of the dorm.

"I'm here." Laylea raised her hand. Whatever trouble she was in, she would face it head on. Hiding was getting old.

Emotions weren't really a demon thing, so she wasn't expecting to be able to read anything from Morioka's face. The speed with which the woman headed for them frightened Laylea more than any scowl the captain could have offered. Ms. Crow jogged to catch up to her and then passed her to take a good look at Laylea.

"You're okay?" she asked.

Laylea nodded. She glanced up as Dizzy flew out of the branches overhead and landed on Oscar's shoulder. Laylea goggled at the bird. She had shifted into Ms. Crow and saved Oscar. How could she and Ms. Crow both be here at the same time? Had Laylea imagined it?

Dizzy cawed. KC and Oscar both attempted to not notice the raven.

Laylea suddenly felt choked up. Whether she'd imagined Dizzy in the hallway outside of the Executive Wing or not, Ms. Crow had definitely been there. She'd saved Oscar's life. Having trouble looking into Ms. Crow's earnest face, she managed to say, "Thank you," before her throat closed with emotion.

Dizzy crowed. Oscar tried to finish Laylea's thought and got it all wrong. "Thank you for not being upset that we're in a closed dorm."

"I'm just glad to see you all healthy and in one piece." Ms. Crow smiled at him. "Dr. Fenn activated a ventilation flush, so it should be safe to go back to your own dorms soon."

"You were amazing, Ms. Crow." Laylea shot a grimace at Oscar. He should be more grateful. Laylea had no doubt he would be dead if Ms. Crow hadn't saved him. He'd said as much.

"Yup. You are an amazing teacher, Ms. Crow," KC interrupted. "Captain Morioka, what are you doing here?"

Morioka was watching Oscar and KC like they were hiding something. Laylea wondered if she could see Dizzy, too. But the demon turned to face Laylea without saying anything about the bird. "One of Adrien Denier's interns informed him that you were in the zoo, causing trouble."

"She was saving everyone from a madman!" KC objected.

Oscar added, "Lots of kids would have died if it weren't for Lee."

Laylea wasn't sure her race through the party had been worth it. KC and Oscar seemed to have handled things fine without her help. Ms. Crow deserved as much credit as any of them. She said so. "Oscar would definitely have died if it weren't for Ms. Crow."

Dizzy screeched and launched from Oscar's shoulder at Laylea's words. KC and Oscar shook their heads at Laylea. They wanted her to stop talking. Why wouldn't they want Ms. Crow to get credit?

Laylea turned to Ms. Crow. The librarian looked confused. She straightened her blue cardigan and cleared her throat. "You've been through a lot, Lee. With everything that's happened today, you might be misremembering things. I appreciate the thought."

"No," Laylea interrupted her. "I'm fine. I—" She fell silent as the universe shifted, and a second Ms. Crow stood where Dizzy had been hovering.

The new Ms. Crow straightened her orange sweater exactly as the librarian Ms. Crow had straightened her blue sweater and offered a sad smile. "Don't tell her." She raised a hand to stroke the single braid she had tied off with a blue ribbon, exactly as her twin

293

sister had. "Lizzy thinks she killed me. It would destroy her to know the truth."

Dizzy wasn't a ghost. Nobody had killed her. Laylea looked to KC and Oscar. They both offered apologies with their eyes. She suddenly had a lot of questions, and she couldn't ask them, not if she wanted to keep Dizzy's confidence. But, really, how much worse was the truth if it were a kindness to leave Ms. Crow believing she killed her sister?

"I…I did fall pretty far," was the best she could think to say.

Dizzy murmured, "Thank you."

Laylea nodded, keeping her eyes on Morioka. "But I'm all better now. How can I help?"

"You've done quite enough, Lee." Morioka's tone was like ice. "DJ Delcampo called Denier's other intern crazy. He said he saw you in Mer dorm just before he was called upstairs." The captain turned her impassive face on KC.

After several moments of consideration, Morioka asked, "You are her friend. Was Lee upstairs?"

Understanding dawned in Oscar's face. He poked KC. She glared at him.

Dizzy leaned down to speak in KC's ear. "Tell her that Lee was with you the entire time."

KC barely managed to keep from shooting her questioning look at the new Ms. Crow. "Lee has been with me since… since… well, she was dragged off to detention—"

Morioka sighed. Laylea winced.

"And then she and I went to Mer when the alarm went off. We've been helping with first aid ever since. Together." She added the last as an afterthought. "She couldn't have gone upstairs."

"Until Dean Gorse is found, Adrien will be tempted to punish first, investigate later," Morioka began.

"Oh!" KC blurted. "There is no Dean Gorse."

"We've heard quite enough alternate history from you, Ms. Dells." Morioka lent KC's fake name enough weight that Laylea wondered if she knew the truth.

KC slammed her mouth closed so hard her teeth clicked. Oscar laughed and clarified, "No, there really is no such person as Bertram Gorse. Gorse is Gorshkov. After his OD on Lake Shore Drive, Grandpa Delcampo paid to rearrange his face and install him as the dean."

Morioka's glare might have burned Oscar through her sunglasses. KC squeaked to his defense. She held up her wrist, pulling the ID bracelet off. "We have proof. Lots of proof. These are the hidden records. It's not Lee's fault we got caught."

Ms. Crow—the one everyone could see—gasped. It was a little late and a little forced. "Could Gorshkov have been the horse that rampaged through ST and destroyed all of Robby's hard work?"

All three kids gaped at her. Laylea grinned. "That's awesome."

A pounding noise made every conscious person in the room turn to stare at the wooden back of the clothes closet entrance. Muffled shouting could be heard from the other side. Ali handed an ambu bag off to Emerald and shouted, "Come on in," as she strolled to the door. She glanced over her shoulder at the copse.

Ms. Crow held up a hand and whisper-shouted, "Give us a minute."

Ali nodded.

"You have to go, Lee," Ms. Crow said. "I'll send your schoolbooks up, so you can continue your studies."

"No. What?" Laylea protested. KC and Oscar closed in, standing with her against the adults.

Morioka held out her hand. "I'll make good use of the evidence you collected. Say goodbye to your friends, Lee. For your safety, I'm taking you upstairs."

"If Denier can't find me, won't he assume that means I'm guilty?"

"A number of students are being taken for medical treatment upstairs." Morioka turned her shaded gaze on KC again. "Isn't that right, Ms. Dells?"

"Yeah, plus all the kids who ran out searching for fresh air," KC agreed.

Morioka blinked at her, looked at her waiting palm, and back up at the girl.

Oscar took the ID bracelet dangling from KC's hand and dropped it into Morioka's waiting palm. KC nodded reflexively as she stuttered. "Oh. Yeah. Lee got… got uh, a lungful trying to drag Oscar to the dorm, right?"

The invisible Ms. Crow prompted, "But she was with you until after the smoke stopped."

"But she was with you. . . me, until we saw the smoke clearing. Then she needed air."

"I got better." Oscar pulled Laylea into a hug. He whispered in her ear, "Go save Shala."

KC's face scrunched up in a superb pout as she wriggled under Oscar's arm to join the group squeeze. "Tell DJ—" She faltered. "Tell him I need a new bracelet."

Laylea nodded. "Sure. I'll tell your brother you love him."

KC grimaced and then sobered. "Be careful. Denier is dangerous."

"He's not the only one," she replied. Then she squeezed her friends tightly. "Look out for each other. I'll be back."

Ali's voice rose as the floor rumbled. "Oh, thank phoenix. You figured out how to get the doors open." She was looking over at them. Her next word was a little quieter. "Incoming." She saluted.

Laylea saluted back. She held KC at arm's length and turned so her friend's back was to Dizzy Crow. She looked KC in the eyes, though her words were for the woman behind her. "Thank you for saving Oscar. If you were my sister, I'd be really proud of you."

Dizzy gazed at Ms. Crow with too many emotions on her face for Laylea to read.

KC raised her eyebrows. "You have no idea what my brothers were like. . . oh." She stopped talking as she remembered KC Dells had no family. She shot a glance at Morioka and Ms. Crow and added, lamely, "Before they all died."

Dizzy turned a sad smile on Laylea. "It's complicated."

Laylea snorted. "Tell me about it."

Dizzy just sighed, "You have to go, Lee."

KC grabbed Laylea into a hug, and then shoved her away. "You've gotta go."

"Come with me." Morioka strode out of the copse, moving farther from the slowly opening door. She stooped in the darkness beyond the trees. When she stood, she held a bear over her shoulder in a fireman's carry. The bear was easily twice her size. She gestured for Laylea to join her. "Quickly."

"Is that Toby?" Laylea asked. "I thought he was—"

"There's no time for questions." Captain Morioka wrapped an arm around her waist and hissed, "Don't shift." Then the tiny Asian woman leapt into the air and spread her leathery wings.

The looks on KC's, Oscar's, and both Ms. Crows' faces couldn't have scared Laylea more. She wrapped her arms around Morioka and Toby and squeezed her eyes shut tight.

45

There are days in life that you want to imprint on your brain, so you'll never forget them. This was not one of those days. Toby was wholly unconscious. He must have been, to lay so limply over Morioka's shoulder. Out of instinct or to comfort herself, Laylea stroked his fur. She focused on his musky scent and kept her face buried in his back while Morioka flew.

Morioka's shoes clicked lightly on the tile floor of the antechamber under the Kovid Seal Pool. Laylea remembered the little room from Emerald's seance a bazillion years earlier. She cringed when her bare feet touched down. It was cold. Though the uncontrollable shivers that ran up her spine had little to do with temperature.

Morioka released her waist once Laylea had her feet under her. "Get the door. Stay close."

For all it looked like it might crumble to splinters if she breathed too hard, the door opened without a sound. Silver light wormed its way to the dank little space under the stairs. Laylea held the door so Morioka could get through and then followed close on her heels as the woman led her up the stairs, along the short ramp, and down the path into the children's area of the zoo. The moon was nearly full, but it was low in the sky. Laylea guessed she had been unconscious for several hours. She listened hard but couldn't hear any sounds of humans. The party must have wrapped up.

At a hiss from Morioka, Laylea hustled to catch up and then passed her, sprinting by the statues of KC's uncles, along the thick evergreens, and into the clearing outside Toby's cage. Ms. Lagat waited beside the giant, hollow tree trunk doing martial arts moves in slow motion, her long skirts swaying around her ankles. A hazy figure flowed in concert with her. When Morioka strode into the clearing, the hazy figure dissipated in a faint blue flash. Ms. Lagat hurried to Toby's cage and pushed open the gate, holding it as Morioka ducked through.

The captain laid Toby at the base of a grand old bur oak. Ms. Lagat rearranged the bear into a more comfortable position. She moved a bowl with water closer to him. Captain Morioka returned to the gate.

A faint coo sounded just above Laylea. She looked up. Far overhead, a small, dark figure flitted through the branches of the bur oak. It was no gently cooing dove. That darting silhouette belonged to Kyle.

Laylea turned her back to the enclosure as she whispered, "Guillaume?"

The coo came again, moving away from her, toward the crinkly, old shifting master and Toby. Laylea spun. She whispered, "Merci, Monsieur Lagat."

The coo turned into a trilling song and then faded into the night.

Captain Morioka approached with one arm out, gesturing for Laylea to come to her. "You make strange friends, Lee Woodford." Morioka pulled her in, holding her close. "But without them, you'd be dead. So, I will let the vampire live."

Laylea's mouth dropped open. "You know..." was all she could manage before Morioka leapt into the air.

"Detective Nellwin broke into a police vehicle to alert me of your peril."

Captain Morioka knew about Kyle. Laylea had no idea what to say. Luckily, any discussion was impossible at the speed they were flying. Laylea clutched at the captain and buried her head in Morioka's magic trench coat, only to feel her forehead pressed against surprisingly warm scales smelling of rich loam, smoke, and security. Laylea should feel frightened for Kyle. The one thing everyone knew about Morioka was that she kept her city demon-free. But Morioka just gave Kyle a pass, and Laylea couldn't find it in her to feel anything but relief that now she wasn't the only one keeping Kyle's secret.

"You can let go now." Morioka set Laylea on the cracked asphalt of the alley behind The Office. After a moment, Laylea managed to pry her fingers loose.

Dawn crept over the city with her rosy, fresh-washed light. Laylea's stomach growled. She couldn't remember the last time she'd eaten anything, and she'd had a busy day and night. The Flores Panaderia down the street started cooking early. Maybe she could knock and talk them into giving her some of their sweet bread straight from the oven. She turned to head out to the street, only to come up short when Morioka snagged the collar of her LPSS jumpsuit.

Laylea squawked. "I'm just gonna run over to the panaderia. I'll be right back."

"Seb will fix you something."

Laylea crinkled her face. "He doesn't serve food."

With a gentle but insistent push, Morioka directed Laylea through the gate and into the small back patio of the bar. "He has food in his apartment upstairs. He will bring it down."

"Seb lives upstairs?" Laylea tried to look at the windows over the bar, but Morioka wouldn't stop herding her inside.

Amal held the back door open for them. "Welcome back, Lee."

He followed as the demon frog-marched Laylea along the hallway and into the bar. The members of Team Wyrdos, her Chicago family, sat scattered around the room. Junior and Diejuste were on the floor by the front door, twisted into the same yoga position. Eleven-year-old Diejuste wore a plaid skirt and light blue button-down shirt like she'd started going to a private school. She yawned, and Junior giggled as he followed suit. His twisted position showed off a spectacularly ugly red, white, and blue cardigan embroidered with sparkly firework designs.

At the far end of the bar, Dee sat with three deskpadds arrayed in front of her. The speed with which she typed and swiped on them and her armpadd would have earned high marks from KC.

The only noise came from a booth in the back, where Orin and Lucio played some kind of violent game. Cards flew out over the tables nearest them. The bitter smell of coffee floated on the air from their table and from behind the long bar.

Seb stood behind said bar, wiping the brass rails. He was the first to catch sight of her. He reverse-nodded his chin at her and turned to flip on the kettle. The box of tea bags and a cup waited by the empty condiment containers.

The sound of the kettle alerted Dee. The detective tapped each of her screens and folded them into each other. She put the whole stack into a bag beside her and approached. "You got caught."

Laylea sucked in a breath, ready to take the lashing. She'd earned it. Junior reached her before Dee could start in. He swept Laylea off her feet into a hug that reminded her how hard it had been to breathe in Brock's smoke. When he'd squeezed enough, he set her on her feet but didn't release her. "Are Oscar and KC and your other friends okay? Do we need to go get them?"

Laylea grinned sheepishly at Morioka over his shoulder, since he wasn't supposed to know anything about the Lincoln Park Shifter School. The captain almost sighed as she looked at the others closing in on them. Apparently, she made a decision and answered for Laylea. "Her friends are safe because Lee risked her life and anonymity to catch the man who released deadly smoke throughout the school."

"The underground feeds are in an uproar," Dee reported. "The smoke-out was not sanctioned. Parents are furious. There is also a run on N. Rumors are flying that a key ingredient is in short supply."

"What are the wolves saying?" Amal asked.

Dee shoved a stray lock of curls out of her eyes. "They're the worst. They're demanding to know why their kids weren't removed from the school beforehand."

"Of course they are," Lucio scoffed from where he stood, peering out the front door.

Laylea's head spun. The Wyrdos were talking about the shifter community like they'd always known about them.

"Maybe the smoke doesn't affect wolves," Amal suggested.

Laylea's eyes teared up as she remembered KC collapsing next to Oscar and all the Sphinx kids—wolves included—lying still, as if dead, in the hallway outside their dorm. Her voice cracked as she said, "It affects the wolves, too."

"Oy!" Seb tapped the bar beside the tea cup. "Come have a rest, Lee." He glared at the others until they made room for her to hop up on a stool. He opened the box of tea bags for her. She picked through the selection, not seeing the flavors through her tears.

Orin spoke up from where he was gathering playing cards off the floor. "And you saved them too, even though they've been jerks to you."

"Not all wolves are bad."

Nobody heard her as Morioka asked, "What is the key ingredient? And why is it missing?"

The only key ingredient we know about is sligh nuts," Lucio pointed out. He kept opening the door and letting the cold, early morning air in.

"It's not sligh nuts," Dee said. "It's something else."

"What else is there?" Amal asked.

"It's blood," Laylea said as Seb poured hot water over her randomly chosen tea bag. The rising steam reminded her of all the kids who had died wearing gas masks. "Blood is the resource. Shifter blood is a key ingredient in N. They were getting it from the kids at LPSS. We kinda eliminated the guy who was giving them access."

"Eliminated?" Dee asked, concerned.

"We didn't kill him," Laylea clarified. "He's just gonna be a horse for a while. And the folks who run LPSS don't respect shifters who can't shift anymore."

Lucio scoffed. "That's not cool."

"Although," Laylea looked up at Dee and then quickly dropped her gaze. "I did kill the guy who invented N."

That silenced everyone.

Little Diejuste, the goddess in a girl's body, slipped between Dee and Junior to hop onto the stool beside Laylea. "Ya didn't kill nobody." She laid a hand on Laylea's arm and tilted her head, her eyes bright. "It was a family matter. Sometime, people blame others because it's too hard to hate da ones ya love. You didn't kill nobody, cherie."

The endearment reminded Laylea of Guillaume. She'd like Guillaume to meet Diejuste. They'd get along.

"Yeah," she muttered. "Well, Dr. Brock's son said I killed him." Remembering she hadn't seen most of them since she freed the girls from Brock's house, she added, "Oh, yeah. This guy, Brock, locked me in a death closet before I went back to school."

Heads nodded all around. Of course, Dee and Morioka would have told them. Dee, her voice still cold, said, "And he was arrested and taken to prison. He was alive when you left for school."

"Then some asshole, not you, killed the bastard before the Captain could question him." Lucio held a hand up for a high five. When he got only stares, he sobered. "Oh, yeah. That could be good news or bad news."

Morioka picked KC's ID bracelet from the pocket of her magical trench coat and tossed it to Dee. "It's good news. They've lost their genius and their money. Gorshkov is gone."

Laylea quickly corrected her. Her hand shot to her collar and the one aerosol tube remaining there. "Gorshkov isn't dead. He's just a horse. I don't know how long this serum works."

Several eyebrows went up at her words.

Dee looked up from examining the bracelet. "You found Gorshkov?"

"Yeah," Laylea confirmed. "Gorshkov was the dean of my school. Amelia..." she caught Junior and Amal's eyes. For the others she added, "A ghost we know, sprayed him with this stuff to make him shift." She held out the tube. "Brock designed this, too."

Junior choked a little as he asked, "Is Gorshkov Deanna's father?"

Laylea nodded. "He didn't know the wolf pack had her in a coma. He was only giving them money and access to the school because he thought they were healing her."

"So, he's not dead?" Orin questioned, his brow wrinkled as he tried to keep up.

Lucio's pretty face was scrunched as well. "And the crew behind N still have his kid."

"Which means they can still make him do whatever they want," Orin concluded. "Right?"

Amal stepped forward, into the mix. "Except we know where she is."

Laylea felt her whole head fill up with grief. Tears welled in her eyes as she realized why Oscar's sister was in the sleep lab, too. "Dee!" She hopped off the stool. "You have to tell Sanna that Shala isn't dead."

"She knows." Dee sighed. "She knows someone is using their daughter to make her husband vote their way."

Laylea grabbed Junior's arm. "We have to go to the sleep lab. Right now. Come on." She tried to drag him toward the hallway. "We can save Deanna and Shala and all the rest."

Dee finally reacted. "Shala is in the sleep lab?"

"Yes." Laylea stomped a foot, frantic to get to the lab. "We can cut off their funding and political coverage if we go now and rescue them."

"Lucio, you're with Morioka. You cover the back entrance of that lab." Dee stuffed KC's ID band in her bag. "Orin, Diejuste, gather first aid supplies. We're going to need them. Amal, go with Junior and Lee. Get the girls out first and then go back for as many others as you can. I'll get Bailey here. Put on your earpieces!" She hollered the last over her shoulder as she ran out the front door.

Why was Dee going to get Bailey? Laylea barely had time to think the question while she raced to the back storeroom, pushing to keep up with Junior while Amal's long legs carried him far ahead. He had the door to the closet open. Laylea and Junior raced in, already holding hands. Junior grabbed Amal's hand, and the brownie pulled the door shut.

46

_L_aylea could feel something was wrong before Junior opened the closet door. The pressure from Seb's shelves and cleaning supplies disappeared. Nothing replaced it. The last time the three of them had travelled to the lab, they'd fallen out of the closet because it was so full. This time, Junior opened the door to an empty room.

No beds. No machines. No sleeping people.

"What the hell?" Junior froze in the doorway.

Amal slipped past him. He muttered, "They knew we'd figure it out."

"What? No." Laylea tripped into the room, looking around as if she could manifest Shala, Deanna, and the rest.

"How could they possibly?" Junior struggled to peel the ear patch from his armpadd.

Amal had been heading for the door. He spun around to face them. "Brock came to the bar to hire you, right, Lee?"

Laylea nodded. Her mind was racing. She had to fight past the words _Are they dead?_ screaming in her brain to explain, "He didn't really hire me, though. It was just a trick to get me into his house."

"Did Denier order him to catch you? Ha!" Junior managed to get the ear patch released but fumbled and dropped it on the floor.

"They saw Lee shift into a dog when we broke in here last May." Amal easily peeled the ear patch from his padd and slapped it behind his ear.

"So, Denier figured out it was Lee?" Junior blew on his ear patch to clean it and pressed it onto his skin.

Amal swiped his armpadd to connect with the other Wyrdos. "Abort. The sleepers are gone." His gaze focused on Laylea. "But he didn't move the sleepers right away. They were still here seven months ago, before the Brock incident."

"Did he just move them, because she escaped the school?" Junior asked.

Amal headed for the door again. "Or did he move them because Brock's son got out of control?"

Laylea lost control. She shouted at her friends, "What if he didn't move them at all? What if they're all dead?"

"He needed them, Lee." Amal laid a hand on the door. "He wouldn't kill them."

"You can find out," Junior added, less reassuringly. "Are their ghosts here?"

Laylea didn't answer. She should have thought of that herself. She turned, facing each direction, muttering her mantras, and begging the universe for answers. Before she'd reached north, a single bitter presence filled her awareness. Her nostrils flared at the sour combination of tobacco, wet tweed, and death. She raised her head and still saw nothing. But the room wasn't empty anymore. A suffocating presence that had been Dr. Maurice Brock filled the space that once held his victims.

He was alone. If Denier had killed the sleepers, he hadn't done it here. For a moment, fear and hope battled in Laylea's heart. And then she remembered that Dr. Maurice Brock would have no more victims. Her heart positively rejoiced at the good she had done by getting him locked away. Her joy radiated in the spirit realm. It burned Brock like his own poison smoke.

And it angered him.

He rushed her. The anger solidified him just as it had given Isa enough solidity to shatter his pretty ceramic figurines. Ghostly hands wrapped around Laylea's throat. Her flesh burned where he touched her skin. She gasped. Death was literally upon her. His grip loosened a little as she giggled at that thought.

"Laylea!" Junior's voice sounded distant. He was scared. It scared her.

She needed to find joy, find the reasons to live that kept her going in the darkest times. She should think of flying with her father, of reading with Bailey on the front porch, of wilding with her friends. Instead, her soul filled with despair for Oscar and Sanna and Brenda and...

Amelia. Amelia knew this place. Amelia could help her.

She screamed for the ghost, "Amelia!" With all her psychic will she called for the deathly cold of the grieving mother to come to her.

"Where is she? What is she doing to you?" Junior called.

In the distance, beyond the searing pain of Brock, Laylea felt Junior's cries. She heard Amal talking but couldn't make out the words. She could barely see them through the dark haze that was Brock. Or was it her vision blacking out because she couldn't breathe?

She croaked out, "Amelia, help me!"

"She's trying to get her here." Junior grabbed Amal away from his watch at the doorway. "Amelia!"

"Amelia!" Amal joined him, and the two yelled for Amelia. "If it's not Amelia, who's hurting her?"

"Lee!" Junior reached out to her. "Grab my hand!" He pushed through the darkness, one hand nearly reaching her.

She wanted to grab her friend's hands. She was too drained to raise her own. She needed Junior. She needed to get free before Brock drained her life. Brock felt her need. He released her for just an instant. The amorphous figure spun and slapped Junior with his stinging anger. The boogeyman's son fell back, crashing to the floor and sliding along the linoleum.

Brock was back on her faster than humanly possible, but Laylea had gotten a moment of freedom, a moment to suck some oxygen into her lungs.

He cried out in pain. The cry morphed into words. "Who's got you, Lee?"

"Amelia!" Amal kept up the cry as he helped Junior to his feet. "Lee, how can we help you?"

Laylea didn't know how they could help. But their concern told her how to reach Amelia. She used up the last of her oxygen and her energy to scream into the empty room, into the universe, "Deanna is missing!"

"I hear you. It's not Amelia that's got you. And. . . and the sleepers aren't ghosts. They're alive!" Junior's words spewed out as fast as his thoughts. "It's…it's not… Gorshkov isn't dead. It isn't him." His eyes spun, searching the room for answers. Suddenly, his gaze shot to Amal and then back to Laylea. This time, his voice rang out, clear and triumphant. "It's Brock."

The hope that filled her battered at Brock. His grip loosened enough to allow her a breath. But, Laylea was too weak for words. She threw her head back and howled. Brock doubled down. He lifted her off her feet. His ghostly fingers dug into her throat.

Amal's deep voice reached her as though from another room, even though she could see him standing not five feet away. "Brock? The asshat who kidnapped and killed little girls before inventing the drug that's destroying our city? That Brock?"

Laylea gurgled an attempt at a howl.

"Cool." Junior grinned. "What kind of karma you think he's got?"

Amal stepped up beside Junior. Laylea saw his aura shining silver and growing. "Not to shock you," the brownie said, "but Brock's karma sucks."

Then Amal—the brownie, the dealer of karma—snapped his fingers.

Silence rang so loud it deafened Laylea. Time slowed as she felt herself falling. The instant before her knees would have slammed into the linoleum, icy cold arms wrapped around her, soothing the burning flesh at her throat and lowering her to the ground safely.

Laylea's body shook as sobs rumbled up from where they had trembled, trapped inside her. Tears poured down her cheeks. The cold aura held Laylea and let her fall apart. Then Junior was there, kneeling beside her, his warm hand brushing away her tears.

When she could, Laylea asked, "Where... where is he?"

Amal's deep voice carried from where he was peering into the hallway again. "Brock is not here anymore. He's traversing the veil and gauntlet." There was no remorse in Amal's tone as he added, "Without our friend Dee's assistance, he's going to find the journey unpleasant."

Laylea reached a hand out to grasp Junior's joyfully god-awful sweater. Then she leaned back into Amelia and asked, gently, fearfully, "Where is she?"

There were no words in the ghost's response. She'd used up her life-force defeating her husband, just as Guillaume had depleted his stopping the bullet intended for KC. Amelia took Laylea's awareness with her into a dark space. Laylea felt herself surrounded by the hazy impressions of another mind. She smelled gasoline, fear, sweat and antiseptic. Vibrations rumbled through her body. She was thrown left and then brought to center again. Shapes formed in the darkness that remained when she opened her eyes. Heat radiated against her skin from all the bodies crowded around her. As the scene floated away, Laylea could feel clarity coming to the slowly waking mind.

Then the vision faded, and the cold faded, and her grief faded.

"They're alive," Laylea gasped. "They're in a van or train car or... or...they're moving." She looked up into Junior's worried gaze. "And they're waking up."

Amal crossed from the door and reached a hand down to help her up. "If you can move, we've got to go. There's not much out there, but someone's running our way."

Laylea took his hand and stood. Junior had to join her because she couldn't manage to let go of his sweater. The three hurried to the closet as the sound of footsteps reached them from the hall. Junior and Laylea stepped into the empty supply closet as Amal turned back to face the room for a moment. His shoulders rose and fell with one deep breath. The doorknob shook. They heard the beeps of an electronic code being entered.

Amal took another breath. Then he raised a hand and snapped his fingers. A golden sparkle shimmered in the room at a level where each of the beds had stood. It faded as Amal stumbled into the closet. He leaned on Junior for support while the boogeyman pulled the hollow door closed.

47

The carefully arranged supplies in Seb's storage room closet tumbled out with the trio as Laylea and Junior tried to hold Amal up. Unbearably weak herself, Laylea released her death grip on Junior's cardigan to help keep Amal from crashing into the crowded shelves. A mop clattered to the ground behind them as Laylea tried to brace herself.

Footsteps echoed in the hallway outside. Laylea tried to remember who had been left behind. Her head spun as if she were still caught up in the struggle between Brock and Amelia. She knew the trauma of the past day was catching up with her. She also knew she couldn't give in to it. Amal was sucking in air like all the students she'd left choking in the school's corridors.

Orin burst through the open doorway as she and Junior got Amal settled on the ground. He backed up again as Amal's long limbs splayed everywhere like a Great Dane puppy's legs.

"Here. Lay his head on these." Laylea swept a stack of sweatpants off the shelves into her dog bed. She snatched a bottle of water from another shelf.

Orin slipped in and cleaned up the mess that had escaped the closet. "What happened?"

"Was it a ghost?" Junior asked. He crouched beside the dog bed, his hands out to keep either of them from falling over.

Orin stopped what he was doing. "A ghost attacked Amal?"

Laylea and Amal shook their heads. She twisted the cap off the water bottle and took a swig before holding it to Amal's lips. When Junior saw her hands shaking, he took over helping.

"Two ghosts. Brock tried to kill me." She stuttered a laugh. "Again."

Amal's breathing evened out. He pulled himself together and took the bottle from Junior, his back supported by the shelves. "Karma got him."

"Yeah, but what did you do after that?" Junior asked. "That's what drained you."

Amal stretched out his legs. His feet stuck into the hall. "I tried to reach through the residual karma in the room to boost justice."

"Of course. I mean, obviously." Junior rolled his eyes at Laylea, who found she was almost too tired to grin back.

Orin, another brownie, had some idea what Amal was talking about. His face crinkled in disbelief. "Like in the whole world?"

"For that room." Amal drank some more and clarified for Junior and Laylea, "All those sleepers with good karma should find luck turning their way. All those working for Denier who kept them asleep and stole their lives will find their shoelaces breaking at the worst possible moment. In theory."

"Shit, man. I'll go get you a candy bar." Orin picked his way over the tall man's legs.

Junior leaned over Laylea and fished for something on her shelves. "I can dole out karma to the deserving, too, you know."

He pulled a blanket from the shelves, shaking it open with a flourish before draping it over Amal. Then he handed Laylea a rawhide with a grin. "You're both heroes. And you should get some sleep. There's not much else we can do tonight."

A shadow fell across him. "This morning, you mean." They looked up to see Dee standing in the doorway. Laylea shoved the rawhide under her butt in a hurry, searching the hallway behind her.

Bailey didn't appear as she expected. Dee raised an eyebrow. "I couldn't bring him. Denier's people were following me. Morioka spotted them as I was leaving."

Laylea took a breath, but Dee cut her off. "I didn't lead them to your place. Once Amal reported the lab was empty, I turned around." She leaned over Junior to hand Laylea a white, waxed-paper bag. "Got you a breakfast sandwich from the Flores Panaderia. Eat. Get some sleep. Junior, let's start going through the data Lee got us and see if we can figure out where they're taking the hostages."

Dee dodged Orin and Diejuste in the doorway. Amal snored. Dee snorted at the sound.

"Ungrateful bastard." Orin tossed a Snickers bar to Laylea. Diejuste knelt and started untying Amal's shoes.

Junior ruffled Laylea's hair just as if he were scratching her puppy ears. "You're okay?"

Laylea nodded. "I'm okay."

He laughed. "You really have to make a bedroom closet at that school, so I can visit you."

"Don't worry about that," Dee said from the doorway. "Lee is not going back to that school."

"Yes, I am." Laylea shifted to set the Snickers on the shelves and avoid Dee's eyes. "I only left to avoid Denier."

"Denier will know if you go back, Lee," Orin said. "He's got people watching the bar."

"I can't help my friends from here," Laylea protested.

"It's too dangerous." Orin stepped over Amal's legs to get closer to her.

Laylea shrugged. "I'm fifteen. I wasn't supposed to live this long anyway."

A collective gasp made Laylea aware that she shouldn't have said that.

Dee's voice could have cut glass. "I took you to the water. I told you you're not dying anytime soon."

"Then," Laylea searched the adult faces filling the little closet, "why are you so scared of Denier?"

Dee blinked. Fear shot across her features for just an instant before her cold mask descended. "Because death isn't the worst thing he can do to you."

Laylea had no response to that. Denier hadn't killed Shala or Deanna or Brenda's father. But they all had family that could help Denier. Laylea had Bailey—an unfathomably powerful witch. But nobody knew that. Did they?

She also had everyone around her who had stayed up through the night to be there when Morioka brought her back from LPSS. If Denier was watching the bar, he might know what they meant to her.

She looked up into Dee's gaze. "I understand."

Initially, Laylea ignored Junior's raised eyebrows. But then she reconsidered. These weren't just adults. These were her friends. They wanted to make the world a better place, just like she did.

She answered Junior's unspoken questions. "Dee's afraid Denier would use me as a hostage, too."

"Even da shifters know Morioka," Diejuste said. "He surely knows by now dat Morioka would do anything to keep you safe."

"I get that." Laylea lowered her voice, looking at Amal, unconscious because of how much he'd given for any chance of helping the sleepers. "But my friends at school aren't safe. Even my enemies aren't safe at LPSS. Why do I get to be safe and leave them in danger?"

"Because you have us," Junior insisted. "When we know how to make them safe, too, then you'll go back."

"Junior," Dee barked, a hint of the banshee in her tone.

Orin added, "She's just a kid."

Junior stood and turned to face the detective. "You treat her like a kid, but you won't let her be a kid."

"I know I'm a kid." Laylea stood. "But, I'm a wyrdo, too. I'm part of this team, a part of this family, right, Diejuste? The gods say I'm part of this family."

"That they do, Lee."

"I found Gorshkov. My friends helped me find him. I promised them I would find Shala and Brenda's dad. But then, I will go back because we've learned for certain that the creators of N have woven it into the running of the Lincoln Park Shifter School. The secrets are there. The answers are there. N isn't just a dangerous drug, you guys. It's a weapon. And my friends are the best chance we have at figuring out the endgame. So, I'm going back. Either I go back with your support and I sleep near a closet so Junior can bring you in to help me, or I go back on my own."

"Lee," Dee said. "You are, as you said, fifteen years—"

"I'm with Lee," Junior interrupted her.

"We're not against her," Orin argued. "We're just saying she's young."

Diejuste stood in the doorway. "She got an old soul."

Dee insisted, "The school is dangerous. I sent her there once, I won't—"

A deep, sleep-thickened voice rose from beside Laylea. "She's not going back tonight."

"This morning," Orin corrected Amal.

Amal turned a flat gaze on his friend. "This morning," he said, "she needs some rest because she used up a lot of energy to find out that the sleepers were still alive. She did it using a skill that none of the rest of us have. Consider that, Dee." He held up a hand before the others could start arguing. "Later. Now, Lee and I are going to share her sandwich and get some sleep. Go away."

He resettled with his head on the sweatpants that Laylea had piled in her bed and reached over his head to take the waxed bag from her lap.

"Come on, Junior." Dee tapped the doorframe. "We can at least cause some trouble on the dark web and distract Denier for a bit."

"Hey." Orin headed out the door. "I'm great at causing trouble."

Junior took half of the sandwich from Amal and handed it to Laylea. He adjusted the blanket over Amal, blew a zerbert on Laylea's cheek, and then slipped past Dee. Diejuste followed him.

Dee watched as they finished the sandwich. When they were done, Dee gathered the trash and headed out the door. At the last moment, she turned back. She let her mask drop, and Laylea could see the exhaustion behind her eyes. "You did a good job, kid."

Then she left Amal and Laylea alone in the storage room.

Despite how mad she was at Dee, Laylea's psychic tail wagged so hard at the unexpected praise from Dee that she burned into a shift so that her real tail could thump against the sides of her plush bed. Her jaw cracked in an enormous yawn that brought tears to her eyes.

She circled clockwise twice and counterclockwise once before she remembered her rawhide. She collected it in her teeth and resumed her spinning before settling on the very edge of her bed, cuddled up in the crook of Amal's neck. A billion new mysteries spun through her head before they settled into the comforting certainty that, like the sleepers and the kids in LPSS, she wasn't alone. She had friends, and together, they would make everything right with the world.

Eventually.

CHARACTERS

- **Adele Lagat** - *see Lagat, Adele*
- **Adrien Denier** - *see Denier, Adrien*
- **Ahanu** - student, thunderbird, Mer dorm
- **Ali** - student, hawk, Mer dorm
- **Amal** - brownie, co-owner of Brown's Resale, member of Team Wyrdos
- **Audra** - student, sailfish, Centaur dorm
- **Bailey Hillen** - grad student, witch, Laylea's brother, aka Bailey Woodford
- **Barrett, Elan** - sociology teacher, wolf
- **Bayard** - Laylea's biological brother, dog
- **Belle Suttrick** - student, Mer dorm, Miro's sister
- **Benniker** - zoo guard, wolf
- **Benny McBride Greene**- student, turtle, Sphinx dorm
- **Bertram Gorse** - *see Gorse, Bertram*
- **Bianchi, Enrico** - music teacher, wolf
- **Big Mo** - student, maned wolf, Centaur dorm, aka Maurice Braga
- **Brandy** - neighbor of Laylea and Bailey, true-human

- **Brenda Samborsky** - student, works in Executive Wing, python, Mer dorm
- **Brian** - student, gorilla, Sphinx dorm
- **Brian Samborsky** - former PE and health teacher, python
- **Britny** - student, goat
- **Brock, Maurice** - pharmaceutical scientist, tick
- **Cal Christopherson** - former student, wolf, Centaur dorm
- **Caliban Meillissene** - student, linden shifter, Mer dorm
- **Carrie Marshall** - student, wolf, Mer dorm
- **Chef Tod** - LPSS chef, Shetland pony
- **Chloe Serra** - student, moose, Sphinx dorm
- **Clark Hillen** - former conditioned force soldier, pilot, Laylea's adopted father
- **Conner Stone** - student, wolf, Mer dorm
- **Correnti, Toni** - shop teacher
- **Crow, Elizabeth** - librarian, counselor, Raven shifter, aka Lizzy
- **Deanna Amelia Gorshkov** - former student, sleeper, Lippizaner
- **Dee Morton** - homicide detective, banshee, member of Team Wyrdos
- **DeGee, Douglass** - contractor, lion, Griff's father
- **Denier, Adrien** - Council Enforcer, wolf, KC's godfather
- **Dizzy** - raven, invisible to most people
- **Diejuste** - voudon loa riding Jane Delphine, member of Team Wyrdos
- **DJ Delcampo** - Daniel Joaquin, wolf, KC's brother
- **Dove Betts**- student, tiger, Mer dorm, twin to Reggie
- **Durrah, David** - former LPSS doctor, head of special testing
- **Dustin Huono** - student, wolf, Sphinx dorm
- **Emerald** - student, singer, selkie, Sphinx dorm
- **Etienne** - zoo docent, disenhanced shifter
- **Eugene** - student, wolf, Sphinx dorm
- **Fan Hu** - *see Hu, Fan*

- **Fenn, Sidney** - school doctor, gorilla
- **Garcia, Jharrel** - police officer, 44 division, medium
- **Ginger Havanish** - missing girl, lion
- **Gorse, Bertram** - dean of LPSS, Lipizzaner
- **Grandpa Delcampo** - dean of Montana Shifter School, wolf, self-declared Alpha of the Americas, KC's great grandfather, aka Luis
- **Griffin DeGee** - student, gryphon, Sphinx dorm, aka Griff
- **Guillaume** - former librarian, former disenhanced zoo docent, dove
- **Harper Pemberton** - student, rhesus monkey, Centaur dorm
- **Isa Owens** - missing girl, pig
- **Jagger deRio** - student, wolf, Sphinx dorm
- **Jase Batka** - student, wolf, Sphinx dorm, grandson of the Detroit Alpha
- **Jay Doe** - recovering Conditioned Force soldier, Laylea's "uncle"
- **Jeannie Nellwin** - doctor, Kyle's wife, KJ's mother
- **Jeffers** - grocery bagger, neighborhood basketball player, cyclops
- **Jimmy Smith** - musician, student, wolf, Mer dorm
- **Josh** - Laylea's biological brother, dog
- **Julia Jimenez** - student, wolf, Sphinx
- **Junior Leo** - apartment manager, boogeyman, member of Team Wyrdos
- **Kadota** - student, orangutan, Centaur dorm
- **Kara** - student, Centaur dorm, dating Reggie
- **KC Dells** - student, wolf pretending to be a coyote, aka Karly Carlotta Delcampo
- **Kenda Moran** - missing girl, horse
- **KJ Nellwin** - Jeannie and Kyle's kid
- **Kyle Nellwin** - homicide detective, vampire, believed by some to be dead, Jeannie's husband
- **Lagat, Adele** - shifting teacher, pigeon

- **Laylea Hillen** - student, dog, Mer dorm, member of Team Wyrdos, aka Lee Woodford
- **Leda** - student, egret, Centaur dorm
- **Lee Woodford** - see *Laylea Hillen*
- **Leslie Corgana** - missing girl, cricket
- **Lucio** - brownie, co-owner of Brown's Resale, member of Team Wyrdos
- **Luke, Oliver** - councilmember, leopard, Oscar's father
- **Luna** - neighbor of Laylea and Bailey, true dog
- **Madam Fan Hu** - Laylea and Bailey's landlady
- **Madame** - French teacher, spider
- **Marcos** - clerk at the Chicago assessor's office
- **McCobb, Randee** - teacher, PE & Health
- **Merrilynne** - student, koi, Mer dorm
- **Milly** - dancer, student, mouse, Mer dorm
- **Milo** - Laylea's biological brother, dog
- **Morioka, Yaksha** - Captain of Chicago PD 44 division, demon, dragon, member of Team Wyrdos
- **Muldoon, Sigrid** - chemistry teacher
- **Murph** - student, cheetah, Sphinx dorm
- **Ned Biggerson** - knitter, The Office regular
- **Nemo** - a canine neighbor of Laylea's and Bailey's, true German shepherd
- **Nicky** - server, neighborhood basketball player, bonobo/gorilla
- **Olivia Schwermin** - missing girl, cow
- **Orin Morton** - co-owner of Brown's Resale, brownie, Dee's brother, member of Team Wyrdos
- **Oscar Luke** - student, leopard (black panther), Sphinx dorm
- **Parkson, Jon** - police officer, true-human
- **Patrick DelValle** - student, wolf, LPSS student alpha, Sphinx dorm
- **Peter** - student, fox, Mer dorm
- **Raederie Rivers** - student, selkie, Sphinx dorm

- **Reggie Betts** - student, tiger, Centaur dorm, twin to Dove, dating Kara
- **Rehyan Linnehan** - student, flamingo, Mer dorm
- **Rhea** - Laylea's biological mother, dog
- **Rhemy** - Laylea's biological brother, dog
- **Riley Betts** - former student, tiger, Dove and Reggie's older sister
- **Riva** - student, sloth, Centaur dorm
- **Robby Brock** - handyman, tick
- **Sanna Luke** - artist, leopard (black panther), N addict, Oscar's mother
- **Seb** - bartender at The Office
- **Shala Luke** - former student, leopard (black panther), Oscar's sister, aka Tishala
- **Sher Hillen** - doctor, witch, Laylea's mother, aka Katherine Coogan
- **Sierra** - Denier's intern Beta, wolf
- **Squirt** - student, sea squirt, aka David Safotu
- **Theresa** - student, lion, Centaur dorm
- **Tippy** - 30lb terrier in Laylea's neighborhood
- **Toby** - bear in Lincoln Park Zoo
- **Tori** - office supervisor at Northeve Labs, friend of Laylea's
- **Trask** - supervisor of Consortium Biotech Division, true-human
- **Vaughn Howe** - student, wolf, Sphinx dorm
- **Walter Bowman** - Consortium therianthologist, Laylea's biological father, true-human
- **Wanda Bargo** - LPSS administration, elephant
- **Woodford** - Laylea's brother, killed by the Consortium, true dog
- **Yaksha Morioka** - see *Morioka, Yaksha*

AFTERWORD

Thank you for reading *Shifter Ghost*. I hope you had fun. If you did, please go to Amazon or Goodreads or your fabulous blog and write a quick review. Reviews are really important to an indie author.

Sign up at wyrdos.net to be the first to know all the latest on my books and audiobooks. I promise I won't inundate you with mail and I will not share your email with anyone. Just ask my sisters. I never share.

READ ON

Start the next book in the series right now. After being stuck in The Office for three months, Laylea's battle with Denier steps up, the school is in danger again, and Laylea has to grapple with all of the secrets she's been keeping. I give you, *Shifter Witch*.

SHIFTER WITCH

A WYRDOS UNIVERSE NOVEL

1

*L*aylea sat on her favorite stool in her favorite place in the city and wished with all her heart that she could leave. She wanted to run through the streets of Chicago with paws pounding rough pavement, cold lake air blowing her ears back. She wanted to run to the zoo and find her school friends partying around the depressed bear's cage. She was fifteen years old. She needed to run. It didn't matter where, really. Just somewhere outside of this bar.

It had been three months since she'd broken the number one shifter rule. Again. And there was no denying it. She had shifted in the middle of a party at the zoo. She couldn't have had more witnesses if she'd tried. Now, the Midwest Shifter Council would do something awful to her if they found her.

So, her brother Bailey had trapped her in The Office, where all their adult friends hung out. Natural and supernatural patrons mingled safely there, most unaware of who was what. Nobody looked particularly weird or *wyrd*, as Laylea thought of supernatural creatures.

The only weirdo in the bar was her, a fifteen-year-old girl who wasn't allowed to leave.

"That was an awfully big sigh, my friend." Jeannie, her tutor, lifted her deep brown eyes from the book in front of her with a perplexed expression. She brushed a spray of braids out of her face, then tied them back with one of the many colorful hairbands on her wrist. "Whatcha thinking about, Leenie?"

"Hm?" Laylea looked up. She realized she'd been turning the pages of her book without actually seeing any of the words.

"Jeannie to Leenie, where did you go?"

The nickname reminded Laylea that she was stuck in more than one prison. Everyone here knew her as Lee Woodford, which wasn't her name at all. She was Laylea Hillen. Though Hillen wasn't hers from birth either. Her bio-mom had hidden her with the Hillens when she was six weeks old. Then the Hillens had hidden her here, in Chicago, with only her brother to protect her while they went off to find and fight her bio-father, Walter Bowman.

Laylea Bowman.

Yuck.

She'd be happy being Lee Woodford if it kept her from ever becoming Laylea Bowman.

"A song for your thoughts, Leenie." Jeannie sipped her cranberry and soda.

Laylea tried to come up with some lie, since she couldn't share anything she'd been thinking with non-shifter, non-wyrdo, adult Jeannie.

Before she could, the door to the bar opened behind her tutor, flooding the dim room with midday sun and a chill October wind. The tiny hairs on her human forearms stood up as she envisioned busting out that door and through her brother's magical forcefield. She'd tried before. She'd never made it out.

Her psychic tail wagged as Junior Leo, the twenty-six-year-old bastard son of the boogeyman, came in and looked around. He pulled off a pair of knit gloves and stuffed them into the satchel he wore across a particularly obnoxious pumpkin-orange sweater featuring black triangles for the jack-o-lantern's nose and eyes. Junior's eyes adjusted to the darkness, and he grinned, first at Laylea, then at Jeannie. Finally, his eyes rose to Seb.

The bartender was pulling a draft for another customer. He didn't look up. The ice in Seb's Scottish-accented voice challenged the cold from outside. "No. The glög is not ready. Won't be selling any today."

Junior slipped onto Laylea's stool, shoving her off the far side as he kept his gaze on Seb. "The cops looking for a parking spot outside will be so disappointed."

Cops. Right.

She picked herself up and took off for the back before Seb could give her "the look".

Laylea had to hide whenever cops showed up. Cops, or wolves.

It was chilly in the bar's courtyard. Since Laylea's clothes did not shift with her, she lost a lot of them around the city. In order to save money, she bought misprinted fan gear in bulk. Her current, cheap, size one sweatsuit cheered "Go Cobbies" instead of "Go Cubbies," and it wasn't nearly as warm as her fur would be. If she got cold enough, she'd shift. Even in her fur, she didn't want to be stuck in the court-yard. She tapped the dog door with one ugg-booted foot. The little door thwapped open and shut.

Laylea curled up on the loveseat the brownies had maneuvered into the courtyard during their last spurt of redecorating. The cush-ions crackled as she climbed into one corner and pulled one of Ned Biggerson's blankets around her. Of all the regulars, Ned was the only one you might suspect of being a wyrdo. The man was enormous. Seb had built a special chair to hold Ned's weight. The man could be found in that chair every weekday evening, knitting away and nursing a beer. The greens and browns of Ned's blanket mimicked the colors of the protective tarp overhead and the tree growing at the corner of the courtyard.

Laylea spotted an egg lying on the cobblestones at the base of the tree trunk. It was October seventh. How would a baby bird survive a Chicago winter? She crawled out of the blanket and over the arm of the loveseat to look closer. The little thing, not as long as her pinkie, must have fallen from the nest she saw in the branches not far up.

She decided she could probably climb as far as the nest without too much trouble. She'd just tuck the egg in one of the pockets of her specially made collar. But when she tried to fit it in, even after removing her key and notebook and a vial of antiserum, she realized the egg would be crushed between her neck and the dog tag reading, "Lee."

There would be plenty of room to tuck it in a bra, if she weren't so flat-chested that she didn't bother wearing one.

With a grunt, Laylea pushed to her feet. She spun around and ran for one of the tall stools that littered the little courtyard. She dragged it over to the tree while cradling the delicate egg against her chest. The cushion fell off, and she decided that was a good thing. She didn't want it slipping while she was standing on it.

With the chair positioned, Laylea wrapped her arm as far around the tree as she could reach. She'd have to climb one-handed. She stabilized herself with her elbow as her feet found nooks strong enough to support her small body. It was slow going, but she only had to climb a few feet before she was high enough.

With the nest an arm's length above her, Laylea braced herself and stretched up. Unable to see inside it, she tilted her hand toward the nest. The warm egg slowly rolled out of her palm.

A figure hit the tarp overhead.

Laylea startled.

The egg bounced off the edge of the nest and fell past her, past the chair. It smashed on the cobbles beside the contents of her collar. Laylea slid down the bark and hit the chair before she, too, tumbled to the stones. Her shin broke with a terrifyingly loud crack an instant before an equally painful burn exploded through her body. She shifted, leaving her a twelve-pound bundle of fawn-colored dog laying in a pile of sweatsuit beside the remains of what should have one day been a bird. It may have been painful, but shifting healed all her wounds. Still, she licked at her furry shin.

She turned her brown eyes from the shattered egg to the figure slipping through an opening between the tarp and the tree. One wing caught on the edge, throwing the bat off balance. The tiny creature stuck his other wing out, caught the air, and spiraled into a flash of blinding light.

Laylea turned away, but not before the pain in her eyes spread down to her toes. She shifted back to human.

Kyle landed delicately on the cobblestones, the quiet tap-flap of his sandals touching down the only indication that he hadn't executed a perfect shift-landing. While Laylea yanked her Cobbies sweatshirt straight, her heartbeat-challenged friend stood there in his neat blue jeans, blue plaid flannel, and red and blue Cubbies zip-up, adjusting the bill of his Blackhawk's ball cap and wearing a grin almost as wide as Ned's shoulders.

He'd been a vampire for two years and he was already better at shifting than Laylea who'd known what she was since she was eleven. She stuffed her jealousy down. He'd never asked to be a wyrdo.

Detective Kyle Nellwin had been shot while working a homicide case. His partner, Dee Morton had been there. She chased the shooter. When she got back, Kyle's body was gone. Dee should have been the one to help him through the transition. But, somehow—the brownies would say it was karma—Kyle had stumbled upon Laylea after a vampire had healed his bullet wound and stolen his soul.

He survived the transition but barely. In the course of that long night, he and Laylea had discovered that Kyle didn't just get nutrition when he drank blood. He got memories, too. He got all of his maker's and a few of Laylea's.

She helped keep him fed through a connection at a blood bank. Or she did until she was sent back to the Lincoln Park Shifter School and then was trapped in the bar. She looked him over. His face was deep black, not ashen or sunk in. It was the middle of the afternoon, and his hood was back. He'd been feeding. She wondered how.

"Hey Fuzzface," he said, grinning.

She grimaced at him. "Nice shift."

Kyle got his grin under control and dug into his hoodie pocket. He tossed a Milkbone to her. "I've been practicing."

Laylea tucked the Milkbone into her collar for later and said nothing, kneeling to collect the rest of her belongings. She'd have to get supplies to clean up the poor baby bird.

Kyle crouched beside her. The largest bit of shell glowed white against his dark skin as he lifted it from the mess. "What happened here? "

Laylea laughed through her frustration. "I tried to put an egg back in its nest. I'm no better at saving then I am at shifting."

He sighed. "Sometimes, my friend, you need to ask for help." He went to the dumpster in the alley and called back, no concern for anybody hearing them. "Like that time I asked you for help when I was turning and scared out of my wits."

"Well, you had an ancient vampire's memories swirling around in your head," she muttered under her breath. Aloud, she said, "You figured out shifting all by yourself."

"Actually," Kyle admitted returning with a fast-food wrapper to gather up the little corpse, "Adele Lagat's been helping me."

Laylea sat up and stared at him. "Ms. Lagat? The shifting master at school?"

"Yep."

There was only one way that could be true. Laylea's breath came faster. She stood and walked over to put the loveseat between them.

Kyle couldn't tell anybody that he was a vampire because vampires were demons—supernatural creatures who feed on humans. And Captain Yaksha Morioka had vowed to keep her city demon-free. He hadn't even dared to tell his wife and daughter, much less Dee or any of the other wyrdos that hung out at The Office. And he'd bound Laylea in a promise to never tell them.

Which meant he'd taken the information directly from Adele Lagat's blood. He'd fed not just from a live human, but from someone she knew.

Laylea turned and stomped to the door.

———

2

*L*aylea reached the door before she remembered why she was in the beer garden. There were cops inside.

"Lee." Kyle's voice came from a distance.

Laylea spun to face him as he came back into the beer garden from the alley. She rubbed the tiny cloth lizard foot the Mom had sent her, charmed to protect her from magic. It didn't protect her from Bailey's stupid spells. It didn't protect her from anger.

"What's wrong?" Kyle sat on the loveseat. "You have a dire emergency inside? Can't spare me some time?"

She dropped her eyes. "You fed on her?"

"Ms. Lagat?" Kyle denied this with a laugh that declared the very idea absurd. "No, Lee. She offered to give me lessons. We kept running into one another at Toby's enclosure, and she recognized what I am. It was silly to deny it. I would never feed on a friend... again." He offered her a silly grimace at the reminder of the one time he'd bitten her.

"You've been hanging out at the zoo?"

He chuckled. "With Toby, mostly. He seems lonely and sad. I know I'm lonely and sad. We get along. He reminds me of KJ's teddy."

"You get along with a bear," she said.

"Yeah. He's a very smart bear. Which brings me to why I dropped by." Kyle hopped up from the loveseat and hurried over to slide the cinderblock in front of the door. The cinderblock typically held the back door open on nice days. The hairs on her neck stood up until he toed the dog door, making it clear he hadn't trapped her outside.

Kyle led Laylea over to the tree, far from the door. "You should know, I'm the reason Toby got into the school last July when Brock's kid gassed everyone."

Laylea had stopped the gas. But she'd fallen down a stairwell and had no memory of how she'd gotten back into the school. Her friends said that the bear had carried her through the halls until he succumbed to the dissipating gas.

"I let Toby out of his enclosure," Kyle admitted. "And then, I followed him. I saw the stone stairs under the lion."

The stone stairs led into the Lincoln Park Shifter School.

A knock sounded at the back door. Junior's voice called, "Lee?"

"If you need help, go to Toby. You can trust him. And I'll stay close."

The door rattled.

Kyle whispered, "Please be careful when you go back."

"I'm not going back to school. I'm not allowed."

Kyle only smiled enigmatically in response. Then he hopped just enough to lift his sandals off the ground and flashed into a bat again.

Laylea wondered idly if Kyle had been drinking from Toby. What memories would he ingest from a sad black bear?

"Lee? Let me out." Junior knocked shave and a haircut on the door. "It's me."

She hustled to the door and dragged the cinderblock out of the way. The door opened so suddenly, it hit her in the head. Laylea tumbled ass over tea kettle, landing as her doggie-self in a pile of clothes.

Junior tried to hide his giggles behind one hand. "Sorry."

He didn't sound the least bit sorry. But he did offer her a Milk-bone. She glared at him with her furry face until he set it on the clothing in front of her and backed away.

"I came out to let you know that the cops are gone, and the brownies are here. Orin's cast is waterproof so nobody can sign it. He's pretty bummed about that."

Laylea looked up from her snack to tilt her head at Junior.

"Yeah, I agree," Junior said. "Any normal person would be bummed their arm is broken." He grinned. "He's being extra nice to everyone in hopes that good karma will help him heal faster."

Orin, Amal, and Lucio were brownies. They dispensed karma. Orin should know better than to try to manipulate it.

"Also," Junior pulled an envelope from a pocket. "You have a new letter from Ms. Crow."

Laylea sat up. She wriggled out of the puddle of sweatshirt and stood on her hind legs to take the envelope. Ms. Crow was the Lincoln Park Shifter School librarian. She had been sending Laylea books and assignments along with notes from her best friends, KC and Oscar. She wanted Laylea to keep learning as much as Laylea wanted to keep learning.

Secret classes, like shifter sociology, she had to study on her own in the storeroom. After a huge blowout with Orin when he was trying to help her with math, Junior had hired Jeannie to tutor her in everything a normal kid would learn in school.

It was ridiculous. Jeannie was a world-class neurogeneticist. She only worked on the hardest or, she said, most interesting, cases around the world. She and her daughter had moved into the city a few months ago and Jeannie had started hanging out at The Office in the afternoons since her daughter's preschool was nearby. When Junior had asked her to tutor Laylea, she'd agreed eagerly, for some reason Laylea couldn't figure out.

Junior was a good friend. He never treated her differently when she was a dog. Everyone else would have opened the envelope for her. Junior respected her privacy. He strolled over to the loveseat while she stood on the envelope with one front paw and broke the seal with the other. Getting the letter out was challenging, but she had a lot of experience from exchanging letters with her parents.

Lee!

The brief letter began in Oscar's messy print.

Is it true? Are you coming home? Why didn't you tell us?

Ali is starting a new semester-long Wilding! Bonus points for any team that gets scolded by Ms. Davies whose application to transfer to the Montana Shifter School was REJECTED again!

Oscar

KC had added a slightly more legible postscript.

P.S. Britny found a patch of catnip growing near Toby's enclosure. It doesn't affect Theresa or Reggie. But it makes Murph and Oscar highlarious! We'll save some to show you. How do you know Mr. DeGee? Come home! Come home! Come home!

KC

Laylea tilted her head at the letter. Her ears rotated forward and back as if she somehow hadn't heard them right. She tried to flip the letter with her nose. It was too flat against the ground. She tried her teeth and then a paw. It wouldn't give.

BAM

Human Laylea screamed a little. Junior giggled. He bowed when she turned to see him standing at the end of the loveseat he'd dropped to make her shift.

"Thanks." She turned back and flipped the letter over with her facile fingers. The back was blank.

She flipped back to the front and read it again. As she did, she grabbed her clothes and pulled them on. The letter made no more sense on the second read. Griffin DeGee was a classmate of theirs, but there was no way KC would call him Mister.

"You wanna go back in?" Junior pulled a little silver flask from another pocket and shook it. "I stole a sample of Hopleaf's glög. Thought you might want to see Seb's reaction."

"Hell yeah." Laylea definitely wanted to see Seb's reaction. Glög was serious business.

She jogged over to the dumpster to toss the envelope. A tiny spark bit her hand when she hit her brother's forcefield. She swallowed a gasp and sucked back the tears that wanted to fall at the unfairness of her prison. She'd only shifted in front of humans because she was trying to save all the kids in school. Why should she be punished for that?

Of course, that wasn't exactly true. And she knew it. She shifted because she was startled and scared and had no self-control. She could have stayed human and saved everybody.

"I got ya." Junior lifted the lid of the dumpster and held a hand out for the envelope. "Let's go inside. The brownies will cheer you up."

Laylea didn't want to be cheered up. But she pouted her way over to the back door with Junior beside her. When he laid an arm across her shoulders, she got an idea.

She let out an enormous sigh. "You know what would make me feel better?"

"What can I do to make you feel better?" Junior ushered her into the back hallway.

"I bet a taste of glög would make me feel lots better." She held her hand out for the flask.

Junior lifted it out of her reach. "Ha! No way am I going to punish your taste buds with inferior glög." He danced down the hallway, yelling back at her, "And there is no way I'm getting on Seb's bad side during glög season!"

It was worth a shot.

Laylea slipped into the storage room to stash the weird letter in her bookbag. She'd have plenty of time to parse it out later. She had nothing but time.

ALSO BY GWENDOLYN DRUYOR

WYRDOS Urban Fantasy Series

WereHuman 1: The Witch's Daughter

WereHuman 2: The Warrior's Son

WereHuman 3: The Hunter's Heir

WereHuman 4: The Wizard's Mutt

Voices of Reason (AVAILABLE FREE TO NEWSLETTER SUBSCRIBERS)

Shifter School

Shifter Witch

Shifter Moon

Free Wishes

Dee

Laylea

Junior

Doug vs. The Boogeyman(EXCLUSIVE TO MY NEWSLETTER)

MOBIOUS' QUEST Fantasy Series

Geoffrey's Queen

Hardt's Tale

First Edition, July 2022

Library of Congress Control Number: 2022907611
Print ISBN 978-1-948421-19-5|
Ebook ISBN 978-1-948421-18-8 |
audiobook ISBN 978-1-948421-20-1

Editing by Leslie Schipa

Published in the United States of America.

Wyrdos.net

www.ingramcontent.com/pod-product-compliance
Lightning Source LLC
Chambersburg PA
CBHW071046250626
47159CB00002B/385